C. KEVIN THOMPSON

the *Letters*

Expanse Books

©2020 C. Kevin Thompson

Published by Expanse Books,
an imprint of Scrivenings Press LLC
15 Lucky Lane
Morrilton, Arkansas 72110
https://ScriveningsPress.com

Printed in the United States of America

All rights reserved. No part of this publication may be reproduced, stored in a retrieval system, or transmitted in any form or by any means—for example, electronic, photocopy and recording— without the prior written permission of the publisher. The only exception is brief quotation in printed reviews.

Paperback ISBN 978-1-64917-054-5

eBook ISBN 978-1-64917-055-2

Library of Congress Control Number: 2020940048

Cover by Diane Turpin, www.dianeturpindesigns.com

(Note: This book was previously published by Mantle Rock Publishing LLC and was re-published when MRP was acquired by Scrivenings Press LLC in 2020.)

All characters are fictional, and any resemblance to real people, either factional or historical, is purely coincidental.

Scriptures marked NIV are taken from the NEW INTERNATIONAL VERSION (NIV): Scripture taken from THE HOLY BIBLE, NEW INTERNATIONAL VERSION ®. Copyright© 1973, 1978, 1984, 2011 by Biblica, Inc.™. Used by permission of Zondervan

Published in association with Jim Hart of Hartline Literary Agency, Pittsburgh, PA.

PRAISE FOR "THE LETTERS"

Fans of Frank Peretti will enjoy *The Letters*, a tender, suspenseful, thought-provoking page-turner.

— JANET GRUNST, AUTHOR OF SELAH
AWARD WINNER, *A HEART SET FREE*

The Letters is an inspiring story of hope and forgiveness. Filled with mystery and messy relationships, this story will keep you turning the pages until you reach the surprise ending.

— KIMBERLY ROSE JOHNSON, AWARD
WINNING AND MULTI-PUBLISHED AUTHOR
OF THE LIBRARIAN SLEUTH SERIES

C. Kevin Thompson gifts readers with a well-written, fast-paced story that includes imperfect but likeable characters. With unexpected twists, *The Letters* is one of those rare novels that keeps us in suspense until the very end. A tale that challenges us to consider the spiritual realm, *The Letters* offers hope and also reminds us that we're never alone.

— DAWN KINZER, AUTHOR OF *BY ALL
APPEARANCES* AND THE DAUGHTERS OF
RIVERTON SERIES

C. Kevin Thompson's newest Christian suspense takes us from the mean streets of New York and the depths of despair through a series of happenings where nothing and no one is what they seem, to a realization of God's unrelenting love.

— PENNY RICHARDS, TWO-TIME WINNER, TEXAS ASSOCIATION OF AUTHORS BEST HISTORICAL MYSTERY OF THE YEAR.

Wow! NCIS meets Peretti. I'm a sucker for a good story, and I loved this book. It entertained me, made me think, and, best of all, ministered to my soul.

— BUCK STORM, AUTHOR OF SELAH AWARD FINALIST, *THE MIRACLE MAN*

The Letters is a heartwarming tale expertly packaged with fragmented pieces of heartbreak, loss, true love, and joy. It's a journey where we remember not all have peace on earth and goodwill toward men. Yet, it's never too late to believe in the Hope of Christmas.

— CALEB ROCKE, AUTHOR, *AS SEEN IN A MIRROR: BEGINNING OF THE END*

The inspirational truth woven through this novel can only be described as challenging the heart. *The Letters* grabbed me from the first page and kept me turning them until the end. The surprise twists brought a smile and sometimes caught me off guard.

— CINDY ERVIN HUFF, AWARD-WINNING AUTHOR, 2019 SELAH FINALIST

For the Fatherless

May this little book
cause your numbers to dwindle

ACKNOWLEDGMENTS

There is one thing I have learned as a maturing writer. For someone to say, "Yes, we wish to publish your manuscript," is a truly humbling experience. For when you have been through the entire process a few times, you realize just how much equity—both financial and sweat—a small group of people have poured into your story just so others may enjoy it.

There have been a great many people who have "poured themselves" into this work.

First, thank you to Kathy and Jerry Cretsinger of Mantle Rock Publishing, for taking a chance on a guy writing what amounts to a female reader's book. Apparently, having lived in a house with a wife and three daughters paid off. I also want to thank the rest of the MRP staff: Diane Turpin, for the book cover design; Kathy McKinsey and Pam Harris for the editing work; and all the behind the scenes people who help with the little things that keep the machine running smoothly.

Second, I want to thank Jim Hart and Elizabeth Kim at Hartline Literary Agency for rooting for me, encouraging me, giving guidance, lending advice, and pretty much keeping my feet firmly planted on planet Earth. It's been a fun ride so far, but we have so much farther to go.

Third, I want to thank my wife Cindy for her continued support and being not only my fan, but my best confidant. Like another Charles in 1843 England, I hope this "little book" haunts our house pleasantly as well as all the readers who open its pages.

Fourth, I want to thank my family for their support and encouragement. And to see our grandchildren not only take on a love for reading, but to see them "writing stories like Papa T" just may be the best legacy a writer could ever leave.

Last, but definitely first and foremost, I wish to thank Almighty God, My Lord Jesus, and the Holy Spirit, for not only life in the here and now, but life everlasting too. Not to mention life amongst the Creation as well as life in the Spirit. Until you've tasted and seen that it is good, then you cannot begin to understand.

Just ask Dorothy.

Or Heather.

Or Malachi.

Or Rachel.

They can explain it to you.

PROLOGUE

Where did it begin?
Or where did it end?
That is the better question.
For somewhere in the heart, during a time filled with turmoil,
A story emerged.

It's an account that will baffle the imagination of many.
A story no one will want to believe.
It will be dubbed a legend by some.
A fairy tale by others.
A lie by most.

However, what you are about to read is a story of passion…
And a story of deceit.
A story of rejection…
And a story of redemption.

Ultimately, however, it is a story of love.
For this is my story.
—Rachel Hamar, December 25, 2019

Wednesday

December 10, 2014

CHAPTER ONE

West 173rd Street
Washington Heights, NY

I slammed the car door shut and dropped my car keys onto the cold pavement. Shuffling the grocery bags from one hand to the other, I crouched in a pretzel-like fashion, trying not to keel over in my high heels.

Stupid keys.

Picking them up, my thigh muscles burned as I rose and fumbled for the one I needed, attempting not to crush the eggs or shatter the glass jars of spaghetti sauce clanking together in revolt.

A stiff winter breeze battered my face as I trudged up the four blocks of sidewalk to the entrance of my five-story apartment building.

No bigger than a wide alley designed to look like a courtyard, the entrance led to eight fractured, concrete stairs, eroded by years of ice-melting salt in the winter, blistering heat in the summer, and a million trudging feet.

The steps spread wide under two forty-year-old doors. Their

glass panes, arranged in nine squares and each framed in wood, had a slightly melted, made-in-the-seventeenth-century look about them.

Multi-colored Christmas lights, designed to be festive and joyous, stretched around the main entrance like an archway. Even they twinkled in a melancholy, exhausted manner. Every third light or so, burned out.

Definitely the entrance to the abode of paupers, not princesses.

I looked over my shoulder at the street.

You know, I could stumble and fall down these stairs. Bust my head wide open. Cracked eggs everywhere. Broken jars of spaghetti sauce adding to an already gruesome scene…

And would anyone care?

I lifted my face toward the sky. Little spits of icy rain raced past the spray of light from the lamppost and pelted my face and coat. The stiff breeze flowing down the street suddenly changed direction and chased me inside the courtyard, assaulting my senses with the smell of cigarettes.

A nameless, foreign-looking man I'd never seen before stood on the third-floor fire escape to my right, leaning over the railing. An occasional flick of his half-spent smoke sent ashes cascading down like snowflakes. His tattered wife-beater, low-riding jeans, and exposed boxer briefs, depicted a picture of self-imposed misery.

I glanced in his direction for a few, lingering seconds.

Just look at that dude. Isn't he cold?

I turned away when our eyes met. Feeling a sudden vulnerability, I scooted up the steps and jammed the key into the lock.

Instead of offering to help, he'd probably rob me while I was on the ground, sprawled out, unconscious in a pool of Ragu.

I scurried inside, veered right into the mailroom, snatched my mail from its box, and hurried up the stairs.

Slipping through the front door of my apartment, I forced the door shut and locked it with a tad more fervor than usual.

I hate living here.

With my hand still on the dead bolt, I allowed my forehead to thump against the door casing as I tried to slow down my breathing.

"I hate living here! Did you hear me?" My lament echoed off the walls into a sea of silence.

I slogged to the kitchen with a sigh, tossing my keys, my purse, and the mail on the couch.

Opening the refrigerator door and depositing the eggs into their normal station, I noticed that except for last night's paltry leftovers, a couple of beers, and a few condiments, the fridge was barren.

I stared into it, leaning on the door for support. Its contents a ready commentary on my life.

Worthless.

Paltry.

Desolate.

I looked heavenward. "I can't do this anymore."

After changing into some sweats and grabbing a glass of water, I flopped down on the couch and thumbed through the mail. Junk mail got flipped to the floor. Bills got opened, examined, and remanded to the coffee table. Due dates were noted. How each one would be paid on time became the question of the hour.

It was then that an envelope, sandwiched between a department store flyer and an advertisement for a local pub, caught my eye. I plucked it from the stack and turned it back and forth, examining both sides. I held it up to the light.

Handwritten. Addressed to me. But no return address.

Then, I saw something inside.

Looks like a folded piece of paper.

I started to open it when my cell phone rang.

"Hello?"

"Girl, you sure are hard to reach."

I smirked. "No, I'm not hard to reach. I'm just always at work. If I'm not at the bank, I'm at the restaurant. If I'm not at the restaurant, I'm at the bank. I have no life, Joanie."

"You're not the only one. I just picked up my third job today. That's why I called you."

"Third jo—" I couldn't even complete my thought. All I could do was exhale. "Where?"

"Goldman's Gifts and Cards. In the mall. It's just on Sundays & Mondays during the holidays."

"What? Those are our only nights off." I huffed. "See what I mean? You already work during the day at Manningham's. Then you leave straight from there and tend bar. Now, you're working our nights off too?" I hurled the remaining mail across the living room. "It's hopeless."

"Did something happen today? You seem more intense than usual."

I forced out an exasperated sigh. "It ain't just today. It's every day. Look at us, Joanie. I'm thirty-five years old. You're thirty-seven."

"Yeah. Don't remind me."

"That's my point." I sat up and wiped my face. "We're not getting any younger. Our rent is almost two thousand dollars a month. We have seven hundred square feet. That's it. Seven hundred." I stood and plodded over to the front window. "Your dad's new place in Lincoln Park has a kitchen bigger than this apartment." I pulled apart the front curtains. The dreary sky matched my mood. "He's got closets bigger than our bedrooms. And, on top of that, we live in this horrible part of the city. Why? Because that's all we can afford."

"Hey, speaking of working nights, aren't you supposed to be at the restaurant tonight?"

Yeah…about that… "I called in."

"Called in? What's goin' on? You never call in."

"I don't want to talk about it."

"Listen, I'm taking you out. I don't work at the bar tonight, some issue with the liquor license, so we're gonna celebrate. And that'll give us some time to chat."

"Celebrate what?"

"My new job, for starters. That'll be an extra hundred dollars a month we'll be able to throw at a bill. Maybe more. And if I do a good job, they said they might keep me on after the New Year. So, we are gonna celebrate. And just maybe, if we're lucky, we'll meet some guys, get drunk, who knows? What do ya say?"

I let the curtains fall back into place. "Woo. Hoo."

"Well, okay, then. If you don't want to come, that's fine. I'll invite Ginger and Lacey. I'm sure they'll be happy to celebrate with me."

I walked over to the couch and flopped onto my back. "You go ahead. I'll just ruin it for everybody anyway."

"Rachel, what's wrong?"

"Nothing." I covered my eyes with my left arm.

"You've been depressed for a long time, Rach. You know it. I know it. And they say the holidays make it a lot worse. And like I keep saying, you really need to see someone. Somebody that can help you get through it."

"With what? We just got the electric bill. It's a hundred dollars higher than last month. So, good thing you got that extra job, I guess. But someday, we're gonna run out of hours in the day and days of the week. And we don't have the room for another roommate."

Joanie didn't respond right away. "Look, I've known you for over half your life, and we've been friends the entire time. That means I probably know you better than you know yourself. So, just spit it out. What's really bothering you?"

I puffed out a grunt. "Everything."

"Could you be a little more specific?"

I stalled, stifling a tear. I don't want to talk about it.

"Rachel? You still there?"

She's not gonna give this up.

"Hello? Can you hear me?"

"I got laid off today. Okay?"

"From the bank?"

"Yes, from the bank. Restaurants don't lay people off. They just keep cutting your hours until you quit."

"Well, excuse me for caring."

I pinched my eyes together, squeezing out a tear. "I'm sorry."

"Is that why you called in tonight?"

"Yep."

"Did the bank give you a reason why?"

"Oh yeah," I said, pinning the phone against my shoulder. "They said they 'hated to lose me,' and 'what a great employee I've been,' and 'if the economy was better,' they would have kept me, and blah, blah-blah, blah-blah."

"But why did they lay you off?"

"I really don't know, but I'm supposedly getting a small severance package for being such a good employee."

"That doesn't make sense."

"None of it does anymore."

"They didn't give you a reason?"

"All they said was they needed to cut back. They laid me and two others off. Said they'd give me good references, though."

"Well, that's a good thing, I guess."

"Not really. It doesn't matter if you're a good employee anymore. Doesn't do any good to try. Being good, doing the right thing, it's all a joke."

"Now, hold on, girl. Don't be talkin' like that. You know we'll get through this. We always do. And anyway, Justin said he would help if we ever needed it."

"Oh, wonderful. Ask your old boyfriend for money." I laughed. "That's a great idea."

"What are old boyfriends for?"

"Nothing, Joanie. Absolutely nothing. That's why we dump them."

"Maybe for you, but for me? I always keep the lines of communication open."

"You string them along?"

"No, I just call them from time to time, and when I ask, they come runnin' with smiles on their faces and cash in their wallets."

"That's so not cool."

"But it works."

"So does robbing a bank."

"Well, that would be dumb. Robbing a bank is illegal. But, using old boyfriends who have no sense? That's what I call smart."

I could envision Joanie tapping her temple as she spoke. She always thought she was "smart like that." I sat up and twisted my frame, pulling my knees close. "Nobody on this planet calls using your old boyfriends smart. What they do call it is psychosis. We learned about it in Psychology 101, Professor Dietrich's class. Remember? City College?"

"Oh, I remember. Worst two-and-a-half years of my life."

I wiped my eyes with my shirtsleeve. "Look, I know you care about me, but I'll be fine. I just need to be alone."

Joanie paused again. "There's more, isn't there? It's not just the bank job that's got you all upset, is it?"

I sniffed. "It's nothing that concerns you."

I could hear shuffling in the background. The sound of keys jingling, doors opening, and little chiming bells filled my ear. "Rach, you're freakin' me out a little."

I inhaled deeply, but I couldn't contain it anymore. I finally broke down and sobbed.

"Hey, I'm comin' home. I'll be there in a few minutes. Okay?"

I didn't argue. "Okay."

CHAPTER TWO

West 173rd Street
Washington Heights, NY

Joanie entered our apartment talking to someone, telling the person she'd talk later. I assumed she was on her phone. She was always on her phone. I swear the woman would die of boredom if cell phones were ever banned from existence. It made me wonder how she survived growing up. Then, I remembered middle school and reminded myself she almost didn't make it after her dad left.

Guess talking on a cell phone isn't that bad after all.

I was flat on my back, on the couch, left arm over my eyes. A box of tissues rested on my stomach. A pile of used ones littered the floor.

And I didn't care.

Joanie sounded winded as she locked the door behind her. I didn't have to look to know what she was doing.

Scanning the living room.

Mouth opened just a bit.

Probably wondering why the mail was all over the place.

I finally heard her bend over with a mild groan.

She's picking up the mail.

"So, I see you're not interested in Weston's Holidaze Extravaganza this Saturday…or McGillicutty's Happy Hour pub special…hmm, I might just take that one."

"No."

"No? No, what? I can't have the advertisements?"

"No, I'm not interested."

Joanie voiced an affirming mumble. "And I see the electric bill you referenced."

"I don't know how it can go up that much. We're never home."

"I'll look into it. And what's this?"

I lifted my arm and glanced out of the corner of my eye.

Joanie was holding an envelope up to the light. "There's no return address, but it's addressed to you."

I dropped my arm back down. "Probably some company wanting to offer me a trip to the Caribbean 'if I just sign up for their 45-minute presentation on how to buy a million-dollar condo in the Hamptons.'"

Joanie chortled. "I'm sorry, Rach, but they won't be sending anything like that to this neighborhood." She held out the envelope. "Here, you need to open it. Maybe it's a flirtatious message from a secret admirer."

"I don't have any secret admirers."

She set the envelope down on the coffee table. "Can't imagine why…but, whatever." She walked around the table and plopped down at the far end of the couch.

I pulled my knees up and made room for her.

"I think I know what's got you so upset today. I mean, besides being laid off."

"Figured it out, huh?"

"Yeah. On the way home." She paused. "It's the date, isn't it?"

I didn't answer.

I didn't have to.

She knew.

"It was twenty years ago today…when Billy died."

I glanced over the couch at the clock.

7:32 p.m.

On that day, about seven-thirty, Billy and I were eating supper at that fast food restaurant he liked so much.

I could picture the place like it was yesterday. I wonder if Burger Meister is even there anymore…

Stupid name for a restaurant, but they did have great fries.

Joanie turned to face me. "I know it's gonna be a long night, but I'm here for you." She patted my knee. "I want you to know that."

By eight-thirty, Billy and I were in the woods.

All alone.

That beautiful meadow. Illuminated dimly by the half-moon Billy pointed out to me, along with the stars.

The gurgle of the tiny creek was like a lullaby. The leaves had all but fallen, and a soft breeze whisked through the barren branches of the trees lining the mountainside.

The feel of winter kissed our exposed skin. The stars, high over the mountaintop, twinkled just like the diamonds I sang about as a little girl.

Lying in the bed of his pickup with sleeping bags wrapped around us, I could feel Billy's chest rise and fall with each breath.

His excited heartbeat pulsed in my ear.

Billy was right. It was heavenly.

Even for a fifteen-year-old girl.

And that's when things went so wrong.

Why did I tell him? Why then?

I'll never forget the look on his face.

The surprise. The jolt. The—

Joanie jerked me out of my daydream, shaking my leg. "Rach? Did you hear me? I cancelled my plans. When I remembered, I called and told Ginger and Lacey we'd celebrate some other time."

I wiped my eyes again. "Do they know?"

"No. I wouldn't tell them anything unless you said it was okay."

"They probably think I'm crazy."

"It doesn't matter what they think." Joanie sank back into the couch. "I'm sorry. I admit…I forgot."

"I wouldn't expect you to remember." I covered my eyes with my hands. "The date doesn't hold any significance for you."

She lifted her feet and set them on the coffee table. "Do you ever wonder?"

"What life would have been like if Billy was still here?"

"Yeah."

"Every day. Especially today."

Thursday

December 11, 2014

CHAPTER THREE

West 173rd Street
Washington Heights, NY

*I*mmersed in a horrible nightmare, I awoke.

My sweats were damp. My sheets were untucked from the mattress and twisted into a tousled heap.

I had been in those same woods. Twenty years ago. Reliving the event, hoping for a different outcome. All the "What ifs?" I'd imagined over the years coming to life in my dreams.

What if I'd grabbed the gun, preventing Billy from aiming it at Daddy?

What if I'd wrestled Daddy more? Jumped on his back? Stood between him and Billy?

What if I'd never told Daddy I was staying with Joanie that night? Just told the truth instead?

What if I'd been stronger? Told Billy we shouldn't? Realized that if he truly loved me, he'd wait?

What if our last names hadn't been Hamar or Baldwin?

What if we'd never gone out? Had never fallen in love?

What if I'd never gotten pregnant?

What if…?

A thousand, fateful scenarios, created by years of misery, knitted their way into my slumber. My mind tried to save Billy. Yet, tonight, like every other night, all my dreams ended with the same, inevitable conclusion.

The clock peered at me from the nightstand. Its red numbers heckled me.

2:04 a.m.

I got up, angry. Even the simplest, most basic pleasure a human being had—sleep—was being taken from me.

Just like everything else.

Billy. Daddy. Momma. My baby. My home. My friends. Everything I knew twenty years ago. Gone. Ripped away from me by decisions in and out of my control.

I was tired of being on that side of the ledger.

Accounts Payable.

The side where the assets always leave. Always get depleted. Sometimes withdrawn by force.

Yet, they never get fully replenished.

And my account was running dry.

It was almost empty.

And seriously, for the first time in my life, I contemplated closing it.

Forever.

There just wasn't anything coming into Accounts Receivable anymore.

Nobody seemed to fund that side.

Except Joanie.

But I'm afraid I'm draining the life right out of her account too.

I peeled off my damp clothes and slipped on a tank top and shorts. I left the sweats on the floor and walked into the kitchen. The clock on the microwave joined the jeering crowd.

2:10 a.m.

Daddy was in police custody at 2:10 in the morning twenty years ago.

I was lying next to Momma in the hospital. My hand on hers.

Later that morning, she was on her way to Cincinnati. St. Patrick's Psychiatric Hospital. A long way from Noring, West Virginia.

Momma stayed at St. Patrick's for about eight months after Billy died. Her six-month stint was extended for two thirty-day periods. When the judge learned that Momma had gotten worse instead of better, he ordered her to be transferred to the care of the main physician at the hospital. In layman's terms, the judge washed his hands of Momma. He handed her over to the head physician to be "handled."

Feeling they had done all they could do for her, the head physician applied for her to be moved and take part in a fledgling program with supposedly great promise, involving what would later be called dialectical behavioral therapy and interpersonal therapy. They would add psychodynamic psychotherapy to her plate after about a year.

The hope was to get Momma to realize that even though she believed she saw other people in the room—specifically, Jesus, Joseph, and Mary—she didn't have to voice it to others. She didn't have to talk to those people. Out loud. If she just kept it to herself and only spoke to people who were actually in the room, it would help others see her as normal.

I was told all she did was laugh in their faces and ask, "What's normal?"

Good question.

So, at the request and recommendation of the doctors in Cincinnati, Momma was accepted into the Long Island Psychiatric Center in Deer Park, New York.

And that is why I'm here. In the City. Eking out an existence.

Momma was all I truly had left.

CHAPTER FOUR

West 173rd Street
Washington Heights, NY

I leaned against the kitchen counter, nursing a beer. Actually, it was nursing me more, I think. I hardly ever drank. Socially, now and then. Nothing like Joanie, though. But in her defense, she worked as a bartender. So, what do you expect? It's like thinking the people at McDonald's never eat hamburgers and fries.

Get real.

It was past four now. By this time, twenty years ago, I had been escorted back to the police station from the hospital in Noring. I sat in a filthy break room, snacking on a bag of potato chips and watching Officer Truitt read his police magazine.

His life was okay. His shift ended at seven. He'd be rid of me in a few hours, Then, he'd get to go home and get on with his life, go to bed, get some sleep, go wherever he wanted, marry whomever he chose, have children—

Stop it!

You need to stop!

All this remembering…

Recollecting…

Reminiscing.

This twenty-year prison.

Twenty years of heartache…

Of pain…

Of despair…

It needs to stop.

I plodded out into the living room and collapsed onto the couch. Sitting there, holding my warm beer, tears pooled at the corners of my eyes as I imagined what my life would have been like with Billy by my side…for the millionth time.

Would we have stayed in Noring? Would we have moved? How many children would we have had? And our first one…was it a boy or a girl?

Stop! Stop doing this to yourself!

Joanie's right.

You need help.

I chugged the last few swallows and pulled the bottle away. Looking at it, I wondered if this was how people became alcoholics. It wouldn't be that hard. Drowning your sorrows, they call it. Trying to escape the hurt.

The loneliness.

Life.

I get it.

I set the bottle down on the coffee table when my eyes caught a glimpse of the envelope.

The one addressed to me in a particular kind of handwriting.

I stretched and snatched it off the table, flipping it over as I did.

Sealed shut, but nothing on the back.

I looked at the front again.

Addressed to me. But no return address.

By someone who knows I live at West 173rd Street.

I studied the postmark.

Jericho, New York. Postmarked two days ago.

But I don't know anybody from Jericho.

I tore it open.

Inside, folded up like a letter, was a white sheet of paper. Eight and a half by eleven. Nothing fancy.

One side was blank. Nothing on it.

On the other side, there were scribbles. Short, jagged marks, like someone used the paper to sharpen a pencil before starting a pencil drawing on a different sheet of paper.

I studied the front and back, looking for anything else. But there was nothing else to see.

I held it up against the lamplight, thinking there might be some coded message written in a watermark or some erasure that might lend a clue.

Instead, nothing.

I chuckled.

Wow, girl, you've watched way too many episodes of CSI.

I dropped my arms, holding the paper and envelope in my lap.

Who would send me something like this?

It's just weird.

Really weird.

I hoped it wasn't that creep on the fire escape from last night.

But he didn't look like the letter-writing type.

I sat for the next several minutes, trying to think of who would send me a piece of paper with penciled scratch marks on it in an envelope with no return address.

And, who lived in Jericho?

Baffled, I finally folded the paper and shoved it back in the envelope.

I got up, turned off the light, and tossed the parcel into the trash.

Then I went to bed.

Weird.

CHAPTER FIVE

West 173rd Street
Washington Heights, NY

Joanie called me at ten-thirty.

She had heard me get up and bang around in the kitchen earlier that morning because it wasn't easy being quiet in your very own seven hundred square feet of The Big Apple. Plus, she knew me well enough to know I'd be awake most of the night.

So, she let me sleep in.

I know how she thinks too.

"You don't have a job anymore, and you're getting a severance package, so why get up? Especially after a rough night?"

However, she thought I would be up by ten-thirty.

She was wrong.

"I was thinking," she said, all chipper and bouncy. "You ought to go see your mom."

I could hear machinery in the background, which made it hard to hear. "Can you speak up? I can't hear you over all that noise." I lied, though. I was just avoiding an answer.

"Hold on. Let me step inside a minute." I could hear a door open and her breathing increase. "That infernal forklift. You go out into the warehouse to take your break, and he cranks it up. It's almost like he waits for us to go on break. You can't hear yourself think sometimes."

I yawned. "So, why did you wake me up?"

"I thought you should go see your mom. You haven't been there in a while. Now, you have a little time on your hands. Take a day and go see her. It might cheer you up."

"Or it might make matters worse."

"Why do you always have to be a glass-half-empty kind of person?"

"My glass hasn't had anything in it for years."

"All the more reason to go see her. If nothing else, it might cheer her up."

I stretched and groaned, pinning the phone with my head against the pillow. "I need to get up and go look for a job."

"That can wait."

"Until when? We get evicted? You know how this works. Even if I got a job tomorrow, it'll be at least two weeks before I get my first check."

"Didn't you say you were getting a severance package? We'll use some of that if we have to."

"Yes, I'm getting one, but they didn't say when. And it's only three months of pay."

"Well, there you go. That's more than enough to cover one day with your mother. We'll be okay, Rach." Joanie sighed into the phone. "Besides, if things get really tight, I'll track my dad down and demand some cash. He owes me."

"You need to forgive him, Joanie. You can't keep holding on to your hate like you do."

She laughed and sighed at the same time. "I'll get rid of my hate when you snap out of your twenty-year-old-funk. Deal?"

Touché.

"He did help us, you know," I said. "That night we showed up after I ran away from foster care. Remember? He was really nice that night. And he didn't have to give us all that money."

"Again, that was twenty years ago. After that, I never heard from him much." It sounded like she was shuffling papers. "When I turned eighteen, the birthday presents stopped coming, Mom's child support stopped coming…everything stopped. It was like he was just waiting for me to become a legal adult so he could finally leave us for good."

"But wait a minute. When I ask you how your dad is doing, you always tell me he's doing fine. You've even told me about things he's said and done over the years."

"Yeeeah," Joanie said with a wince in her voice. "I made all that up."

"Why would you do that?"

"Because it's easier to make up stuff than tell you the truth." She paused again. I could sense the emotion in her tone. "Look, he was the one who screwed up my family. And for what? That bimbo he met at work? The one who eventually left him after they moved to Chicago?" She sniffed. "She even left Mr. Peabody behind. Remember him? The dog my dad hated?"

My heart hurt for her. I had no idea. "Sounds like you need to see a therapist too. Maybe we should go together." Get a discount. Two for one.

"Oh, I'm good now. I'm over it."

"Doesn't sound like it."

"Mom's happy. If she's happy, I'm happy for her. Although I never would have predicted it…marrying that creepy-looking A/C repair guy."

"Mullet man…I remember him. How are they doing? And have I been getting the truth about them, or has it all been lies?"

Joanie laughed. "I've been telling you the truth about them.

And yeah, Mr. Mullet finally cut that dumb thing off. Actually, he turned out to be an okay guy. They've been together ever since. And he treats Mom well."

"I'm glad to hear that."

"Proved to me one thing. You can't judge people by their appearance. You just—hold on a second." Joanie spoke to someone else with her phone pressed against her chest. She does it all the time. "Hey, Rach, I've got to get back to work. They apparently can't run this place for five minutes without me."

"Movin' up the corporate ladder?"

"I wish. But please do me a favor? Go see your mom. If not for you, for her. For me? Will ya?"

I sat up on the edge of the bed. "Okay. Okay. I'll go. Maybe it will be good to get out of this apartment."

"Call me when you're on your way home. We're goin' out tonight. Just you and me. You need some life in them bones, girl."

I got up and walked into the bathroom. "I have to work tonight."

"Seriously?"

"Before today, you weren't the only one around here working more than one job."

"Tomorrow night then?"

"Don't you have to work?"

"I'm taking it off. Haven't had a Friday night off in forever."

"I guess it's a good thing I'm getting a severance check, huh?"

"Oh, now you're making me feel guilty."

"You know Friday nights are the busiest for me at the restaurant, right?"

Joanie grumbled something inaudible. "Geez. Try to help a friend…"

"All right. I'll talk to the manager tonight. Tomorrow night might work." Lord knows I really don't want to be there…not this weekend.

"Done. Okay? It'll be my treat."

"Don't you have to go back to work?"

"Don't forget to call me. I want to hear how your visit went."

"Yes, Mother."

I WENT downstairs to get the mail.

After all that talk about my severance check, I wondered if it might have arrived. I was told, when they laid me off, the check would be in the mail. In banking terminology, though, that meant seven to ten business days.

Probably ten.

That way, they could hold on to their cash just a little longer. Pennies more in interest. Fatten the bottom line, cent by cent.

I opened the mailbox, and the only piece of mail was a white envelope. Similar to the one from yesterday. No return address. Generic stamp. Postmarked in Jericho, NY, with yesterday's date. I held it up to the light.

Just like the other one.

As I walked upstairs, I opened it. Inside was a folded sheet of paper. Unlike the one from yesterday, this one not only had scribbles—this time in crayon—but it also had some crudely written letters scrawled in a couple of places.

Two capital A's and two capital B's.

No obvious order.

Looked like the handwriting of a small child.

I bolted through the apartment door and raced to the garbage. I fished the other letter out, shook the coffee grounds off the paper, and wiped it down with a dishcloth. It was stained, but whatever was written there, across the page, was still legible.

I sat down on the couch and smoothed the first one out on the coffee table before laying today's letter next to it.

Looked like the same paper. Same kind of envelope. Same postmark.

My name and address were printed by hand. The handwriting didn't look familiar. It looked feminine, but not overtly so.

The envelopes had different dates stamped on them. One from yesterday. The older one from the day before that.

They arrived on different days, so they were probably mailed on different days.

There was different writing on this new page. Two letters. A's and B's. One "A" is near the upper left-hand corner. The other is in the bottom left-hand corner. One "B" is along the top, near the upper right-hand corner. The other was below it, in the bottom corner. What looked like the beginning of another letter near the middle of the page.

I leaned against the back of the couch. "This is so weird," I said to myself. Maybe somebody made a mistake. Sent it to the wrong address. Wrong person.

I could understand someone making that mistake once, but twice?

And with no return address, even if I rejected it, there was no way to return it to the sender. "So, the person sending them wouldn't even know they were going to the wrong address."

But, they have my name on them…

I could understand if the address was correct but the letter was addressed to a former tenant. Simple case of wrong address. But, whoever is sending these knows my name.

And knows I live here.

I started to freak out a little. Like a fish in a bowl. Being watched from every side. Someone was messing with my mind.

Well, if that was their intention, it was working.

I jumped up, closed the curtains, and checked the door locks.

I looked up at the corners of the room. I checked every

picture, every clock, every little hole in the wall put there by former tenants.

No button microphones.

No nanny cams.

Nothing.

None that I can see any way…

CHAPTER SIX

Long Island Psychiatric Center
Deer Park, NY

 entered the parking garage of the Long Island Psychiatric Center in my Dodge Neon. Slate grey, except for the trunk lid and back bumper. They were forest green.

Yeah. Forest green.

And no, I didn't have an accident.

I bought the piece of junk that way two years ago. Five hundred bucks. 127,000 miles. Nearly bald tires. Was probably a decent car off the showroom floor in 2002, but by the time it reached me, the old girl had been ridden hard, suffered an accident, and spewed black smoke from her tailpipe when you accelerated.

Sadly, it was all I could afford.

Finding a space near the back of the lot, I parked and toyed with the idea of leaving it unlocked with the keys resting on my seat.

Maybe someone would steal it, if tempted enough, so I could get the insurance money.

Eh, probably not.

There is nobody in this city that desperate.

I strolled in the front doors of the psychiatric center. In the lobby, centered behind a small, raised fountain, stood a Christmas tree that must have been twenty feet tall. Adorned in white lights, red bows, and an angel on top, it portrayed an elegance that seemed out of character for such a facility.

But it was pretty.

I approached the main desk. "Hi, Miss Hamar," the receptionist said.

Sarah Sinclair had been the receptionist for almost eight years now. Nice African American woman. Married. Two kids. Both girls. She was going to school part-time to get her Business Administration degree so she could "run this place someday." Her lapel sported a pin with a famous snowman's smiling face. The caption underneath read: Happy Birthday!

"Hi, Sarah." I signed my name on the clipboard. "How are you doin' today?"

"It is what it is. How long has it been, Miss Hamar? Since you visited your mom?"

That a girl. Cheer me up.

I handed her my driver's license. "Too long. I'm working two jobs now." Well, I used to have two…but I'm not gonna stand here and bore you with all the details. "Time's been a little tight, you know?"

"Oh, I know all about that. Workin' here, goin' to school, raisin' a family. Do you ever think it shouldn't be this hard? I mean, tryin' to survive, make ends meet? Seems like people shouldn't have to work two and three jobs just so they can have the lights on at night."

"It's tough. But, at least we have lights, right?" Something Freda Hotchkiss, my foster parent from many years ago, taught me. "Always be thankful for what you have," she'd say. Easier said than done, though, Freda. "Could be livin' in some sad place in another part of the world where women like you and me are sold to the highest bidder."

Sarah began bouncing her head up and down. "You see, that's why it's always good to talk to people. You get different perspectives." She clicked away at the computer mouse. "You're right. You are absolutely right. We think we got it bad. But we really don't. It could be a whole lot worse."

Yeah. Such words of wisdom. If only I could believe them too.

"Just like these people in this place, right?" Sarah continued. "Have I heard some storeeeez, honey." My visitor's pass printed out, and she handed it to me. "It does keep you humble."

But what about when that story is yours, Sarah?

No doubt, one of those "storeeeez, honey" is probably about my momma.

That's when humbleness turns to humiliation.

Big difference.

I took the pass without responding to her comments. "Thanks. Have a great rest of your day."

"You too."

Walking away, I peeled the paper backing off and slapped the pass on my chest.

Let's get this over with.

I STOOD at the door of Momma's room. Locked and secured, I peered inside through the square windowpane. The wire mesh embedded in the glass made me feel like Momma was more of a criminal than a patient. I knew it was "for everyone's safety," but sometimes, perspective was more powerful than reality.

A metal-framed, single bed, bolted to the floor in the corner of the room, was made. Appearing to sleep on top of her blanket, Momma faced away toward the wall.

A nurse stepped out of the room next door and saw me. "May I help you?"

I turned and faced her.

"Oh, Miss Hamar," Nurse Swanson said. She'd been working this floor for over a year now. Good person. Really cared about the patients, which was comforting when you were the visiting relative. "How are you doing?"

"Okay. And you?"

She peeled off her rubber gloves. Red felt antlers attached to a green headband, almost fell off her head. She repositioned them. "Well, except for this confounded thing that won't stay on top of my head, it's been a good day." She fiddled with the decoration again. "Are they straight?"

I nodded. "As straight as they're gonna get, I'm afraid."

"Dollar store item. What should I expect, huh?"

I smiled and thumbed at the door. "How's she doing?"

"Today? Quiet. Been sleeping for a while now."

I watched through the window as the nurse spoke. Momma moved a little. Repositioned herself. "Can I go in and wake her?"

"Sure. Allow me." She motioned for me to step back. "I need to check on her anyway." She gave a light rap on the door and opened it with her key. "Dorothy? I've got someone here to see you."

Momma remained unresponsive.

"It takes a few minutes sometimes for her to get her bearings after these new meds." She walked over and gently rubbed Momma's arm. "Dorothy, somebody's here to see you."

Momma took a deep breath. She moved her head and yawned but didn't open her eyes. "Tell Rachel I'll be with her in a minute." Her words were slight, a little slurred, but intelligible.

Nurse Swanson jerked her head around at me, her words a mere whisper. "How did she know it was you?"

"Maybe she heard my voice outside the door."

Nurse Swanson nodded, accepting my answer as a possibility. She stepped aside and allowed me to get closer. "I'm going to close the door. If you need anything, just press the nurse's button. You know the drill."

"Thank you."

Momma inhaled a quick breath. "Thank you, Lilly."

"You're welcome, my dear." The nurse winked at me and closed the door. I just watched Momma lie peacefully on her bed for a few seconds before attempting to wake her.

"Momma." I tenderly nudged her arm. "It's me. Rachel." I sat on the edge of the bed.

She rolled toward me a little and squinted as her eyes tried to adjust to the shards of light cutting through the outside window. She beamed and reached up to caress my cheek. "Sweetheart, I'm so glad to see you."

"I know it's been a while, Momma. I'm sorry for not comin' more often."

She didn't answer right away. Instead, she kept brushing my cheek with her fingers. "But you needed to today, didn't you?"

I tipped my head at an angle. "Yeah. How did you know?"

"I can see it in your eyes. They're sad."

With those words, the tears, dammed up inside in a feeble effort to appear strong for my mom, started to leak through the cracks.

"It's okay, baby girl." She pulled me down and hugged me tight around the neck. "I know. I know. Yesterday was a difficult day. I felt it too."

I hugged her for a short while before sitting up. "What do you know about yesterday?"

She gazed at me as if I should know. "It's been twenty years, hasn't it? Since Billy Baldwin died."

"Did I tell you that?" I stifled a sob.

"No, sweetheart." She stroked my cheek again, this time

wiping a tear away. "Do you remember the night you visited me in the hospital? The night it happened?"

How could I forget? "Yes."

"You remember tellin' me about how your daddy had been arrested?"

I nodded.

"I was trying to get up out of bed as I recall," she said, attempting to recollect that evening. "I wanted to go see your daddy in jail…is that right?"

"Yeah, but the nurses wouldn't allow it."

She nodded ever so slightly. "I don't remember much after that."

"That's because they shot you full of medication. It knocked you out in about two minutes."

"I do remember waking up the next morning. They were getting me ready to go to St. Patrick's. I asked what happened to you and your daddy, and the nurse told me that Elmore had killed Billy, and that he'd been arrested for murder. And you were at the police station, probably giving a witness statement." She offered a thin-lipped smile. "That's how I knew."

"I see."

"And of course, later you told me about the pregnancy…and the abortion…"

Yeah. I offered a smile that came out more like a frown. "That was a rough patch." I patted her arm. "But it seems you've come to terms with it."

Momma bit her lip. "You can never come to terms with ending someone's life, Rachel. I truly believe that. You just have to learn how to live with it somehow."

I blinked and sat up a little straighter.

Maybe that's my problem.

I haven't figured out how to live with it yet.

"I can't believe your daddy, though. He knew that Baldwin boy had struck his head on a rock. He should have rushed Billy to the hospital right then. Billy might still be alive today if he'd done it."

I squinted at her with concern and bewilderment. "Who told you that?"

"Oh…I must have heard it from somebody. But your daddy did hesitate, didn't he? And when Billy fell down, grabbing his head, your daddy waited, acted like leaving Billy out there might be the best option. That's what he did, isn't it?"

I listened to her describe the scene. It was like she was standing over my shoulder that night while I knelt beside Billy, rocking back and forth, praying and wishing he would just get up.

A cold chill slithered through my body. "Momma, I'm not sure those details ever came out in any discussions we've had over the years. I know I never told the police how Daddy waited, like he didn't know what to do. And I definitely didn't tell them how he considered leaving Billy's body out in the woods to make it look like some kind of accident." I wiped the tears from my face. "They didn't ask, so I didn't tell."

"But it came out in the trial, didn't it?"

Yes. It did. "I've always thought it was those facts that hurt Daddy the most."

"You should always tell the truth, Rachel Leah. 'The truth shall set you free.' Otherwise, what is covered up will be shouted from the rooftop." She smiled. "Or the witness stand."

"Did you talk to Daddy? Did he tell you about that night?"

"I got a letter from your father about a month after he was sentenced to life in prison. He apologized for everything, but he never got specific."

"Well," I said, wiping my cheeks again, "it didn't matter anyway. That jury was determined to use Daddy as the scapegoat so they could keep the peace. All they wanted was to keep the Baldwin family from tearin' up the town."

"Rachel," Momma said, turning a little more to face me, "we

can tell the truth, but we can't control what others do with it. That's their business. I mean, look at Pontius Pilate. He had the truth standing right in front of him, and all he did was wash his hands. So, you see, sweetheart? You speak the truth. What they do with it is something they'll have to live with…in this life and the next."

"But they sent Daddy to prison for the rest of his life."

"And rightfully so."

"But it was an accident, Momma."

"You can tell yourself what you wish, sweetheart, but when your daddy was drivin' through those woods, tryin' to find you, he kept sayin' he didn't know who was out there in those woods with you, but whoever it was, he was gonna get him. 'Nobody takes my daughter out in the woods like that,' he said."

"Did Daddy tell you that?"

Momma poked her bottom lip out and shook her head. "But it's true."

"How do you know that? Were you there? In the truck?"

"No. I wasn't."

"So how do you know what he said?"

"Well, for starters, I knew your daddy. Better than you did, I might add. There wasn't a boy in all of Randolph County that was good enough for his daughter. Why do you think he was so adamant about you goin' to college and gettin' a degree? Bein' the first Hamar in his family to go to college?"

"I did, you know."

"I know, and I'm so proud of you," she said, reaching up and grabbing my face with both hands. "And that's what your daddy wanted. He wanted you to get out of Noring. Get away from—"

"The Baldwins."

Momma held my face for one long second before dropping her hands. "That crazy family wasn't the only reason, but they were definitely at the top of the list."

"Daddy said we 'reminded him of the past.' That's what he

said that night in the woods once he learned who Billy's daddy was."

"Did he tell you the story? Of Abigail Baldwin and Henry Hamar?"

I nodded. "That was the past we reminded him of, apparently."

"Did he also mention that Abigail Baldwin and Henry Hamar were in love?"

"Yes."

"That they would sneak out into the woods to have their little trysts?"

"Daddy didn't mention that part, but I've kind of put two and two together over the years."

"Their relationship was a tragic love story. It created over a century of hatred between the two families that still lingers today."

"Why didn't anybody tell me or Billy about it? We had no idea. We fell in love innocently."

"The families both agreed that if they simply coexisted in Noring without ever havin' any interactions, they could keep the peace. I guess nobody considered that their offspring could fall in love with a member of the other family and go undetected in such a small town."

"I tried to tell Daddy I wasn't Abigail, and Billy wasn't Henry. But all Daddy said was, 'If I see it, surely the Baldwins will too.'"

"Sweetheart, you were right. You and Billy were not Abigail and Henry. You two were children. They were adults. And they lived in a different time. Different rules when it comes to family. However, Daddy was also right. You and Billy may have been just fine for the rest of your lives. No feuds. No hatred. Just love. But the Baldwin family and your Daddy would only see Abigail and Henry. They would be reminded of how a young man and woman fell in love over a hundred years ago. How she got pregnant out of wedlock. How they both ran away to live in another state but never got married. How this scandal caused both families to point a finger at the other side and blame their heathen child for poisoning the mind of their innocent one.

"They would recount the day Abigail returned home pregnant, with two children in tow, accompanied by a tale of how Henry abused her. How one of the members of the Baldwin family traveled to Arizona, hunted down Henry Hamar, and murdered him in cold blood. How he was subsequently arrested, tried, and hung for his actions. Wild West style.

"They would remember how, in retaliation for the death of Henry Hamar, the Hamar family sent a lynch mob to the home of Abigail Baldwin, stormed the house, tied up Abigail along with her children while the baby was left in its crib crying, and then set the house ablaze."

Momma paused and gripped my hand. She shook her head slightly. "Honey, those were frightful times. A month later, all five Hamar men responsible for their atrocity were arrested by U.S. Marshals and eventually sentenced to prison. At that moment, the die was cast. The families vowed to destroy each other.

"So, when your daddy said you and Billy were just like Abigail and Henry, he was telling the truth, from the perspective of the family history. Your relationship would have opened up old wounds. It would have caused too much trouble for you and Billy. And it wouldn't have been fair for your little one."

"So, that's why Daddy said we needed to end it immediately. Not so Billy and me could be happy, but so the families could live with their hatred."

"Your daddy hated the Baldwins. Nothin' was ever truer," Momma continued. "Most of it was just tradition. I tried to get him to let it go, reminding him that not one Baldwin had ever done anything to him personally, and that he shouldn't hold grudges against people he never knew."

I stood and walked over to the corner of the room. The conversation disturbed me. "So, when Daddy found out Billy was related to the Baldwins, there was never gonna be a chance of us staying together? Ever?"

Momma sat up on the edge of the bed, holding her head with one hand and balancing herself with the other. "Had Billy left when your Daddy said to leave, he might have survived the night. Had you not been pregnant, he probably would still be alive, provided you two never saw each other again. However, when you two told your daddy you were pregnant, and Billy was the father, there was no way Elmore Hamar was ever going to allow Billy to live. One way or the other, Billy and that baby were doomed if your daddy had anything to say about it."

"But at the very beginning, before Billy fell and hit his head, Daddy was trying to get me to leave. Had I obeyed and not argued with him, we would've just left Billy in the woods." I peered at Momma. Her words didn't make sense. "Billy would've just gone home, and Daddy and I would've gone to the hospital to see you."

Momma peered at me with sad eyes. "Rachel, honey, you're thinking about what happened that night. I'm thinking about what would've happened in the upcoming days and months. Do you think your daddy would have lived peaceably with Billy and the Baldwins, knowing that you were not only pregnant with Billy's child, but also you'd probably never make it to college because of it? Do you honestly believe your father would have just lived with it if you had to stay in Noring indefinitely? And be forever tied to the Baldwin family?"

The Daddy I knew and loved could have. But Momma seemed to know a different side of Daddy. And she was right. Once word got out about the pregnancy, the people who knew the story of Abigail Baldwin and Henry Hamar would have stirred things up just like they did in that courtroom the day I testified, causing such a ruckus that the judge had to postpone the trial until the next day.

"Momma, I miss Billy so much. He wasn't like all the other people in his family. He was different. He didn't even get along with his two cousins at school. They picked on him mercilessly. He hated that side of his family."

Momma patted the bed beside her with her hand. "Here. Sit with me."

I wiped my face with my shirtsleeve and sat down.

She draped her arm around me. "No matter how much you replay those events, no matter how much you mourn, Billy isn't coming back."

"But I loved him, Momma." I bent over and buried my face into my hands. "When will those feelings go away?"

She pulled me close. "Oh, sweetheart, you never want them to go away completely. They remind us of so much."

"I know." Anger rose inside me. I sat up straight. "That's why I want to forget."

"Honey, it's not healthy to only remember the good things. We learn from pain. We learn from heartache. We realize from the bad times how blessed we are in this life when the good times do roll around, and they remind us that this was not how it was all supposed to be." She paused. It was as if something inside her ordered her to stop. She took a deep breath before releasing it with a bit of an edge. "That's what happens when sin enters the picture."

Sin.

That three-letter word.

The one that promised so much.

But only took.

"Momma, it's...it's more than that. That was twenty years ago. And I'm still dealing with some pretty bad things right now."

"I heard."

"Heard what?"

"That you lost your job at the bank."

I twisted my torso toward her. The look on my face must have been amusing because Momma laughed. "How did you…?"

"God told me." She placed her hand on my arm and patted it like she had done a million times. "I've been prayin' for you ever since."

"Listen,…you know I love you, and I want nothing more than to see you get out of this place, but Momma, you're gonna have to—"

"Stop talkin' about God? Is that what you were gonna say?"

I grimaced. "Somethin' like that."

"Well, you're not the only one who thinks that way. The nurses say the same thing. So do the orderlies. Even my doctor tells me as much. But at least he admits a healthy faith can be a good thing." She offered a tired smile.

"That should tell you something, Momma. If everybody is saying your actions are not…"

"Normal?"

"Well, yeah. If everybody is saying your actions aren't what other people usually do, then it must mean something, right?"

Momma looked away and retracted her hand. Her gaze dropped to the floor. "It's amazing how folks will give God some of their lives, when it's convenient. However, to give him all of their lives, the way Jesus commanded us, and see the world for what it truly is, through God's eyes instead of their own, that, somehow, seems like lunacy."

"But it's true, Momma. You'd be out of here by now if you'd just keep it to yourself." I placed my hand on her shoulder. "I'm not asking you to stop believin' or anything like that, so don't get me wrong, okay? But just don't say anything around these people. Make them think you don't see Jesus, Joseph, and Mary anymore. Make them think you're better. Healed. Normal again."

Momma faced me again and peered into my eyes as if she was conducting an eye exam. "You want me to lie in order to get out of here."

"Not necessarily. Just don't be so forthcoming, that's all. They don't have to know everything."

"Rachel, if you name a pig Rose, is it still a pig?"

"What?"

She pursed her lips like she was frustrated with me. "If you name a pig Rose, or Violet, or Daisy, is it still a pig? Or does it become a sweet-smelling flower?"

I had to admit it. I missed Momma's backwoods simplicity sometimes. "Yes, Momma. I get it. It's still a pig."

"So, when you tell me to not be so forthcoming, what you're asking me to do is only tell enough truth to manipulate my situation. In this case, enough so that I can get out of here."

"Exactly."

"Yet, I'll still be the abnormal lunatic who sees and speaks to Jesus, Joseph, and Mary." She gave a half-hearted shrug. "Call me Daisy, Rachel. But when I walked out of here, I'd still be a pig. Not to mention, I'd be trusting in my own ways rather than God's."

"But, Momma, do you really think God wants you to be in this place?"

"Well," she said, brushing her slacks, working out the wrinkles, "that's just it. *I* don't think I need to be in here. You obviously think the same. But the people who sent me here have other conclusions."

"That's why you need to tone down the God stuff. You don't have to stop talking to God, just don't broadcast it to everybody around you. Keep it personal."

She stopped the brushing and looked up at the outside window, which was eight feet above the floor and not big enough to crawl through. "Why was Paul allowed to be imprisoned, chained to a prison guard twenty-four hours a day? Why was

Peter crucified upside down? Why was John exiled to the island of Patmos for the rest of his life? God could've gotten them out, saved them, so why didn't He?"

"You're asking the wrong person."

"Well, when I see Him face-to-face someday, I'm gonna ask that question. But I suspect one of the reasons was to show that God could do miraculous things even when it seems all hope is lost. So that we're reminded of who's in control. So we don't pat ourselves on the back too hard, congratulating ourselves for how smart we think we are. At least that's how I feel about it." She turned her eyes to me. "I believe God can use me here." She began to chuckle. "And what better place for God to be than in a crazy house operated by a bunch of skeptics?"

I listened, becoming more convinced by the minute that trying to reason with her wasn't going to produce anything but anxiety for me.

"Momma, did you hear about Joanie?"

"No." A downcast aura swept across Momma's face. I don't think the change of topic pleased her. "Is she still living with you?"

"Yep. We have to live together. We'd never be able to afford a place in the city on our own."

"Have you met any attractive young men of late?"

"Mom, I'm thirty-five. If I meet young men, people start looking at me like I'm some kind of cougar."

She smiled. "Honey, I didn't mean twenty-something young. You have to remember, at my age, thirty-five is young."

I clasped my hands together. "Well, the answer to your question is no."

"How hard have you been tryin'?"

"Momma, I don't think that's any of your business."

"I just want to know what's goin' on in my baby's life, that's all. And to know how to pray too."

"Well, it seems you have a hot line to Heaven. Can't you just pick it up and call whenever you want? Get the latest, up-to-the-minute reports on me?" I watched Momma's face switch from pleasant to annoyed. "I mean, you knew about the bank job. You knew about Billy. About what Dad was thinking before he met us in the woods—"

"It doesn't work like that. And I don't take too kindly to your irreverence. I just care about you, Rachel Leah. But, if your love life is too private to indulge your mother, then we can talk about something else." She looked at the outside window again. "How's the weather looking today?"

I rolled my eyes. "You know, Momma, you can still be a real smart aleck sometimes."

She smiled. "When I try."

CHAPTER SEVEN

Long Island Psychiatric Center
Deer Park, NY

Momma and I visited for about another twenty minutes. She showed me the letter Aunt Sue wrote her a couple of weeks ago.

Wow. Did that open up old wounds.

The morning after Billy died wasn't the first time Momma had been admitted to St. Patrick's Psychiatric Hospital. It was the third time. When she was sent there the first time, I was nine years old, and Aunt Sue helped take care of me because Daddy worked long hours. I practically lived with Aunt Sue and Uncle Ronald during those couple of weeks. They did everything. Helped get me ready for school. Made sure I got home safely. Took me to doctors' appointments, tutoring, wherever I needed to go.

They did it again three years later when Momma was admitted the second time.

After Momma was released, they put their house up for sale and moved in the middle of the night to North Carolina. Momma didn't even know where they had moved for six months until she received a letter from Aunt Sue, explaining the entire affair, naming our family as the sole reason for their exodus.

Aunt Sue and Uncle Ronald were the only remaining kin in the area. Once they were gone, my family became the last members of the Hamar clan to live in Randolph County.

So, when Momma got sent to St. Patrick's for the third time, the morning after Billy's death, it created issues for me. Daddy was in jail for Billy's murder, and Aunt Sue and Uncle Ronald lived in another state.

Joanie and her mother pleaded with the social worker to allow me to stay with them, but "the law is the law," he said. And with that, Bill Summers, my case manager, moved me to the foster home of Wilbur and Freda Hotchkiss four days before Christmas.

Bill Summers had tried calling my aunt and uncle to ask them to help, but I knew the answer to that inquiry before he ever dialed their number. And since I never heard the outcome of Mr. Summers's call and ended up in foster care, my suspicions were confirmed.

They wanted nothing to do with their niece.

But that was okay. The feeling was mutual.

As it turned out, Aunt Sue had been sending Momma about three to four letters a year. Momma said she believed they were guilt offerings. My aunt's way of apologizing for not being more assertive with her husband in order to take care of kin.

"Momma, there's one more question I have before I go."

She grinned. "Only one?"

"That day, the day Billy died, Officer Wells, the officer who used to take me to see you in Cincinnati, told me a story. According to one of the nurses at the hospital there in Noring, when they brought you into the emergency room that evening, you were telling them you needed to leave. You kept saying—"

"My daughter was in trouble and that she needed me."

"Yeah. Something like that. But, I don't think Billy had even picked me up from Joanie's house yet when you were taken to the hospital."

Momma just shrugged as if she knew more than she was revealing.

I searched her eyes. "How did you know I'd be in trouble?"

She offered me one of her patented motherly smiles. The kind Moms give you when they want to say, "I told you so." Without lifting her arm, she pointed toward the ceiling.

"Oh. You're tellin' me God told you that too?"

"He didn't tell me what exactly. Just that you were in trouble. Had they let me go and find you, who knows what might have happened? I might have been able to stop things before they got out of hand."

It was true. If there was anyone Daddy would have listened to that night, even in the presence of a Baldwin named Billy, it was Momma.

I didn't say anything else about it.

The trip down memory lane had made sure any and all healed wounds were reopened.

I hugged Momma, and we said our goodbyes. She wanted to escort me to the front lobby, but she knew they'd never approve it, so she pushed the button and called for the nurse.

Nurse Swanson offered to walk with us to the elevator, but Momma could tell I was uncomfortable with that. So, she told me goodbye and made me promise to come back sooner. I did and left.

Once we exited the room, I motioned for the nurse to follow me down the hallway.

"What is it?" Nurse Swanson said.

I squared up my stance and looked Nurse Swanson in the eye. "What kind of medication is she on?"

"I'd have to pull up her charts to be sure."

"The reason I'm asking is because she just told me some things in there, things she shouldn't know, things she really had no way of knowing, like she's become clairvoyant or something?"

Nurse Swanson looked away, avoiding eye contact at first. "Well, I can say one thing. She's been a busy lady."

"Busy? What's that supposed to mean?"

"You know how she talks to…" Nurse Swanson looked up and down the hallway. "People? In her room?"

I nodded and motioned with my hand. "Go on."

Nurse Swanson leaned against the wall. Her voice softened, got quieter. "I've walked by her room on more than one occasion and heard her talking. The first time it happened, I thought she had a visitor. Thought it might even be you since you're the only outside person who comes to see her.

"When I stopped and looked inside her room, I saw two men standing next to her."

"What were they wearing?"

"I couldn't tell. The light coming through the window was really bright. All I could see were their silhouettes."

"How do you know they were men?"

"Truthfully, I didn't. I just assumed they were because they both were much taller than your mother."

"What did you do?"

"I was wondering how they got in there, so I opened the door to introduce myself. But when I did, your mother was the only one in the room. She was still standing in the same place, but there was no one else there. I apologized for the intrusion and walked back out."

"What did my mom do?"

"She just looked at me and smiled."

"She never said anything?"

Nurse Swanson shook her head.

"Then what?"

"I closed the door and looked through the window again. But that time, all I saw was your mother."

"Nobody else was in the room?"

"No." She looked up and down the hallway again. "I've never told anyone about that incident until now, so please don't tell anybody. But you're her daughter, so…I thought you should know."

I leaned back a little and squinted. "You know, I think you're the first person, besides my mother, who has actually seen someone when Momma was talking to this Jesus and Joseph."

Nurse Swanson narrowed her eyes. "And you know about Mary, right?"

I did.

At first, long before I was born, Momma used to talk to Jesus.

Shortly thereafter, Joseph was added to the conversations.

Then, Mary.

Jesus, Joseph, and now Mary.

Sometimes all three of them at the same time.

This newest phase of her psychosis, Mary, started about fifteen to twenty years ago. The doctors said they believed it was her mind trying to fill in gaps. They told me trauma often proved to be the trigger in these cases. When a traumatic event takes place, the mind creates a safe haven, a place, which could be stored in a memory, created out of a hodge-podge of memories sandwiched together, or completely made up. That safe haven could take on any form. An actual place. A thing.

Even a person.

About two years after my abortion, on one of my visits with Momma, I finally told her the rest of the story. She knew I had been pregnant. That much had been revealed to her. But when she learned of the subsequent abortion, she went bonkers. She became unruly. She wailed and kept saying repeatedly, "Oh, God, I was hoping it wasn't true." I had to leave, and the orderlies and nurses had to restrain her.

I walked out of the room feeling horrible.

It was definitely a low point in my life. A life filled with numerous moments of dragging the bottom.

The doctor believed the trauma of that revelation could have been the trigger.

It probably was.

I didn't visit again for six months. I kept in contact with her doctor at the time, Dr. Winnegan, and he updated me whenever I called, but we both felt it best that I stay away until Momma requested to see me.

Six months later, she did.

But I still felt terrible…

~

I FELT a hand on my shoulder. "Rachel," Nurse Swanson said, "are you okay?"

"Yeah. And yes, I know about Mary." I patted her hand before she removed it. "There haven't been any others show up, have there?"

"No. Just the three."

"And please tell me everyone has been cordial to Momma despite her…beliefs?"

"Oh, yes. Most certainly."

"Good. Because I remember how the orderlies in Cincinnati treated her when they found out she saw and talked to Jesus and Joseph. I overheard one of them tell another how he asked Momma to let them know when Pharaoh or King David showed up, and they'd roll out the red carpet."

Just lowlifes being insensitive.

"I'm so sorry. But no. No one here would do such a thing. They'd be canned in a New York minute. The doctors here would never allow it."

"That's good to know." I inhaled deeply and gave a comforted nod.

"There's one more thing." She checked the hallway one last time. "Remember when I called your mother a busy lady a few minutes ago?"

I nodded. "Uh-huh."

"About...two weeks ago..." She began counting with her fingers. "No, three weeks ago, your mother started telling her doctor about another physician in the building. What was weird about it, though, was she knew things about that doctor no one could explain."

"Like what?"

"Turns out, they were personal things. Real personal. She told a story about this other doctor and how he was meeting up with one of the nurses, usually after hours, you know, after his shift was over, but sometimes it was happening while they were on the clock too."

"So, what? They were hookin' up?"

"Having an affair, actually. Both were married."

"What's so alarming about that? Happens all the time." Just ask the last bum I dated. His wife wasn't too happy when she learned about the removal of his wedding ring when he frequented the bar where Joanie worked.

"Well, that's just it. Nobody knew about it. And since then nobody has been able to come up with a justifiable explanation as to how your mother found out. Yet, she did. And she relayed some pretty distinct details that were later admitted to by the doctor and the nurse. She pretty much had everything correct."

I looked in the direction of Momma's room. "Maybe she overheard somebody else talking about it."

"Like I said, nobody knew about it. Or so they said. This

whole story has been the buzz for the last three weeks. We've had newspaper reporters here, snooping around. We even had one sneak in, posing as a guest of a patient he knew."

"They didn't allow them to interview my mom, did they?"

"Oh, heavens no. They haven't been allowed to talk to anyone, except the hospital's spokesperson. The hospital administration is still beside themselves. The professional ethics handbook is cut and dry. If you do what they were doing, especially on the grounds, you're gone. Losing Dr. Stephenson was huge. He was one of their biggest names in the research department. He had written scads of magazine and journal articles, published several books, which are used in university campuses all over the country, in the higher-level psych programs. His name alone secured a lot of money in medical grants. It's been a big blow to the center, I hear. And he lost his adjunct teaching position at some college in Minnesota."

I looked at Nurse Swanson, my disbelief written on my brow. "In a place this big? Nobody knew? Nobody saw anything? Nobody noticed a twinkle in their eyes when they were together?"

"Apparently not. Nevertheless, when the news broke, the hospital administration had to investigate. Everybody who worked with the doctor and the nurse said they hadn't seen or heard anything. The nurse who was involved finally admitted that they had a regimented schedule of when they got together in order to avoid detection.

"Turns out, they didn't work on the same wing. So, they didn't have a great deal of interaction at work." Nurse Swanson leaned toward me, and in a whisper said, "He had a house rented in Pennsylvania. He would tell his wife he was attending this conference and that conference when, in fact, he and Nurse Rivers were meeting there. Apparently, she told similar stories to her husband so she could get away."

"And everybody, no doubt, wondered how a fifty-something-year-old woman like my mom, who is a resident at the same hospital, found out about something nobody else suspected."

"Exactly."

"Did anybody ask her?"

"Oh, yeah. The hospital administration's investigator came here and interviewed her," she said, pointing at the door. "Asked her all sorts of questions, according to your mom."

I glanced in Momma's direction again. "Does she ever get out of this room?"

"Sure. She has to be escorted by someone, though. All the patients on this wing do."

"So, she does get out? Take walks? That sort of thing?"

"Yes, ma'am. And visits the doctor in his office. Goes outside for fresh air breaks. Even goes to the cafeteria once a week for lunch. She's about ready to start going twice a week."

I closed my eyes, trying not to cry again.

I'm so sorry, Momma. That's no way to live.

Nurse Swanson placed her hand on my shoulder again and patted it gently.

"So," I said, trying not to break down, "it is a distinct possibility that someone could've been talking about that doctor and nurse? Then, my mother overhears them on one of her fresh air breaks or in the hallway or wherever? And when the news breaks, they blame it on the crazy, long-time resident because the people from whom my mother received her information all denied knowing anything, making it their word against my mom's?"

She shrugged. "I guess that's a possibility."

"Why say you know anything about such a volatile situation when a crazy person can take the fall?"

"I know that sounds plausible, but that's also a lot of what ifs, don't you think? All those things—fresh air breaks, visits to the doctor's office—were all designed to ease her back into a normal routine. She didn't leave her room without an escort. And if she did hear about that incident in a hallway or outside, don't you think the nurse or orderly would have too? And don't you think your mom would have said, 'Nurse So-and-So or Orderly Such-and-Such was there. He or she heard it too. Ask him? Ask her?'"

She had a point. Juicy news like that would have spread like wildfire. It would have been all over social media.

Gossip at its finest.

"But Miss Hamar, I want you to know, your mother's actually been doing very well recently, despite all the hubbub."

I pointed at the room. "Of course she is. She's asleep half the time."

"No. She's actually awake more than not these days. You just caught her right after she took her morning meds. She took them a little late this morning because of one of those fresh air breaks. She said she wanted to enjoy the fresh air with a clear head, so she went outside before breakfast today."

"How many times a day does she take meds now?"

"Used to be four when she first got moved to this wing. Then it was three. Now, it's two. Early to mid-morning, after she's had something to eat, and then sometime after dinner. Usually before she goes to bed."

"Could I get a list of those meds?"

"Follow me. I'll pull her chart."

CHAPTER EIGHT

En Route to Santorino's Italian Grill
Long Island Expressway

The ride back to Manhattan from the Long Island Psychiatric Center went by quick, probably because I kept replaying all the conversations from my visit over and over in my head. As one discussion morphed into another, a realization became clear to me.

Unless they moved Momma or released her, I was never getting out of New York City.

Not unless I wanted to leave her. Never see her again.

And that I couldn't do.

She was the only family I had.

SEVEN YEARS into his minimum twenty-five-year sentence for second-degree murder, Daddy got into a fight with another inmate in the prison yard. I was twenty-two at the time, and from what I was told, Daddy did a number on that guy.

I can only imagine. Those sledgehammer-sized fists of his had created legendary stories in Noring, West Virginia.

As a result, he was moved from the Northern Regional Jail and Correctional Facility in Moundsville to the Mount Olive Correctional Complex.

However, like any place where people reside, news can travel fast when the lips are loose. Word got out that Daddy beat up a gang member who had stolen some of his belongings. The report said Daddy actually saw the man go through his stuff. He initially reported it to the officer on duty, but by the time the officer arrived, the gang member was sitting on his own bunk, reading a magazine. Daddy's stuff was gone, no doubt being held by someone else.

So, when Daddy got his opportunity, he confronted the man in the prison yard. They had words, and Daddy told the man he expected his belongings back on his bed by nightfall or else. The gang member laughed in Daddy's face and told Daddy he wasn't man enough to whip him, so he wasn't worried.

Wrong answer.

Daddy sent the twenty-eight-year-old man to the hospital with multiple fractures to his jaw, a fractured skull, damage to his pancreas, and severe ligature marks around his neck. Apparently, it took six correctional officers with Tasers to get Daddy to release the man's throat and pull him off.

The gang member died the next day.

Daddy was tried and convicted of first-degree murder and moved to Mount Olive.

But his troubles didn't end there.

Four months later, Daddy was shanked by another gang member, a friend of the man Daddy killed. The man walked up behind my dad, and with a filed-down piece of welding rod, he stabbed Daddy in the back, puncturing his lung.

They got into a scuffle, but Daddy never had a chance.

I believe Daddy actually welcomed death. I think that's why

he urged Billy to pull the trigger twenty years ago when Billy stood by his truck with a shotgun leveled at Daddy's chest.

In Daddy's mind, it would have solved everything.

Billy would have gone to prison. Our relationship would have been over. And Daddy would have died and finally been put out of his misery.

Everything solved with one shot.

But that's not how it went down.

That gang member simply messed with the wrong person. And Daddy took out years of frustration on him, knowing he'd eventually forget to watch his back one day.

Hoping someone would finally do what Billy could not.

So, as I said, Momma was all I had left.

If she ever passed away, I'd be all alone.

NYC it was.

For now.

CHAPTER NINE

Santorino's Italian Grill
Third Avenue
Manhattan, NY

I arrived at work early and decided I might as well grab a bite before my shift started. I didn't generally eat where I worked, but I decided to break my own rule on a day when it seemed all the rules didn't apply anyway.

Two letters without a return address.

A doctor and a nurse having an affair despite knowing the consequences of breaking the rules of the ethics manual.

A clairvoyant patient hearing from God and reporting her findings like an undercover reporter.

A nurse seeing multiple people in a patient's room only to find her eyes were playing tricks. Or were they? She didn't report it to anybody because she was afraid they'd exchange her nurse's scrubs for a room down the hall from Momma's.

And a jacket that's really straight.

As you can see, the day had already been trying enough. Why not go all out? Go for broke? Break all the rules?

Joanie would applaud me right now.

"Finally!" she would say. "You're livin' it up."

Oh, yeah, sister. I'm paintin' the town red. I'm eating Italian. Such a wild child.

At my request, Penny, one of my coworkers and one of four waitresses on the afternoon shift, placed me at an outdoor table so I could people watch. A hobby I enjoyed.

The only hobby I had.

I found it fascinating to observe people. Especially this time of year. The Christmas decorations up and down the avenue. The crisp air. The promise of the holidays. Even when you were down and depressed from a trip to a psychiatric hospital, the feelings aroused by the festive music brought a smile somehow.

Single people, pairs, groups, all made their way here and there, to and fro, while I wondered what they were thinking about, talking about, where they lived, where they worked…

All those questions you think of but never get any real answers when you "people watch."

It was all speculation on your part. Half-educated assumptions based on superficial observations, like clothes, jewelry, mannerisms, gait, and the shopping bags a person carried. It's like judging a book by the cover without ever taking the time to read what's inside.

Kind of like how we interact with people we don't really know.

As they walk up to you at a bar, in a coffee shop, or at the crosswalk.

The cordial smiles. The quick, cautious glances.

The desire for the bartender to interrupt and toss the stranger out.

The wish for the barista to take and make your order so you can leave.

The impatient tap of the foot at the intersection, waiting for the little illuminated man on the blinking sign to start walking.

Anything to stop the madness of feigning interest.

Superficial. Paper-thin. Conversations.

The scratch-the-surface kind of stuff we're willing to tell anyone because it's safe. "I'm a Pisces. I live on the island. I have two cats, Kibbles and Bits. I like long walks on the beach."

Blah, blah, blah.

Nobody really knows anybody anymore.

Not in my world, at least.

I wasn't even sure I knew everything about Joanie, and she was the closest friend I've ever had…

Well, so much for the joyful mood of the season.

Penny interrupted my roller coaster of emotions with a glass of water. "Rachel, I've never seen you eat here before. Is this your first time?"

"Yep."

"Really? You know they give us food half price as an employee, right?"

"Sure do. Just never been a big Italian fan."

"No way. You work here and don't like Italian?"

"I said I wasn't a big fan. I didn't say I hated it."

Penny inhaled deeply. "I just love the smells. The pizza. The lasagna. All of it."

"You see, I do too. But by the end of my shift, I've smelled it so much, the last thing I want to do is eat it."

"We better get your order in, then," Penny said, taking another deep, exaggerated breath, "before you intake too much of this…this…bliss."

I responded with a girlish giggle. "Yeah, you're right."

Superficial. Paper-thin. Conversations.

"So, what will it be?"

I had perused the menu, but nothing excited me. "What's the special today?"

Penny glanced at her watch. "Lunch special still has about

forty-five minutes left. Italian meatball sub. The dinner special tonight is gonna be chicken cacciatore, by the way.”

“Thanks, but no thanks.” I spied other people’s plates. “What’s that guy eating? That looks pretty good.”

“Uh, looks like the eggplant parmesan. Hold on.” Penny strolled over to the gentleman and asked him if she was correct. He responded to her, she nodded, and walked back over to my table. “Yep. I was right.”

“I’ll have that.”

Penny scribbled it down. “Got it.”

As Penny stepped away, she stopped, spoke to the man with the eggplant parmesan, and thanked him for his help. Once she cleared the doorway, the man looked over my way and smiled.

I returned the gesture.

“Is this what you ordered?” He pointed at his meal.

I nodded. “Yes. It looks really good.”

He gave me a thumbs-up signal. “Tastes even better than it looks.”

“Great.”

He waved and went back to his dinner.

Superficial. Paper-thin.

I watched him slice his meal into pieces.

I’m a Scorpio, by the way…If you’re into that sort of thing.

I finally turned away and observed the crowds traipse up and down Third Avenue.

A couple of minutes later, Penny brought me a basket of freshly baked bread sticks and a few pats of butter. She also set down a glass of wine.

“I didn’t order wine.”

She turned her head slightly and smiled. “No, but the eggplant parmesan at table sixteen did. He said to tell you that you can’t eat that dish without a really good Primitivo or Zinfandel.”

“Seriously?”

"Yes, ma'am. That's a $22 glass of wine, so sip it. Slowly."

I glanced in the direction of the man. A smile spread across his face. He nodded and went back to his meal.

"I think you have a not-so-secret admirer there, Rachel."

"Whatever. Not the first time a guy's bought me a drink."

Penny peeked over her shoulder at the man before leaning closer to me. "Oh, so you get this all the time? Guys buying you expensive wines? It happens so often you don't give it a second thought?"

I chuckled to myself. "It happens quite often, actually, but for the most part, the drinks are cheap, and the guys are cheaper."

"Did they look anything like this guy?"

Suit. Short hair. Knows how to hold a fork and knife. "Not even close."

"And that drink ain't cheap either. You wouldn't have ordered it."

"You're right. I can't afford wine like this."

"Well, girlfriend, maybe your luck is changing."

I took a quick glimpse at the man again. He was eating and watching the people like I had been a few minutes ago. "Bye, Penny. Don't you have some tables to check on?"

"I do. I'll be back in a few."

I wiggled a wave with my fingers and took a sip of the wine. Smooth, indeed. Definitely better than beer or the watered-down drinks at Joanie's bar.

I set the glass down and returned to my people watching.

About ten minutes later, Penny brought my meal and set it down in front of me.

"I have to say, that does smell good," I said. "The guy at table sixteen says it tastes even better than it looks."

"Well, darlin', it's gonna taste real good now. Prince Charming picked up your tab."

"What? No. No. He can't do that. Tell him I said thank you, but I really would feel better if—"

"Too late, sunshine. He's already paid for it. His table isn't mine, so I didn't know until after the deed was done."

Just then, the man stood. I expected him to look our way, smile, maybe even come over and begin a conversation about the weather or the fact that he drove into the city from the suburbs. But instead, he rose from his seat, pushed his chair under the table, and left.

Penny, watching the whole thing unfold like I was, pursed her lips. "Hmm. That's refreshing."

"How is that refreshing?"

"A man buys you one of the most expensive wines on the menu to go along with your meal—the same meal he had—and then pays for the whole thing himself without coming over here to get your phone number or your name? How is that not refreshing?" Penny picked up my empty water glass. "And they say chivalry is dead."

"I don't like handouts."

"Handouts? Get off your high horse, Queen Bee. What I just witnessed was sheer heaven. Renews your faith in people. Everybody wants something these days. Nothing is free, even if it's advertised that way."

Just then, the man returned to his table.

"Well, *Yente*," I said. I watched him out of the corner of my eye. "It appears we've been played. Looks like the ol' 'Oops, I forgot my phone or my keys or my wallet or my glasses' routine. And then he looks over in this direction, makes his way over to the table, and then asks for my phone…"

As I spoke, the man did indeed retrieve his glasses off the table and slipped them into his blazer's inner pocket. But he never looked our way. He simply left like he'd done before. No eye contact. No smiles. Waves. Nods. Nothing.

Not superficial at all.

Instead, slightly intriguing.

Penny laughed when he exited the restaurant. "Yep. You're

an expert. You ought to write a book." She reached down and picked up a dirty plate from the empty table next to mine. "You sure had him all figured out."

"You just blew your tip."

"No worries. According to Maddison, he did that too, for both of you."

Penny stopped and circled back to me. "Oh, and by the way, Dr. Phyllis, if you didn't notice, he didn't have a wedding ring on either."

"That doesn't mean a thing. Trust me."

"It's true he could have just taken it off, but he didn't know you were coming in here, did he…Hmm? Just sayin'."

True enough.

He was nice.

Maybe too nice.

At least, that's what I told myself as he crossed Third Avenue and strolled down the street.

LATER THAT EVENING, business picked up. Ten waitresses and six waiters, and we were still having a hard time keeping up with the demand. Not a good thing in the restaurant industry. You want a steady business. You want repeat customers. You want them to walk away happy. But when you're slammed, the wait time has grown to over an hour, and you're down two people, everything drops. The patience of the patrons. The stamina of the work staff. The reviews from the Yelp crowd.

And the tips.

I was smiling. I was apologizing. I was giving people free dessert for waiting so long. I was taking twenty percent off the bill if an order was wrong. All the things we're trained to do.

On good days, tips in a restaurant like this push twenty-five percent. Sometimes even more if you got a happy tourist looking to make someone's day.

But on the harried days, you're lucky if you get fifteen.

Then, there are the jerks. On this night—of all nights—one of my patrons gave me a virtual tip. That's right. The man wrote on the tip line these words:

Here's your virtual tip of 20% to match the virtual resemblance of service.

Then, when you looked down at the total, he had only paid for the meal. The tip was literally virtual. Non-existent. *Nada*.

Had I known, I would have given him a sneezer.

But instead, I raced around, taking care of my customers as best I could because I always try, even when people hate me.

I came to work wondering if I should just do this full-time. But now, I was thinking tonight may not be the best night to make such a decision.

However, my severance package from the bank wasn't going to last forever.

If I did work full-time at the restaurant, I'd make about as much as I did at the bank…

Provided I worked at least fifty hours a week…

And most of it would be cashed out in tips…

"It's a thought," I said aloud while filling someone's drink.

Penny stayed on for some overtime and to help out. When I blurted out those words, she stopped and leaned over to me. "What are you thinking, princess?"

I chuckled. "Did you hear that?"

"Sure did."

"I was just wondering if I should do this full-time."

"I thought you had a job at the bank?"

"Yeah. Had a job."

"You got fired?"

I shook my head. "Laid off."

"That stinks."

"So, now, I'm looking for another job."

Penny scooped some ice from the ice machine and filled a glass. "My brother works at a bank. I could talk to him. You were a teller, right?"

"Yep," I said, my lips making a pop sound.

"Is that something you still want to do?"

"I'm not sure."

"Let me know. I can talk to him and see if he has anything available."

I raised my shoulders with an animated shrug. "Sure. Why not? Can't hurt. Worst he can say is no, right?"

"I'll call him tomorrow." She pulled out a serving tray and began to load it with drinks. "Hey, you want to go get a drink after closing? Now that you don't have to get up early?"

I wasn't much of a partier. Never liked alcohol that much, and liked the party scene even less. But everyone was telling me to get out more. Even Momma wondered if I had met any "young men" lately.

Hard to do that in our apartment complex. Locked inside, staring at the TV.

"Sure," I said. "We could go to Joanie's bar. She's on tonight. We'll get her employee discount."

Penny lifted her tray. "I'm in."

Friday

December 12, 2014

CHAPTER TEN

West 173rd Street
Washington Heights, NY

I awoke to the sound of the delivery truck outside my bedroom window. Its back-up beeper blared up and down the street, piercing my ears despite the box fan's attempt to block out the noise.

I lifted my head and strained to see the clock.

9:52 a.m.

Oh my.

Joanie's already at work. Manningham's Construction.

I don't know how she does it.

Penny and I stayed at the bar until one-thirty, and Joanie closed down and walked in the apartment door at three. Then, back up at six-fifteen to be at Manningham's by seven.

Her industrious nature made me feel like a moocher. That annoying friend who always seems to lose the good-paying job so she never has any money to throw at the bills.

I had a good job.

Not anymore, though.

I was a good employee, they said. "Unfortunately, you're just a casualty of budget cuts."

Yeah. The collateral damage of the bottom line.

Money over people.

That always makes you feel special.

While bigwigs get golden parachutes, the little people get tossed from the plane with a goodbye and a promise of a water landing in ten business days.

I rolled over and stretched as the phone rang. I snagged it off the base. "Whoa," I said as I picked it up, feeling a little hungover. "Hello?"

"Rachel, it's Penny. You got a minute?"

I rolled onto my back and grabbed my head. "Yeah. What's up?"

"I just got off the phone with my brother. He said they don't have anything right now, but they do have a person who's leaving in about two weeks. She just turned in her two-week notice yesterday, and they're gonna put the job out on all the online job sites later today. But he said for you to set an appointment and come in to see him personally. And to make sure you bring your résumé. If he thinks you'll be a good fit, then he said you could apply officially at that time. This way, you don't have to waste your time if he or you decide it's not gonna work."

"That's awesome. Thank you so much." She gave me his phone number and the name of the bank. "I owe you one."

"No, you don't. That's what friends are for. Now, all I ask is, just don't go in there and make me look like an idiot." She laughed.

"Thanks, I think."

~

I MADE myself a cup of coffee and went to get the mail. On the way down the stairs, I decided I'd better revise my résumé before I called Penny's brother and set up that appointment. With my luck, he'd want to meet in two hours, and my résumé would be four years old.

With the mail in one hand and my coffee cup in the other, I sat down in front of the computer and turned it on.

While the machine whirred to life, I sorted through a flyer for local supermarket and a couple of presorted envelopes with only return addresses pre-printed in the corner. No notable names were typed above those return addresses. And of all things, they were both marked "urgent."

Yeah. Hurry! It's so time-sensitive, we mass-mailed it.

A couple of bills. A small catalog of women's clothing addressed to Joanie. Not much else.

I tossed the mail on the floor, and a white envelope peeked out from inside the clothing catalog. I reached down and snatched it from its hiding place.

Same kind of envelope as the two I'd received over the last couple of days. Addressed to me. No return address. Stamped in Jericho, NY. This one was postmarked yesterday.

I opened the letter and unfolded the page. Instead of scribbles, a drawing of stick-figured people emerged. It appeared to be done in pencil. The drawings were crude. The hands of the two figures were nothing more than circles with lines extending from the edge of the circle.

The lines must be the fingers.

The head was another circle. The hair looked a lot like the fingers of the hand. Two dark dots represented eyes, and a curved line, turned upward, was the smile. The bodies were just lines. So were the legs, with feet that looked identical to the hands.

One figure was considerably bigger than the other. Above the smaller figure was the handwritten word, ME. Over the other, the word DADDY, printed in the same handwriting, an adult's handwriting, as the address on the envelope.

The two stick people were standing near a tree of some sort. At least, that's what it looked like. Another vertical line with an unsophisticated triangle sitting on top of it. Above the triangle about two inches and not connected to anything else, two lines extended into the air, forming what looked like a "V."

A bird, perhaps?

I studied the picture.

It seemed to me that some poor child had sent a meaningful picture to somebody. Probably intended for a father serving overseas, or maybe an incarcerated man. Or maybe a divorced father no longer living under the same roof.

But not me.

I'm not a Daddy.

Or a Mommy.

But I could have been.

I inhaled deeply. A swell of emotion flooded my body.

I need a distraction.

I folded the letter up and stuffed it in the envelope.

I added it to the other two residing in my nightstand drawer.

Get that résumé done, Rachel. Maybe they'll give you a significant raise over the last job, and you can move out of this crummy neighborhood.

I plopped down in front of the computer.

"Just don't make me look like an idiot," Penny said. I tapped at the keyboard. Clicking the mouse. The adding and updating of my multi-faceted skill set. The arrangement of strong sentences, depicting my rich pool of talent and keen intellect. Attaching reference letters from past employers, even one from the knucklehead who just laid me off because of budget cuts.

"She's an excellent co-worker," one letter said.

"She's a hard worker," said another.

"She was an asset to our team," the knucklehead said.

Superficial. Paper-thin.

Blah. Blah. Blah.

Words on a page. Never truly revealing the person inside.

If I was such an excellent, hard-working asset, then why let me go?

That's what I'd ask me if I was doing the interview. And you know what my answer would be?

Ask those lying dweebs at my old job. How should I know?

~

TWO HOURS LATER, I clicked Save and blew out a sigh of relief. It was amazing how much stuff can be added to a résumé in four years.

I took the last sip of coffee from my third cup, set the mug down, and picked up the phone. I dialed the number Penny gave me.

"Sun Ridge National Bank. This is Jocelyn speaking. How may I direct your call?"

"I was asked to call this number and request to speak with Sandy Worchiewicz?"

"Thank you. Please hold."

"Tha—" And before I could be cordial, the elevator music flooded my ear as the mellow, female sales lady told me about Sun Ridge's new IRA accounts.

Jocelyn has such a warm personality…like that of an answering machine.

Superficial. Paper-thin.

The sales lady droned on. "With Sun Ridge, it's easier than ever to escape your past, secure your future, and enjoy the here and now with—"

"Thank you for holding. This is Sandy, how may I help you?"

"Hi, Sandy, my name is Rachel Hamar. I was asked to call you for the purpose of setting up an appointment with Mr. Henshaw concerning a teller position?"

"Yes, he informed me you might be calling," she said. I could hear computer keys being manipulated in the background. "I have a nine-thirty open on Monday, as well as a four-thirty slot that afternoon. Otherwise, it will be Thursday or Friday of next week. Will either of those work into your schedule?"

"I'll take the nine-thirty."

"Perfect. When you come, please bring with you a copy of your résumé, copies of any reference letters, and contact information for those references, as well as your driver's license and your social security card."

"Anything else?"

"Have you already applied for the position online?"

"Actually, I was told to wait and meet with Mr. Henshaw first."

"You may want to bring with you any needed information in case you need to go online from here and apply, but..." Sandy said, her demeanor taking a sudden detour into pleasantness. "May I make a suggestion?"

"Certainly."

"If Mr. Henshaw said for you to come in first, before you apply online, I suggest you go ahead and apply online. That way, when he offers you the job, you can say it's already done."

"But he is just interviewing me at the request of a mutual friend. There's no guarantee he's going to—"

"Honey," Sandy said, her voice lowering to a half-whisper, "take it from someone who knows. If he asked you to meet with him face-to-face, the only way he won't hire you is if you go in there and totally mess it up."

"But, he told me—"

"Sweetheart, you can do what you want, but Mr. Henshaw is the regional manager. He oversees seven branches in the Manhattan and Long Island area. He doesn't have the time to do the hiring himself. He's got branch managers and assistant branch managers who handle that for their own buildings. So, because you're going straight to his office, you're bypassing a bunch of people in the hiring process, not to mention all the people applying online."

Penny said her brother worked in a bank. She never said he was a big shot. "I didn't realize that. All right then. I'll get right on it. Thank you, Sandy, for your help."

"Sure. And if you don't mind me asking, how did you come across this posting being it's not even online yet?"

"Like I said, as it turns out, we have a mutual friend." I wasn't about to tell Sandy who it was.

Superficial. Paper-thin.

Sometimes no information is the best course of action.

"So, it was a personal reference..." She sounded as if she was logging this information into the computer.

"Yes. Thank you, Sandy. I'll see you Monday. At nine-thirty."

"When you come into the main lobby, go to the elevators on your right. We're on the fourteenth floor."

Fourteenth floor, huh?

Nice.

CHAPTER ELEVEN

Antonelli's Pizza Emporium
Lexington Avenue
Manhattan, NY

I looked around the restaurant as Joanie and I sat ourselves. "You know I work at an Italian restaurant, right?"

"I know. I know," she said, "but you've got to try this place. Their pizza is the best in town."

"And you also know I'm not a big fan of Italian, right?"

"Yeah. So?"

"Yet you're taking me to an Italian place?"

She shrugged with her hands turned upward. "Is it a crime?"

"No. It's just—"

"It's just what? You're not a fan. I get it. But you do eat Italian, right?" She huffed. "I saw you eat a whole can of Chef Boyardee one time."

"When we were thirteen. My family was poor. Remember? I ate a lot of Chef Boyardee back then. We ate a bunch of Ramen noodles too. Boxed macaroni and cheese. PBJ's. All the culinary hits."

"Look, I told you yesterday I was taking you out. My treat. But if this isn't cool, we can just go back home, if you want." Her face turned sad. "I just wanted to celebrate my new job, and I thought that since you have an interview Monday, we could go ahead and celebrate that in advance too."

"We're fine. I can eat Italian two nights in a row."

"You had Italian last night?"

I nodded as a waiter approached our table.

Joanie leaned over, trying to squeeze her words in before the waiter welcomed us. "Why didn't you—"

"Ladies, welcome to Antonelli's. I'm Roberto, and I'll be serving you this evening."

Joanie gave our twenty-something waiter a once over. "One can only hope."

Roberto smiled and winked at Joanie. "Our special tonight is chicken alfredo for $12.99. Half orders are $8.99. And our pizza special is a Mexican taco pizza. Can I get you ladies something to drink? Mixed drink? Wine, perhaps?"

"I'll have water, please," I said.

"And you, Miss?"

"What do you suggest?" Joanie leaned closer to him and read his name tag out loud. "Roberto."

"Depends on what you like?"

She frowned. "I'm trying to be a good girl tonight."

"Then mixed drinks are probably out. Probably wine too?"

"Probably."

"We have the usuals. Soda, tea, water."

"Give me a Sprite."

"I'll be right back with those drinks." Roberto stopped at the table behind us to answer a question.

"So," Joanie said, watching Roberto as she spoke, "anything exciting happening in your life that I need to know about?"

"I got another one of those letters."

"Those letters? Oh, like the one the other day? Wednesday, was it?"

"Actually, I got one yesterday too."

She peeled her eyes away from our waiter. "What were those like?"

"Similar. But different."

"That helps. Could you be more specific?"

"The one from yesterday was a lot like the one you saw, but had a couple of letters written on it. Two A's and two B's. It was like a little kid learning how to write the alphabet.

"Then, the one from this morning had a drawing. Two stick people. One larger than the other. The smaller one had the word ME written above it in what looked to me like an adult's handwriting. The bigger stick figure had the word DADDY written above it."

"In the adult handwriting too?"

"Yeah. All capital letters. The two figures were standing next to something. A tree, I think. And above the tree, it looks like the drawing of a bird."

"Daddy, huh?"

I nodded.

"Was the smaller stick figure a boy or a girl?"

"I couldn't tell by the drawing."

"Daddy…? That's still too vague to figure out who sent it."

"I'm just afraid somebody has the wrong address, and these are supposed to be going to some father, like a guy in the armed forces or something. Maybe even a divorced husband. But all those possibilities still don't explain the fact that they are addressed to me."

"Yeah, that is weird," Joanie said as the waiter approached.

"All right," Roberto said, all cheery and pleasant. "A water for you, and a Sprite for you. Are you ladies ready to order?"

"I sure am," Joanie said. "I'll take a slice of that Mexican taco pizza with a side of Roberto to go." She batted her eyes and reached out, touching his little notepad and brushing her fingers across his as she did. "And I don't care about the cost."

Oh. My. Word. Check, please?

"One slice of the special," Roberto said, jotting it down on his pad, "and one special slice." He ripped off the bottom of the page and handed it to Joanie. "I get off at eleven."

Joanie took the piece of paper and flipped it around for me to see. She winked.

A phone number.

There's a hotel across the street, guys. "If it was me, I'd be dialing that number right now to make sure it's not the one for time and temperature."

Joanie wrinkled her brow. "Do they even have those numbers anymore?"

"Don't worry, *señorita*," Roberto said. "It's real. Go ahead. Call the number."

Joanie beamed a giddy smile and whipped out her phone. She punched in the number and waited.

"See?" he said. "Put your hand on my back pocket. It's vibrating right now."

I have to admit, I'd never seen Joanie speechless before. Nor had I ever seen her blush. But right that moment, with her right hand extended halfway, she was both.

Maybe I need to leave.

She touched his back pocket and giggled before yanking her hand back. "It's vibrating all right."

"I never play when it comes to the possibility of *amor*," Roberto said.

"You sure don't," she said.

"Uh, I'll tell you what," I said. "You can put my water in a to-go cup, and I'll just catch a cab, if that's okay. It's getting a little uncomfortable in here for me."

Joanie smacked me playfully on the arm. "Oh, stop it. We're just playing. Isn't that right, Roberto?"

"*Eres la única que quiero, mi princesa.*" He gave Joanie one long, desirous look.

I picked up my purse. "*No comprendo* but I'm sure that's my cue to leave."

Joanie reached out and grabbed my arm. "All right, show's over, Roberto. We're about to lose our audience."

"Got it." He looked me squarely in the eye. "So, do you want me to put your water on her bill?"

I peered at the both of them. It was weird how they switched from overtly flirtatious to a normal patron and a normal waiter. Before I could respond, Roberto offered an innocent smile. Joanie started to snicker under her breath. She lowered her head and began to laugh louder.

"Okay, so what's goin' on here?"

Now, they both were laughing together. Apparently at my expense.

"Oooh, I get it. You two know each other…" I looked back and forth between the two of them. "That's why you brought me here, to play this little game. Good one."

"I did think my hand on his pocket was a nice touch," Joanie said.

"A nice touch?" Roberto said. "That doesn't explain it well enough."

Those words sent the two of them into hysterical laughter.

"How do you two know each other?"

Joanie cleared her throat and rubbed her face, trying to calm down. "Rachel, I want you to meet Roberto. He works at Manningham's. We met about two weeks ago. He came into the office to see the owner about something. Our eyes met. We started talking…" As Joanie explained, her gaze slowly shifted from me to him. "…went out for lunch one day, then a couple of days later, we had dinner."

"You two are dating?"

Joanie smiled with her teeth showing. "Surprise."

"Well, for a best friend, you sure know how to keep secrets."

"You're not mad, are you?"

"Of course not. It's just…two weeks?"

"Well, actually, up until yesterday, we were just going out to lunch or dinner, that sort of thing. Either during work or right after work. Whenever we could squeeze it into our busy schedules. But yesterday, we both admitted that there's something going on between us. Some kind of chemistry neither of us has felt before." Joanie reached out and took Roberto's hand. "It's like that magic you hear people talking about all the time. You can't explain it. But you know it when you see it, feel it."

"Well…" Now it was my turn to be speechless. "I, uh, am happy for the two of you. A little, uh—"

"Stunned?"

I began nodding in agreement. "Most definitely."

"I thought that since we were going out tonight, I could introduce you to him at the same time."

"Italian, huh?"

"Had I just told you I had a boyfriend, it wouldn't have been near as much fun."

"But…wait a minute." I jerked my thumb in Roberto's direction. "How old is he?"

"I'm thirty-one."

I scanned his person. "No way."

Roberto sucked in his stomach. "You think I'm older?"

"Oh, no. Actually, I thought you were about twenty-two, twenty-three? Maybe twenty-five?"

He relaxed his stance and wiped his brow in a dramatic way. "Whew. That's good. I was afraid I was getting too fat."

"Trust me. You're not fat."

"You got that right," Joanie said. "And he's ambitious. Tell her, Roberto, what your plans are."

Roberto inhaled and cleared his throat. "I've been at Manningham's for six years now. I've applied for their engineering program. They'll send me to school if I promise to work for them after I graduate with my master's in engineering. I already have a bachelor's degree in business. So, I thought, why not? I love working there."

Joanie's grin blossomed even bigger. "Not only ambitious, but good looking and smart."

"That's why I was in the office that day." Roberto looked at Joanie, and I could tell they were head over heels for each other. "I went there to talk to the man in charge of the program, and that's when we met."

I studied the two of them for another brief moment. "I hope everything works out for you, Roberto. But I have one thing to ask of you."

"Shoot."

I placed my hand on Joanie's arm. "This is my best friend. Please treat her right. She deserves it. Don't string her along. Don't be a player and cheat on her behind her back. Don't put college and work ahead of her. Will you promise me that?"

He dropped his notepad to his side. "Yes, but I have to admit, I feel a little intimidated right now."

"Let me put it to you this way then," I said. "My dad went to prison for murder. While he was in there, he killed another man."

Roberto's eyes grew wider. And a little troubled.

"And I am his daughter. I am a Hamar through and through. Do you get where I'm comin' from, Roberto?"

Roberto placed his hand on my shoulder. "I do. And you have nothing to worry about. I really like your friend, and I think she likes me too." He looked at Joanie. "We've both decided to take this slow. We've both been through enough bad relationships. We'd like to see this one turn out different."

I covered his hand with mine. "Glad to hear it." I could see a worrisome look surface in those brown eyes of his as I stared at him intently.

Roberto fumbled for words and glanced around the dining area. "I…probably had better take your order and get to my other tables before they fire me. We can continue this conversation later, if you wish."

I removed my hand and chuckled.

"That wasn't very nice, Rachel," Joanie said.

"What? I can't have a little fun too?"

Joanie glanced at Roberto's face and laughed. "She's kidding, Roberto. She'd never hurt a fly. Although all that stuff about her dad is true."

Roberto peered at me with a more troubled look.

I pointed back and forth at his notepad and Joanie. "I'll have what she's having. Pizza, I mean. No sides."

Roberto blurted out a relieved chuckle, scribbled it on his pad, and walked away.

"Isn't he great?" Joanie said.

"Seems to be, but…"

Joanie's girlish grin switched to defense mode. "But what?"

"You know the rule, girlfriend. Never get your honey where you make your money. It's a recipe for disaster."

Joanie waved me off like I was nuts. "It ain't like that between us. He works in a completely different department. If we broke up, we'd probably never see each other again."

"I'm just sayin'. Don't say you weren't warned."

"Okay, I won't." Joanie's eyes followed Roberto across the dining room. "So, you already had Italian this week?"

"Yep. Last night."

"Where?"

"At work. Before shift. I'd never eaten there before, so I thought I'd try it."

"What did you order?" Her eyes shifted from Roberto to me. "And please tell me it wasn't pizza?"

"Actually…" I smiled. "I had eggplant parmesan. It was really good." Then, I smiled even bigger. "I also had a glass of wine with it."

"That's pretty fancy for a woman with no job."

"Didn't cost me a thing."

Joanie took a sip of her drink. "You get your meals free there?"

"Not exactly."

"What does that mean?"

"Okay, so I was sitting at this table…" I went on to explain the story about the man who ordered the eggplant parmesan and bought my meal, making sure I had a $22 glass of wine to go with it.

Joanie leaned forward and placed her hand on my forearm. "Please tell me you got his number?"

"Nope."

"Did he get yours?"

"Nope."

"So, you let a man who bought you a $22 glass of wine get away?"

"Guess so."

Joanie lowered her head and shook it in despair. "You're gonna be an old maid, Rachel." She tilted her head so she could see me out of the corner of her eye. "Sitting in a rocking chair someday, holding a cat, wishing you'd called out to him as he left the restaurant and walked down that sidewalk."

"Thanks for the encouragement."

Joanie gripped my arm tighter. "Hey, maybe he paid for his meal with a credit card. You could get his name."

"I've got his name." Penny made sure of that. "And yes, he did pay with a credit card."

"But you didn't get his phone number?"

"I didn't."

"Maybe that's why you're still single."

I offered a wiseacre smile. "Oh, that's right. You're the expert on relationships now."

"Nice. So? What's his name? Where does he live? Where does he work? How was he dressed?"

"He had on a business suit. That's all I know."

"Are you going to pursue it at all?"

"Maybe."

She shot me a befuddled look. "What are you waiting for?"

"Just let me handle this, okay?"

"Okay, okay," she said with her hands raised in surrender, "but don't wait too long. He may buy some wine for somebody else tomorrow. Somebody a little more aggressive?"

"Don't you even think about it."

"No, no, no. I wasn't talking about me. Why would I want to mess things up with Roberto? I was talking about somebody like me. You know the type."

Yes, I do. "I'll take that under advisement."

"Is there anything else you're not telling me that I should know about? Did you win the lottery? Move out while I was at work? Join the Peace Corps?" Joanie spotted Roberto at another table, and her eyes followed him.

"I do have that interview Monday."

"Yeah, for that teller position you told me about, right?"

I nodded. "As it turns out, Penny's brother is the regional manager for Sun Ridge National."

"Small world, huh?"

I took a swig of my water. "Penny told me that so long as I don't go into that meeting looking and acting like a real imbecile, I pretty much have the job."

"You see? I told you everything would work out." She turned to face me again. "That's great news."

"Yeah, it is. Of course, I don't officially have the job yet, but…"

"Is there anything I can do to help?"

"Just make sure I wake up when you do Monday morning? In case my alarm doesn't go off?"

"Done."

Saturday

December 13, 2014

CHAPTER TWELVE

West 173rd Street
Washington Heights, NY

After we left Antonelli's, I went home. Joanie went to the bar across the street and waited for Roberto to get off work.

I told Joanie not to wake me in the morning. The way I looked at it, I probably only had the weekend to sleep in. Monday morning, I'd have my interview. If what Sandy from Sun Ridge told me was true, I'd undergo all the fingerprinting and background checks that afternoon. I might be on the payroll as soon as Tuesday morning. I was already bonded. Surely, they wouldn't have me go through all that again.

So, sleep in I did.

When I rolled over to check the time, it was 10:47 a.m. I smelled coffee and knew Joanie was up.

Slipping on my robe, I plodded into the kitchen, rubbing my eyes and yawning. Joanie was buttering a piece of toast. "You just get up too?"

"About a half hour ago."

"What time did you get in?"

"Two."

"You know nothing good happens after midnight, right? Especially with a guy." I plopped down into one of the chairs at the kitchen table. "That's what my momma used to tell me. Take it from me. She was right."

"When were you ever out past midnight with a man?"

"All right, so you got me there. But it's true." Billy and I didn't need to wait until midnight. Matter of fact, we couldn't. Daddy definitely would have known something was up.

"I got the mail. You got two of those letters today. Both are postmarked Friday."

I looked around the kitchen. "Where are they?"

"On the coffee table."

I got up and hurried into the living room. I wasn't sure why, but I was a little excited, but apprehensively so.

I sat down on the couch and opened both letters. The postmark and the name on the front looked identical to the others. They also were identical to each other. From the envelopes, you couldn't tell them apart.

I fished out the folded-up piece of paper from the first one and opened it up, smoothing it out on the table. I did the same with the second one. As it turned out, I apparently had them backwards.

The first letter I opened had another drawing. This time, the stick figures were more defined. And in color. Colored pencils, it looked like. The heads had hair. The little child, a boy perhaps, had short brown hair. The older, taller person had hair that looked black but with gray lines in it. I could only imagine the person, who looked like a man, must have had hair that was turning gray. Again, the names ME and DADDY were inscribed above the stick figures, but this time, they appeared to be written by the hand of a child, not an adult.

Behind the two stick figures stood a house with what looked

to me like an in-law suite off to one side. The house was a two-story, or possibly a tall ranch-style with lots of windows. There was a long driveway leading up to a front door, perhaps? And like the previous picture, there was a tree off to one side covered in green leaves. A more distinct bird rested on one of the branches.

The difference between this one and the other picture resting beside it was the people in the background. The little artist seemed to be drawing a scene from a family reunion or maybe a birthday party in the second picture. I counted fifteen people in the picture. They all stood in front of the house, spread out across the front yard, facing the same direction, like they were posing for a picture.

Except for the additional people in the second picture and the precision of the artist's hand, by comparison, the second picture wasn't very different from the first one.

You could tell, though, this little girl or guy was getting older, more confident, and the dexterity and acumen were increasing.

This child is drawing his or her daddy pictures of their house. Of their family... The father must be somewhere... Iraq? Afghanistan? Riker's Island, maybe?

Joanie sat down beside me, chewing on her piece of toast. She tapped the second picture with her finger. "I like that one better. Whoever drew it is a better artist."

"It's not a competition. Here, I'll show you." I went into the bedroom and retrieved the other letters from my nightstand. I spread them out in the order I received them. "See? They all seem to be from the same person, judging by the envelopes. Looks like a little boy to me."

"Don't you find it strange?" She pointed to the third drawing I had received yesterday and the words ME and DADDY written by what had to be an adult's hand. "That an adult—who obviously is helping this kid, based on this handwriting right here—

would address several letters to you? With no return address?" She concluded with a wave of her hand. She picked up her toast again. "That's the part that's really odd."

"Yeah." My response leaked out as more of a thought than a verbal confirmation.

"Maybe you should go to the post office in…" Joanie picked up one of the envelopes, "Jericho and see if anyone has seen a person mailing these letters. It's got to be the mother, right?"

"Or a prankster."

Joanie pursed her lip in a thoughtful way. "Well, that's a whole 'nother deal right there. I was thinking this was just a legitimate mistake somehow. But if someone is playin' a game, then who knows who it is and why?"

"And that would make identifying the person mailing them even more crucial."

"Right…But wait a minute." Joanie took another bite and brushed the crumbs from her fingers. "What if they are being mailed from somebody's house? Who's to say the person is actually taking them to the post office in Jericho?"

I frowned. She was right. If this was a prank or something worse, the culprit would probably be smart enough not to walk into the post office and have his mug all over the security cameras. "So, going to the post office would probably be a waste of time."

Joanie chomped another bite of her toast. She held up a finger and chewed quickly. "You could still give it a shot. Who knows? Maybe this person dropped them off there after all. At least see if they can help you."

It was worth a try. I glanced at the clock on the wall.

11:21 a.m.

We'd never make it before noon. "Maybe I could go there Monday after my interview."

"I'd go with you, but I have to work." She leveled her eyes at me in fun. "Then, I have to go straight to the bar and help get things ready for Monday Night Football and half-priced wings."

"Sounds like fun."

"Want to come? Half-priced wings? Besides, I need someone to talk to. Somebody who's not trying to hit on me all night or talk to me about the game."

"Why don't you ask Roberto to join you?"

"He has to work too."

"And why does he work two jobs? Manningham's not paying him much either?"

"He makes okay money. More than me. But he's saving for school."

"I thought he said they would send him to school?"

"They are…or will…or are gonna…" Joanie rolled her eyes at her momentary lapse of proper English. "Anyway, I guess the school is pretty intense. They recommend that you don't work a job during schooling, if you can help it. So, he's saving up for it."

"You gotta love an industrious man."

Joanie smiled big. "I do." And with that, she shoved the last bite of toast into her mouth.

Monday

December 15, 2014

CHAPTER THIRTEEN

Sun Ridge National Bank
Columbus Ave.
Manhattan, NY

I rode the elevator up to the fourteenth floor of the Sun Ridge Building. Sun Ridge National Bank had branches all over The Big Apple, but its corporate offices were here on Columbus Avenue and occupied floors ten through fourteen.

The doors opened, and directly in front of me was a desk, a little taller than your standard office desk but lower than the front desk of a ritzy hotel. A woman, mid-forties, shoulder-length, brownish-blonde hair, and enough make-up to keep the Avon lady flush, sat behind the desk and was on the phone. She appeared to be having an off-the-books, hush-hush conversation.

When the doors opened, she looked up, became more clandestine, and abruptly ended the call just as I reached her desk. "Can I help you?"

"Good morning. You must be Sandy. I'm Rachel Hamar."

"Yes, yes." Sandy stood and extended her hand. "It's good to meet you."

I shook her hand. Firm grip for a woman. "I know I'm a little early."

"Actually, Mr. Henshaw likes it when people are early. Let me call and let him know you're here."

"Perfect."

Sandy punched a button, and her phone immediately began to ring. Before Mr. Henshaw answered, she picked up the receiver. "Mr. Henshaw, your nine-thirty is here…certainly, sir, I will." She hung up the phone. "If you'll follow me, I'll take you to his office."

"Thank you."

Sandy stepped out from behind her desk and pointed down the hallway. "Mr. Henshaw's office is this way." Her three-inch heels clicked on the shiny tile floors until we rounded the corner and hit some carpet. "How long have you been in the banking business?"

"About four years."

"And what was your position?"

"I was a teller."

"And where do you work?"

Present tense. Past tense. I'm not gonna differentiate for her. "First Trust."

"That's one of the bigger banks in the city. If you don't mind me asking, why would you want to leave them to work here?"

I do mind you asking. "Bigger isn't always better, Sandy."

"That's what I hear."

Superficial. Paper-thin.

Fill in the dead air with something to pass the time, an attempt to get some morsels for the coconut telegraph while you're at it.

Sandy reached the last door on the left and gave it a hearty knock.

"Come in," said a male voice from inside.

Sandy opened the door and walked through, still holding the doorknob. "Mr. Henshaw, Rachel Hamar to see you."

I strode through the doorway, past Sandy, trying to show how authoritative I could be without appearing arrogant. Something I read on a blog about interviews.

Hope they were right.

I saw a man standing behind a desk. I assumed the suit he wore could've paid a month's worth of rent for me. He looked just like Penny, just taller, darker, and more handsome. With a wall of windows behind him, overlooking Central Park, it gave the office a wonderful view and provided a bit of an intimidating backdrop.

"Welcome to Sun Ridge, Miss Hamar," Mr. Henshaw said. He walked out from behind his desk and shook my hand. "I'm James Henshaw. Penny speaks highly of you."

"Likewise," I said, returning the gesture.

Another man, sitting in one of the chairs facing the desk, didn't turn around initially. Instead, he stood and turned to face us as I was shaking Mr. Henshaw's hand.

"Miss Hamar, this is Gordon Ames. He's the branch manager of the flagship branch on the first floor."

I shifted my focus to the other man. "So glad to mee—oh, I believe we've met already."

The man smiled and shook my hand. "I believe we have."

"You two know each other?" Mr. Henshaw said.

"Not really," I said nervously.

"We had a…late lunch, or early dinner, together," Gordon said. "Well, together is a bit of a misnomer."

Mr. Henshaw's expression of confusion grew each time Gordon gave another detail.

"I work part-time at Santorino's Italian Grill…"

"Yes, with Penny," Mr. Henshaw said. "She told me."

"Well, I arrived early to work one day last week and decided to get something to eat before my shift started—"

Mr. Henshaw raised his right hand and motioned for me to pause. "And let me guess. Gordon was having a late lunch there, I presume?"

Gordon nodded. "Remember that report you requested for the Feds? It took more than a couple of hours to put together. We didn't get finished until after two o'clock that day. So, I decided I was going to treat myself."

"What a small world we live in," Mr. Henshaw said. He motioned to the empty chair. "Please, Miss Hamar. Have a seat."

Gordon offered me his seat and slid over to the one on the far side.

I sat down, crossed my legs, grabbed my résumé, and handed it to Mr. Henshaw. I reached back into the folder and pulled out another copy. "I have one for you too, Mr. Ames, if you'd like?"

"Thank you," he said and took the document.

Mr. Henshaw quickly scanned the paperwork and set it down. "Miss Hamar, I know Gerald Jones, your former bank president-slash-employer. First Trust is an established bank, and under Gerald's leadership, it has grown steadily over the years. However, of late, they've made some…how shall I say it?" He looked at Gordon, rested his elbows on the desk, and pressed his fingertips together. "Financial moves that proved to be unfruitful. As a result, they have indeed suffered a hit." He sighed and tapped my résumé with his finger. "You mentioned here you were laid off because of budgetary cuts, is that correct?"

"Yes, sir."

"Well, I can vouch for Mr. Jones. That wasn't a falsehood. As a matter of fact, I predict he will be dismissing more personnel before it's all said and done."

"Mr. Jones did assure me that it had nothing to do with my performance. I was just some of the low-hanging fruit, you know?"

"I do. I got laid off from my first three jobs in my early years. Low man on the totem pole. The banking business can be a tough gig sometimes, even on a good day."

We all laughed one of those casual group laughs people take part in when they're in a nervous meeting with people they really don't know.

"How long have you known my sister?"

"About a year. That's when I started working at the restaurant."

"Gotta love Penny. She's a free spirit. And a good person."

"Yes. I agree wholeheartedly. We tend to see things eye to eye more so than the other employees there. We often go out for drinks or something to eat after hours or before shift."

Mr. Henshaw gently nodded as he listened. "I see you have been in the banking business for four years. Was that all as a teller?"

"Yes, sir."

"Do you have any aspirations of moving up the proverbial ladder, if the opportunity presented itself?"

"Actually, I had plans to apply for the assistant head teller position at my old job. I had heard the lady was going to retire by year's end." I shrugged my shoulders. "That was the plan, anyway."

Mr. Henshaw looked over at Gordon. "Mr. Ames, do you have any questions for Miss Hamar?"

"I would like to put her through our teller test after this interview is over."

"Do you have any objections, Miss Hamar?" Mr. Henshaw said.

"No. But what's a teller test?"

"It's something we do here at Sun Ridge. Not all institutions do it, but we feel it helps us identify strengths and weaknesses as well as give us an indication of the applicant's abilities. Think of it like a typing and computer test for a secretarial position. We give you different scenarios, different programs, et cetera, and monitor your abilities. As you can well imagine, we get all kinds in here applying for teller positions. People who have never operated a calculator before, people who've never handled money or had to make change." He rolled his eyes. "It's frightening what's out there these days."

"In other words," I said, "it weeds out the good interviewees who don't have the skills to back up their rhetoric."

Mr. Henshaw looked at Gordon with a huge smile. "Penny said I'd really like you. She said you were a no-nonsense kind of person."

When you've been through what I've been through, nonsense makes no sense. I smiled. "Guilty as charged."

"No, no, I like that, actually. In a world of superficiality, straightforwardness is energizing."

Wow. And he's not wearing a wedding ring either. "I couldn't agree more."

"Gordon," Mr. Henshaw said. "Did you have anything else to add?"

"I was just going to say the teller test has two parts, written and practical. Think of it as a practicum, of sorts. We ask you some questions, and then we put you through some dry runs with money to show us your teller skills. Just use the procedures and protocols you've learned at First Trust. If we hire you, we'll train you on how we do things at that time."

"Sounds easy enough."

Gordon perused my résumé again. "You do come with high recommendations, Miss Hamar. I think we can probably skip the written part, don't you think?" He held up the letter from my old boss and looked at Mr. Henshaw.

Mr. Henshaw nodded again and intertwined his fingers together. "Gerald Jones is old school. He doesn't hand out a recommendation unless you've earned it."

Well, what do ya know?

"Do you have any questions for us, Miss Hamar?" Gordon said.

"I did apply online. I figured it was the appropriate thing to do. However, I didn't see anything on there about hours, pay scale, benefits, that sort of thing."

"We can discuss those things after your test," Gordon said. He glanced out of the corner of his eye at his boss. "I think some of those items are negotiable, so I'd hate to give you hard and fast figures at this time."

I looked at both men before answering. "Very well. Nobody's signed on any bottom line just yet."

The corners of Mr. Henshaw's mouth lifted. He leaned forward and lifted his intertwined hands to his chin. "Penny said I was going to like your spunk."

I was a little taken with the comment. "Was she right?"

He dropped his hands back to the desk and chuckled. "I get the feeling she was downplaying that side of you." He pushed himself away from the desk and stood. "Gordon, if Miss Hamar is anything close to what Gerry wrote in that recommendation letter, I expect her to be on our payroll by the end of business tomorrow. I'd like to get her in here ASAP to work alongside Mildred before she retires. Get a feel for how we do things here at Sun Ridge."

Gordon and I stood simultaneously.

"Very good, sir," Gordon said.

"Miss Hamar, good luck on your test." Mr. Henshaw extended his hand.

I shook Mr. Henshaw's hand, hopefully not for the last time, and followed Gordon Ames out of the office.

CHAPTER FOURTEEN

Sun Ridge National Bank
Columbus Ave.
Manhattan, NY

I'd never taken a practical teller test before where I actually handled money, answered questions based on situations one might encounter, all with the bank manager staring over my shoulder.

It was quite interesting, actually. I stood behind a bank teller's window. In place of the window sat a TV monitor. When Gordon pressed play and began the test, the videotaped customers walked up to my teller window. I pretended to be on the other side. As the customer handed me certain things in the video, Gordon would supply those items and watch me handle them, pausing and playing the video at the appropriate times.

The first customer handed me a deposit slip and some cash. I was instructed to explain my actions as I proceeded so Gordon would know why I was doing what I was doing.

A second individual walked up and asked to see the bank manager. I directed her to the information desk.

On and on the test went, fifteen customers came and left, each with his or her own set of needs.

When the fifteenth person walked away, Gordon shut down the system. "All right, I think I've seen enough."

"Umm…That sounds kind of ominous."

Gordon chuckled as he shut off the TV monitor. "Quite the contrary, Miss Hamar. You did very well. First Trust has trained you thoroughly."

"That's good to know."

"Let's slide over to my office, and if you wish, I can start the hiring process."

"I got the job?"

I heard a stifled snicker escape. "If you want it, it's yours." A half-smile formed on the right side of his mouth. "Of course, that's provided you pass all the background checks, fingerprinting, so on and so forth."

"No worries there. And how long does all that take?"

"Depends on how many arrests you've had over the years. How many aliases. That sort of thing."

"Only the one bank robbery…oh, well, there was that one bounced check I wrote at Macy's last year…" I offered a playful grin. "Just kidding."

Gordon smiled and motioned with his arm toward the door. "This way, please."

He followed me out the door and pointed down the hallway. "Last office on the right." He led me past several offices and what looked like a break room. Unlike Sandy, he didn't feel the need to ask me filler questions. Instead, he strolled a little fast for me and my heels. I kept up as best I could, trying not to look like a lumbering bumpkin from Wes Virginny wearing stilettos for the first time.

As we passed people walking the other direction, all eyes were on us.

Who's that with Mr. Ames? What's her name? I can't believe

she wore that dress. Or those heels. She's what? Thirty-five? Forty? I don't see a ring.

I could see the questions in their eyes. I could hear the comments being made behind a cupped hand. We've all been there.

Superficial. Paper-thin. Conversations.

Their eyes gave them away. Their whispers too.

Momma once told me, "When people cover their mouths with their hands while their eyes are on you, only evil abounds."

In that singular moment, Gordon and I were surrounded by evil.

He breezed through his office door, which stood open, and walked straight to his desk. "Come on in." He peeled off his suit coat, hung it up on the nearby coat rack, and depressed a button on his phone while motioning at the chair in front of his desk. "Make yourself comfortable."

I watched him in awe. It was just like in the movies. Corporate executive, big office, phones with intercoms, an actual coat rack with coats hanging from it, pictures of famous people on the walls. Well, in this case, they were famous quotes by famous people.

"Yes, Mr. Ames." The voice in the intercom sounded familiar.

"Sandy, can you come to my office, please?"

"I'll be right there, sir."

"Was that the Sandy from the fourteenth floor? The lady who escorted me to Mr. Henshaw's office?"

"Yes."

"You don't have your own secretary?"

"Mr. Henshaw likes all the hiring to run through one person."

"So, she works two jobs?"

"Kind of." He sat down. "Even though Sandy works at the front desk and acts as a receptionist for those on the fourteenth floor, her real function is as Mr. Henshaw's personal secretary.

The fourteenth floor doesn't get many visitors, and if it does, they are already meeting with someone. Mr. Henshaw put her out there in the lobby when the other lady resigned. Saved the bank some money."

Money. The bottom line of a bank. "She seems nice."

"Oh, she is. You just want to watch what you say in her presence. The lobby has ears."

I lowered my voice and peeked over my shoulder. "Busybody type?"

"No worse than what we're doing right now."

Ouch! It was true. I had to admit it. We do gossip about the gossipers, don't we? Of course, when we do, we're doing everyone a public service by warning them about the gossipers and everything they do to keep the pot stirred.

That's what we tell ourselves, anyway.

"I apologize," I said.

"For what?"

"My mother once told me that gossipers come in all shapes and sizes. To tell them apart, just look for the hand by the mouth." I modeled for him what I was saying. "Apparently, I fit the description."

"Well, your mother sounds like a wise woman. It's easy to do. To get caught up in all that stuff."

I winced a little. "Was that a test too?"

Gordon smiled just as Sandy knocked on the door and walked in.

"Sandy, I believe you've met Miss Hamar?"

"Yes, sir." She smiled at me.

"I'm going to need you to begin the hiring process. She will be taking Mildred's place."

"I'm on it." Sandy leaned over slightly, placed her hand on my shoulder, and winked. "Welcome aboard."

I patted her hand. "Thank you."

Sandy walked out, and Gordon shuffled some papers on his desk.

"Miss Hamar, while we're waiting for the paperwork to arrive, tell me a little about yourself."

"Well, first, only telemarketers and credit card company mailers call me Miss Hamar. My friends and colleagues call me Rachel."

"So noted. We do prefer to call each other by first names when having casual conversations. However, when in more formal settings, we usually refer to each other by titles and last names."

"Of course. So, do you want the *Reader's Digest* version or the extended play?"

"Cliff Notes, actually, would be great."

"I grew up in a small town in West Virginia. I became an orphan at the age of fifteen and was placed in foster care. I rebelled against the system and ran away just a few weeks after being placed in a home. I lived on the street for four years—about ten months in Cincinnati and the rest here in the city—before I finally moved into a halfway house for women in the Bronx. My mother was moved to the Long Island Psychiatric Center during that time, and that's why I've remained in The Big Apple."

Gordon's face was able to hide his astonishment at first, but by the time I concluded, the look of bewilderment peeked out from behind his professional eyes and mouth. "Your mother's at LIPC?"

"Yes."

"Is she okay?"

"She seems fine to me. That's probably because the way she acts is all I've ever known. But the doctors have diagnosed her with schizophrenia. They say she's not normal."

"I'm sorry to hear that." He shifted in his seat. "And what about your father?"

"It's a long story. But when I was fifteen, my dad was arrested and tried for murder."

"He's in prison, then?"

"He was. He was murdered in prison several years ago."

Gordon leaned back in his chair. He rubbed his goatee. "That's quite a story, Rachel. I'm sorry about what you've had to endure. I hope this job will help you break out of that cycle."

"Well, you know how it is in this town. Pay is okay sometimes, but the cost of living is tough."

"I do. I've struggled to work my way up to this job. Only been in this chair for four years. Lots of nights and weekends leading up to it."

"You have family, Mr. Ames?"

"I do. I have a daughter. She's finishing up college this year. I also have an older son who is presently serving in the Navy and stationed in Japan."

I looked at his finger. No gold band. And about what? Ten years older than me? Maybe eight? "That's nice. Having a family, I mean."

"I've always believed family is who we are. Without it, we're just numbers on a page. Faces in a crowd. The neighbor in apartment 2-B."

Huh. Hadn't ever thought about it quite like that.

"Families are also the thing that keeps us sane when life gets crazy. They keep us humble when we get full of ourselves. Keep us levelheaded when we get angry. Keep us up when life gets us down."

I smiled slightly. I wanted all those things. Wished for all those things. Had only experienced glimpses of all those things in the past.

Maybe that was why I'd been sad for so long.

Nobody had been there to balance out the insanity, anger, and depression.

CHAPTER FIFTEEN

West 173rd Street
Washington Heights, NY

I parked two blocks away from the apartment complex. All the spaces near the front entrance were taken, compliments of the corner *bodega's* Monday afternoon specials. Every Monday. Even holidays. Garcia's half-price specials attracted hundreds of people to the store. With the purchase of twenty dollars or more, excluding beer, liquor, and cigarettes, of course, one could walk away with twice the groceries. It was the poor man's BOGO paradise.

Looking forward to peeling off my high heels and putting my feet up, I normally would have grumbled about the extra steps. But I felt good about the day. Things seemed to be turning around for me. Gordon said he would call me just as soon as they received my security clearance. He was hoping for tomorrow, but figured Wednesday was a more reasonable expectation. So, I was to plan on starting Thursday morning, unless I heard different.

I exited my car and strolled up the street, breathing in the brisk afternoon air. It seemed cleaner somehow. Probably wasn't. Just the effects of my good mood, I figured.

A good mood has a way of tempering your vision, skewing it to the positive side of life. I guess that's why people take every medication known to man, legal and illegal, or drink themselves to the bottom of a bottle. Each person trying to find that mood that makes everything better.

I knew how they felt.

As I rounded the corner toward our front entrance, the man wearing the wife-beater t-shirt and displaying some creepy tattoos stood on his emergency stairwell, flicking his ashes. He spotted me and watched me like a hawk. I snatched a glimpse twice before reaching the doorway. Goosebumps zigged and zagged across my skin. I felt like he was undressing me with his eyes.

No matter how good a mood you're in, some things never change.

I grabbed the mail and noticed another anonymous letter amongst the flyers and credit card offers.

Closing our apartment door behind me, I dropped my purse and the other mail on the coffee table and plopped down onto the sofa. I ripped the envelope open and pulled out yet another white sheet of paper. Instead of the drawing of a house with a little child and a dad standing outside by a tree like the last couple of pictures, this picture was of the DADDY sitting in a big chair. The child sat on his lap. Next to them, on both sides of the dad and the little child, other people were sitting in similar chairs, all facing the same direction.

Behind the row of chairs, a blue sky with white, puffy clouds filled the background. Several birds were in the sky, flying every which way. And again, above the two main characters were the names DADDY and ME, written in a child's hand.

The picture was a little more precise.

The stick people were more defined.

The birds were starting to look more like birds. Although a couple of them looked more like dragons.

The child's hair was getting longer.

This kid is getting older and older with each letter…

I sighed. Maybe I should go to Jericho. Try to find out if anybody at the post office knows anything.

I peeked at my watch. 3:32 p.m.

Maybe I will swing by that post office, then I can go celebrate my new job with half-priced wings at Joanie's bar.

CHAPTER SIXTEEN

United States Post Office
425 N. Broadway
Jericho, NY

I walked inside the cramped little post office. One tired-looking, female postal worker stood behind the counter with a customer before her. Her blonde hair was pulled up in a ponytail, and she had the dark circles you get when you're about a hundred hours behind on your sleep.

Three other people stood in line, and I joined them as the fourth.

This was good. If someone was bringing these letters inside, the workers should know who it is, right? And if these letters are being mailed, how many carriers could a small branch like this have?

I stood behind a man who had already checked his watch three times since I got in line. The customer at the counter kept asking questions about the package she was sending, and the man in front of me was about to explode.

"So, if I mail this first class, what's the difference between that and two-day delivery?" the customer at the counter said.

The man in front of me couldn't contain himself. "The difference is how many days it takes to get there!"

The woman at the counter slowly turned and glared at the man, unappreciative of his eavesdropping.

"What?" the man said, lifting his arms in a questioning manner. "This place closes at five, lady. We'd like to get through the line before that happens."

I took a gander at the clock on the wall. 4:18 p.m.

The woman at the counter faced the postal worker again, but her voice got louder. "I get so tired of rude people, don't you? Oh, what am I saying? You work for the post office. You must deal with rude people all the time."

The postal worker just smiled. She couldn't say anything. Not verbally, anyway. But her eyes answered loud and clear.

The man in line growled in frustration. He stormed past me and out the door, mumbling expletives as he did.

The woman at the counter watched the entire scene out of the corner of her eye. When the man left, she plunked down some money on the counter. "I'll send it first class."

The postal worker tapped at the computer screen in front of her. "Some people have a hard time with patience. It's a sign of the times, I think." She slapped some postage on the package and handled the money. "Everybody's in such a hurry. They have to have everything move faster. Fast food. Fast pass lines. Faster internet service." She handed the woman her change. "Nobody seems to know how to slow it down anymore."

"Boy, don't you know it. Well, you have yourself a splendid day, and thanks for your help."

"I'm going to try. You have a good rest of your day. Next person in line."

∾

SEVEN MINUTES LATER, it was my turn. I pulled out my letters and laid them on the counter along with my driver's license. "I know this might be a bit of a different request, but as you can see, these letters are being mailed to me. They all have the same address. My address. However, there is no return address. All of them have been stamped here, at this post office, so it appears the person mailing these letters lives around here. He or she may even come in here and drop them in your mailbox in the lobby."

The postal worker behind the counter, with a name tag that read 'Wanda,' picked up one of the letters and examined it. "So, what's your question?"

"Is there any way you can help me determine who is mailing these?"

"Ma'am, I wish I could help you, but whoever's mailing these obviously doesn't want you to know who's sending them."

"And that's strange, right?"

Wanda bobbed her head from side to side while her face scrunched up. "It could be." She opened an envelope and pointed inside. "May I?"

"Sure."

Wanda pulled out the sheet of paper from the letter that came today. She unfolded it, and her eyes widened in surprise. "Oh. I was expecting a letter. This looks like a child's drawing."

"And if you look at the rest, they're all the same. From what appears to be a child. At least, that's what I think."

Wanda opened the others, careful not to get them mixed up. "Who's Daddy?"

"I don't know. I'm not married. I have no children. And my father is dead. So, the only explanation I can come up with is that these pictures were intended for some man...a soldier overseas, perhaps?"

"Yet, they are addressed to you."

"Weird, huh?"

"I wish I could help you...," Wanda said, flipping over one

of the envelopes, "Miss Hamar. You definitely have a mystery on your hands."

"Have you seen anybody coming in here, mailing these?"

Wanda frowned with a shake of her head. "We have hundreds of people come in here every day. And besides, who's to say they mailed them from our lobby? They could've mailed it from their house. They could've put it in a drop box within our zone. They could've enlisted the help of someone else to drop them off. They could've even mailed it from their place of employment." She offered a resigned shrug. "There's really no way to tell."

"But don't you have surveillance cameras for this sort of thing?"

"We do. But again, even if we saw a person with an envelope in his or her hand that looked like one of these, it would be impossible to find out which person was doing it. These envelopes aren't anything special. We get hundreds just like 'em every day."

You're telling me you guys can't look at the video for me?"

"I'm sorry, but to view the video system, you're gonna need some cops and a warrant."

"I don't have to see the videos myself. I just wanted you all to review them."

"Ma'am, if this person was doing something illegal, then we would comply, with a warrant. But right now, we have no reason to do so. All this person is doing is mailing letters. Nothing illegal about that." She placed the letters back in their envelopes and handed them back to me.

"But what if this child is being held against his will?"

Wanda lifted one eyebrow. "Then, I suggest you go to the police."

"What if I hired a private investigator?"

"To see the videos, he's still going to need the police and a warrant."

"Then, maybe that's what I'll do. Go to the police."

"If it was me, that's what I'd do. The pictures are strange enough. But the fact that they are being mailed to you makes it even more bizarre. I mean, one letter might seem like a weird thing, but how many do you have now?"

"Six."

"That's way beyond weird, in my opinion."

CHAPTER SEVENTEEN

DJ's Sports Bar & Grill
Manhattan, NY

I sat at the bar, holding a beer, wishing I had just gone home. Joanie tried to talk to me when she could, but half-priced wings on a Monday night during football season seemed to be a big deal to a lot of people. The place was packed.

And loud.

"I went to the post office today," I said, almost yelling.

Joanie wiped down the area two seats down. "The one in Jericho?"

I nodded instead of yelling again.

"And?"

"Didn't find out anything. Not that I expected to."

"They couldn't help you at all?" Joanie accepted an order from one of the waitresses.

"They said if I came back with the police and a search warrant, then they could let us see the security cameras."

"Are you gonna go to the police?"

"I don't know. I'm afraid they'd laugh me right out of the precinct if I did."

Joanie filled a couple of glasses with beer and set them on a serving tray. She flagged someone down.

A skinny waitress wearing her version of a Hooters outfit strutted up to the counter. "Thanks, Joanie," she said, taking the tray.

I waited for her to leave and then pointed in her direction. "What's up with the costume?"

Joanie shrugged. "It's all about the tips. And the guys in this place on a Monday night love two things: a good football game and tight shorts."

"Seems…Neanderthal."

"Call it what you will, Rach. But when she walks out of here tonight, she'll be carrying over five hundred dollars in tips."

"Five hun—" I interrupted myself, realizing I was shouting even louder than before.

"That's not an average night. But on nights like this? Five hundred easy." Joanie looked around the bar. "May be closer to seven hundred."

"All because of the shorts?"

"No, not just the shorts." Joanie presented a sly smile. "But they probably bring in an extra twenty percent."

I took a swig of my beer. Okay. So, she's a hooker…of sorts.

"Besides, she's one of the best," Joanie continued. "Probably gets ten phone numbers a night handed to her, in some of the most imaginative ways too."

"When you're dressed like a bar-hoppin' street walker, then I guess that comes with the territory, huh?"

"A girl's gotta do what a girl's gotta do."

But she doesn't have to lower herself into the meat department.

"Are you gonna have any wings?"

I had a menu sitting in front of me, and I'd promised myself I was going to celebrate my new job. Yet, in spite of it all, I didn't feel exuberant. "What do you recommend?"

"Well, you don't like spicy food, so I'd stay away from the hot wings. You might like the garlic parmesan. You've also got to try the house special wings. It's a sauce you'll love."

"Sold. Six of each?"

"Coming right up."

THE WINGS WERE LONG GONE, my second beer was almost finished, and the crowd was thinning. So was the noise. My ears rang, and my rear end was tired of this hard bar stool.

"You know, if you want people to stay longer, you should invest in more comfortable chairs."

Joanie's eyes became saucers. She lifted her hands as if I'd solved an ancient mystery. "I know, right? I've been saying that for months. The owner says they're thinking about it, but these chairs were part of the original bar before he bought it. 'They give the place some nostalgia,' he always says."

"No. They make me want to get up and leave."

Joanie plucked her cell phone from her back pocket and checked the screen. "Speaking of leaving, aren't we out late tonight? It's after midnight."

I lifted my beer and gulped the last couple of ounces before tipping the empty bottle in a half-hearted salute. "This is me being a wild child. Celebrating a new job."

Joanie walked down to the end and lifted the portion of the bar, exiting from behind it. She motioned for another woman to take over for her.

She sat down next to me and tossed her dishrag on the counter. "I'm really happy for you on this new job. Banking seems to be your thing. You like working in that field."

"It pays well, and it's something I feel comfortable doing.

I'm not sure it's what I envisioned myself doing for the rest of my life, though."

"Do any of us get to do what we really want to do?"

"I'm sure some people do." I pointed to the television. "Those players seemed to be enjoying their jobs."

"Yeah, but how many football players never make it to the pros?" She pointed at the TV. "And those guys? They don't get to play forever. It's not like they retire at sixty-five playing that game."

"Is this conversation going somewhere?"

"I just worry about you. That's all."

"Aw, shucks, Joanie, that's so sweeeeet."

"Knock it off. I mean it. You scare me sometimes. And I know these last few days have been really hard. Now, with these stupid letters showin' up, it seems you can't catch a break. There always seems to be something draggin' you down."

"I wouldn't say they're dragging me down. I just wonder who's really sending them. My biggest fear is that there's some stalker out there messing with me."

"Kind of like *Criminal Minds*?"

I slumped in my seat. "Well, I hadn't really considered it being a serial killer…until now." I feigned a smile. "Thanks."

"I didn't mean it that way."

"But now that you mention it, there is that one guy in our complex. Hispanic-lookin' dude, always wears a wife-beater…"

"The guy on the stoop? With all the tattoos?"

"Yeah. Always smokin' cigarettes."

"Okay…I know who you're talkin' about. You hardly ever see him unless he's standing out on the stoop."

"And he's always watching you, kind of like a vulture in a tree branch."

Joanie slapped the bar. "You know, I hadn't thought of him. He's just creepy enough to do something like this."

"I've wondered about him too. But these letters don't seem

like something he'd send, you know? I would expect half-naked selfies or something, but not children's drawings."

"Unless he's not right in the head. He could be a grown man, but mentally, he could be a child." Joanie shrugged. "Have you ever heard him talk? I haven't."

It was true. I'd never heard him speak. Never saw him anywhere else except on the stoop, smoking cigarettes, watching me as I came home. I'm sure he watched other people too. But one thing was certain. I never saw him leave the building. Never saw him enter it either.

Strange.

Yet, the more I thought about it, there were probably others I didn't witness come and go either.

Joanie grabbed her dishrag and wiped the counter, like she needed something to do. "Maybe we should find out which apartment he lives in and confront him," she said.

"Are you nuts?"

"He's either guilty or not guilty. Wouldn't you like to know which one?"

"Yeah, sure. But I'd rather stay alive than know the truth about tattoo man. No offense." Joanie was right, but I had no intentions of actually confronting the man. However, if I went to the police… "I should go to the cops instead. Maybe they can help me figure it out?"

"They're the ones who probably should talk to tattoo man anyway."

"Yeah. They have guns."

Tuesday

December 16, 2014

CHAPTER EIGHTEEN

New York City Police Dept.
33rd Precinct

I didn't sleep well.

It wasn't because of a lack of fatigue.

It was those crazy letters.

Visions of the man in the wife-beater scribbling on some paper, stuffing the picture into an envelope, and smiling, with his gold teeth shimmering in a devilish way, made me nervous.

More visions of a faceless serial killer, wearing a dark hoodie, stalking my every step, spying on me through a pair of binoculars from across the street, following me to work, learning my patterns, and waiting for the most opportune time to abduct me certainly added an edge to my nightmares.

Thanks, Joanie, for that one.

I got up when Joanie did and felt horrible doing it. I still couldn't figure out how she did it, getting home at two or three in the morning from the bar and being back to work by seven at Manningham's. After a week, I'd collapse from sheer exhaustion, which made me worry about her. How long would it be before her body simply shut down in protest? I did it one night, and mine was already creating a picket sign.

With Joanie gone, I sat at the kitchen table. One hand holding my head and the other wrapped around my coffee mug. The hammer inside my skull was trying to pound its way out.

Our conversation at the bar last night, and my earlier meeting with the postal worker, sent me thinking. Why hadn't I involved the police? Or at least a private investigator? I knew I needed to do something.

And when the mail came that morning, it sealed the deal for me.

HERE I WAS AN HOUR LATER, three blocks away from the apartment, on Amsterdam Avenue, strolling into the 33rd precinct of the New York City Police Department. After answering a few questions from the officer at the information desk, it was determined I needed to speak with a detective.

I was escorted to a room filled with desks. It reminded me a little of the police station back in Noring, just bigger, more crowded with furniture and equipment, and a lot more people doing their police…stuff. I had to admit, I half-expected to see Donnie Wahlberg and Tom Selleck walk by.

Silly girl.

You watch entirely too much television.

"If you'll have a seat, I'll get Detective Bowen," the officer said.

I sat down in a chair by a desk. A photograph of a woman holding a baby rested in a picture frame, strategically placed to be seen at all times. An empty coffee cup and a computer monitor displaying the NYPD crest gave the desk that "coply" feel. A small LED Christmas tree, no more than five inches tall, was plugged into a USB port. Its fluid wave of colors, from green, to red, to white, to gold, to silver, and back to red again, added a little holiday cheer to what otherwise looked drab and sterile.

The smell of burnt coffee and fresh disinfectant didn't help either.

A woman wearing slacks and a dress shirt walked up beside me and leaned forward just a touch, reaching out her hand as she did, the gold badge on her waistband signifying her status. "Miss Hamar?"

"Yes?"

"Hi, I'm Detective Nicole Bowen. Would you like a cup of coffee?"

"Uh, no, but thank you."

She pulled out her desk chair and sat down. White woman. Brown hair, shoulder length. Greenish, almost brown eyes. Maybe my age, probably a little younger.

Definitely stays away from the donuts.

The detective picked up the old, empty coffee cup and tossed it in the trash can against the wall and replaced it with a new, steaming cup of Joe. "I understand you have a dilemma you are trying to solve?"

"I guess you could call it that."

She looked at me with eyes that said, "I'm listening."

"Okay, so, uh, I'm a little nervous. Been a long time since I've been in a police station."

"You've had dealings with NYPD before?" She sipped her coffee as the last word drifted off into a question.

"Oh, no, no. No. I, I, uh…When I was fifteen…my father accidentally killed my boyfriend. Back in West Virginia. That was twenty years ago. Because of that, I spent a bunch of time at the police station there."

"Where in West Virginia?"

"Noring."

"Continue."

"Well, anyway, between the police station and the court-house, I've had my fill of legal drama. That's why I hesitated coming here."

"Well, right now, Miss Hamar, we're simply having a conversation. All I'm trying to do is determine if you're in the right place. If so, we'll help you any way we can. If not, then I need to get you to the right people or department. So, my first question in that pursuit is, what is your home address?"

"West 173rd Street, Washington Heights."

"It seems," she said with a comforting smile on her face, "you're in the right place. For now." She took another sip. "The officer who brought you in here stated that you had a concern about some letters you've been receiving in the mail? Can you tell me about those letters?"

"Yes." I opened my purse and pulled out the now seven letters received so far, the seventh arriving earlier this morning.

Another crudely drawn picture. This one depicted a man sitting in a chair with a child sitting in his lap, on his right knee. Another child, bigger and older, sat on the man's left knee. Instead of labels telling me who each person was, there was something like a caption across the top of the page: ME AND MY BROTHER SPENDING TIME WITH DADDY.

It was a simple pencil-like drawing. No color in this one.

I handed the seven letters to the detective. "I have them stacked in the order I received them. The first one is on top. The one from today is on the bottom."

Detective Bowen counted the letters and checked the post-marks. "You've been receiving these for a week now?"

"Yes."

"But the mail doesn't run on Sunday."

"I got two on Saturday. One for Saturday. And one for Sunday, I'm guessing? I put them in the order I thought they should go based on the pictures inside."

"Pictures?" She started to open the first one.

"Each envelope contains a picture. Each picture is a little more detailed than the previous one."

She studied the first picture before turning it around for me to see. "This looks like a child learning how to write…well, except for the handwriting at the top. That looks like an adult's."

"That's what we thought too."

"We?"

"Me and my roommate. Joanie Harrington. We've been friends since elementary school."

"Is she someone who likes to pull pranks?"

"What? No. She's not sending these."

"How do you know?"

"Well, let's put it this way. She knows I'm here. And I don't think she's dumb enough to allow me to get the police involved if she was pulling a prank. Besides, she knows what I've been through over the years. If she was the one sending these to me, she knows I'd probably kill her."

"Well, I hope you understand. I had to ask."

"I get it."

"And, let's not talk about killing people in a police precinct. Doesn't go over too well in here," she said with a wave of her hand. "It's kind of like yelling 'Bomb!' on a plane, you know?"

"Sorry. Figure of speech."

The detective opened the remaining letters and studied each drawing. "Do you have any idea who these people in the pictures represent?"

I shook my head. "I have lain awake at night trying to figure that out. At first, I thought some mother, perhaps, or a grandmother, was sending them to a father who was not at home. Like a soldier or an incarcerated man, maybe? Someone who would like to receive pictures from his son, but—"

The detective pointed at the picture in her hand. "How do you know this is a boy?"

"I don't. I just assumed based on the length of the hair in the later drawings. But, I guess it could be a little girl."

"If these were being directed at a father who is away for some reason, like you suggested," she said, flipping over one of the envelopes and then holding it up, "why would they be addressed to you?"

I shrugged. "That's the part we can't figure out. Even if the person who lived in the apartment before us was the intended recipient, why would they be addressed to me?"

She flipped through the drawings, being careful not to mix them up. "Well, it's very apparent this child is getting older. The pictures start out as if the child is a baby." She picked up the first letter. "My son is three now." She pointed at the picture on her desk. "If you handed him something to write with when he was a baby, he'd scribble away at the paper for a few seconds before trying to eat it. Now that he's three, he'd probably produce something more like this." She picked up the second letter. "So, I can see the progression here." She grabbed the last letter. "See how much more defined these lines are than these, for example?" She set it down next to letter number four.

"We noticed that progression too. We also tried to determine the age of the child based on the drawings."

The detective examined the last letter. "I'd say, based on this last one, the child is probably nine or ten. Maybe a little older, but it's hard to tell."

"And this still doesn't explain why they are coming specifically to me."

"That is the $64,000 question, isn't it?" She opened her lap drawer and pulled out a magnifying glass. She held it up for me to see. "Sherlock Holmes. He's the reason I got into law enforcement. Wanted to be a detective since I was twelve."

"I hope you're as good as he was."

She smiled but didn't respond. She examined the letters more closely. "Do you know anyone who has a child this age?"

"Sure. I have friends who have children, but I see them once in a while. Makes no sense for them to send me pictures like this through the mail anonymously. They could just bring them to work or give them to me when they saw me."

"What about relatives?"

"I have no relatives with children."

"No siblings?"

"No. I'm an only child."

"Tell me about your parents."

I knew she would ask about them eventually. The woman with the problem is always the suspect in the beginning. "Well, I told you about my dad and what happened to him. He was sent to prison for the murder of my boyfriend when I was fifteen. Daddy lost his temper and beat Billy up. Struck him in the head with the butt of a shotgun twice. Caused blood clots. Billy died right in front of me." I stopped and inhaled to keep from crying. "Then, about seven years later, my daddy died in prison. Got stabbed by another inmate as an act of revenge."

The detective lifted her eyes from her examination and turned to look at me. "I'm sorry to hear that."

"As for my mother, she's a resident at the Long Island Psychiatric Center."

The detective's eyes widened a little.

"That's why I live here. To be close to my mother."

"May I ask why she is a resident at LIPC?"

"She's had mental issues for years, according to the doctors. Since before I was born. She was diagnosed with schizophrenia at first, but they've added several other psychoses to her list of maladies."

"Has she ever been a danger to others?"

"No. At least nothing I've ever witnessed. But she goes off into these…episodes…trances…whatever you want to call them. She thinks she's talking to Jesus, Joseph, and Mary."

The detective's eyebrows arched as if something made sense to her. "Is your mother a religious person, then?"

"Religious wacko, you mean? A nut? That's what the doctors think. My daddy did too. He was trying to get someone to get her to stop acting that way. It started with her talking to Jesus as if He was in the room, standing right in front of her. Daddy hated it when she would start talking to or about Jesus. Then, one day, she started talking to someone named Joseph. That continued for several years. Then, about fifteen years or so ago, she added someone named Mary to the list. The doctors believe that as her condition worsens, she will continue to add names until she's talking to a room full of imaginary people."

"I'm sorry to hear that, Miss Hamar." She set the magnifying glass down. "Sounds like you have been through a lot."

"You don't know the half of it. That's why I need this case solved. It's starting to freak me out a little, and I've been through enough for one person. I don't need some wacko stalker adding his version of crazy to the mix."

She offered a contemplative smile. "When your father got arrested, it was just you and your mom at that point?"

"Not exactly." I explained to her what happened about the night Billy died, the subsequent trial, and my stint in foster care before striking out on my own. She asked clarifying questions along the way. I tried to keep it brief, but it took the better part of thirty minutes to relive it all.

"You spoke of an aunt and uncle living in North Carolina. Do they have children? Could these pictures be from them?"

"They do have children, but not this age. They're all grown, married with kids of their own."

"Could your aunt and uncle be sending you pictures from their grandchildren, perhaps?"

"I don't know why they would. Their grandchildren are older now. It would be weird. I know my aunt keeps in contact with my mom. They're sisters, but she'd have no reason to send me old pictures from her grandchildren, especially without a letter enclosed explaining everything."

The detective rummaged through the letters one more time. "Do you mind if I make copies of these?"

I gave an uncertain shrug. "I guess."

"If you're not comfortable with it, I understand. If I take the case, I'll just need to be able to access them whenever necessary. Also, if you get any more, I'll need to see those too."

"You can make copies. That's fine."

"And you'll bring me any others if you get more?"

"Sure. Anything to help figure this out."

She gathered up the letters, keeping them in order, and stood. "All right then. I'll be right back."

Several minutes passed. I watched as people streamed in and out of the room. Others sat at desks. Some on cell phones. Some on landlines. Some having discussions. Some staring at computer screens and tapping keyboards. Apparently, some conversations were more serious than others. I heard one person mention a homicide in one conversation while in another discussion, people were smiling and referencing the football game last night.

Hey, that guy looks familiar. I think he was at the bar last night.

"All right, Miss Hamar," Detective Bowen said, stepping around my chair and sitting back down at her desk. "Here are your letters."

I took them and stuffed them back into my purse.

"I just got done speaking with my sergeant. He wants me to look into your case."

I jerked my gaze upward. "Really? Wonderful."

"You seem surprised."

"Honestly, I didn't think you all would care that much." I pointed at the homicide conversation. "I mean, you guys seem to have bigger fish to fry."

"We do have a full plate, but this case intrigued Sergeant

Visiano. I think because we could have a case involving a child, we want to make sure there's nothing heinous going on."

"That's been my one big fear too."

"Let me look into it, and I'll keep you informed. Do you have a good working phone number where you can be reached?"

I gave her my cell number.

"Perfect." She stood, and I rose with her. "Thank you, Miss Hamar. Here's my card. If you receive any more letters or find out any additional information that may help us figure things out, please call me."

"Thank you." I took the card and shook her hand.

"If you just follow Officer Hankins, he'll escort you to the front door."

Officer Hankins smiled and waved me on. "This way, Miss Hamar."

Wednesday

December 17, 2014

CHAPTER NINETEEN

Sun Ridge National Bank
Columbus Ave.
Manhattan, NY

A few hours after I left the police station, I received a call from Sandy at Sun Ridge. She informed me I could start the next morning. So, here I was, bright and early, Wednesday morning, sitting in Gordon Ames's office, with my legs crossed and a legal pad and pen in my hands, ready to start the next chapter of my banking life.

"We're just waiting on Mildred, Miss Hamar," Gordon said.

"Please, call me Rachel."

"That sounded more like a plea than a request."

"I guess it did. It's just, when people call me Miss Hamar, it reminds me of my Old Maid status."

"Well, forgive me if you think I was implying anything but simple courtesy and professionalism."

I lifted my hands in protest. "No, no, no. I knew you didn't mean anything by it. I don't think anyone really does. It's just a hang-up on my part. Twenty years ago, I had plans to marry my boyfriend. We were…," I smirked at the thought now, "crazy in love. Two teenagers who didn't know any better."

"I take it you broke up?"

I inhaled deeply and tried to keep my eyes from pooling. "He died."

The blood drained from Gordon's face. "Miss…Rachel, I'm sorry. I didn't know."

"It's okay. You're right. You didn't, and I wasn't offended."

A knock sounded at the door, and Gordon lifted his eyes from me to that direction. "Mildred." He stood and offered her the seat beside me. He seemed relieved by the interruption also. "Please. I'd like to introduce you to Rachel Hamar. Rachel, this is Mildred Hollingsworth."

Mildred, a sixty-something woman with dyed black hair, moseyed around behind me and eased herself into the chair to my left. She turned toward me and held out her hand. "Hi. Nice to meet you. I heard some good things about you." Her accent caught me off guard. Sounded a little southern for someone living in New York.

"Same here," I said, returning the handshake. "And as I understand it, I've got some big shoes to fill."

"You do, dear. You do. This man expects me to do everything."

"Mrs. Hollingsworth," Gordon said, "please don't scare her off before she starts."

"I'm just being truthful, Mr. Ames. Would you rather I lie?"

Gordon pointed at Mildred. "You see? Ever since I came to Sun Ridge, I've had to deal with this."

"He just doesn't like it when I tell the truth. It sometimes makes him look bad, that's all," Mildred said, leaning over toward me. "If it makes him look good, then he wants me to go up on the roof and blab it through a bullhorn."

Gordon's eyebrows danced as if Mildred wasn't exaggerating as much as one would think.

Mildred chuckled at Gordon's lack of response. "I love it when he's speechless. But he knows not to press me too much." She leaned over and looked at me as if over a pair of eyeglasses. "It also helps to know where all the bodies are buried."

"Yes," Gordon said, interrupting her show, "Mrs. Hollingsworth's been with Sun Ridge for...what? A hundred years now?"

"If that's the case, then I look good for my age." Mildred laughed, and all her oversized teeth glistened. "Almost twenty-three, actually. I did have a life before Sun Ridge." She turned toward me. "I retire on my twenty-third anniversary." She grinned in excitement and scrunched her shoulders like a small child. "In two weeks."

"I sure envy you," I said. "I could use a retirement about now."

"Couldn't we all?" Gordon said. "Mildred, Miss Hamar will be taking your place, so I hope you won't taint her too much in these last couple of weeks."

"Now, Mr. Ames, you know I'm just yanking your chain. A girl's gotta have a little fun before she sails off into the sunset. I mean, seriously. What are you going to do? Fire me?"

"So long as you don't cross any lines."

"Have you ever known me to cross any lines, Mr. Ames?"

"I can't say that I have, but you've never been two weeks away from retiring either."

Mildred's smile looked more like an acknowledgement. "Fair enough."

"Getting back to the purpose of our little get together here, I would like Miss Hamar to shadow you for the next two weeks. I'll need her to be trained to take your spot after you leave. She's worked as a teller for the last four years, so she has experience with that aspect of your job, but she will need to be shown the managerial side as well. She has expressed interest in becoming a head teller eventually."

"Managerial?" I said.

"Yes. Mr. Henshaw wanted to give you the opportunity to become the head teller. Mrs. Hollingsworth has been in that position before and knows how we do things. She's also run the loan department. So, you have two weeks to glean as much expertise from her as possible."

Mildred flashed a tight-lipped, I-feel-sorry-for-you smile. "Be careful what you wish for."

"Mildred, you can head back downstairs. I need to speak with Miss Hamar before I send her down."

Mildred nodded and stood. "I'll see you on the first floor."

Once she cleared the doorway, Gordon waited a few seconds, and then he started tapping at the computer keyboard. He pointed at the screen. "I just wanted to make sure she was getting on the elevator."

He spies on his employees with the security cameras? "If I may be so bold, Mr. Ames..."

"Please, Gordon."

"Gordon, if I may be direct, it's a little unnerving that you don't trust one of your long-standing tellers to follow a simple directive." I pointed at his computer. "Do you make it a habit of watching us from here?"

Gordon lifted his eyes from the screen. "Mildred is Mr. Henshaw's mother-in-law."

"But Mr. Henshaw wasn't wearing a wedding ring."

Gordon lifted is left eyebrow and tilted his head.

"I...I mean, I just noticed that he wasn't..." I grabbed my ring finger and made a circular motion around it. "It's a girl thing."

Gordon smirked. "She's actually his former mother-in-law. Mr. Henshaw's wife left him for another man two years into their marriage. Mildred was beside herself. She hated the other man more than she disliked Mr. Henshaw. She disagreed with her daughter and actually fought for Mr. Henshaw when it came time for divorce court. She helped save him from having to pay alimony."

"Interesting."

"And as for Mildred, that explains her…uh…How shall I put it? Spirit? Boldness? *Hutzpah?*"

"I was thinking more along the lines of guts, maybe even audacity?"

"She definitely feels like Mr. Henshaw owes her something. If I had been here, in this position, I never would have agreed to hire her." Gordon held his hands up. "I mean, she's a good lady and employee, don't get me wrong. I just don't think working with relatives in this business is a best practice. But since you'll be working closely with her, I need you to know that she thinks she runs the place sometimes. Mr. Henshaw has had to have multiple meetings in his office with her over the years…" He feigned a pleasant smile. "Ones I was privileged to attend."

"I see."

"That's one of the reasons why she no longer runs the loan department. She didn't want to loan money to anybody, regardless of the credit rating, unless she knew the individual personally. Believe me, that list was small."

"I'll keep all this in mind when she trains me."

Gordon put his finger to his lips. "Mum's the word. We did not have this conversation."

"What conversation?"

His head bobbed up and down. He winked and pointed at me. "That's why I like you."

Speaking of that…

"Gordon, may I talk about something that's not related to this job?"

He offered a half-shrug. "Sure."

I crossed my legs the other direction and leaned forward just a little. I clicked my pen, trying to think of how to begin. "I never was one for beating around the bush, so I'm just gonna throw it out there."

He blinked.

"The other day…at the restaurant…you bought my dinner, and I never really got to thank you for it."

He took a deep breath, like a wave of relief washed over him. "Oh, think nothing of it. I'm not sure what came over me, but I felt like it was the right thing to do." He lightly brushed the tip of his fingers over the keys of his keyboard. "Besides, drinking only water with that eggplant parmesan seemed criminal."

I lowered my gaze to my notepad. "I see. Well, thank you." I looked up again. "It was delightful. I can't say I've ever had a wine that expensive before."

"It's not the price that makes good wine…or wine good. It's the company."

"I see. So, knowing which wineries are good at what they do helps make informed decisions, I assume?"

"I suppose, but I was actually referring to the people with whom you drink your wine."

Really? I know I blushed a little. I looked back down at my notepad in a futile attempt at covering it up. "I would agree. Good company makes everything better."

Gordon inhaled as his eyes fixated downward, his fingers no longer tracing the keys. "Yes."

NOT MUCH ELSE WAS SAID AFTER that. Gordon finally stood, took in another calculated breath, and escorted me downstairs to find Mildred. When we spotted her, he shook my hand, wished me well, and motioned for me to proceed while he circled back to the elevator.

Mildred, watching me say goodbye to Gordon, pointed at a door at the far end of the teller area. She opened it and let me inside "the hen house," as they called it. I followed her to window number four, and she kept her eye on Gordon until he disappeared into the elevator.

When the elevator door closed, she spun around on her heels. "So, did you get the lowdown on me?"

"The lowdown on you?"

"Oh, come on. I may be old, but I'm not dead. And I'm definitely not blind. Why else would he keep you in his office after I left?"

"He just wanted to make sure I understood what my role was going to be here. I guess when he talked about managerial responsibilities and my eyes got the size of hubcaps, he got a little nervous."

Mildred studied me. "Did you get his phone number?"

"I don't think that's any of your business."

"So, you did?"

"I'd rather not talk about it."

"So, you didn't? Doesn't surprise me."

"What's that supposed to mean?"

"Gordon's a widower." She tapped her ring finger. "His wife passed away about three years ago. Pancreatic cancer. He wore his wedding ring up until about six months ago."

That's why he mentioned good company…

When drinking wine…

He wasn't talking about me.

He was talking about his wife.

He misses her.

I struck a nerve when I told him about Billy's death.

I closed my eyes and expelled a remorseful sigh.

"You didn't know about his wife?"

I shook my head. "No."

I didn't know.

But I knew how he felt.

CHAPTER TWENTY

For the first time in forever, I parked right in front of our apartment building. I didn't have to walk multiple blocks. A pretty incredible feeling, especially considering how my feet throbbed. It's amazing how quickly your feet get used to sandals and flats and forget what it's like to wear heels.

Standing on the fire escape, in his usual place, stood tattoo man. Instead of the wife-beater t-shirt, he wore a black hoodie. Same jeans. Boxer briefs exposed. He had the hood pulled down over his face, and his head hung down as he leaned on the railing. I couldn't see his face, but the cigarette, hanging from his fingers, glowed red against the evening's shadows.

Must be some life.

I actually felt sorry for him. He seemed lonely. In a tough guy sort of way.

Slogging through the main doors, I grabbed the mail and went upstairs.

Just as I rounded the corner on our floor, the man in the hoodie emerged from the apartment at the end of the hallway.

My blood froze.

With the hoodie still over his head, he locked his door and headed my way.

He sure looks bigger and taller up close.

As he approached, he stepped to one side and motioned for me to pass. "After you," he said in a much deeper voice than I expected.

Skeptical and nervous, I bowed my head a smidgen. "Thank you." I scurried past and fumbled for my keys.

Finally steadying my hand enough to jam the key into the lock, I glanced down the hallway, half-expecting to see him behind me, brandishing a weapon.

Instead, nobody was there.

I closed and locked our door and placed my ear against it.

Nothing.

I peeked out the peephole.

All clear.

I sat down on the couch and yanked off my shoes. I glanced back at the door.

Maybe I misjudged the guy. Maybe he's just like every other person in this God-forsaken building. Poor. Lonely. And despondent.

I flopped back against the couch and massaged my right foot while I sorted through the mail.

It was the typical fare, but I didn't care about the junk mail or the flyers or the bills. All I wanted to know was if a small, white envelope addressed to me resided amongst the stack.

Sure enough, another envelope sat snugly between a book of coupons and the cell phone bill.

I opened it, wondering if Detective Bowen would rather I wear gloves like they do on *CSI* so they can check for fingerprints.

Inside, another picture emerged. This one looked like the little child had gone to a football or baseball game. Or maybe even a concert. There were people everywhere on the page. All forming a circle. Or was it a semi-circle? It was hard to tell. The people, hand-drawn and more detailed than in the previous pictures, seemed to depict a crowd that would have continued onto the next page, going both left and right. Yet, they all were wearing what appeared to be the same thing. Almost like fans at a football game wearing all one color to show unity and create an intimidating atmosphere for the opponent. Inside the masses, in the middle of the circle, were fifteen people, themselves standing in a circle. Kind of like a huddle. But they faced outward. Faced the crowd.

Down in the front, on the far side of the masses, an arrow pointed to a smaller person. On the end of the arrow, the word ME was written in the hand of a child, not an adult.

This child has a front row seat.

People of all ages surrounded the kid.

I ran my hand through my hair. I didn't know what to make of it. Or what to make of any of this anymore. I wanted to simply toss the letters in the garbage. Forget they had ever arrived. Ever existed.

But I knew I'd probably get one tomorrow.

And the next day.

And the next.

That's how my life went.

Events. Horrible events. Troubling events. Ones that would cause the average person to fold. End it all. They kept happening. Robbing me of what little joy came my way.

I sat there staring at the picture. My eyes moistened as my spirit took one more step downward.

You've been through enough, Rachel Leah.

No one should have to endure the heartache and pain you have.

Someone once said, "Life's not fair."

I could handle "not fair."

But what about when life is cruel? I didn't come from money. I didn't grow up with the proverbial silver spoon in my mouth. And I know I'm not the sharpest knife in the drawer.

I'm average.

A nobody.

A number in someone's system. Nothing more. Nothing less.

That's just how life is these days.

It was then I remembered the business card Detective Bowen handed me at the police station. "Call me if you get any more letters…"

I wiped my eyes and rummaged through my purse. I retrieved the card out of my wallet and got up to grab the phone.

Looking at the card, I wondered if she had been able to find anything out concerning my case. I punched in the number.

"Detective Bowen."

"Hello, Detective, it's Rachel Hamar. I just got home and found another letter in my mailbox."

"Postmarked from the same place?"

I snatched the envelope off the couch and double-checked. "Yes."

"Addressed to you?"

"Yes."

"So, that much hasn't changed. What about the letter itself?"

"This one's like the others. Just another drawing, but it's a different picture. Different scene."

"How so?"

I described the drawing to her.

"I'll need to get a copy of that as soon as you can get it to me."

"I can bring it by around lunchtime tomorrow."

"Great."

I switched the phone to my other ear. "Have you had a chance to work on this case at all yet?"

"I did request a warrant for the security camera footage from the post office. The postmaster promised to wait for me until I could get there to pick it up. I plan on looking at it first thing in the morning." She sighed a little. Sounded tired. "One step at a time, Miss Hamar."

"Of course. Well, I'd appreciate it if you could keep me informed."

"Absolutely. And if you receive any other letters after today, just do what you just did. Call me, and we'll arrange to make copies. And, if anything else surfaces that may help us piece things together, please do not hesitate to contact me. Day or night. My cell phone's always on."

"I will."

A glimmer of hope.

The only thing that's kept me going all these years.

A belief that things have to improve.

One person's life cannot be all bad, all the time, every day.

Eventually, the sun has to come up.

The dark clouds must dissipate.

The rain can't fall forever.

I hung up, looking at the picture in my hand.

"Please, God, can something good come out of this for a change?"

Thursday

December 18, 2014

CHAPTER TWENTY-ONE

New York City Police Dept.
33rd Precinct

Detective Nicole Bowen clicked the mouse, pausing the video from the post office in Jericho, New York. She leaned in for a better look, rubbed her eyes, and squinted. She wasn't sure if the grainy resolution was causing the headache or if lying awake at two in the morning was the culprit.

All she knew was this: the stalker she'd been bird-dogging for the last three weeks suddenly quit. It was as if the man decided to go on vacation. If it was a man at all.

The stalker posted videos to an obscure Moldovan-based web address, guarded by a string of servers scattered throughout Europe and Asia. Videos of girls and women in Central Park. Joggers. Dog walkers. Park bench readers. Even a woman helping her four-year-old daughter learn how to ride a tricycle.

These victims, oblivious to his actions, were alerted to the videos by "friends" who had been tagged in the videos. The Central Park Cameraman, the moniker media outlets had given the slime ball, used his victims' social media accounts as a means to invite others to watch.

It worked. When the friends saw the videos, they contacted the victims. When these victims, all female, saw the videos, every one of them had the same reaction. They felt violated, unsafe, and creeped out. "If we were so unwittingly videotaped in the park," one victim said, "where else were we being watched?"

Their residences had been swept for bugs and video devices by law enforcement. All their residences and businesses had been cleared. That much was a relief. But as another victim told Detective Bowen, "I feel like a prisoner now. I've shut down all my social media accounts. I've switched cell phones and got a new number. I even withdrew my two-year-old daughter from day care and quit my part-time job. I'm afraid to leave my house for fear I'm being filmed. Or worse. I find myself going to that website to see if I'm on there again in some new video I haven't seen yet. It's maddening. My husband and I are thinking about moving out of the city now. I'm not sure I can live like this, especially if you can't catch this guy."

That last sentence is what had Detective Bowen staring at the ceiling in the wee hours of just about every morning since, including this one.

Security cameras in and around Central Park failed to catch the guy in the act. It was as if he knew where the cameras were so he could carry out his perverted activity undetected.

Now, there was this case about the mysterious letters sent to another woman. She had to admit it was a completely different M.O., but the thing that had her sitting at her precinct computer at six o'clock in the morning was the fact that another woman, Rachel Hamar, felt the same way.

Watched.

Spied on.

Unsafe.

Just like the women in Central Park.

And West 173rd Street wasn't that far away from Central Park.

Bowen reasoned if these two cases were related, they just might have enough information to begin profiling this scumbag geographically. Maybe narrow down his center of operation, locate the lowlife, and get him off the streets. And since the Central Park Cameraman case had gone cold, these letters being given to another woman in a different location would explain why all the video uploads to that skanky Moldovan website stopped.

He might be changing his angle. He might know law enforcement is on to him, so he was stalking in a different way.

The timing fit.

But that's about all that did.

So, here she sat, sipping on her second cup of coffee. Watching the security camera footage of the post office lobby, via the warrant from Judge Roberson. People walking in. People walking out. Mailing letters. Carrying packages. All she wanted to do was connect the dots. Gain a lead. Catch a break.

Bowen stopped the video near the end of Day One, which was the day before the first letter arrived in Rachel Hamar's mailbox. She believed that if the letters were arriving post-marked, the person would have to mail them at least a day in advance.

If he mailed them there at all.

He could have mailed them from his house. A drop box along the street. Given it to a friend to mail for him. Even stashed it amongst a pile of outgoing mail at his place of employment.

She knew the chances of catching this joker walking into a post office were slim to none, but she had to start somewhere.

Bowen leaned back in her chair and held her cup of coffee, allowing the warmth to seep into her fingers. She took a sip as the video counter ticked the seconds ahead.

About fifteen minutes after the postal worker locked the doors to the counter area, a man wearing a white t-shirt, shorts, and tennis shoes entered the lobby and dropped a piece of mail into the slot on the right marked Outgoing Mail. Then, he turned and headed for the front door. He pushed it open, stepped through the doorway, and vanished.

Bowen almost spit her coffee across her desk. She set her cup down, choked the mouthful of coffee down, and paused the video. She rewound it several times and watched the man vanish over and over again.

She switched to the security camera on the outside of the building. It showed the man walking through the front door of the post office. A few seconds later, she saw the front door open, but no one walked out.

There's only one way in and out for patrons. And it's not like he met up with someone on the inside and exited through the back with one of the postal workers.

She watched him grab the door from the inside. She watched him push the door open. She watched him step through the doorway.

And disappear.

And that's impossible.

She leaned forward and studied the video frame. She rewound it again and studied it frame by frame. Every angle available showed her the same thing.

The man went inside, but he didn't come out.

She flopped back into her chair, baffled by what her eyes told her.

Maybe he simply exited the doorway and rounded the corner quickly. The frames did skip ahead a few seconds. It wasn't a continuous video. Maybe he just walked out. No magician. Just a flaw in the technology.

She leaned forward again, grabbed the pen resting on a notepad, and began jotting down notes.

Need to watch other days of footage to see if the same thing happens at the same time every day.

Need traffic cam footage of area in front of post office.

Where does he go when he walks out?

Where did he come from?

Just then, a voice from behind wrecked her train of thought. "Working hard, I see."

Detective Bowen eased back into her chair and turned to face her partner, Detective Richard Kessler. "What are you doing here? Aren't you supposed to be on vacation?"

"Yes. But we got back early. Thank God."

"Trouble in paradise?"

"No. Family reunions are great. We got there Sunday after-noon. You know? That park I told you about?"

"Oh yeah, Leavenworth?"

"Letchworth."

Bowen snickered. "Just kidding."

"Well, let me tell you, by Tuesday, it felt like Leavenworth. I mean, I love Barbara and her family. Don't get me wrong. But like most families, she's got a couple of fruitcakes who make the rest of us feel uneasy, you know? Like you can never really unwind."

"So, you left early?"

Rick nodded with pursed lips. "We told them we needed to get back. What we needed was a vacation from the family reunion."

Been there. "Why are you here at all? Aren't you off until after Christmas?"

"I keep a second pair of glasses here in case I break my regular pair on the job." He walked over to his desk. "I broke my other pair playing volleyball Tuesday night. But it's all good. Gave us another excuse to leave early."

Nicole pointed at him. "That's what's different about you. Glasses are missing."

Rick opened the lap drawer. "Aren't you in a little early this morning?"

"Couldn't sleep. We caught another case. Could be related to the Central Park Cameraman."

"Same M.O.?"

"Not exactly. But the timing fits."

Rick grabbed his glasses and slipped them on. "I wish I could help you right now, but Barbara and I are planning a day of movies and restaurant hopping. Been years since we've done that."

"Restaurant hopping?"

"Yeah. We go out for breakfast, then we pick a matinee to go see. Then, we hit somewhere for lunch before going to another matinee. Then, it's dinner and another movie. We used to do it all the time when we dated and were first married. Since we've had kids, I think we've done it once, maybe? Was a long time ago."

"Sounds like fun. You two have a blast. I'm sure this new case will be here when you get back."

"That bleak, huh?"

"I think bizarre is the better word."

"Can't wait."

CHAPTER TWENTY-TWO

The Columbian Coffee Shop
Columbus Ave.
Manhattan, NY

It felt good. Getting up around the same time Joanie did. Showering. Fixing some breakfast. Packing a lunch. Getting ready for work.

I know some people would have loved to have the time off. Getting laid off with a small severance package would have translated into one word: Vacation. Use up the severance, then go back to work. Joanie even encouraged me to do it. Take some time. Go enjoy life. Visit Mom. Take some day trips. Take a cruise. Go back to Noring and visit old friends.

Just get away.

All visiting Mom did was upset us both.

And day trips...to where? With whom? I didn't have anybody, except Joanie, and she worked all the time.

And the suggestion of a cruise was even more ridiculous. Besides, I get seasick on the ferry.

Then there was that last option. I kept asking, "Who wants to go back to Noring?"

I'd spent the last twenty years running from Noring.

Running from the memories.

Running.

You get tired when you run.

And when you run a long time, eventually you collapse.

That's why working was so important. I needed a distraction. I needed an escape from the running, if that makes any sense at all.

Running from the running…

As PART of that convoluted process, I stood in line at The Columbian Coffee Shop, holding my little tear-away tab.

Number 47.

The big red, electronic numbers on the wall read "42."

I watched the people behind the counter taking orders, making drinks, grabbing little over-priced baked goods out of a display case, taking people's money, handing back change, yelling "Welcome to The Columbian Coffee Shop!" to every patron who walked through the door in a half-hearted, mechanical manner.

The indie coffee shop experience at its capitalistic finest.

"Number forty-three!"

A young girl at least ten years younger than me strutted up to the counter with an expensive purse over her shoulder and her cell phone in her hand. Without looking up from the screen, thumbing it like she was angry at the phone, she blurted out her order to the guy behind the counter. He asked all the clarifying questions. Regular or decaf? Hot or Iced? Leave room for sugar and cream? Whip/no whip? Yada, yada, yada…

If someone walked in and asked for black coffee, they'd

probably tell that customer they didn't know how to make it.

"Number forty-four!"

The door behind me opened, and in walked Gordon Ames, wearing his suit and carrying his briefcase. He untied his overcoat and scooted to his right, out of the doorway.

I watched him yank a number from the little dispenser on the wall. Apparently, he's been here before.

I started to slink behind the tall man standing beside me, hoping Gordon wouldn't see me. After my conversation with Mildred yesterday, I felt silly. I had taken the whole glass of wine and eggplant parmesan thing way too far. I thought maybe he had purchased my dinner that day to open up the proverbial door.

The possibility of getting to know each other.

A simple, harmless, generous gesture, translated by me as a possible flirtatious act.

Just to see where it might lead.

Yesterday, in his office, he didn't come right out and say it was just business or that he was just being nice. He did say something about good company. And wine being better with said company. And it being the right thing to do.

So, how's a girl to translate all those signals?

He's a widower, Mildred said, who still wore his wedding ring for over two years after his wife passed away.

I suppose being forward with a woman might seem awkward.

Getting back on the horse called Dating after years of leaving the old girl in the barn can be disconcerting.

Trust me.

I know.

"Rachel?"

I looked up, trying to act surprised to find anyone I knew standing in line. "Oh, hi, Gordon. How are you this morning?"

"I'm good. You come in here often?"

"Nope. First time. I used to go the other direction to work.

Now that I come this way, I thought I'd try this place."

Gordon slid over next to me. "Like most of the coffee houses in the city, they boast about having the best coffee of them all. I can't say I disagree. The coffee here is better than some of the others I've tried. But to say it's the best…?" He shrugged his shoulders. "I'll let you weigh in. Tell me what you think."

"I'm not a connoisseur. As long as it tastes okay, I'm good."

"I see you have your number."

I held it up and smiled. "Forty-seven."

"When they call your number, if it's not Heather, allow the next person in line to go ahead of you and swap numbers with them. She's the best coffee maker they have here. The others don't take the time to make it right every time. She does."

"Which one is Heather?"

"The little blonde with the pony tail."

Blonde, huh? Ponytail?

"I remember one time, this guy made my drink. It was awful. I brought it back in, and Heather remade it. It was perfect. From that day forward, when I stop by here, if she's not behind the counter, I walk out."

"You haven't given anybody else a shot since that day?"

"Nope."

"And how long ago was that?"

"About a year ago."

Hmm. He talks about her like he's…infatuated…even if it's just a little… "She's what? In college?"

"Just graduated. Actually looked at banking for a short time during her freshman year, but changed her mind and decided to go pre-med. She'll be leaving here next summer and rollin' up those huge medical school tuition bills."

"Number forty-five!"

He seems to know a lot about her. Too much for a barista, if you ask me.

Sigh. I thought he would be different.

"She's rooming with my daughter right now. She's been a good friend to Elena."

My eyes must have bugged out. "Oh, so you actually know her outside of…here?" I pointed at the walls.

Gordon smiled but in a pained manner. "Well, yeah. She and Elena have known each other since high school. Her family really helped Elena and me through a rough patch. They're good people."

"A rough patch?"

Gordon looked down toward the floor. "My wife passed away a few years ago. Cancer. Heather and her family became good friends during that time. They're like extended family. We get together for all the holidays. It's been nice."

"So, that's why you hold out for her to make your coffee."

Gordon looked at me as if I'd just spoken some forgotten language. "Yeah."

After seeing the look on his face, I wanted to slink out the door and crawl into the nearest garbage can with a lid.

Hello, doofus. Not everyone is a lowlife. Some guys actually have morals.

"I'm sorry, I just misunderstood."

Gordon's expression, puzzled by my previous statement, suddenly lit up. "Ohhhh…you thought I had a thing for Heather?" He started to laugh.

I bobbed my head from side to side slightly and winced. "Maybe a little."

His laughter sank deeper into his gut. He placed his fist over his mouth. "Oh, now that's rich."

"What is?"

"To think a twenty-something, cute, blonde barista would give an old guy like me the time of day." He shook his head while he continued to control his hilarity. "I'm flattered that you would think that highly of me."

"Well, to be honest, I wasn't."

His eyes got bigger.

"Number forty-six!"

"You thought I was…a what? A pervert, or something?"

"No. Not at all. You just seemed a little too interested in her, but it all makes sense now."

"Oh, a stalker, then?"

"I think we need to change the subject before I really regret having this conversation more than I already do."

"Number forty-seven!" Heather stood behind the counter, waiting for her next customer.

Gordon gently grabbed me by the arm and escorted me to the counter. "Hi, Heather."

"Hi, Mr. Ames. What can I get for you? The usual?"

"Actually, it's not my turn yet. This is Rachel. She's new at the bank, and I wanted to introduce her to you. Can you take care of her for me? She's a friend."

"Of course. What would you like, Rachel?"

It was happening so fast.

In a mere few minutes, I went from being alone to thinking my boss was depraved to being his friend.

Can you take care of her for me? She's a friend.

A friend.

I don't have friends. Not plural.

"Uh, I, umm, just regular coffee. Black."

Gordon leaned forward to get a better look at my face. "I didn't peg you as a black coffee kind of person."

"I'm not. I just really want to…leave."

He wrinkled his face and waved me off like I was being ridiculous. "Please, go ahead and order it the way you like it. My treat."

Out of the corner of my eye, I saw Heather smile. She could tell what was going on.

I inhaled deeply and held it. "Mocha caramel iced latte, skim, no whip, extra mocha…and a shot of whiskey, if you have any."

CHAPTER TWENTY-THREE

United States Post Office
Jericho, NY

etective Nicole Bowen backed her unmarked sedan into the first parking space outside the drug store next door. Except for an alley-like smattering of additional parking spots between the two buildings, the vantage point offered her an unobstructed view of the post office entrance.

A man got out of the vehicle two spaces down and walked up to the passenger side. Fifty-something. Graying hair. Razor stubble gave the impression he hadn't shaved today. He cupped his police shield in his hand and waved it at her.

She unlocked the door, and he climbed inside.

The man reached out his hand. "Detective John Witherspoon. Nassau County PD. Second Precinct."

Nicole shook his hand. "Detective Nicole Bowen. NYPD. Thirty-third. I was the one who contacted you."

"And we appreciate that, by the way."

"It's your jurisdiction here. These letters show up in ours, but we have reason to believe they originate here. So, that makes us partners, of sorts."

"Yes, it does." He pointed at the folder on the dash. "May I?"

Nicole waved her approval. "Not much in there yet. Just copies of the letters sent so far and a surveillance photo." She checked the clock on the dashboard. "I've watched the security camera footage for the last ten days. Every day, except one, he showed up right around closing time. Always dropped off a small, white envelope into the mailbox, exited, and—"

"Vanishes, right?" Detective Witherspoon's left eyebrow lifted as his right one dipped. "I read the report."

"Just write 'em like I see 'em. You're welcome to challenge it. I'd love for someone to find whatever it is I'm missing. All I know is, he appears to mail these letters every day around the same time. Always at the same place. Which means, we've got less than ten minutes before they shut down for the day. He likes to show up right at closing time."

"When all the workers are in the back?"

"Seems so."

"But the lobby's still open." Detective Witherspoon set the folder down in his lap. "Pretty slick move, if you ask me. No one would suspect anybody at that time of day." Fishing out a picture of the suspect, he held it out, away from his face, like his eyes needed special accommodations. "Judging by the door frame, he's probably six foot. Maybe more. Dark hair. Some kind of white uniform shirt with some writing on the sleeves. Were you able to get a clear image of that emblem?"

"On-Time Couriers. Main office is located in Brooklyn."

"Never heard of 'em."

"Neither had we. But we looked 'em up. They seem legit and reputable. However, when I spoke to their manager, he said he was new and didn't know all the couriers yet. They have over fifty. He looked at that photo and said this guy was at work this morning. Had to look up his name, though. Flip it over."

He did so. "Kenneth Singh."

"We found his apartment, but nobody was home. I've got an RP sitting on it in case we miss him here."

"What do we know about Mr. Singh?"

"Not much. Just moved to the City six months ago. Born in Jakarta, Indonesia. Is here on a work visa, and speaks four languages, including English. Rents an apartment in the Bronx. Information beyond six months is sketchy."

Detective Witherspoon huffed. "Gotta love sketchy. Makes our job so much easier."

She scanned the parking lot. "I'm thinking one of us should be inside. The other here."

"I'll take the inside." He checked his watch and slipped the picture into his coat pocket.

"Don't spook him."

"Detective, I've been doing this job a long time. And the older I get, the less I like to run. So, don't worry that pretty little head of yours. I've got this." He opened the door and crawled out. "I'm on channel seven."

He shut the door, looked both ways, and allowed a pick-up truck to pass before crossing the parking lot.

"Don't worry your pretty little head." She closed her eyes and inhaled deeply. *Good thing I'm a civil servant.*

DETECTIVE BOWEN FLIPPED her radio to the correct frequency. "Radio check. Come in, Witherspoon."

She watched him adjust his earpiece. "Loud and clear. Let me know when you see our suspect approach the building, then follow him inside."

I've been doing this a long time too, Detective. Don't worry your pretty little head. "Ten-four."

Several minutes passed, and she studied every person

walking toward the post office, near it, or by it. For those who approached from far away, she lifted a pair of binoculars to her eyes and checked. One face, then the next. A grandma holding the hand of her granddaughter as they crossed the street, turned, and walked toward the grocery store. A businessman in his suit, standing along the sidewalk, hailing a cab. A bold soul in a t-shirt, shorts, and flip flops despite the chill in the air, crossing the post office parking lot and entering the drug store next door. A young punk with the penguin walk and sagging jeans to match, leaning against a car, acting like he was waiting for someone.

There.

Approaching from the other side of the grocery store. A tall man. About six foot. White uniform shirt. White pants. A white something in his hand.

Looks like our guy.

She depressed the radio transmitter pinned to her shirt. "Suspect heading your way. About to round the corner in front of the grocery store."

She could see Detective Witherspoon peer out the doorway and then step back. "Roger that."

The man identified as Kenneth Singh rounded the corner and headed straight for the post office's front doors.

Bowen watched the suspect look around as he got closer and closer. A little too suspiciously for her taste. What if he's got an accomplice? A lookout? Someone to alert him if they spot cops lurking in the shadows?

She quickly dumped the contents of the suspect's folder onto the seat beside her, grabbed the now empty manila folder, flipped it inside out to hide the NYPD crest, and got out of her car, using the folder as a prop. Just in case there was someone watching.

Detective Bowen traversed half the distance between her car and the post office when the suspect flung the door open and entered. She grabbed her mic. "Suspect just walked in."

Quickening her step, she closed the gap and entered to find

Detective Witherspoon holding out his badge, asking the man to stop and not drop the piece of mail into the slot. "Put your hands against the wall and drop the letter on the ground," he said.

Kenneth Singh appeared confused. "What is happening?"

Bowen stepped inside and cleared the lobby of two other patrons before standing on the other side of the suspect, blocking the doorway.

"I need you to drop the letter, Mr. Singh."

"Okay, okay," Singh said. He opened his right hand, and the letter fell to the floor. "How do you know my name?"

"Put your hands on the wall." Detective Witherspoon had pocketed his badge and placed his hand on his holster.

Detective Bowen did the same. "We don't want any trouble," she said. "We just need to ask you some questions. But first, we need to make sure you're not carrying any weapons."

"Weapons?"

"Please, Mr. Singh," Witherspoon said. "We can do this the easy way or the hard way."

Singh's puzzled look appeared to be transforming to one of frustration. "I didn't do anything wrong." He faced the wall and slapped his hands against it like he knew the drill.

Witherspoon frisked the suspect, starting with his torso. "You didn't answer the question, Mr. Singh. Do you have any weapons?"

"What question?" Singh said. "She said you needed to know if I had any weapons. Apparently, you're already checking."

Witherspoon pinned Singh against the wall, grabbed one of the suspect's wrists, and twisted it behind his back. He slapped on a cuff before yanking his other arm down and fastening it to the other cuff. Witherspoon then leaned in close to Singh's ear. "Don't get smart with us. We can make your life miserable if we want. But we're trying to be as cordial as possible. It's your call."

"You call this cordial? It's because I look Middle Eastern, isn't it?"

Detective Witherspoon bent over and picked up the letter. "No." He inspected it and held it up, nodding at Detective Bowen. He spun Singh around and pinned him against the wall. "It's because the person mailing these letters is up to no good."

Bowen took the letter from Witherspoon. Same name. Rachel Hamar. Same address. West 173rd Street. Washington Heights. She held it up for Mr. Singh to see. "How do you know this woman?"

"What woman?"

"Rachel Hamar?" Bowen said, pointing at the envelope. "The woman addressed on this letter?"

"I don't know her. I just mail the letters. That's my job. I get a bunch of things to deliver every morning. I'm like the UPS man. See?" He nodded at his sleeve. "On-Time Couriers. That is who I work for. You can ask them."

"We already have," Bowen said. "The thing we want to know is, who is giving you these letters? You've stopped by here every day around this time for the last ten days or so, mailing a letter just like this." She continued to hold it up.

"I don't know where they come from. I swear. I am given things all day to deliver."

Witherspoon snatched the letter from Bowen's hand. "But why here, Sunshine? At this post office? Why not one close to your job?"

"I mail it on my way home."

"Your way home, huh?" Bowen said. "You live in the Bronx, Mr. Singh. On-Time Couriers is located between here and your apartment. That makes Jericho, New York, one gigantic detour."

Singh huffed in exasperation. "You don't understand. We not only have to deliver the items they give us, but we must follow any special instructions too. Like, if a customer wants a package delivered to a person's home after twelve noon because they know the person receiving it works in the morning and will not be home." He shrugged as if it was obvious. "We have to do what the patron wants. We must follow their instructions."

"You're telling us that whoever asked you to mail this letter asked you to mail it from this specific post office?"

Singh nodded. "I make it my last stop of the day since there is no special time of the day specified. The drive back helps me unwind before I get home."

She looked at Detective Witherspoon. "That would explain why he comes every day around five."

"But it doesn't explain the disappearing act."

"True." She stepped closer to Singh. "Where do you go when you leave here?"

"I told you. I go home."

"How do you get there?"

"Same way I get here. By motorcycle."

"Where's your bike now?"

"In the parking lot."

"I didn't see you ride up on one. You walked."

Singh scrunched his brow. "You were spying on me?"

Witherspoon shoved the letter in Singh's face. "You betcha, scumbag. We've got a woman who is worried sick because you're mailing these things to her. So, what do you know about these letters?"

"I told you. I don't know anything about them. I just mail them."

"Well, Mr. Singh, since you don't know anything," Bowen said, reaching out for his arm, "we're gonna need to take you in for questioning. Maybe your memory lapse will improve on the ride in."

"Are you kidding me?"

"Not in the least."

CHAPTER TWENTY-FOUR

New York City Police Dept.
33rd Precinct

"Hello?"

"Miss Hamar, this is Detective Bowen."

"Please tell me you have good news."

"I have news. But I'm not sure if it's good or not. We intercepted the man who has been responsible for mailing the letters. We apprehended him with another letter and have brought him in for questioning. I'm assuming this letter is the one you would have received tomorrow."

"Okay. Well, I got another one today, and I think you're going to want to see it. It's different from the others."

"Can you bring it to the precinct?"

"Right now?"

"If you can. If not, I'll send someone to come get it."

"No, I can do it. I'll be there in a little bit."

Detective Bowen hung up the phone. "She's on her way. She got another letter today. Probably mailed yesterday."

Detective Witherspoon sipped his coffee. "You know, it doesn't matter where I go. My precinct. Here. The Feds. The little Podunk police station back home. The coffee always tastes the same."

"Yeah. Weak. And burnt."

Witherspoon, taking another sip, acknowledged her response with a grunt and pointed. "Why do you think that is?"

"No one ever washes the coffee pots out. Or the makers, for that matter."

He scrunched his eyebrows and pondered her answer. "You might be onto something."

"Have you ever seen anyone clean those things? All I ever see anyone do is empty the pot, dump the basket, and add more coffee and water."

"But doesn't the custodian do that?"

"I've never seen one do it. And I work all hours in this place."

"Now that you mention it. I worked graveyard for over two years, and you're right. I never saw anyone clean it." He looked into his cup. "My dad was a cop. He said this was what grew hair on your chest."

"He lied. I drink the stuff all the time." She lifted her hands. "No hair."

"I'm gonna have to see some evidence, Detective."

"And I'm gonna have to file an SH complaint with IA."

"You brought it up." He chuckled and motioned toward the interrogation room. "Want to see if our Mr. Singh wants any coffee?"

"You can." Bowen stood. "I want to see if Mr. Singh will live up to his last name."

"Oh, now, you see?" Witherspoon said, pointing at Bowen. "I

didn't peg you as a comedian. Just goes to show we never know about people."

They walked down the hall, and Bowen opened the door. "I'll be here all week." She allowed Witherspoon to enter first.

He looked at Kenneth Singh and thumbed back in Detective Bowen's direction. "Did you know she was a comedian? Funny girl."

Kenneth Singh's exhausted expression became one of puzzlement. "When can I get out of here?"

"Do you have some pressing appointment, Mr. Singh?" Bowen said. She sat down opposite her person of interest and set a folder and a laptop down on the table.

"No. I just want to go home."

"In due time, Mr. Singh, or can we call you Kenneth?" Witherspoon said.

"I don't care what you call me. I just want to go home. I'm tired, and it's been a long day."

"We have a few questions to ask you, Kenneth." Witherspoon patted the laptop resting on the table. "I want you to watch something for me."

Bowen opened the computer, entered a password and immediately, the lobby of the U.S. post office in Jericho appeared on the screen. "Do you recognize this location, Kenneth?"

"Yeah. Of course. It's where you two arrested me. Falsely arrested me, I might add."

"No one's arrested you, Kenneth. Not yet," Bowen said. "We just brought you in for questioning. See," she said, pointing at his hands, "no handcuffs. If you were arrested, you'd still have them on."

"And they'd be secured to that little silver hook there," Witherspoon added.

Detective Bowen tapped the mouse pad and the picture sprang to life. "This is the security camera footage from the post office. This is from yesterday. Just watch."

In the frame, they watched Kenneth walk into the lobby, look both ways, then drop a letter into the slot in the wall before heading for the exit. Witherspoon held up his finger, and Bowen paused the video.

"Did you see that, Kenneth? As you walked inside, you looked both ways before mailing the letter. Why did you look both ways?"

Kenneth eyed Witherspoon before looking at Bowen. "We're always taught to mind our surroundings. We are delivery people. Other people know we sometimes carry things of high value. So, we are taught to look around. Be suspicious. Of everybody."

"I can buy that," Witherspoon said. "So, did you know there was something valuable in that letter?"

"No. Was there? I had no idea what was in it. For all I knew, it could have had a check or money order in it."

Witherspoon, seeming to be okay with the answer, glanced at Bowen. She shrugged and tapped the keyboard again.

The picture showed Kenneth exit through the lobby door.

Bowen paused the video and pointed at the screen. "Kenneth, you see yourself exiting the lobby?"

Kenneth's bushy eyebrows knit together again. "Yes."

"Look at the time stamp below. What does it say?"

"Twelve minutes after five. And forty-two seconds."

"Good. Now, when I push Play, the video is going to show three things. First, it's going to show you exiting the post office lobby. Second, it's going to switch from this security camera to the one outside, looking across the parking lot. Then, it's going to synchronize the two cameras and show one on one side of the screen and one on the other. Okay? Ready?"

"Sure."

Detective Bowen began the next sequence of footage, showing Kenneth push the inside of the lobby door. The door swung open, but no one stepped outside in the second camera angle. When the synchronized videotape appeared, it showed the inside of the lobby on the left, and the outside of the post office on the right. When Kenneth Singh pushed the door open, all three of them saw that same door open outward, toward the parking lot.

But no one exited the lobby.

And the door swung shut.

Detective Bowen paused the video and peered at Kenneth. "Did you notice the time stamp, Kenneth? There's no break in the video. It's a continuous feed, even when the two angles appear side by side."

Kenneth scratched his cheek. "I don't know what happened. As you can see, I'm here. I did not disappear into thin air."

"No, Kenneth," Detective Witherspoon said. "You didn't. Not for good, that is. But you did here," he said, tapping the monitor with his fingernail. "Can you explain that for us?"

"No. I can't."

"Can't? Or won't?"

"I cannot. I have no explanation for you."

"Let me help then." Witherspoon sat on the edge of the table. "I think you know someone at that particular post office. That would explain why you drive all the way to Jericho from the Bronx to mail a letter that could be mailed in a hundred different locations. All of which are closer to your apartment."

"I already told you. The specific instructions for mailing that letter say it has to be at this post office," Kenneth said, pointing at the monitor. "If I mailed it from somewhere else, it would eventually get back to my boss, and he would fire me."

"But that doesn't explain the disappearing act, Kenneth. However, a person working on the inside would. And if you left out the back of the post office like an employee, then that would explain why you never appear on the parking lot camera."

"But wouldn't you see me turn around and head back toward the mailroom on the other one?"

Witherspoon lowered his gaze. "You're right, Kenneth. We

would. We should. But we don't. We've checked it. As a matter of fact, we've checked the last nine, ten days, however long it's been since you started delivering these letters. You never double back."

Kenneth turned his hands upward. "You see? I've been trying to tell you. I'm just the courier. Nothing more. Nothing less. And I cannot help it if your cameras malfunctioned. I am just a courier, trying to make a living."

"Is it normal for a courier to get the same delivery every day? What I mean is, your company has over fifty couriers working each day, delivering all kinds of packages, letters, envelopes, that sort of thing. You have delivered every letter to this post office. Why not some other courier?"

"Our manager likes consistency. He says it makes our jobs more efficient. Since I delivered the first letter, I now know the way. I can deliver it faster than a new guy who's never driven out here before."

Witherspoon looked at Bowen. "Makes sense."

"I believe him," Bowen said.

Kenneth blinked. "So, can I go now?"

Witherspoon tossed a small wave at Bowen. "It's your precinct, Detective."

She stood and closed the laptop. "A word?"

"What about me?" Kenneth said.

"Just sit tight," Bowen said. "We'll be back in a few minutes."

"Well, can I get something to drink? I'm thirsty."

"We have coffee," Witherspoon said.

"I'd rather have water."

"I'll see what I can do."

Both detectives exited the room and closed the door behind them. Bowen motioned Witherspoon away from the interrogation room windows.

"You know, we really don't have much on this guy," Witherspoon said.

"True, but I might be able to get a judge to allow us to hold him until after five o'clock tomorrow. If the letters stop, then we know there's something shady about Kenneth."

"And if another courier shows up with another letter, then our buddy Kenneth just might be telling us the truth, the whole truth, and nothing but."

"Exactly." Bowen huffed a sigh. "We still need to track down where these letters are coming from and how the courier service is getting them."

"All right, this is what we do," Witherspoon said. "You see if you can get the judge to allow us to hold Kenneth here to keep him from delivering anymore letters to the Jericho post office. I'll go sit on the post office tomorrow and see if we get anyone else dropping suspicious white envelopes off. And if you can get me info on this On-Time Couriers outfit, I'll also pay them a visit in the morning and try to find out how the courier is getting the letters."

"Keep in mind, Witherspoon, that the entire reason I took this case in the first place was because I believed it might be tied to a stalker case I've been investigating."

"Right. The Central Park Cameraman. You think Singh is your stalker?"

"I guess we'll know a little after five o'clock tomorrow afternoon."

I WALKED the short distance between our apartment and the 33rd precinct, wondering. I passed businesses and people and didn't even remember or recall getting that far down the block.

What did the new letter contain?

Who was the man they believe might be responsible?

Detective Bowen mentioned some stalker, trying to assure me that for right now, the two cases were not related.

But why bring it up unless there was a possibility?

Should I be watching my back everywhere I go?

When Detective Bowen called, I was sitting on the couch in mild shock. The letter in my hands, received in the mail earlier today, didn't display a crudely drawn picture of something I had no idea how to interpret. Instead, this time the letter was more like an actual letter.

It wasn't addressed to me, though. I mean, the envelope was, just like all the others, but not the paper inside.

It really wasn't addressed to anyone. It was more like a little girl's Dear Diary entry:

Today, I played in the meadow with my friends. There is so much to do and see there. You would love it. The flowers are so colorful. When they blow in the wind, they look like they are dancing. There are animals everywhere too. All of them are so friendly. I fed a bird some seeds we had found on the ground. He ate them right out of my hand! Daddy said he thought the bird liked me because I guess it doesn't do that with everybody. That made me feel special.

By the time Detective Bowen called, I had read the letter at least ten times. On my way to see her, I must have replayed the letter another ten times in my head. Yet, as I entered the precinct, I still didn't know what to make of it.

I was cleared and escorted to Detective Bowen. She was talking to another man, dressed in a shirt and tie. He held a cup of coffee and kept readjusting the badge clipped to his belt.

He looks like another detective.

I didn't say anything. I just stood by Detective Bowen's desk and waited for them to finish their conversation.

A couple of minutes later, the man left, and Detective Bowen walked over and shook my hand. "Hello, Miss Hamar."

I simply handed her my letter and plopped down in the chair beside her desk.

"This looks troubling," she said, taking the envelope from me.

I stared straight ahead at the wall. "It's all troubling."

Bowen didn't respond but instead opened the envelope and began to read.

Once finished, she gave a small groan and picked up a letter off her desk. She then held it out. "This is the one we confiscated from our person of interest. Read it and tell me what you think."

I raised my eyes and just stared at her for a couple of long seconds. "You haven't opened it yet?"

"No. It's your mail. I thought it best to wait and let you do that. However, judging by this one and the change in the overall letter itself, I'm thinking this new one may be similar since it apparently was intended to be the next one delivered."

My eyes went back and forth between the letter in her hand and her concerned eyes. "You said there might be a stalker."

"Look, Miss Hamar—"

"Please. Rachel."

"Look, Rachel, I shouldn't have mentioned that case. As of right now, I have nothing, I repeat, nothing to tie these two cases together. I'll admit, it was the other case that made me interested in yours, but the more I investigate yours, the more it's looking like they are not related after all."

"Are you certain?"

"One hundred percent? No. But right now, I'm about ninety-nine percent convinced. Especially if this letter is like the one you just brought me."

I hesitated then took the piece of mail from her.

Detective Bowen sat down at her desk and offered me a pair of scissors. "Poor girl's letter opener."

A smile leaked out, but I waved her off. "Did you need this envelope for fingerprints or anything?"

Bowen shook her head.

I ripped the envelope open.

"If you want me to read it after you're done, that's fine," she said, placing the scissors in her lap drawer. "If you'd rather I read it instead, I can do that too."

I didn't respond. I just unfolded the letter, and something dropped to the ground. As I bent over to pick it up, she jammed her hand against my shoulder. "Don't. Allow me."

She got down on one knee and pulled out a latex glove from the pouch on her belt. Using the glove like a paper towel, she picked up the item. Turning her hand over, she displayed a pressed flower, flattened about as thin as it could be. The edges of the flower had turned brown, like it had been picked a while ago, but the majority of the color remained.

Yellow.

A buttercup.

Detective Bowen must have been watching my facial expressions. "Are you all right?"

"I'm not sure."

"What do you mean?"

I fell back into my chair and drew in a measured breath. "It could be a coincidence, but my favorite flower is the—"

"Buttercup?"

I bit my lip.

"Who would know that?"

My grandmother.

She used to call me her Little Buttercup.

I'd forgotten about that.

"It has to be someone who knows you well."

I shrugged in defeat. "My mom, obviously. Joanie, maybe, but I can't remember if I've ever told her that."

My dad knew, too, but that doesn't matter anymore.

"Would your mom or Joanie go to such elaborate lengths to try and deceive you like this, even if it was done merely as a practical joke?"

"No. Not them. Not like this. Not this long." Besides, where would Mom get buttercups?

"Does anyone else know?"

Joanie knew how much this whole ordeal was bothering me. But she wouldn't do such a thing. She knew I'd kill her if it turned out to be her. Besides, she was the one who suggested I go to the police.

"About the buttercup being your favorite flower?"

But Joanie did play that little prank with her new boyfriend the other night.

She seemed to really enjoy punking me like that.

"Miss Hamar? Are you hearing me?"

Maybe it was his idea. How long did she say they had been dating?

How well does she know this guy anyway?

Detective Bowen said this case could be tied to a stalker case she was investigating.

Could Roberto be the stalker?

Detective Bowen placed the flower on her desk. "Rachel?" She reached out and touched my arm.

I heard a voice speaking. I finally heard my name.

"Rachel?"

I yanked my gaze in her direction. "What?"

"I was asking you some questions. Did you hear me?"

"I—I was thinking about how Joanie played a little joke on me the other night."

"What kind of joke?"

"She wanted to introduce me to her boyfriend. They played a prank on me. I think it was her way of trying to lighten things up for me…and introduce me to her new boyfriend at the same time. She knows how hard it's been over the last few days."

"Is she a prankster?"

"No. But it could've been her boyfriend's idea."

Detective Bowen pointed at the letter in my hand. "Could they be doing this together?"

"I don't think so. Joanie was the one who suggested I contact you."

Bowen sat silent for a long moment. "What about the boyfriend? What do you know about him?"

"Nothing, really. He supposedly works with Joanie at Manningham's Construction."

"What's his name?"

"Roberto. I don't know his last name."

"Well, a new person suddenly enters your life via your best friend. Acting as her new boyfriend? That could be something." She tossed the glove into the wastebasket. "I'll need to check him out." She jotted down some information on a notepad. "Got any idea how old this Roberto is?"

"He said he was thirty-one."

She scribbled more notes.

I set the envelope down next to the flower and straightened out the folded piece of paper in my hand. It was another Dear Diary-style letter. Just like the one I'd read less than an hour ago. However, like the one previous, it appeared to have been written by a child.

Today, I played in the meadow again before dinnertime. Daddy says this kind of flower always reminds him of me. He said it's always bright. It's always alive. And it smiles on a sunny day. I picked one so I could press it to always remind me of this day.

Daddy said that if I wanted to, I could go to the meadow tomorrow and pick a whole bunch of them. Then he said I could bring them back to the house so they could be put in a pretty vase.

I can't wait!

When I read the last couple of lines for the second time, I dropped the letter and bolted from my chair, shivering as I arose.

"Rachel. What's wrong?"

"Get that letter away from me." I marched over to a window overlooking the street below. I hugged myself tight and began to rock.

Back and forth.

Back and forth.

I heard Bowen groan as she plucked the letter off the floor. Then, a long silence. "I'm not seeing it, Rachel. Does it have something to do with the flower?"

I nodded like a crazed lunatic.

"What about it? Why does that have you so rattled?"

The memory of me, bounding through the fields, the wind blowing my hair, my dress, my bare feet…it all brought tears to my eyes.

The walks. The afternoons. They were good times. Happy times.

Picking buttercups, making sure the stems were long so they could get a drink from the bottom of the vase. Handing them to my grandmother and watching her smile spread from ear to ear.

The afternoons sitting at the kitchen table, sipping tea, thinking I was so big and grown up.

The overnight slumber parties in the living room, munching on popcorn and promising not to tell Mommy how late we stayed up.

The kind of over-the-river-and-through-the-woods story-book tales you long to tell your own children someday on a long winter's night by the fire. I had always remembered those days, but for some strange reason, I had forgotten about the flowers.

How would anyone know about those times? I hadn't told anyone about those trips to Grandma's house.

I finally turned to see Bowen standing a few feet away,

rereading the letter. "No one knew about that except Grandma and me."

"Knew about what?"

"I used to walk to my grandmother's house when I was a little girl. When the buttercups were in bloom, I always brought her a bouquet. She would cut the stems and place them in a special vase. She said it was for my flowers only."

"Couldn't she have told someone about all this?"

"I suppose. But she told me that it was our little secret. That's why she called me her Little Buttercup. It was her pet name for me. No one has ever called me that since. Not even my mom."

"Is your grandmother still alive?"

I shook my head.

"How old were you when she passed?"

"Nine, I think. Maybe ten."

"Was she your maternal or paternal grandmother?"

"Maternal."

"Then, she could have told your mother."

"But where would my mother get buttercups? Assuming she's the one sending the letters. She's in LIPC. She doesn't go anywhere without an escort."

"Good point."

"And why would she send me a letter like that?"

"Good question." Bowen stepped closer. "I want you to come look at the man who we caught mailing the letter and tell me if you've seen him before. He's sitting in our interrogation room."

I inhaled and nodded at the same time. It was more of a mechanism than a response. I was trying not to break down into a blubbering idiot.

"Follow me."

Detective Bowen led me down a hallway and around a wall. Just a few feet away sat a room with windows. The shades were half-drawn.

"Let's stand right here and pretend we're having a normal

conversation," Detective Bowen said, gently grabbing my arm and turning me so I could peer over her shoulder. "See that room behind me? The one with the shades and all the windows?"

"Yeah. There's a man sitting at a table, drinking a glass of water."

"Wearing a white shirt, right? Dark hair. Looks like he might be from India?"

"Is that the man who has been mailing these letters to me?"

"Look at him. Have you ever seen him before?"

I watched him. He took another sip of his drink then flopped back into his chair and glanced at his watch. He rubbed his eyes. Seemed frustrated. "No. I've never seen him before."

"Are you sure?"

Hoping against hope they had found the person responsible, I did not want to pin this on an innocent man. "I'm sure."

"What about the shirt? Have you ever seen anyone wearing a courier shirt like that before?"

"No. Is that what he is? A courier?"

Detective Bowen nodded. "He claims someone gives the letters to his company. He is given the letters by his supervisor with specific instructions to mail them at the post office in Jericho."

"He's mailed all the letters so far?"

"Apparently."

"Then he should know who's dropping them off at the courier service, right?"

"No. He claims he gets them from his supervisor along with all the other deliveries he has to make."

I tilted my head. "Then his supervisor should know who's bringing them in."

"That's one of the things we're working on."

I crossed my arms tighter.

"We're gonna figure this out, Rachel."

I nodded, but inside, I wasn't so sure.

Friday

December 19, 2014

CHAPTER TWENTY-FIVE

The Columbian Coffee Shop
Manhattan, NY

I didn't sleep much. How could I when twenty-five-year-old images of my grandmother kept replaying over and over again? My mind would not stop reliving the days spent with Grammy. Picking buttercups. Baking cookies. Taking long walks through the woods. Grammy used to say that was what made being a grandma "grand."

Those memories, some of the best ones I have, led to an entire train of thought from my childhood. A trek through time, conjuring up memories long forgotten.

Friends who moved away.

Relatives I had never met, talked about by my parents in casual conversations.

In each instance, the recollections became more obscure. More troubling. The train of thought was becoming a train wreck.

Why couldn't the letters have been about those things? Help me recall the times I'd gladly forgotten? Why did they have to attack one of the most vivid, wonderful memories I had growing up?

These letters caused my memories of Grammy and the time spent with her to seem creepy now. Like someone was watching me pick those flowers when I was a little girl. Standing behind a tree or kneeling behind a bush. Spying on an innocent child through binoculars or worse, a camera lens.

As I stood in line at The Columbian Coffee Shop, watching the baristas race around behind the counter, I couldn't help but wonder if someone was pointing a camera lens at me at this very moment.

I peered toward the door and scanned the crowd before facing the counter again. Everyone seemed just like me.

In a rush.

In need of coffee.

Wanting to be left alone so they could thumb their smartphones in peace.

Except for the loud mouth to my right, talking through his Bluetooth earpiece. Like we all wanted to hear his half of the conversation.

And why do people like that have to yell as if the person on the other end is across the street?

Sometimes, technology isn't helpful. It's just annoying.

"Number sixty-five!" the little blonde barista with the pony-tail said.

I held up my number and flagged her down, weaving my way between two tourists. "That's me, Heather."

"Oh, hi, Rachel. What can I get for you?"

I pointed at the sign behind her. "I want to try one of those peppermint mocha frappe thingies with the candy cane sticking out of it. Large. Five-gallon bucket size, if you have it. Gonna be a long day, I'm afraid."

"Aww. I'm sorry to hear that." She took my money, grabbed

a cup, and scribbled my name on the side along with the drink info. "Why's that?"

"Couldn't sleep last night. A lot going on in my life right now."

"That sounds troubling."

Troubling. The title of my life story. "I guess that's a pretty good way to put it."

"I'm not trying to pry or sound like some matchmaker, so please don't take this wrong, but didn't Gordon Ames say yesterday you were working for him now?"

I smiled. "He did."

"Gordon's a good man. If you're having problems, he's got a level head. I know he's helped me through a lot. He would be objective too. He really doesn't know you that well, so all that I-can't-be-honest-because-I-don't-want-to-lose-her-as-a-friend stuff doesn't apply."

"Yeah, but he's my boss."

"True, but he's not like other guys. Trust me. I've known his family for several years now. His daughter Elena has told me stories you wouldn't believe."

"Like what?"

Heather started preparing the drink. "Stories of how women, including our neighbor next door, have been trying to hook Gordon up with their friends. They all say the same thing about him. He's intelligent. He's accomplished. He's got a great job. He has deep feelings about certain subjects. He's a great conversationalist…"

"But?"

Heather flipped a switch, and the blender growled as it chewed up the ice. She then motioned for me to meet her at the end of the counter. "They say when they try to get him to go to their place, or try to go to his, he shuts it down before it starts."

"What's that got to do with talking to him about my problems?"

She wagged her finger for me to come closer. "If he's not that kind of guy, then he won't use the getting-to-know-you-better conversation as a springboard to other things. Make sense? And it won't make your business relationship weird either. Trust me on this. He will keep it professional. He'll be like a counselor who just so happens to work at a bank…and happens to be your boss."

"I don't know. I just started working there. It's only been a couple of days."

Heather stepped over and shut the blender off. She grabbed my cup, poured the Frappuccino into it like she'd done it her entire life, and grabbed a lid. "Whip cream?"

"No, thank you."

She slapped the special lid on, jammed a candy cane down through the little hole off to the side, and handed it to me. "Look. I'm not saying you have to talk to him. I'm just saying if you need someone who can be objective, Gordon's your guy."

"All right. I appreciate it."

Heather gave me a warm smile and a quick wave with her fingers before spinning around to look at the red numbers on the wall. "Number sixty-eight!"

CHAPTER TWENTY-SIX

On-Time Couriers
Main Hub
Brooklyn, NY

Holding a cup of coffee from a local bodega, Detective Witherspoon strolled into an open delivery bay door, which was part of a large, industrial row of buildings. He scanned the doorway and peeked inside. Approximately twenty people, all of them younger except for two, scurried around like squirrels on a freeway. The two older men stood off to one side. One was holding a clipboard, and the other kept pointing at the hurried employees, who were all wearing the same type of shirt Kenneth Singh wore back at the 33rd precinct.

Witherspoon knew they needed answers, and soon, or they would have to cut Singh loose. They were on thin ice as it was, holding him for twenty-four hours. However, the district attorney agreed that the letter found in Singh's possession was sufficient evidence to hold him for twenty-four hours.

But only enough for twenty-four hours.

That was why Witherspoon was standing at the bay door at seven-thirty in the morning.

No rest for the evidentiary-challenged.

According to Singh's description, Witherspoon was guessing the man with the clipboard was Mr. Hahn, the manager/owner of On-Time Couriers. He entered the bay door and headed straight for him. "Excuse me? I'm looking for Mr. Eugene Hahn." He grabbed his coat lapel with his free hand and flashed his shield. "I'm Detective Witherspoon, Nassau County PD, and I just want to ask him some questions about some parcels that have been delivered by his company over the last several days."

The man with the clipboard motioned for the other man to get lost. "I'm Eugene Hahn. What can I do for you, Detective?"

"Is there somewhere we can go that's a little more private? And quiet?"

Mr. Hahn pointed to a paneled cubicle in the corner. "We can use my office."

"Perfect."

Mr. Hahn led Detective Witherspoon into a small office and circled around a small desk piled high on one side with shipping invoices. He offered Witherspoon the lone chair in front of the desk.

Witherspoon motioned toward the stack of papers. "Looks like business is booming."

"We can't complain. But my secretary went out on medical leave, so I have to do my job and hers for now." He patted the two-foot high mound. "This is hers. Two days' worth of invoices. I will be here all weekend processing them."

"The joys of running your own business."

"It comes with the territory." Mr. Hahn huffed. "Detective, as you can see, it's the Christmas season, and we are very busy, so how may I help you?"

Witherspoon set his coffee cup down on the desk and reached into his coat pocket, pulling out a sheet of paper, a photocopy of one of the letter's envelopes. He handed it to Mr. Hahn. "A woman has been receiving letters like this one over the last several days. She's received ten so far. All of them are addressed just like this one. All of them have been mailed from the post office in Jericho. And all of them have been delivered by the same person, an employee of yours. Kenneth Singh."

Mr. Hahn's eyes widened with a question. "It's funny you should mention him. He didn't show up to work this morning."

"That's because we are holding him for questioning."

"He's been arrested?"

"No. He's just being detained. That's why I'm here. According to Mr. Singh, these letters are arriving here from some other place and person. They then are assigned to him to deliver with specific instructions to deliver them each day to that post office in Jericho only. Mr. Singh says he delivers them at the end of the day because it's easier for him to do so."

"I can vouch for Kenneth. I remember him being assigned letters like this one. I'd have to check to see if he was assigned all ten of them."

"He claims he did deliver them all."

"Okay, so you already know that. Why are you asking me then, Detective?"

"Who has been giving these letters to your company for delivery? You must have a person who receives these items and processes them, correct?" Witherspoon tapped the stack of invoices.

"We do. But we have stores all over the city. Even a couple in New Jersey. We operate to some degree like UPS or Fed-Ex, just on a much smaller scale. People bring their parcels to our stores. We have people who then pick up those parcels and deliver them here. This warehouse is our hub. From here, the couriers deliver the packages."

"What about packages that get delivered outside the island? Or the state?"

"We don't accept any deliveries that are outside of our area. Our selling point is that we guarantee same day or next day delivery, depending on what the customer pays for, or we give them their money back. For anything outside our area, we send them to the nearest UPS or Fed-Ex store. That's how we distinguish ourselves from those guys."

Witherspoon picked up his coffee. "How many stores do you have?" He took a sip.

"Fourteen."

"You must have a tracking system, right? Once a package, or letter," Witherspoon said, pointing to the paper in Hahn's hand, "is processed in your store, doesn't it get a bar code or something? So you can track it?"

"Like I said before, we're like UPS and Fed-Ex, but on a smaller scale. We are in the process of purchasing just such a system. Hope to have it in service by the beginning of next year."

"So how do you track parcels?"

Mr. Hahn picked up his clipboard. "The old-fashioned way."

"You log everything, then?"

"We do."

"Can you show me the logs for Kenneth Singh? And would we be able to backtrack these letters to the person who originally dropped them off if we follow the paper trail?"

"Possibly. Come with me." Mr. Hahn stood and led Detective Witherspoon across the warehouse and into another room stuffed with filing cabinets. Each cabinet drawer affixed with a sticker demarking a length of time. Each span of time differing based on how much the file drawer could hold.

Mr. Hahn waved his arm at the storage system. "Now you see why I need a digital tracking system." He studied the postmark on the paper in his hand and searched for the right cabinet. "Since your letter would have been postmarked yesterday, it would've been delivered the next day, I'm assuming," he said, still looking. "That would mean it got dropped off to us either the day it would have been postmarked or the day before."

"Is there anything I can do to help?"

"Do you have the postmarks on the other letters in question?"

"I can call and get them."

"I'll tell you what. Let's do it this way." He pointed at a filing cabinet. "Here we go." He opened the drawer. "This drawer holds the logs for the correct day of the letter you have in your possession." He dragged a small table close, yanked out all the manila files, and set them on top of the table. "All I ask is that you keep these in order by the date at the top right."

"You got it."

"I'll search this next folder. It holds all the logs for the day before the postmark on your letter. What you're looking for is a log entry about a letter that has a destination of Jericho, New York."

Witherspoon drew in a deep breath. "Piece of cake."

"We'll see. But first, while you get started, I need to get the rest of my people out on their routes." Hahn held up his clipboard again. "I'll be back in a few minutes."

"No problem."

WITHERSPOON RIFFLED through folder after folder, page after page. Twenty minutes later, Mr. Hahn came back and dug into the cabinet next to the one Witherspoon was searching.

Shortly after arriving, Hahn pulled out a piece of paper and held it out. "Here you go. It appears the letter in question was delivered to our store in Queens."

"You got to be kidding me," Witherspoon said. "I've been looking in the wrong drawer?"

Hahn offered a shame-faced grin. "Sorry."

Witherspoon huffed and took the invoice. "Queens, huh? There's a post office in Queens. Why not mail it there?"

Mr. Hahn shrugged. "Why do people do anything?"

"True."

"There are handwritten instructions on that invoice to mail the letter only at the post office in Jericho. That means the person working at the store would have also affixed a note to the letter with the same instructions. That's how we get details and instructions to our couriers."

"But how do you affix them? Wouldn't a sticky note come off?"

"Yes. That's why we do not use those. We have shipping labels we write on that can be peeled off without tearing the envelope or package. Starting next year, this whole system will be digitized. No more handwritten notes on invoices and labels."

Witherspoon nodded.

"Do you have any other postmarks we need to check?"

Witherspoon pulled a list of dates from his breast pocket and handed it to Hahn.

Hahn exhaled noisily as he opened another drawer. "I suppose you will need copies of these too?"

"I will."

CHAPTER TWENTY-SEVEN

Manningham's Construction
West 43rd Street
Manhattan, NY

*D*etective Bowen parked her car down the block and traversed the sidewalk leading to the front doors of Manningham's Construction. Wanting to keep her occupation undetected, she entered the building with her blazer buttoned up, her badge covered.

The beginning measures of a Christmas song fell from the speakers embedded in the ceiling as she strolled through the doorway. The sound of a smooth saxophone belted out the notes to "I'll Be Home for Christmas."

Wearing a headset and speaking to someone on the phone, a receptionist, dressed in a red blouse, with images of snow and pine trees woven into the fabric, and a pair of black slacks, stepped out from behind her counter-like desk. She dipped a spoon into a cup of yogurt and ate between sentences. When the front door opened, she didn't turn to see who had walked in right away, and instead, picked up a magazine off a small table.

Detective Bowen allowed the door to close behind her and waited for the woman to acknowledge her. She unbuttoned her blazer and snatched her shield off her belt.

Finally, the receptionist turned. When she saw Bowen standing in the middle of the small lobby with her NYPD shield extended, she nearly dropped her breakfast. "Oh. Excuse me, Louise, but someone just walked in," she said into the headset. "Let me call you back." She reached up and pressed a button on the earpiece before setting her yogurt down on the desk. "I apologize, Officer. I didn't hear anyone come in. How may I help you?"

"I'm Detective Bowen with the NYPD. I need to see one of your employees. His first name is Roberto, and I don't have a last name yet."

"Oh, you're probably talking about Roberto Casillas. He's the only Roberto who works here as far as I know."

"Good. I'm going to need to speak to him."

"Sure. Just one moment." The woman dialed a short number. "Hey, Eddie, can you find Roberto and send him up to me, please? Thanks."

Bowen clipped her shield onto her belt. "Thank you."

"He's not in any trouble, is he?"

"No. I just have a few questions I need to ask."

"That's good. He's a good guy. Hard worker. Wants to be an engineer."

Bowen nodded and smiled, trying to be patient. "Is there a room we can use that's kind of private?"

"Sure. When he gets here, I'll take you down to the conference room."

Just then, Roberto strolled through the door to the left.

"Oh, well," the woman said, "speak of the devil. Right this way."

Bowen held out her hand and displayed her shield. "Roberto Casillas, I'm Detective Bowen, NYPD. I have some questions I need to ask you, and she's offered a conference room down the hall for us to use."

Roberto's eyes squinted slightly as he processed what was happening. "Am I in some kind of trouble?"

"No. Not at all."

The receptionist led them down a short hallway and opened a door, flipping on the light all in one motion. "Here you are. I don't think anyone's scheduled to use this right now."

"Perfect," Bowen said. "Thank you. This shouldn't take long."

The woman smiled and left.

Roberto walked inside but remained standing.

Bowen motioned to a chair on the other side of the conference table. "Have a seat." She closed the door.

Roberto moved to the other side of the room but remained standing. "I didn't do anything, Detective. I wouldn't do anything wrong. I'm getting set to start working on my Master's Degree in Engineering. I'd never do anything to mess that up."

Bowen held her hands up. "Whoa, now. No one's accused you of anything. But I do have some questions." She motioned again. "Please, sit down."

He finally complied with her request.

She did the same opposite Roberto and retrieved a notepad from the inside pocket of her blazer. "I don't want to take a lot of your time, so let's just get to it. First, do you know a woman by the name of Rachel Hamar?"

"Yes. She's my girlfriend's roommate. Why do you ask?"

"I understand you and your girlfriend, Joanie Harrington, played a prank on Rachel a few nights ago at a restaurant? Antonelli's?"

"Yes. It was a harmless one. Joanie wanted to introduce me to Rachel. I work a second job at Antonelli's, as a waiter, and I couldn't get off work that night. So, Joanie said, 'Why don't I bring Rachel to you, then? We can pretend to flirt with each other as a waiter and a customer. Have some fun with it.' That's pretty much how it went down."

"Pretty much?"

"Well, Rachel started to get uncomfortable with our flirting. She was going to leave, but Joanie finally told her the truth."

"How long have you and Joanie been seeing one another?"

"About three weeks or so. We both work here." Roberto pointed his thumb over his shoulder. "She's here, if you want to talk to her too."

Detective Bowen shook her head. "That won't be necessary right now." She glanced at her notes. "But while we're on the subject, what is her position here?"

"She's the lead foreman's secretary. Her office is in the back of the building."

Bowen jotted something down. "Is that where you work too?"

"Now it is. I used to go out on the construction crews. They stage out of a different location about twelve blocks away. I've helped build several buildings in Manhattan and Long Island over the last three years. But when I told them I wanted to join their engineering program, they moved me here to be closer to the engineering department. Kind of on-the-job training while I go to school."

"That's how you and Joanie Harrington met?"

"I saw her for the first time when I came to apply for the college loans. The lead supervisor helps head up that program. He's the liaison between the dreamers and the doers."

"Dreamers and doers?"

"That's what they call the engineers and the construction crews here."

"I see. And you decided you wanted to switch? Go from being a doer to a dreamer?"

"Yes, ma'am."

"And it so happened that Joanie Harrington worked in that department."

"I didn't know she did at the time. I'd never met her before the day I came here to apply."

Bowen flipped through her notebook. "You two just hit it off?"

Roberto shrugged a little and smiled. "I guess you could say that. We've been seeing each other ever since."

"But you didn't know her before that day?"

"No."

"Did you know Rachel Hamar before then?"

"No. I never met her until that night at the restaurant."

"Did Joanie ever talk about Rachel prior to your meeting at the restaurant?"

"A couple of times. She wanted me to know she had a roommate. She also said something about how Rachel had been a friend of hers for a long time, but that's about it."

Bowen wrote that information down in her notes. "What about since you met Rachel? Has Joanie said anything else about her?"

"Not much. But she did say she was concerned about her. When I asked why, she said something about how Rachel was going through a lot right now."

"Did she get specific?"

Roberto's eyebrows rose. "Oh, she did say something about some letters. From what I understood, Rachel was receiving letters from someone she didn't know. It was confusing to the both of them. Now that I think about it, Joanie did mention that she had encouraged Rachel to contact the police." Suddenly, his face displayed a look of enlightenment. "That's why you're here, isn't it?"

Bowen formed a big smile. "What can you tell me about those letters?"

"Nothing. I've never seen them. Joanie's never talked about them in detail."

"Have you ever been over to Joanie's apartment?"

"No. Joanie said she's embarrassed by it. I guess it's small and not furnished very well, according to her. I tell her not to worry about that, but she's a little hard-headed when it comes to those things, I'm finding out."

"But you do know where she lives?"

"Yes."

"And you started dating her about three weeks ago?"

"Yeah. Something like that."

Bowen flipped back several pages in her notepad. "Roberto, where do you live?"

"Secaucus, New Jersey. 45 Meadowlands Parkway. I have an apartment there. Pirate's Landing is the complex."

"How long have you lived there?"

"It's been three years this month."

"And where did you live before that?"

"The Bronx. Single parent home. My mom raised me after my dad left. I've vowed to help my mom after I get hired on here as an engineer."

"Does she still live in the Bronx?"

Roberto nodded.

"Have you ever heard of the Central Park Cameraman?"

Roberto's pleasant demeanor switched to confused. "You mean the guy the police were looking for? The one who was taking pictures of women and posting them to the Internet?"

"So, you have heard of him?"

"Who hasn't? It was all over social media and the news."

"That's true. Do you own a camera, Roberto?"

"Yes…my phone has one." Roberto's eyes widened like he had just remembered leaving his wallet at home. "Are you suggesting that I'm the Central Park Cameraman?"

"Are you?"

"Okay." Roberto sputtered some half-hearted guffaws. "I think this conversation is over." He stood.

Bowen knew she was drawing at straws, but she had to press on. "You've lived in the area long enough. You would know the area as a construction worker who travels between Secaucus, Manhattan, the Bronx, and Long Island. Also, living in Secaucus would afford you the opportunity to slip in and out of Central Park without living around it, possibly being spotted accidentally while just living your life.

"Then, there's the part about you dating Joanie Harrington, the roommate of Rachel Hamar. It started approximately three weeks ago, just in time to switch your MO from filming women in Central Park to harassing a woman with letters." Bowen continued to sit, but she had turned in her chair slightly and had pinned her eyes to Roberto's. "Do my conclusions sound that farfetched, Roberto?"

"You know what I think, Detective? I think you have nothing to go on, and I'm a convenient target. I'm male. I'm Hispanic. And I know the woman involved." Roberto pushed his chair under the table. "But you're wrong, Detective. And I will not allow you to frame me for something I didn't do." He took one step toward the door and then stopped. "And if you pursue me any further with this, I'm going to get a lawyer and sue your department for harassment. I've never done anything illegal in my life. Go ahead. Check it out, and you'll find that to be the truth." He took two more steps. "And I'm not about to start now. I have too much at stake with this job to play some stupid prank and jeopardize it all." Roberto opened the door and slammed it against the wall on his way out.

Bowen leaned back into her chair, tapping the end of her pen on the table.

That went well.

CHAPTER TWENTY-EIGHT

West 173rd Street
Washington Heights, NY

I was so glad to be able to leave work. The day had dragged. Each hour seemed like three. The end of the day had appeared to be running in the opposite direction. And the faster I ran to catch up, the "behinder" I got.

It also didn't help that we were smack-dab in the middle of the holidays.

During this festive season of the year, people who walk into banks have already lost their minds. I chalk it up to the stress. They want everything to go perfectly. They want everything, including their money, yesterday. They also want you to play Santa and give them everything they desire.

Even the bizarre requests.

Like the customer today who brought in her payment statement for a loan she received a couple of years ago. She explained how the money was used to help her daughter and son-in-law place a down payment on their first home.

Now, she wanted the loan rescinded. "There are two

reasons," she said, much like a politician trying to sway an election. "First, they no longer want the house. They're divorced. And second, I can't afford it anymore as the co-signer because I lost my job."

"I understand. Truly, I do," I told her, "but I'm just a teller." I pointed the customer in the direction of the loan department. "Mildred, in the loan department, can help you."

I smiled, knowing how this was going to turn out.

Good luck, ma'am. You're gonna need it.

I know Mildred listened, even lamented, with the customer, because she told me all about it. She patted that poor woman on the arm and offered an understanding nod. Then, politely, without any expression to expose her true beliefs, Mildred reminded the lady of her financial obligations, gave her a few pointers on selling the house to recuperate the money, and wondered who in the loan department approved "this dolt" for anything.

Mildred didn't really care. Her days were numbered. Retirement was the sweet light at the end of her tunnel. A Merry Christmas smile was plastered on her face, I'm sure. Yet, her actions, her body language, like Ebenezer Scrooge from *A Christmas Carol*, told the woman what she really thought about her plight, and Christmas, for that matter:

What's Christmas time to you but a time for paying bills without money; a time for finding yourself a year older, but not an hour richer; a time for balancing your books and having every item in 'em through a round dozen of months presented dead against you?

I know.

Mildred told me all about it and wrapped up the story with her own "Bah! Humbug!" concerning the woman's misfortune.

~

IRONICALLY, however, that's how I felt today.

A year older.

But not an hour richer.

My checkbook laughed at me as I punched out for the day. Like it has for years now. Reminding me that I wasn't much different from the woman wanting to give her loan back to the bank.

At least she got approved for a home loan.

The wind howled at me too. Snowflakes scurried about, announcing the early arrival of the winter storm everyone at work had twittered about all day long. The gusts sliced through my coat, attacking my ill-prepared frame. I leaned inside, snagging my things from the back seat as the frigid air found every exposed surface of skin.

Parked four blocks away, I slammed the door shut and trekked up the sidewalk, holding more dollar store bags than I cared to display. Yet, when I thought about it, wincing into the wind, no one was probably going to mug a person for dollar store trinkets. Now, if I was carrying bags from Macy's or Tiffany's, then I'd need a bodyguard. Especially in this neighborhood.

But if I was carrying bags from Macy's or Tiffany's, I wouldn't be walking up to this dump. Day after day. Month after month.

Entering the apartment building and fumbling for my mailbox key in the process, I finally set a handful of bags down on the dirty, tile floor. I hope there's nothing in here today, I thought as I inserted the key. An empty mailbox would be nice for a change. I twisted the key and opened the slot. Especially since Detective Bowen found the man yesterday with the letter in his hand. There shouldn't be anything but normal, everyday—

When I saw it, I heard a sound behind me. I took a step back, dropped the other bags on the floor, and spun around, expecting to see a menacing person standing in a doorway.

But there was no one else in the small mail room.

Just me.

One envelope rested on the bottom of the mailbox. Face down. Same size as the others.

I gazed into the mailbox, hesitated, and then slowly retrieved the parcel. I flipped it over, and on the front, in the same pen, the same handwriting, the same everything, was an envelope addressed to me. Here. At this address. Correct apartment number. Just like the previous ten letters.

I tore it open.

Another short paragraph was written by the hand of a child. I guessed ten years old? Maybe eleven or twelve? No older than that. But this time, another sheet of paper was enclosed. On it, a hand-drawn picture of what looked like a girl holding a small bear.

Today is my birthday! Daddy gave me a present, and it's the best present ever. It looks just like the one I saw the other day. He was standing on his back legs, grabbing an apple off an apple tree. It was the funniest thing I've ever seen. I drew a picture of him. His name is Buttons. Buttons the bear. I called him that because he has buttons down his back. I can open him up, and keep treasures in there.

I dropped the letter and drawing like they were burning my fingers. I felt dizzy and braced my arm against the wall before slowly sliding down into a troubled heap.

Why is this happening?

Buttons? Really?

I had a stuffed bear.

When I was six.

His name was Buttons.

And he was a Christmas present.

From my mother's church.

I trembled, thinking about the day I opened that gift. I slept with that bear. Took it everywhere I went until I lost it four years later. Momma thought it may have fallen out of the car at the local department store. We went back to get it, but we couldn't find it. No one at the store had seen it either.

Buttons was gone.

The buttercups I had inside the pouch from my latest trip to Grandma's house were gone too.

Then, I thought about the buttercups and Grammy. I could picture myself picking the flowers and gently stuffing them into Buttons so as not to crush them.

The memories.

The correlations between my life as a child and these letters were getting strange.

Outlandish, actually.

I clamored to my feet. My breathing escalated, and a cold sweat broke out across my face. I stuffed the letter, picture, and envelope into one of the bags then gathered all of them in a rush. Running up the stairs, I unlocked the apartment door and plowed inside.

"I thought you were never gonna get home," came a voice from inside the apartment.

I screamed and whirled around. Bags flew every direction as I tried to free my hands and protect myself.

I saw someone sitting on the couch, in the dim light of the end table lamp, staring at me. "Joanie! You scared me to death!" I wiped the hair out of my face and mouth and allowed my purse to slide off my shoulder and fall to the floor. "Since when do you get home this early? Don't you work the bar tonight?"

"I switched days with Rosanne."

"You could have told me." I pressed my hand against my chest. "My heart's about to burst."

Joanie stood up from her stoic position on the couch. A suit-case rested on the floor next to her. "I've got a bone to pick with you."

"What now?" I started picking up the grocery items strewn across the floor. "I told you, I haven't received that severance check yet. When I do, I'll—"

"I'm not talking about that."

I grabbed my purse strap and slung it over my shoulder. "So, what's bothering—"

"Why did you tell the police Roberto was involved?"

"What?"

"A female detective from the NYPD was at Manningham's this morning, questioning Roberto. She accused him of being the Central Park Cameraman."

"Wha—I—I have no idea what you're talking about."

"The detective told Roberto the time frame fit. He could've been the man who was taking pictures of women in Central Park and uploading them to the Internet. Then, about two weeks ago, he changed his M.O. and started sending those letters to you. Is that what you told the police?"

"You're not making any sense."

Joanie took a few steps closer to me. "Did you tell the police about Roberto? Did you accuse him of being involved in sending you those letters?"

I swatted an unruly strand of hair out of my face. "No."

"They didn't ask you about Roberto?"

"No. Not specifically. I mean, they asked me a bunch of questions. They wanted to know if I knew anyone who might want to play a practical joke on me. I told them about the joke you two played at the restaurant the night you introduced me to him. But I never told them I thought he had anything to do with the letters."

"Well, apparently, that detective does. She came to his work, Rach. Now Roberto's boss is investigating him per company policy. They said this would temporarily suspend his participation in their engineering program. If they find anything, they could remove him from the program permanently, even fire him. So, in the meantime, he's back on the construction sites instead of being in the main building."

"I...I'll...call his boss. I'll tell him it's just a misunderstanding."

"No." She pointed her finger at me. "You've done enough damage. You need to get that detective to call and clear things up."

I set the bags on the couch. "Okay. I will. As a matter of fact, I need to call her anyway. I got another letter today."

"I don't care about your stupid letters anymore. All I've done, for practically my entire life, is be a friend to you. A friend for you. A good friend. A friend who's been there through...everything! And this is how you treat me? You go behind my back and accuse my boyfriend of being some serial psycho?"

"I told you, I didn't accuse him of anything. I hardly know him, and neither do you, for that matter."

Joanie's eyes burned. "Roberto is the best thing that's ever happened to me, and you're just jealous!"

"Jealous? Why would I be jealous? I'm happy for you, Jay-Jay."

"Don't call me that. Only my father can call me that."

"All right, all right. But I'm not jealous. I am happy for you. If he's half the man you've painted him to be, then I'm really happy for you."

"Roberto's twice the man. And he's going to make a great engineer. But I may not get to see that happen now."

"I told you, I'll call Detective Bowen. I'll get her to set the record straight. Then, you and Roberto can patch things up."

Her jaw protruded in anger as I spoke, and her fists shook. She huffed harder with each sentence I spoke, attempting to calm herself until it was no longer possible. "He told me he didn't want to see me anymore!"

"Wha—Who? Roberto?"

She pointed her finger in my face again. "You better fix this." Her words slurred as tears began to stream down her cheeks. "Or else."

She turned, grabbed her suitcase, and headed for the door.

"Where are you going?"

"I can't stay here anymore."

"What? You can't just leave." I stepped in front of the door. "We need to talk."

"I can't right now."

"Please, Joanie, don't leave. We'll get this worked out."

She pushed past me and opened the door.

"Joanie, please." I reached out and grabbed her arm.

She jerked away. "Don't touch me." Then, like I'd never witnessed before, she slammed the door shut behind her.

CHAPTER TWENTY-NINE

West 173rd Street
Washington Heights, NY

The echo of the slammed door reverberated off the walls and slowly dissipated into an eerie silence. The squeak of the wheels on Joanie's suitcase rolled down the hallway until it was replaced by the *thunk-thunk-thunk* of it hitting the stairs on the way down.

Soon, that sound was gone too.

All I heard now was the hum of the refrigerator.

And my erratic breathing.

It was happening all over again. My life crumbling before my eyes. Everything that could go wrong doing so. And now, even the one constant, my best friend, was no longer here to help me through it.

I was alone.

Totally and utterly alone.

Was she really going to move out? Over a misunderstanding? We've had worse dustups than this...

Then, it hit me.

This wasn't about me.

It was about Roberto.

I slowly sat on the edge of the couch.

She must really care for him.

I hugged myself.

What have I done?

I slowly rocked back and forth.

There had never been a serious relationship for either of us since Billy died.

And if she felt about Roberto the way I did about Billy…

I'd be furious too.

But this time, I was the problem.

I'm a walking plague.

One that won't die but kills everything it touches.

The rocking back and forth increased.

Why is it always me?

Why can't anything ever work out?

Billy…

I miss you so much right now…

And that's when I fell apart and cried.

Ninety minutes later, the phone rang. I contemplated allowing it to go to voice mail at first, but I thought it might be Joanie.

"Hello?"

"Rachel? This is Detective Bowen. I've got some good news."

She was the last person I wanted to talk to right now. "Yeah. What is it?"

"Well, I thought you'd be a little more excited than that, for starters."

What she said didn't really register. All I could think about was being alone. "Did you accuse my friend's boyfriend of being the Central Park Cameraman?"

"What? No, uh…not exactly."

"What's that supposed to mean? Sounds like you did to me."

"I was fishing, Rachel. That's what we call it. If he was involved in any way, I was pressing him to see if he'd break, make a mistake, say something that would point me in the right direction."

"Unbelievable."

"That's my job, Miss Hamar. Find leads. Follow leads. Solve cases."

"But what happens when people get falsely accused?"

"Falsely accu—What are you talking about?"

"Roberto? Joanie's boyfriend? After your little Q & A session this morning, his boss wanted to know why you were there. When he heard you were accusing Roberto of being the Central Park Cameraman, he started his own investigation."

"But I didn't accuse him. I never even said anything about charging him or bringing him in for questions. All I did was piece some details together that kind of made him a person of interest. That's all. Like I said, I was fishing."

"Well, apparently, his boss doesn't agree with your assessment."

Detective Bowen sighed into the phone. "Roberto must have talked about it with your roommate."

"He did. And as best as I can tell, he broke up with her because of it."

"Well…that's just crazy."

"Crazy?!" I switched the phone to my other ear and jumped up from the couch. "Are you aware Roberto's boss temporarily removed him from their engineering program because of the accusations you made? I guess Manningham's Construction doesn't want to be on the front page of the *New York Times* as the company who gave the Central Park Cameraman a free ride in their engineering program while he continued to terrorize women in The Big Apple."

"That's just an overreaction on their part. I'll clear that up with his supervisors. I'll go there first thing in the morning. I promise."

"And while you're at it, maybe you can find me a roommate? Joanie moved out. And I can't afford this place on my own."

"She moved out?" Another heavy exhalation filled the line. "Look, I'll talk to her too. Try to patch things up between the two of you."

"You know, Detective, I'm not sure I want to pursue this case anymore. It's not only driving me crazy, but it's starting to affect other people who aren't even involved."

"I fully understand, but like I said a few minutes ago, I have some good news that may change your mind."

I picked up a grocery bag and carried it into the kitchen. "Fine. What is it?"

"Detective Witherspoon was following up the lead on Mr. Singh's work. He went to On-Time Couriers and spoke to Mr. Singh's supervisor. Together, they were able to track down where the ten letters originated. Three of the letters were dropped off at the On-Time Couriers store in Queens. Two were delivered to their store in Brooklyn. One was taken to the store in Hoboken, New Jersey. The rest were taken to the store in Manhattan.

"All of them were dropped off with the exact same instructions. And I quote, 'This letter must be delivered to the U.S. Post Office in Jericho, New York, before six o'clock this evening.' And the person dropping it off always paid in cash."

I retrieved two more bags. "And how does that help us?"

"Now, Detective Witherspoon is going to those stores to see if the people behind the counter can identify the person who dropped off those letters."

"Well, I have another one you can track down now."

"Another one? You received another letter? When?"

"Today. In the mailbox like all the others."

"That's odd."

"Right?" I growled in frustration as I dropped the empty plastic bag on the ground. "And I thought you caught the guy red-handed yesterday?"

"We did. However, we have reason to believe now that he *is* just a courier and was simply being used for his services as a courier."

I jammed the bag into the garbage. "So you mean there may be more people involved?"

"It would appear so. We intercepted the letter he was going to mail. The one that you should have received today, and since we nabbed it a day early, you shouldn't have received anything today."

I walked over to the front window and looked at every pane of glass across the street, trying to see if there was anyone looking back at me. "Why did I get one in the mail today when that letter was supposedly never mailed?"

"Excellent question. It could be that the letters are coming to you a day late, meaning it's tomorrow when you'll not get one. We thought the post office was delivering them the next business day. Maybe it's actually two days for some of them."

"That's not true. They've all been postmarked the day before." I walked over and picked up the bag containing the letter, double-checking the latest parcel. "This one is postmarked yesterday."

"What does the letter itself say?"

I read it to her and described the picture.

"Does this bear have any significance to you? Like the buttercup did?"

Tears welled up. I inhaled and choked back sobs bubbling up from inside. "Yes. I had one just like that when I was six. I named mine Buttons too."

"Who would know about this?"

"My mother. The bear was a gift from her church."

"And you said she also knew about the flowers?"

"No, I said my grandma could have told her, but I have no way of knowing for sure."

"You could ask her."

I knew she was going to say that. "Yes. I could."

"But you don't want to?"

I unpacked the last bag. "Let's just say that when I visit her, it's never completely enjoyable."

"Would you rather I talk to her?"

"Are you kidding?"

"Not at all. And I would be very careful. I promise I won't accuse your mother of being anything."

Right now, Momma was the last person I wanted to see. There would be lectures. About how all this ties to some spiritual truth or passage in the Bible. I'm in no condition to deal with that right now.

It just might send me to the rooftop to jump.

I sniffed and wiped my eyes. "Do whatever you need to do. But please, don't upset her. She's been through a lot as well. We both have."

"You have my word."

Saturday

December 20, 2014

CHAPTER THIRTY

Sun Ridge National Bank
Manhattan, NY

 fell asleep on the couch and woke up at three in the morning. From that moment, my mind was flooded with the memories of the night before. A slight wave of nausea swept through my torso as I recalled more and more of the conversation.

I checked Joanie's room to see if maybe, just maybe, it was all merely a horrendous dream.

Her room was empty.

I crawled into bed and stared at the ceiling until six. A million images raced through my tired mind. Each one lowering me a little more into my well of depression.

Then the alarm clock went off, and I started getting ready for work.

Story of my life. Work. Home. Rinse. Repeat.

And on occasion, ruin people's lives.

That's what a plague does.

I finished getting ready, grabbed my keys and my purse, and headed for the door.

I need coffee. Strong, strong coffee.

With a double shot of citalopram.

I EXITED The Columbian Coffee Shop with a hot, steaming cup of hazelnut coffee and headed down the street for work. Sipping it, I realized what Gordon had told me was true. This was the second time someone else other than Heather had made my coffee, and there was *no* comparison. I wasn't sure how anybody could so easily mess up something as simple as a cup of coffee, but if you're a coffee drinker, you know exactly what I'm talking about. There really does seem to be an art to it after all. Heather got it. The others? Not so much.

She needs to be the manager and train the others so they can—

"Rachel!"

I turned to see Gordon waving at me, motioning me toward him.

I met him halfway, but I couldn't muster a smile. "We're gonna have to stop meeting like this, Gordon."

He glanced at his watch. "You're early this morning, aren't you?"

"Couldn't sleep. So, I decided to get up and get ready. Come on in to work."

He peered inside the coffee shop. "Can you hold on a few minutes? Let me grab my coffee?"

"Sure."

"Please tell me Heather's working this morning?"

I shook my head.

Gordon hesitated. "Wonderful. I'll just be disappointed if I buy anything."

I took another sip of mine and then lifted it slightly as if I was toasting a wedding party. "I understand." I smacked my lips and winced a little. "Bitter."

"Like they didn't add enough of whatever it is they add to it, right?"

"Exactly."

He peered inside the coffee shop one more time. "I'm going to break my vow and take a chance. Will you come inside with me?"

I vacillated.

"For moral support? You could add some sugar or cream or whatever you think it needs to yours while you wait…"

I chuckled slightly. "Okay."

"So, how's everything with you?" Gordon said as we exited the shop.

The patented conversation starter everyone uses when they have no idea how to start a conversation.

The shotgun blast of icebreakers.

"How's everything with you?" There has got to be something to talk about if "everything" is on the table, right?

I smiled, laughing inside at Gordon's attempt at small talk as we strolled up the sidewalk toward the bank. "Are you sure you want to ask that question?"

"Now, there's an answer I've never heard before. Or, actually, a question posing as an answer."

"Well, it's the truth. I'm not sure you want to go down that road today. Might want to ask my opinion of the weather instead or what I think about the Giants' chances of making the Super Bowl."

Gordon took a swig of his coffee and frowned at the taste. "You didn't strike me as an NFL kind of girl."

I batted my eyes. "What's the NFL?"

He laughed and tapped his chest. "I'm a Jets fan, so…"

"My condolences."

"Ouch." His eyes widened and eyebrows twisted in feigned misery. "You sure know how to hurt a guy when his team's down."

"Sorry. I really don't keep up on sports."

Gordon smiled. "It's not the job, is it?"

"No." I looked down at the sidewalk. "The job's fine. It's just…"

"Just what? The money? Not making enough? I could look into that if you need me to."

I shot a cautious glance at him. "That's always on the table, if you're offering, but that's not what's bothering me. Well, let me rephrase that." I straightened my gait, trying not to slump at the shoulders. "Money might become an issue if things don't get patched up between me and my roommate."

"Uh-oh."

"There's been some things happening lately. It started before I got the job. No one seems to understand it. No one seems to be able to explain it. Now, I have the police involved, hoping they could figure it out, and that's messed things up even more."

"The police?" Gordon's tone became managerial.

"Don't worry, Gordon. It's not like that. I didn't rob a bank or anything."

"But to involve the police must make it pretty serious, right?"

"Personally, I think they're trying to make something out of nothing important."

"How so?"

I studied Gordon's face for several steps before we reached an intersection. "Are you sure you want to discuss all this? It seems that everyone who comes in contact with me and my story becomes infected with bad luck or bad karma or something…ungood.”

The light flashed, and the crowd began crossing the street.

“Ungood, huh? I’ll take my chances,” he said, leaning over to me and saying it in a more hushed tone because of the crowd. “Besides, I’m pretty good at piecing puzzles together. Maybe I could help.”

“You may wish to refrain until you hear the whole story.”

We reached the bank building, and Gordon punched in the security code on the employee entrance. “Why don’t we go up to my office? You can fill me in on the details there.” Gordon opened the door and waved me through.

“But what about my post?”

“You’re here early, right? And if we’re not done by the start of your shift, I’ll get Mildred to cover for you.”

“I thought she was off today?”

“She was supposed to be, but she wanted Black Friday off, so I compromised with her. She had to work last Saturday and this one in return.”

“She won’t be happy.”

“And I don’t really care. She’s leaving in a little over a week.”

GORDON and I sat in his office. I filled him in on the entire affair, including the story about the letter I received yesterday and the blow up between Joanie and me.

Gordon leaned back in his chair and slowly shook his head. “Well, I said I was good at putting puzzles together, but this one seems like a five thousand piece one to me. Never done one of those before.”

“I told you.” I set my empty coffee cup on the edge of his desk. “Better to hear the story before committing to anything.”

"Oh, I didn't mean I wouldn't try to help."

"There's really not much you can do. The police are still investigating it. Detective Bowen told me last night that they had some new leads on who might be sending the letters."

"So, it looks like this Mr. Singh isn't their man."

"How could he be? He was still being held for questioning when I received the latest letter."

"He could be working with someone. Sounds to me like this is too much for just one person to accomplish anyway, if they want to avoid detection. And the fact that Mr. Singh was caught attempting to mail a letter while another one was obviously mailed without his assistance—all during a time when he was in custody—tells me there are definitely others involved."

"But couldn't just one man be using all these couriers as decoys while at the same time using them to muddy the water? It definitely would make it harder to figure out who's giving the couriers the letters."

Gordon intertwined his fingers and pressed his thumbs together. "I suppose. However, that would then beg the question: Who would go to all this trouble to send those letters to you? And how do they know about your childhood?"

Exactly. That was the most troubling part.

The childhood memories.

Being used against me.

"Those are the questions keeping me up at night. At least, when Joanie was there, I felt a little safer. Like I had someone to talk to about them. Now that she's left, I feel more exposed. Alone."

Gordon leaned forward and rested his elbows on the desk. "Is Joanie coming back to the apartment?"

"I don't know."

He gazed at me for a long moment before dropping his eyes to the papers on his desk. "I have an apartment in SoHo. It's not much. One bedroom. One bath. It's been sitting empty for about twenty days now. If you needed a place to stay until you could build up some cash to put toward something, we might be able to come up with some kind of arrangement."

"Are you offering me a place to live?"

His eyes twinkled a little. "I guess I am."

I turned my head and lifted my eyebrows. "And what kind of arrangement were you proposing?"

Gordon's face drained. "Oh, no, no, no. I...I was not..." He dropped his head and pressed his fingers into his forehead. "Oh, boy. Please don't mistake this as anything but a friend helping a friend. Please. I was just thinking that instead of it sitting empty, I might as well allow someone to use it. That's all." He lifted his eyes to meet mine. "And since you are in danger of losing your apartment, I thought you could...I mean, it's sitting empty. Might as well be put to good use."

His sudden, verbose, innocent-yet-troubled defense made me chuckle inside. "Even though I find your offer very enticing and generous, especially if Joanie does officially move out, we hardly know each other."

"Very true. And do not think that your job is in any way tied to this." He sighed forcefully. "I don't want you to think for one second that I was...that I meant we should..." He dropped his head into his hand again. "The last thing I need is a sexual harassment lawsuit...Gordon, you idiot. Nimble on your feet as always."

I laughed and leaned forward in my chair. "Gordon, relax. You're safe. I was just making sure. No offense, but the last thing I need right now is a relationship. Wait...that didn't come out right. What I meant to say was—"

He held up his hands. "Let's stop. Obviously, this conversation has taken a very unfortunate and uncomfortable detour."

Yeah. Timing is everything.

You can pull your foot out of your mouth, too, Rach.

And you wonder why you're still single?

I sighed. "Agreed. But don't worry. I know you just wanted to help."

Gordon sat up straighter. "I fully understand your aversion to relationships. Ever since my wife passed away, I've been a bumbling buffoon when it comes to talking to women. Unless it's strictly business. So, be assured, I only wanted to help. People have helped me in the past when I was down on my luck, and I've always vowed to 'pay it forward,' if you will," he said, forming quotations with his fingers.

"You vowed, huh? Do you hold this vow as strongly as your vow to not get coffee when Heather's not working?"

Gordon's eyes widened in a mildly shocked manner. "Wow. I guess I should stop making vows, huh?"

"No. Vows suit you. You seem to be a committed person. To the things that really matter, I mean."

He slowly nodded his head more and more. "That's true. I was married for a long time. And if my wife were still alive, I'd be more in love with her today than ever."

"I'm sorry about that, by the way. I, too, know how it feels to lose someone you love."

"That's right. Your boyfriend, if I recall? When you were a teenager?"

I pursed my lips and nodded.

He inhaled a deep breath and held it in as he started to speak. "Listen, although I'd love to help you with your apartment dilemma, I'm thinking now it may be a good idea to take that apartment offer off the table. I don't want things to get weird between us."

"If you don't mind me asking, how much does a one bedroom, one bath apartment in SoHo go for these days?"

"Depends on the location. Mine is $2,595 a month. But they can go up into the four-thousand-dollar range and higher."

"Yeah. That's definitely more than we pay now. And it would be a hefty gift for someone you hardly know. An employee, no less. And no tellin' how long I'd need to stay there to gather up that cash you were talking about."

He stood. "I'll keep my ears open. If I hear of anything, I'll let you know."

Brilliant, Rachel. You just punched the gift horse in the mouth.

All because of an awkward moment.

I stood with a sigh. "I'd appreciate that. Thank you."

CHAPTER THIRTY-ONE

Long Island Psychiatric Center
Deer Park, NY

Detective Nicole Bowen walked into the Long Island Psychiatric Center with her beige, layered trench coat cinched up around the waist by the accompanying belt. She peeled off her gloves and stuffed them in her pockets as she crossed the lobby toward the receptionist's counter, admiring the towering Christmas tree along the way. She'd never been to the LIPC before, and she wasn't sure how they'd react to a law enforcement officer strutting through the door.

She untied the belt of her coat, unclipped her shield from her waistband, and held it up discreetly. Just high enough to clear the top of the counter. "Excuse me, my name is Detective Nicole Bowen. I'm with the NYPD. I need to speak with one of your patients, Dorothy Hamar?"

The part-time receptionist examined the badge and then looked the detective over. "You know, I could probably get one of those off eBay. Don't make me a detective. You should be carrying a picture ID or something, like the Feds do."

"You're not serious, right?"

"As a heart attack. But don't worry, Detective. I'm on it." The receptionist picked up the phone and dialed a four-digit number. She plopped into her seat and pointed to the phone. "It's ringing."

Detective Bowen reattached her shield to her waist, jammed her hands into her coat pockets, and looked away, trying not to speak her mind.

"Yes, Dr. Hausberger, I have an NYPD detective here to see one of our patients." She examined Bowen again. "She's got a badge, if that's what you're askin'." She continued to stare at the detective. "Dorothy Hamar…Hold on, let me ask." She produced a fake smile and covered the receiver. "Can you state your business? Why do you need to see Ms. Hamar?"

"It concerns her daughter, Rachel."

The receptionist uncovered the receiver. "Got somethin' to do with her daughter, she said…I don't know. Here, why don't you talk to her?" She held out the phone. "He wants to talk to you."

Bowen paused for a brief moment and then grabbed the phone. "Hello?"

"Yes, I'm Dr. Gustave Hausberger. I am the senior research fellow here at LIPC. And you are?"

"Detective Nicole Bowen. NYPD. I'm here to speak to Dorothy Hamar. It concerns an investigation involving her daughter, and I thought she may be able to answer some questions for me."

"This has nothing to do with a report the police took from Dorothy a few weeks ago?"

"Sorry? What report?"

"Uh, if you don't know what I'm talking about, then it probably doesn't concern us at this time. If you will wait there, I will be right down to escort you to her room."

"Is that necessary?"

"It is. Dorothy was just moved to our second-most

restricted area a few weeks ago. Visitors who are not immediate family members or on the contact list must be escorted at all times, including into the patient's room. It's hospital policy."

"I see. All right."

~

A BURLY MAN in his sixties, wearing a blue, pinstriped dress shirt with a white collar, a red tie, and khaki trousers, lumbered down the stairs to the right. A white lab coat covered most of his robust frame. Three pens and a mechanical pencil protruded from a vinyl pouch clipped to the chest pocket of his lab coat. A bespectacled man, he exuded all the tenets of nerdiness Detective Bowen expected to see.

He approached with his right hand extended. "Welcome to LIPC, Detective. I am Dr. Hausberger. Have you signed in?"

"I have."

"And did you receive a visitor's pass?"

"I did." Bowen plucked it out of her coat pocket and held it up.

"If you would, peel off the back and display that on your person." He patted his chest on the left side. "That way, you won't get accosted a hundred times on our trek to the ninth floor."

Bowen decided not to argue and did as instructed. She held out the peeled paper and looked around for a garbage can.

"Just hand it to our receptionist. She can throw that away for you."

Detective Bowen offered a fake grin of her own and held it out, enjoying the dramatic turn of irony. "You can handle that, right?"

The receptionist gently grasped it and crumbled it up as she glared at the detective.

Dr. Hausberger pointed toward the elevators. "Right this way, Detective."

"Ninth floor, huh?"

"Yes, our two most restrictive areas are housed on the ninth floor. Makes escaping from this facility harder than if they were housed on another, lower floor."

"Makes sense."

The elevator door opened, and they stepped to the side as two other visitors exited.

"Oh, by the way," Detective Bowen said, "is there a reason why your receptionist has a burr up her butt?"

"Who? Chandra?" He waved his hand, stepped inside, and pressed the number nine. "I think she's just mad at the world. Always been that way. Then she wonders why she never gets promoted, never gets more hours, never gets a raise."

The elevator door closed, and the number indicating the floor increased slowly.

"Hasn't anyone sat her down and talked to her about her attitude?"

Dr. Hausberger shot out a disgruntled snort. "More times than I care to remember. Always has an excuse for her poor behavior and blames us for her inability to better herself." He started chuckling. "She once told my predecessor that the reason why she was rude to people was because she had ADHD. Can you believe that? Telling a world-renown psychologist you have ADHD, trying to use it as an excuse for your poor job performance?"

"What did he do?"

"Gave her a prescription for Ritalin and told her to get back to work. When she started griping about that, he told her, 'This isn't a public school. It's the real world. So, get over yourself, or you'll be reprimanded if I get one more customer complaint.'"

"Did he?"

"No. He left to take a position in Sweden. I got the honor of inheriting the problem. And yes, she's been reprimanded twice since then." The door opened, and they stepped out of the elevator. The doctor pointed to his right. "If you would like, you could file another complaint. That would be her third and give me the necessary ammunition to dismiss her."

"I have to admit, I was ready to arrest her if she refused to call you. Charge her with impeding an investigation. Luckily for her, she picked up the phone."

"Yeah. Lucky for her. Not so much for us." The doctor offered a pained smile and stepped up to the nurse's station. "We are here to see Ms. Hamar. Is she awake?"

"Yes, sir. She just returned from her fresh air break."

"Great." The doctor faced Bowen. "This way."

They passed several rooms. Most were quiet, except for a couple, and those troubled Detective Bowen.

Cries for help rang out from one room. "Please, help me. They don't want to know the truth. They're drugging me. Keeping me here against my will. Please! Help me." The plea repeated over and over.

From another room, a heavy-laden sob emanated from the open hatch in the doorway. An orderly set what looked like a breakfast tray on the ledge and was trying to coax the patient inside to come retrieve the food. But only weeping met the tray. The orderly slammed the latch shut and uttered an expletive as he whipped around on his heels.

Seeing his supervisor approach, he straightened his gait and swallowed. "Oh, good morning, Dr. Hausberger."

"Having trouble with Maya again, are we, Bobby?"

The orderly relaxed a little. "Yes, sir. She's not eating again. I was just going to get Ralph to come help me in case she got physical."

The doctor nodded like he understood. "Just make sure, Bobby, you only walk in that room with compassion. Leave your frustration outside the door."

Bobby huffed a lament. "Yes, sir. We will."

"Very good. Carry on. And make sure the lead nurse is with you."

Detective Bowen felt a shiver streak across her torso and extremities as they both continued toward Dorothy's room. "It takes a special person to work in a place like this, doesn't it?"

"Funny you should say that. I was just thinking the same thing about your line of work a few minutes ago. All the violence you see on a daily basis must taint you."

"I'd be lying if I said it doesn't affect you at all. But when you think about it, what line of work doesn't? The higher the stress level, the more it does. Don't you think?"

The doctor stopped in front of a room to their left and peeked through the window. He inserted a key into the door's lock. "Very true," he said. "I guess we all have a gift or two to offer humanity. The trick is finding it soon enough to make it of some use before we simply get tired of dealing with it all."

Bowen nodded, and the doctor opened the door.

"Dorothy, it's Dr. Hausberger. I have a visitor to see you. May we come in?"

"Sure," came a voice from inside the room.

The doctor opened the door wider and stepped aside so Detective Bowen could enter too.

"Dorothy, this lady is—"

"She's a detective." Dorothy's eyes narrowed, but her gaze was still fixed on the opposite wall. "NYPD. Wants to see me about Rachel, I think."

Bowen turned to Dr. Hausberger with a befuddled look. "Did you tell her I was coming?" she said in a whisper.

"Detective, I didn't even know you were coming to see Dorothy until I got the receptionist's call. What we have here is a bit of clairvoyance. Dorothy has several unique abilities. She can recall things that have happened, and often, they have nothing to do with her life, but instead deal with other people's lives. In addition to that, she understands things as they are happening, sometimes on a very deep level. Her insights are extremely intriguing…and often profound. And of course, like she just demonstrated, she knows things before they happen." He displayed a half-hearted shrug. "We can't explain it."

"That's because you choose not to believe, Dr. Hausberger," Dorothy said.

"And, of course," the doctor said with an exhale, "there's that too."

Bowen eyed the doctor, then Dorothy, then back to him. "I'm sorry, but there seems to be some kind of history here I'm not up to speed on."

"You sure said a mouthful," Dorothy said under her breath.

"Pardon me?"

Dorothy turned to face her visitors. "You said there was a history. You have no idea."

Bowen lifted her hands in confusion. "Is there something I need to know before we proceed?"

"Dorothy has many…special gifts," Dr. Hausberger said, easing his hands into his pockets. "For example, she was able to uncover an affair between a doctor and a nurse who were both on staff here. They worked different floors and never had any contact with Dorothy. We are still baffled as to how she knew all the details. Actually, that's why I thought you were here. To open up some new wounds for the hospital, as it were."

Bowen's puzzled look didn't mellow.

"You see, Detective, it was Dorothy who blew the whistle on the good doctor and nurse. It was a sad day here at LIPC. They were both good people. Good assets for LIPC. Hated to lose them."

Dorothy scratched her head. "That's what sin will do."

"What do you mean?" Bowen said.

"Both of them were married. They shouldn't have been doing what they were doing, and they knew it. Yet they went to great lengths to cover their tracks anyway. But know that your sins will find you out and be shouted from the rooftops. And it isn't just the fact that they were wrong in what they did. Their sin has affected a great many people as a result. Isn't that right, Dr. Hausberger?"

"I would have to agree, Dorothy."

"And how did you find out about it?" Bowen said.

"He told me."

Bowen pointed at Dr. Hausberger. "Who? Him?"

The doctor closed his eyes and shook his head.

"No. God did," Dorothy said.

Bowen stopped. She suddenly understood everything Dr. Hausberger was trying to say without saying it. She also understood what Rachel had told her. How conversations could be uncomfortable with your mother, in a psychiatric ward, when all she does is spout remarks like that. "God told you they were having an affair?"

"Yes, dear. Just like He told me you were coming today. Just like I know Rachel's in danger. Just like I know why your husband left you. Just like—"

"Whoa, whoa. Wait a minute. How do you know about me?"

Dorothy peered into the detective's eyes. "Dear one, He knows all about you. All about your divorce. How it happened. Why it happened. How it's saddened you. Soured you toward men and relationships. A feeling you are passing along to your daughter, I might add."

Bowen stood stone-faced. A disturbing air crept into the room, and it immediately felt colder. "I…I don't think that's any of your business, Ms. Hamar."

Dorothy offered a sheepish smile. "I agree, Detective. I don't know you. You don't know me. But He wants you to know He still cares about you and your daughter, despite everything that's happened."

"Uh, we need to change the subject." Bowen shifted her

weight. "You said Rachel's in danger. Were you talking about your daughter?"

Dorothy's eyes returned to the wall as she nodded.

"How is she in danger? From what?"

"It's not from what. It's from whom?"

"Someone's trying to hurt her?"

"Yes."

"Who?"

"Satan."

Bowen expelled a tired sigh. "Listen, Dorothy, I don't have a lot of time to spend fooling around with religious issues that have no bearing on my case. I just need you to answer some questions for me. Then, I'll leave you in peace."

"You want to know about the letters, correct?"

"How did you—No, who told you…wait a minute. Did Rachel tell you about them?"

"Nope."

Bowen rolled her eyes. "Did God tell you about the letters?"

Dorothy shrugged. "Maybe."

"Dorothy, I need you to tell me the truth."

Dorothy smiled and faced the detective again. "Why? When I give it to you, you don't believe it."

"But how do we know it's the truth?"

"You have eyes to see, Detective, but yet you are blind. Ears to hear, yet, you are deaf. I'm practically telling you everything about your life, everything about the lives of other people, and you stand here in disbelief, thinking I'm the crazy one." Dorothy lifted her hands and turned them upward. "Just look at where they have me now, Detective. On the ninth floor." Dorothy repositioned herself on her bed to get a better look at Bowen. Her eyes softer now. "Do you know how this hospital works, Detective Bowen?"

"Afraid not."

"It's very simple, actually. The crazier you are, the higher you go. There's only nine floors in this hospital, Detective. So, what does that tell you about what they think of me?"

"I'm not a psychiatrist, Ms. Hamar, so I can't comment on—"

"I'm not asking you to diagnose me. All I'm asking is for you to understand. My crime, Detective Bowen, is being a believer. Loving my God with all my heart, mind, soul, and strength. Talking to Him in what many describe as 'troubling episodes of delusion.' At least that's what Dr. Hausberger and his colleagues write on my evaluations.

"Even fellow believers, who visit me, doing charity work, think I'm in need of an exorcism. They think I'm nuts because I can see my Savior. I talk to Him. Spend time communing with Him, and for that, I was diagnosed as schizophrenic years and years ago.

"Since then, God's blessed me with His presence. In my times of trouble, in my times of need, when all others had forsaken me, including my husband, God was there. My Lord and Savior comforted me." Dorothy's eyes shifted to Dr. Hausberger. "And after all that God has done for me, and continues to do, I get sent up the river by man's inability to truly see the world around him."

"Up the river?"

"Yes." Dorothy looked at Detective Bowen again. "Isn't that what inmates call prison?"

"But this isn't a prison."

"Isn't it, Detective? Can I leave when I wish? Can I go home?"

Bowen scratched the back of her head. "Well, apparently, the doctors feel going home would place you or your loved ones at great risk. Is that correct, Dr. Hausberger? You're the expert, and I'm getting a little out of my area of expertise here."

"Well, it is true that—"

"Detective," Dorothy interrupted, "my husband thought I

was nuts. So, he took me to a doctor and told the man I was talking to myself. I told Elmore I was talking to Jesus, which I was. But they didn't believe me. So, the doctor gave me a prescription.

"My husband got it filled and gave it to me. He told me to take it. I refused. As a result, we got into an argument. Elmore told me I'd better take it or else. I refused still. Why? Because there wasn't anything wrong with me.

"So, my husband proceeded to beat me and forced me to take those pills for the first time. I realized at that point how far apart we had grown."

"Did you report your husband to the police?"

"No."

"Why not?"

Dorothy blurted out a reluctant sigh. "Because God told me not to."

"God told you not to…God wanted you to get beaten?"

"Heavens, no. Instead, He told me to take the medication. That it wasn't that big of a deal. He'd see me through. So, I did."

"Did that solve your problems with your husband?"

Dorothy surveyed her little room. "What do you think?"

"Your husband still thought you had issues after that?"

"Yes."

"If I may," Dr. Hausberger said, "since those early days of Dorothy's diagnosis and treatment, her psychosis has expanded. She now exhibits multiple hallucinatory episodes and denies to this day, vehemently, I might add, that she has a problem."

Bowen scratched her head again. "Dr. Hausberger, as you know, I'm a detective for the NYPD. I've been a road patrol officer. I've worked undercover. I've worked on the vice squad. And I've been a detective now for almost four years. I've won commendations and received the Medal of Valor. So, I think I'm qualified enough to ask this question: How is Dorothy a threat to others? I mean, has she ever exhibited any signs of violent behavior?"

"That's a good question, Detective, and the answer to that question, to the best of my knowledge, is no. However, that's not why she's here at LIPC."

"No, Detective," Dorothy said, "I'm a guinea pig."

Bowen pinched her eyebrows together.

Dr. Hausberger cleared his throat. "You see, Detective Bowen, by the time Dorothy got to this facility, she had been diagnosed with several maladies. When her hyper-religious tendencies were linked to those diagnoses, she did become, of sorts, a test case for some new therapies. We were given *carte blanche*, by the judge handling her case when she was in St. Patrick's in Cincinnati."

"Therapies?" Bowen said.

"Medicinal only. Well, there's continual counseling, too, but I assure you, nothing barbaric is occurring. No electrodes or shock therapy or lobotomies. Those are tools of an era long since passed."

"So, we're talking about drugs?"

"For the most part, yes."

"And even though you've tried these new drugs on her, she's still managed to work her way up here to the ninth floor?"

"Sadly, yes."

"But you still didn't answer my question, Doctor. Has Ms. Hamar exhibited any dangerous tendencies that would be deemed as harmful to others?"

"Physical tendencies? No. Psychological tendencies? Most definitely. We are working in tandem with four other psychiatric hospitals around the world to help people like Dorothy. Our work is on the cutting edge of psychotherapeutic—"

"In other words," Dorothy said, her voice monotone, "they've found other religious people who also talk to God, and they want them to stop too. Find a medication strong enough to block out God. That's their real goal, Detective, although they would never admit to it in a million years."

Bowen took a step back. Her eyes searched for answers. Her feet wanted to leave. She wanted to cover her ears and lock Dorothy and Dr. Hausberger in the room.

Dr. Hausberger puffed a tired and annoyed exhalation. "Are we discouraging a person's desire or right to follow or participate in whatever religion they choose? Of course not. Are we attempting to treat that which has been rightly diagnosed as a mental disorder? Yes. All we wish to do is help people like Dorothy live healthy and full lives without exhibiting the psychological maladies which cripple a normal human existence within proper, accepted, societal expectations."

"Normal human existence?" Bowen squinted in confusion. "Within proper...what?"

"Societal expectations. To say it another way, depending on where a person resides, be it America, Holland, Mozambique, you name the place, there are accepted family values that may not be tolerated elsewhere. There are usually accepted, personal responsibilities within the framework of that society's expectations too. These societal expectations may be based on a constitution, or a religion, or a treaty, or some other set of parameters that rule the day. Other populations around the world may find these expectations objectionable, even deplorable. The point is, Detective, cultural mores, namely, where a person lives, dictate to varying degrees what is considered normal human behavior and what is considered to be outside those accepted norms.

"So, what we and these other hospitals are doing is finding ways to handle cases like Dorothy's based on those societal expectations.

"Therefore, how we handle Dorothy here in the U.S. is going to be a little different than if she lived in Holland or Mozambique because their cultures have different expectations when it comes to how an individual behaves concerning, in this case, how one speaks to God. Whatever is considered normal in that society is the accepted practice. Anything outside the norm is viewed as unacceptable."

The detective's eyes shifted from Dr. Hausberger to Dorothy. "What *is* normal, Doctor?"

Dorothy chuckled. "That's a good question, Detective. Keep badgering him with that one. I've asked it for years now. Still can't get a straight answer. All he does is give me that cultural gobbledygook."

Dr. Hausberger frowned. "Paying attention to cultural values is paramount in today's societies, and we must be sensitive to that."

"But what about my culture?" Dorothy said.

"That's what we are talking about, Ms. Hamar. You live in America. Specifically, New York City. There are expectations here that do not apply in a place like Birmingham, Alabama, for example."

Dorothy looked at the detective. "You see what I mean?" She tapped the side of her head. "Thick as pea soup."

"Uh, Ms. Hamar," Dr. Hausberger said, "there is no reason to become mean-spirited."

"Mean-spirited? Mean-spirited…" Dorothy's voice trailed off for an instant and ended with an exasperated huff. "Do you hear yourself when you talk, Doctor? Do the words register up there in that educated head of yours before they come out?"

Dr. Hausberger turned to Detective Bowen. "You see, this is where every conversation concludes. In a tirade of personal attacks and spiritual irrelevancy."

"Spiritual irrele—?" Dorothy bit her tongue. "But Doctor, this spiritual irrelevancy you speak of is my culture. It was not how I was raised initially, but it has become who I am. Doesn't that matter? Or do cultures matter only when they serve a purpose to those who hold the keys to the kingdom?"

"All cultures matter, Ms. Hamar, but within a culture, certain arts, literature, beliefs, even a way of doing things that are territorially unique to that segment of the population are what create that culture and make it distinct from all others. There may be similarities, of course, but nevertheless, each culture forges itself within that region of the world and perpetuates itself by creating those aforementioned arts, literature, and beliefs."

"So, Doctor, by your definition, is Christianity a culture?" Dorothy said.

"In a looser sense of the word, yes. The only caveat would be a lack of territoriality. Christianity is a religion that transcends national boundaries."

"Yet, a Coptic Christian may look a great deal different from an American Evangelical Christian, or a Roman Catholic Christian in South America."

"Yes, I suppose that's true."

"And that's based on culture, right?"

"It is."

"So then, why is my culture of Christianity any different?"

Dr. Hausberger glanced at Detective Bowen. "I'm not following."

Dorothy looked at Detective Bowen. "I believe there is a spiritual world out there. In here. Everywhere. I interact with it. And that's what's gotten me into this situation." She motioned to her surroundings.

"But Ms. Hamar," Dr. Hausberger said, "you claim to talk to Jesus, Joseph, and Mary. Even you must admit that talking to people who have long since left this earth is out of the realm of normalcy of your average Christian culture, especially here in America."

Dorothy sat for a moment. Her expression started as a rebuttal, but she froze. Her hand still in the air. Slowly, she lowered it to her lap as the seconds passed.

"You see," Dr. Hausberger said, "that is the bone of contention we have here, Ms. Hamar."

"No, Doctor. It's not. At least not the way you are imagining it."

"I'm sorry?"

"You think my actions give you permission to treat me because I apparently do not fall within what's considered normal, accepted Christian culture in America, specifically New York City. And may I add, that same 'normal, accepted Christian culture' must be accepted by people who are not Christians at all, if not more so, than those who do believe, even if their belief is of an elementary level." Dorothy paused before looking directly at Detective Bowen. "And maybe that is the entire problem."

"What's the problem, Dorothy," Dr. Hausberger said.

"Because I see what others don't, I'm the oddball. Could it be that the culture has it wrong because it cannot see? Cannot understand?"

"Ms. Hamar," Dr. Hausberger said, "before you throw all Christians in America under the bus, I would proffer the idea that maybe the majority should rule in cases such as these."

Dorothy's gaze switched to the doctor. "That's funny. That's exactly what Pontius Pilate said too…right before he washed his hands."

CHAPTER THIRTY-TWO

West 173rd Street
Washington Heights, NY

I spent the better part of two hours talking to Gordon before relieving Mildred at the front counter. I had to admit. Heather was right. Talking to him was easy. Telling him my story wasn't nearly as challenging as I thought it would be. Even when things became awkward, it felt strangely comfortable.

Especially when he offered that apartment to me.

Now, driving home, replaying the conversation in my head, I could kick myself.

"What kind of arrangement did you have in mind?"

Did I really say that? Did it really come out that way?

What were you thinking, Rachel Leah? Oh, wait. That's right. You weren't thinking.

Great way of putting a nice guy on the defensive.

I can be such an imbecile sometimes.

To add insult to injury, I arrived home to find the only available parking spot five blocks away. A salt-encrusted sedan pulled out into the heavy traffic just ahead, and I had to whip in before the car coming from the other direction beat me to it.

Weston's Department Store was having their Christmas Holidaze Extravaganza. They did it every year, the weekend before Christmas. It always clogged up the streets, and pedestrian traffic grew tenfold. If you like to people watch, this was the place. Everything and everybody came out for this shindig. It was like a *Men in Black* audition mixed with your Black Friday-style holiday sale.

I got out of my car and hiked up the sidewalk, navigating around the icy patches of half-melted, refrozen, packed snow.

Whoever invented high heels should be bound, gagged, and made to wear the stupid things on icy sidewalks.

Standing at the corner, out by the light post, the man who usually wore the wife-beater t-shirt was talking to two other men. All three had coats on, each one depicting a sports team. I couldn't make them out, but I did see a basketball on one of them. They huddled together like they had some serious business to discuss and didn't want anyone eavesdropping.

As I approached, the man from my building spotted me. He smiled and nodded slightly, then turned back to his friends. I tossed a polite smile back in his direction and made a quick left turn into our apartment entrance. The archway of Christmas lights around the doors to the complex still blinked as if they'd just run a marathon.

If they blinked quicker, it would make everyone feel a little perkier.

I stepped inside the mailroom and wondered how many letters I'd receive today. It was Saturday, I thought, feeling a little snarky.

I might even get two, since it's the weekend.

And I was right. Amidst a credit card offer and an advertisement for a car dealership, two letters huddled together, facing each other. Both postmarked yesterday. Both addressed to me.

No distinguishing marks to tell me which one was number twelve and number thirteen.

So, like I'd done for almost two weeks, I went upstairs, plopped on the couch, and opened them both.

The first one was another diary-formatted paragraph.

I had a great day today. Daddy took me, my brothers, and my sisters to the mountains, and we had a picnic. There were a bunch of other people there also. It was so much fun. The meadow is huge. It has flowers of every kind, and all of them were in bloom. Daddy says they never lose their petals. They are always blooming.

When we got there, it was light outside. Off to the side of the meadow, there is a creek. It's not very deep, but Daddy says it flows down the mountain and forms the most beautiful pool. He said he'd take us there tomorrow, and we could swim all day, if we wanted to. I can't wait!

I read the second letter.

Today, we followed the creek down the mountainside. Daddy helped me and the others when the path got too steep. We got to the end of the creek and found the beautiful pool Daddy had told us about yesterday. We swam in the pool for hours. It was wonderful. And Daddy said we didn't have to worry about something in the water nibbling at our toes. Everything here loves us. Even the fish! They would come right up and look at us like they wanted to say "Hi" and carry on a conversation. You could even pet them.

I have to admit. I've never petted a fish before. But they act kind of like dogs and cats. And they love to brush up against your legs.

This child had mentioned things from my past. Buttercups. A

bear named Buttons. Even the meadow with the creek that sounds a little like the one Billy took me to the night he died. This child had mentioned a brother in an earlier drawing, but this was the first-time brothers and sisters had been mentioned specifically. Yet, I didn't have any siblings.

I'm an only child.

So, were those other things just coincidences? Generalities that, when phrased correctly, sound specific enough to be convincing? Like the horoscope that tells you, "Your life is about to change." Then you meet someone new and think, "Oh, wow. It was right."

Or is there more to this?

As I tried to imagine the scene painted for me by this child, I reminisced about the meadow Billy had taken me to that fateful night. If I didn't know any better, this child could have been describing that meadow. But how would he know about it? Or was it a she? And besides, meadows often look similar. Flowers. Creeks. Trees. Grass. I could probably describe one and have fifty people give me fifty different locations of a particular one they remembered.

I set the letter down and closed my eyes. I imagined the meadow. The moonlight shimmering off the creek. The lulling sound the water made. I felt the wind whisk across my skin and escape through the tall pines again, just like I had experienced that fateful night.

I felt Billy's strong arms wrapped around me. His heart pulsing in my ear. So peaceful. So relaxing.

Then, the truck arrived. Billy grabbed his shotgun for protection.

It was Daddy, though.

A conversation ensued.

Daddy's hand was on the door handle of his truck. He was ready to leave and take me with him when he spun around to look directly at Billy. "Baldwin? Your last name is Baldwin?"

"Yes, sir."

"Rachel, you never told me his last name was Baldwin."

"What does that matter, Daddy?"

Daddy ignored me. His eyes focused on Billy. "Isn't this the boy who took you to the movies last fall?"

"Yes, Daddy. But why does it matter what his last name is?"

"You Judson's boy?"

"No." Billy said. "That's my uncle."

"So, you're Matthew's boy, then?"

Billy nodded. "Yes, sir."

"Matthew Baldwin…" Daddy's voice trailed off for a few seconds. "And your grandfather's Matthias Baldwin?"

Billy's brow pinched together. "Yeah."

"Great-grandfather's Jedidiah Baldwin?"

"That's right."

Daddy aimed his thumb at his truck. "Rachel, it's time for us to go."

"Daddy, why did you need to know who his granddaddies were?"

"That's no concern of yours, young lady. Now, get in the truck."

"No."

Daddy's voice became thunderous. He pointed at his truck. "Rachel! Get in this truck! Now!"

"No!"

"Rachel," Billy said, "it's not worth it. Just go. We can talk about it later."

Daddy took several steps toward us and zeroed in on Billy. "Talk about what later?"

Billy's heart must've stopped beating for a long second. His breathing became choppy. I could tell he was scared. "This whole situation. You apparently don't want us seeing each other." Billy lifted his hands as if the answer should be obvious, not wanting to tell my daddy about the pregnancy.

"You're right. I don't. Rachel's not supposed to be here," Daddy said. "And that's another thing. How many times have you lied to me, young lady? How many times have you two met like this when I thought you were somewhere else?"

I shot a stern gaze at my father. The truth was out now. There was no sense hiding it anymore. "More than you care to hear about."

Daddy's breathing escalated. His anger was full-blown now. He stomped towards Billy and grabbed him by the shoulders. "Is this how you thought you'd win my favor? Huh? If you were to ask her to marry you someday, was this how you were gonna butter me and her momma up and ask for our blessing?"

"Let go of him!" I lurched at my father and began pulling on his arm, screaming. "Let go of him! Leave us alone!"

In one quick motion, Daddy shoved Billy away and back-handed me across the face, knocking me to the ground. The sting of whose hand it was hurt more than the blow itself. I grabbed my jaw in agony.

Billy lost his balance and fell backwards, striking his head against a rock protruding from the ground. He let out a sharp cry.

"You're goin' with me now, Rachel." Daddy bent over, grabbed me by the arm, and yanked me to my feet.

I tried to jerk my arm away. "No! I can't believe you hit me! You've never hit me! Ever!" I began striking Daddy in the arm and chest. "Let go of me!"

Groaning and grabbing his head, Billy staggered to his feet and stumbled around to the other side of his truck. He snatched his shotgun and maneuvered around to the front of the vehicle. He stopped, aimed it in the air, and fired.

The shot echoed across the face of the mountain and faded into the night air.

Daddy, struggling with me, turned and gaped at Billy. His speech suddenly became stern but calmer. "You better put that gun away, boy, before you regret it." Daddy pushed me away and marched toward Billy.

Billy chambered another round and leveled the weapon at Daddy's chest. "Stop right there, old man!"

Daddy laughed but didn't stop. "Old man? You better shoot me, boy. You better do it. You better shoot me now."

I frantically jumped to my feet, shouting, "Stop it! Stop it!"

A nervousness overtook Billy. His eyes blinked and twitched, and the gun trembled as his finger slid up and down the trigger.

Daddy didn't stop. He kept shouting at Billy. "You better pull that trigger, boy!"

Billy lifted the barrel of the shotgun and fired a warning shot over Daddy's head. He chambered another round. "The next one goes into your chest, old man."

"No, it won't," Daddy said. He traversed the last few feet, grabbed the gun barrel, and pushed it up toward the night sky.

Billy squeezed off another round.

I screamed. "Noooooooooo!"

Daddy manhandled the other end of the gun with his left hand, jerked it toward him, and in one skillful move, struck Billy in the face with the butt of the weapon, using Billy's momentum against him. He twisted the gun and wrenched it from Billy's grasp.

Billy's nose erupted into a spray of blood as he staggered backwards.

Daddy jammed the butt of the gun into Billy's stomach.

Billy, clutching his nose, doubled over, gasping for air, wincing in pain.

Daddy then lifted the gun high and slammed the butt of the weapon into the back of Billy's head.

Billy collapsed to the ground in a heap.

Daddy, positioning his feet, flipped the gun around, and stabbed the barrel into the back of Billy's head. "You see, boy?

That's not how it's done…unless you're shootin' at quail." He lifted the gun high and reloaded the chamber.

"Daddy, please stop!" I said.

"If you're gonna shoot somebody," he said, ignoring my plea, "at least have guts enough to hit them in the chest or the head. None of this namby-pamby, warning shot crap."

Billy rolled over onto his back and glanced up before squinting, bracing for the worst.

Then, Daddy relaxed his grip, ejected the remaining, unspent slugs before tossing the gun across the meadow.

The firearm clanked when it hit the ground and slid across the damp grass.

Daddy slowly pivoted and glared at me. He pointed at his truck. "We leave. Now."

"Daddy, please…" I was tired of all the fighting. My voice soft.

Billy, still holding his nose and head, managed to get to one knee.

I ran over to Billy, knelt beside him, and placed my hand on his shoulder. "Are you okay?"

"Rachel, just go," Billy said, still looking at the ground.

Daddy took two steps and halted. His arms hung lifeless beside his body. Without turning, he said, "Billy Baldwin, are you aware of your family's history in these parts?"

Billy looked at me and shrugged in confusion. "I don't know what you're talkin' about."

"I'm not surprised. I'm sure your kin have tried to keep it from you just like I've tried to keep it from Rachel. I figured, so long as the two families had no dealings with each other, then maybe we could get by for one generation without trouble."

"So, what are you sayin'? Our families don't like each other or somethin'?" Billy attempted to stand, but fell back to one knee. He shot one hand to the ground for balance and chuckled to himself. "Did we used to have feuds and shoot at each other like the Hatfields and McCoys?"

Daddy, still facing away, spoke softly. "If it were only that simple—"

Just then, the doorbell rang, jolting me out of my daydream, and I shrieked before stifling it with my hand.

"Miss Hamar? It's Detective Bowen. Is everything all right in there?"

She definitely wasn't the person I wanted to see right now. "Yeeees. Just a minute."

I closed my eyes, trying to see Billy's face one last time, but images of him falling to the ground again, rolling over on his back, and losing consciousness were all I could see.

I lumbered to the door and snuck a peek through the peephole before opening it. I did leave it latched, though. "Yes, Detective. What is it?"

"Is everything okay? Your eyes are red. Have you been crying?"

"I'm fine." I wiped my face with my hand. "What do you need?"

"May I come in? Or is this a bad time."

"I'm really not in the mood right now."

"Look, I understand. But I do have some news for you, and you have some letters to show me, right?"

I closed the door, unlatched it, and swung it wide for her to enter. "Please tell me you straightened things out with Roberto's employer."

"I did," she said, closing the door behind her. "He was fine once I explained the whole ordeal to him. He told me he'd stop the investigation, make sure it didn't wind up in his personnel file, and reinstate him to the engineering program Monday."

"Why not today?"

"I don't know. Because it's the weekend, I imagine. But does it really matter?"

"I suppose not." I sat down on the couch.

"I also stopped by to see your mother," she said, sitting down in the chair next to me. "Your mother is a very intriguing woman. A smart one too."

"Did you learn anything?"

Detective Bowen snickered a little. "She's feisty. And she and that Dr. Hausberger have no love lost between the two of them. I can tell you that."

"Yeah, he's a real piece of work too. They go toe-to-toe every time he visits her."

"Wasn't any different today, I'm afraid. However, your mother got me thinking about some things on the way back."

"Like how nuts she is? And why I don't visit her more? And what she talks about when Jesus, Joseph, and Mary pay a visit?"

Detective Bowen smiled, but in a sorrowful way. "She does miss you, Rachel. And she's concerned about you. She told me you were in danger, and her expression was one of genuine distress."

"Did she say how I was in danger?"

She paused. "Your mother said it had something to do with Satan."

"Ah, yes. The satanic plot to ruin my life and send me hurtling to hell. I've heard that warning so many times, Detective, I've lost track."

"Well, all I know is, in her own way, as she argued back and forth with Dr. Hausberger, she seemed coherent, logical, and even made sense to me."

"One doesn't have to be stupid to be nuts. Lots of brilliant people have been crazy."

"And that's just the point your mother was trying to explain, I think. Because Dr. Hausberger doesn't believe in religious things, or chooses not to, according to your mother, he is, by choice, oblivious to another world around him."

"Oh, yes. The spiritual world."

"Yes. That's exactly what your mother called it."

"I know, Detective. I've heard about the spiritual world since I was little. For as long as I can remember, actually." I scoffed. "I'll give Mom credit. She's been consistent. All these years, she's said the same thing over and over."

Detective Bowen scooted back into the chair. "That's what she got me thinking about, Rachel. What if she's right? What if there *is* a spiritual world at work we don't see?"

"Okay, Detective," I said, shifting in my seat. "Now you're starting to worry me."

"But just hear me out."

I waved her off. "Whatever."

"I've been doing this job for many years now. Like I was telling someone recently, I've worked the road, been in the vice squad, and been a detective. I've seen a bunch of bad people do horrible things to other human beings, to animals, and to property. I refuse to believe that humans, all by themselves, are capable of some of the atrocities I've seen."

"Why are you telling me this?"

"Rachel, how can mankind be so ruthless? So uncaring? So unfeeling? So heinous? So conniving? So—"

"So evil?"

"Exactly. This kind of treachery has to be otherworldly. I refuse to believe that every human being is like that. I'm not. You don't seem to be. I know plenty of men who can be jerks sometimes, but I'm confident you'll never find them running a prostitution ring or becoming a serial killer."

"So, where does evil come from?"

Bowen pointed at me. "That was the question I was pondering on my way here. Obviously, we have a choice to make. We have choices to make every day. There have been more times than I care to admit when I believed pulling the trigger and ending the bad guy's life would make everyone's life so much easier. But there's something inside me that convinces me not to. It's as if I'd lose a part of myself if I did. And if I did it repeatedly, I'm not sure there would be any Nicole Bowen left. So, I cuff the lowlife instead and haul him away."

"If you are looking for answers, Detective, you're asking the wrong person."

"I'm just thinking out loud, I guess. I mean, me and a bunch of my friends were off for a three-day weekend about a month ago. We watched, like, five scary movies in a row. You know, the real spooky kind. Evil spirits grabbing people and throwing them against the wall. Furniture moving by itself. Vampires and zombie-looking things jumping from the shadows and killing people left and right.

"The strange part is, we didn't think anything about it. We even made comments about how so many people believe in that sort of stuff. We even watched one of those TV shows with people hunting ghosts, trying to catch some spirit on camera to prove to viewers some kind of spirit world actually exists—"

"Yet," I said, interrupting her, "a woman sits in a psych ward and is labeled a lunatic, all because she claims to actually see the very things the ghost hunters want to capture on film."

Detective Bowen gave a confirming smile. "Your mother's not sounding so crazy now, is she?"

I didn't want to admit it to her, but I'd had the same questions. Numerous times. Wondering how irrational my mother actually was. Wondering if maybe, just maybe, she knew more than all the doctors who were diagnosing and treating her. But I wasn't ready to concede. I wasn't ready to acknowledge anything right now. I was receiving letters from an unknown source, written by a presumed child about things no one should know about. If it weren't for the actual letters resting on the coffee table, then I'd be wondering about my sanity too. "Hey, not to change the subject, but here's the letters I got today. Two of them." I picked them up and handed them to her.

"We're assuming you got two because of the weekend? One for Saturday? One for Sunday?" She took them.

"That's how it went down last weekend."

She read them both. "How do you know the order?"

"I don't really. But the one I handed you first makes reference to a swimming hole and how they were going to go there to swim. The second one describes it. Also, the first one makes mention of brothers and sisters. The second one uses the word *we*, so I'm assuming the brothers and sisters are included. There's been no mention of multiple siblings until these two letters. Only a brother was mentioned before. Yet the person writing these things acts like I already knew about them."

Detective Bowen reread the first letter. "And we have already established you have no siblings."

"Correct. I'm an only child."

"And what about the meadow? Sound familiar?"

"A little. But the meadow I'm thinking of…I only got to see it in the daylight once."

She pointed at the letter. "Did it look like this?"

"Not exactly."

"Meaning?"

"What I remember of that place, the pleasant things, before my Daddy showed up, happened at night."

A sudden look of enlightenment spread across Detective Bowen's face. "That's where your boyfriend was killed, wasn't it? You told me it happened in the woods, but you never got specific."

"The police took me back to the crime scene the next day. I had to explain how it all happened."

"And that, obviously, happened during the day."

I nodded. "So, as you can imagine, the picture of the meadow I recall is quite different from the one this child paints."

Sunday

December 21, 2014

CHAPTER THIRTY-THREE

Goldman's Gifts and Cards
Manhattan, NY

J awoke the next morning hoping I could smooth things out with Joanie now that Detective Bowen had cleared things up for Roberto. Joanie was my best friend, and my roommate. Or at least, she had been. That's why I had to go see her.

I peered down the long hallway of the little indoor mall, which housed Goldman's Gifts and Cards and a dozen other little Mom and Pop shops owned by locals.

Studying the placard on the wall by the main entrance, I found Goldman's Gifts and Cards. Store number seven. Fourth one down on the right.

With a quick glance up and down the street, I moseyed inside and tried my best to look like all the other frazzled patrons.

I knew Joanie was working extra hours due to the holidays, but I couldn't remember when. So, I took a chance on catching her before she got to work. However, when I arrived, the store was already open and filling up with last minute Christmas shoppers. She was standing at the register, ringing up customers.

I contemplated going back home but thought better of it. I needed to see her. I understood that the one bright spot in her dull, sleep-deprived world was Roberto, and I had apparently messed that up big time.

I stepped inside and scurried to the right, turning my back to the cashier's counter. I peeked over my shoulder.

"That'll be $14.52," Joanie said, beginning to wrap a glass ornament in tissue paper.

The customer held out some money.

I slipped down the aisle and spied on her from between a cardboard cutout of a large snowman and a rack of Christmas cards. Perry Como sang "White Christmas" for all the patrons through the speakers overhead.

Joanie made the change and handed it to the woman. "Here you go, ma'am. Your change makes fifteen, and a five makes twenty." She grabbed the handle on the paper sack and held it out for the woman.

"Thank you," the woman said.

"You're welcome. And have a Merry Christmas," Joanie said.

"Merry Christmas to you too." The woman took her bag and walked out.

Joanie helped the next customer in line.

I kept waiting, watching, looking for a moment when I could approach her without others standing nearby. I knew it would be awkward, so I didn't want to make a sce—

"Can I help you?"

The voice from behind startled me. I spun around and almost knocked the cardboard snowman over into a display of crystal ornaments. "Whoa!" I reached for it, but it was too far away.

A man grabbed the snowman and steadied it, like freezing in

place would stop the world from spinning. Finally, he stood the snowman back up and slowly let go, making sure it wasn't going to fall over again. His heroic demeanor changed into one of mild annoyance.

"I'm so sorry," I said. "I was just looking for a Christmas card for a friend, and you scared me. You guys really shouldn't sneak up on customers."

"Excuse me, but are you from corporate?"

"Corpora—No, I'm just a customer."

"I see. Well, the reason I asked was because you seemed more interested in my employee over there than you did these cards."

"You're the manager?"

"Assistant manager."

"For your information, that employee over there is my roommate, Joanie Harrington. I was waiting for your customers to leave so I could talk to her for a minute. However, if you'd rather, I can do that while your customers are standing there, listening to our conversation."

The manager offered a fake smile. "She breaks for lunch at eleven-thirty. If you would so kindly wait until then, I'd greatly appreciate it. As you can see, we're pretty busy."

I glanced at my cell phone and checked the time. "No problem. Do you mind if I set that up with her?"

"Not at all." He walked away.

I turned around, and there, staring at me from behind the counter, was Joanie. No smile, no frown. Just a blank stare.

I walked over to her and pointed back in the manager's direction. "I hear that you're taking your lunch at eleven-thirty. Could I talk to you when you're free?"

"Uh, sure."

"Meet you in the food court? My treat."

"Okay."

I strolled around the little mall with a cup of coffee in my hand, trying not to notice how horrible it tasted.

These people can't make coffee like Heather either.

I finally sat down at the closest table to the front of the dinky food court. Only a few minutes passed when Joanie rounded the corner and sat down across from me.

"Look," Joanie said, "I only have thirty minutes, and I need to make sure I'm back before my break ends."

"Sure. Why don't we get in line, and we can talk while we order?"

Joanie dismissed my idea with a wave. "I'm not hungry, but you can."

"Look, Joanie, I just had to see you and tell you how sorry I am for everything. I never meant for you or Roberto to get involved. You suggested I go to the police. And at the time, it seemed like a good idea."

"Yeah, well…" Joanie chuckled nervously while looking at the table. "That was stupid on my part. That one's on me."

"I'm not here to point fingers, Joanie. I'm here to tell you that Detective Bowen came by the apartment yesterday. She spoke to Roberto's manager. He's stopping the investigation. He's gonna reinstate Roberto to the engineering program. It was all just a big misunderstanding."

"Yeah, I know. Roberto called me last night."

"Soooo? Are you two going to be able to patch things up?"

Joanie nodded. "We already have."

"That's great!"

"Yes, it is."

I watched Joanie fidget with her purse strap and take a glimpse at her cell phone.

"Okay, so why do I feel like talking to me is worse than getting a root canal?"

Joanie took in a deep breath. "Listen, Rach, uh, I know you better than anybody. And I know why you're here. I'm not coming back. So, you can just stop wishing for that." She fiddled with the strap to her purse a little more forcefully. Her voice got a little louder. "When I left your apartment, I went straight to Roberto's to see if we could patch things up. However, because he was being investigated and was temporarily suspended from the engineering program, he ended our relationship. So, I had nowhere to go."

"Where have you been staying?"

"I've been staying with Lacey. She said I could crash there until I got things figured out. But Roberto called me to tell me he had been reinstated, thanks to you. We had a long conversation on the phone before we agreed that the best move for us was for me to move in with him."

"I thought you said you and Roberto were taking things slow? He said it himself. You two had been burned so many times."

"I remember. But that was before."

"Before what?"

"Before…this. Look, Rach, it's time we move on with our lives. You've said it yourself. We're in our thirties and not getting any younger. If we keep living like we've been living, we're gonna grow old together and never experience life."

"And you want to start a new life with him. I get it."

"I hope you understand."

"I understand you wanting to pursue your relationship with him, but I'm not clear on why you feel the need to alienate me, especially at this time in my life. You know what's been going on." I choked back my emotions. "I'm scared, Joanie. And if I have to face this alone…" I reached into my purse and pulled out a small package of tissues. "I'm not sure I can."

Joanie reached across the table and placed her hand on mine. "You're one of the strongest people I know. The stuff you've been through would have killed half the people around here. The other half would have become alcoholics or drug addicts to cope with it. You can make it, Rach. I have faith in you."

I fell back into my seat. "Why does this sound like a farewell address?"

"It's just, with me not living in the apartment any longer, I'm not sure how much I'm going to get to see you."

"Of course." I yanked out a tissue from the package and wiped my eyes. "Every waking moment not spent at a job will be spent with him."

Joanie smiled. "Something like that."

I looked her square in the eye. "He also told you that if you stayed with me, it was over, didn't he?"

"No."

I studied her eyes. "You're lying."

Joanie dropped her head and retrieved her hand. "Roberto didn't say anything of the sort. This has nothing to do with him."

"So, what are you saying? This is all your idea?"

She slowly nodded.

"And what happens when things don't work out with him? Then what? I thought we made a pact to never put ourselves in that situation?"

"We did, but I just can't live like this anymore."

"What do you mean?"

Joanie set her jaw. "You, Rach. I can't deal with…" She pointed back and forth between the two of us. "All this letter business, your mom, your depression over losing Billy, your feelings over losing your dad, the regret of having an abortion…I just can't do it anymore. I can't be there for you like I have in the past. It's drained me to the point where I have nothing left to give. I'm empty. I've lost my zest for life. And I need some time to find it again."

I tried to hold the tears inside, but they escaped. I closed my eyes and stood. "I have to go."

"No, Rachel, please wait. Don't end things like this."
"I didn't, Joanie. You just did."

287

CHAPTER THIRTY-FOUR

West 173rd Street
Washington Heights, NY

could barely see driving home. The falling snow made it more difficult, but my tear-filled eyes were the real reason. Everything was blurry. In all the years of pain, heartache, and abandonment, I'd never been told by anyone I was no longer wanted around.

Even the foster homes wanted me for the money.

I'd always felt like a plague. A bad penny. A curse. But never was I told that to my face.

Until now.

And the thing that hurt the most was who told me. My best friend of over twenty-five years. The one who had plotted and planned and schemed and finagled life with me, for me, and around me.

She was gone. And I was the reason. I was like a leech, I guess. I had drained life from her. Caused her to lose "her zest for life." Even her countenance, her smile, her joy seemed vacant. Hollow. Like she was going through the motions of life without any joy inside.

I guess that's what it feels like when you have a friend like me.

~

I PARKED two blocks away and shut off the engine. The wind howled outside, and I didn't want to get out. I didn't want to go to our old apartment and have to deal with all the memories. I just wanted to sit there and allow winter's bite to suck the life out of me.

Maybe if I just fall asleep in here, the hypothermia will eventually end it all.

I hugged myself and began to rock.

Back and forth.

Back and forth.

Like the night Billy died.

Huddled over his lifeless body.

Begging him to wake up.

Pleading with him to breathe again.

And like that night, the floodgates opened.

Twenty years of pent-up sorrow flowed out of me like never before.

~

A FEW MINUTES LATER, someone tapped on my passenger window with fingernails.

Go away.

The person then knocked.

I turned, glancing out of the corner of my eye, and the man in the wife-beater t-shirt was leaning over, waving at me. "You okay?" he yelled through the closed window.

I debated whether to respond. I finally turned the key and rolled the window down an inch.

"Sorry to bother you," he said. "I just saw you pull up a while ago, but you never got out. Then, when I walked up to see if you were okay, I saw that you were crying."

"I'm fine. Just had a bad day, that's all."

"Oh. Sorry to hear that. Well, Merry Christmas, miss. Hope your holidays get better."

"Thanks." I wiped my eyes.

He motioned a short wave and began walking down the street. Two of his buddies were waiting at the corner. When he reached them, they crossed the street and continued down the sidewalk.

I finally got out of the car and fought the blowing snow right up to the entrance of the apartment building. My wet face grew colder and colder as snowflakes stuck to my drenched cheeks.

As I approached, I looked at the old, rundown structure.

I'll never be able to afford this place now.

What am I gonna do?

Start searching the Internet for a cheaper place to live, I guess.

When I started up the steps, a man dressed like a postal worker blasted through the doorway and jogged down the steps with a purpose. Over his shoulder was a large bag.

"Hey," I said, "aren't you guys supposed to be off on Sundays?"

The man harrumphed. "I wish. When I got this job fifteen years ago, we were off every Sunday. But not anymore."

"Since when did you guys start working Sundays?"

"When people started ordering all their Christmas stuff online."

"I see."

"But only packages, thank God. No first-class mail. We made a pact with a major online company about a year ago. And guess what? New York and Los Angeles got to be the test markets. Lucky us. They just rolled it out in Dallas and a few other places this year. I guess if it goes over well, they'll make it nationwide."

I sighed and kind of mumbled to myself. "That would explain it." I started to walk away.

"Explain what?"

I spun around. "Oh, sorry. I was just lamenting."

"At Christmas." He puckered his lips and nodded, like he understood. "The irony of it all."

I scrunched my eyebrows together.

The mailman shrugged. "Isn't this supposed to be a time filled with joy? And here we are, standing here, total strangers, wishing it was over so we could move on with life."

Wishing it was over?

You have no idea.

"That's why I didn't know you guys worked Sundays. Nobody ever sends me packages for Christmas."

"That's why you were sad?"

"Among other things, yeah."

"So, you don't get any? Ever?"

I shook my head. "Not expecting any this year either."

"Ma'am, I'm truly sorry to hear that." He looked at his bag. "I want to go back in that mailroom and put one of these in your mailbox now."

"That's sweet of you."

He reached out his hand. "Let's make a pact, shall we? We won't allow the busyness of life to get in the way of the joy of the season. What do you say? My wife is always telling me I need to lighten up and enjoy life more."

"Interesting you should say that. Besides the busyness of life, can we include the cruelty of life too?"

"Sure. Whatever gets in the way of our joy. I mean, look at this. It's snowing at Christmastime. Hasn't done that in years. That must be a sign, right? Of something good about to happen?"

I offered an encouraged smile. "I sure hope so." I reached out my hand. "Deal." His firm grip warmed me inside.

"Merry Christmas, ma'am. And may you have a very Happy New Year."

"You too."

He released my hand. "My wife tells me all the time, 'It's not about what's in the packages. It's all about what's in the heart.'"

"She sounds like a wise woman."

He nodded slowly, as if contemplating the thought for the first time. "She is. Much wiser than me."

"How long have you been married?"

"Only four years. Second go around for the both of us. Both of our spouses passed, so it makes this time of year a little tougher, you know?"

Oh, I do.

"Well, I wish you both many years of happiness together."

He reached out his hand again. "Merry Christmas."

"And you, sir." I shook his hand one last time before watching him walk away. I thought about what he said.

It was not about what's in the packages. It was all about what's in the heart.

Seems so trite right now.

It's a wonder we didn't break out in song and do a dance number right there in front of the apartment building.

I walked inside and passed the mailroom before stopping in my tracks.

Only packages? That's what he said. No first-class mail.

"I won't have anything then," I said to myself and took two more steps toward the stairs. "No letters today."

But what if someone did send me a package? There's a first time for everything, right?

So, hesitantly, I checked.

And inside my mailbox sat a small box.

I pulled it out and looked back toward the doorway. I ran

outside and saw the mail carrier hop into his vehicle and mosey down the street.

A package. Addressed to me. No return address, though.

I raced upstairs and sat down on the couch. I dropped my purse beside me and turned the package around in my hand, examining it from all angles.

It had a fancy mailing label with little wreaths encircling the outside. The more I thought about opening it, the more frightened I became.

What if there's a bomb in here?

"Hey, brainless," I told myself, "twenty minutes ago, you were fine with freezing to death in the front seat of your car. A bomb would be much quicker, don't ya think?"

Just open the dumb thing.

I grabbed my keys and used them to slice the packing tape. I opened the delivery box and inside sat a smaller package, wrapped in glossy red Christmas paper.

I pulled it out and turned it over and over. Pretty paper but no label. No writing.

I slid my fingernail down the long sides, slitting the paper. I followed what appeared to be the lid to the box all the way around until the red paper lifted off with ease.

Here goes nothing.

I lifted the lid.

Inside, folded tissue paper encased a letter. This one wasn't in an envelope like the others. The letter was folded like it had been intended to be placed inside an envelope but was inserted into this box instead.

I pulled the letter out of the box and something inside of it fell out and dropped on the floor. I looked down, and staring up at me were several one hundred-dollar bills. I picked them up and started counting.

Two thousand dollars?

"This must be some kind of mistake." I scanned the living

room, expecting Joanie to be standing in a doorway. Big smile on her face.

But no one was there.

I examined the box again. It was addressed to me. Just like the letters had been. Same handwriting. Same kind of letter.

No, wait. I didn't look at the letter.

I grabbed the letter and opened it. Another Dear Diary-like entry.

It's funny how things change as you get older. Just a few years ago, I would have been running around this meadow, chasing the butterflies, picking flowers, giggling and laughing, full of energy. Constant motion. Now, as I sit here in the same meadow, by myself, I have a completely different appreciation for what I see.

The colors are so vibrant. The blue sky. The green of the trees and the field. The flowers. Even the animals. So full of life. I even had a bear cub stroll up to me earlier, nuzzle my hand, give a little growl before returning to its mother at the edge of the forest. Its fur was softer than I imagined it would be. Playful little thing.

Now, I'm lying on my back, looking up at the puffy, white clouds float by. I close my eyes and listen to the breeze kiss the forest branches. I could stay in this meadow forever.

Daddy says it will always be like this. Always has been. Always will be.

So peaceful.

I fell back into the couch and closed my eyes. I tried to imagine what this person described. It had to be a girl. Guys don't write like that. They do chase butterflies, but they don't pick flowers. Boys don't nuzzle with bear cubs. They'd want to wrestle it.

Who are you?

Why are you writing me these letters?
And why are you sending me money now?

CHAPTER THIRTY-FIVE

West 173rd Street
Washington Heights, NY

This one was different. It came in a box. Maybe there are fingerprints or residue or something Detective Bowen can use. Maybe the money can be traced.

I dug my cell phone out of my purse and dialed.

"Detective Bowen."

"Detective, Rachel Hamar." I scooted to the edge of the couch and hovered over the items sitting on the coffee table. "Listen. I just got another letter, but this one came in a small box wrapped like a Christmas present."

"Was it addressed to you like the other letters?"

"Yes. But inside, besides a letter, was two thousand dollars in cash. All one hundred-dollar bills."

"Wow. Who would send you that kind of money?"

"No one. That's just it. I don't know anybody with that kind of money to just give away."

"What about the bank? You work at a bank, right?"

"Yeah, but I just started. It's been less than a week."

"Okay, so probably no one's going to hand out that kind of cash to a new employee." She sighed into the phone. "This case is getting stranger by the minute."

"You're telling me."

"What I meant was, Detective Witherspoon called me late last night. He's been to all the drop locations used to send the letters. He viewed their security cameras and found out those letters were dropped off by different people."

I flopped back into the couch. "Differ—How could that be?"

"Beats me. He said about half of them were delivered by men. All different men. Not two alike. The other half were delivered by women. And same thing there. No two women looked alike. One letter was even delivered by a kid. Looked like a little street urchin. Ragtag clothes, dirty face, the whole nine yards."

"Maybe they're homeless people. Maybe someone's giving them money for delivering the letters."

"We thought of that. Some of the men and women looked like they could have been homeless too. But a couple of them looked like they worked on Fifth Avenue. The man had a suit and tie. The woman had a really nice fur coat and scarf."

"You're right. This is getting strange."

"Witherspoon is trying to track these people down and talk to them individually. Maybe they can tell us something."

"How long is that gonna take?"

"Might take a while. We do have the owner of On-Time Couriers and all his managers on the lookout for any letters addressed to you with directions to be delivered to the post office in Jericho. They were told to stall the person until we could get there."

"All this begs the question. Why not just go to the post office and mail them? Why use these couriers at all?"

"Makes it harder to track everything down. Look at how many man hours we've put into this already, and we're no closer to catching these people than we were when we started."

"Depressing, if you ask me."

"Yeah, well, welcome to my world, Miss Hamar. Listen, I'm on my way over to your apartment. I'll need to take the latest letters and make copies. I'll also need to take that money and have it checked for prints and make sure it's legit."

"Of course."

~

DETECTIVE BOWEN ARRIVED about thirty minutes later and examined the box, the letter, and the money with rubber gloves on her hands.

"You know, I didn't even think about my prints," I said.

"No problem. We've already ruled you out as a suspect." She laughed a little.

"That's comforting."

"Is there any significance to the money at all?"

"None that I can think of." I stopped and rubbed my chin. "Although, it is interesting…I had just left Joanie's work. I saw her for lunch today. Went to tell her how you had fixed things for Roberto, you know? That everything was gonna be okay. But it didn't matter. She told me she was still moving out. So, on the way home, I was thinking about how I'd have to find a cheaper place to live." I waved my hands at the walls. "Because I can't afford this dump now."

"I assume your rent is two thousand dollars?"

"Almost."

"That's interesting, wouldn't you say? Who knows about how much you pay for rent each month?"

"Good question. Joanie, of course. And the landlord. Uh, probably everybody else in this building who has an apartment like ours. I think they all rent for similar amounts."

"That's true. Anyone could get online and figure out how

much you pay each month. That wouldn't be hard, and it still fits the M.O. of an outsider, like the Central Park Cameraman."

"Wonderful."

"The Internet is a blessing and a curse, if you ask me." Detective Bowen slipped the items into large, plastic bags with writing on them. "Is there anyone else you know who might have done this?"

"Actually, I was telling my supervisor yesterday about Joanie moving out." I leaned back into the couch. "I don't remember telling him what we pay for rent, though, but he knew I couldn't afford it."

"Like I said before, if your supervisor wanted a ball park figure, all he'd have to do is look it up on the Internet." Detective Bowen shifted her head and spied me out of the corner of her eye. "Maybe you have a secret admirer, Miss Hamar."

"But that would mean after I left his office, which was around ten o'clock, he would have had to run to the post office in Jericho," I said, grabbing the plastic bag containing the wrapping paper with the label, "because that is where it was mailed from, and get it there by what? Noon? Then the post office had to process it and get it on a truck to get here by today—" I paused. "And besides, the mailman told me just a little bit ago that they only deliver packages purchased online on Sundays. So, this should not have even been delivered today."

Detective Bowen lifted her eyebrows. "Well, maybe it simply got mixed up with those online packages. It was in a box that looks like one."

"I suppose. But that's just one more coincidence in a case full of 'em, wouldn't you say?"

"True enough. But for me, believing your supervisor sent this to you doesn't sound all that hard to believe. He works at a bank. Easy access to that much cash. And I'm sure he puts his own money in the bank where he works. So, you leave his office. He makes a withdrawal for two grand. He wraps it up in this little box and drives to Jericho. That could be easily done by noon. And, think about it: it would be getting to that post office earlier than all those other days. Remember, we caught Mr. Singh mailing it around five in the afternoon, and it still got here the next—" Detective Bowen interrupted her train of thought. A sudden look of puzzlement spread across her face.

"What is it?"

"If your supervisor did mail that box, it can only mean one of two things. Either he's the person behind all these letters, or he heard you talk about the letters and decided to take advantage of the situation and use these letters as a cover for giving you this money."

"But I didn't even know Gordon before I interviewed for the job. And we had only met once before, not knowing we'd see each other three days later."

"You met him before? Not at the bank?"

"I was eating a late lunch at my second job, Santorino's. He was eating there too."

"He followed you?"

"No. He was there first."

"But he showed up at a place where you work?"

"Yeah, but…no. He's not responsible for all these letters. Or this box." I sat up on the edge of the couch and placed my hand on Detective Bowen's arm. "Please, don't mess this up too. Don't treat Gordon like Roberto. I don't want you to even talk to him. Is that clear?"

"I have to do my job, Rachel."

I stood and moved away from her. "And if it means interviewing Gordon, then you're off the job. And tell Detective Witherspoon to stop looking for those people. I'll just figure it out myself."

"Listen, I can check up on Gordon without talking to him. If I see that there's no red flags, then I'll wait and see what Witherspoon turns up. Fair enough?"

"What do you mean exactly? Check up on Gordon?"

"Run reports on him. See if he has anything in his past that may prove useful. Since he's a supervisor at the bank—"

"He's the branch manager."

"Since he's the branch manager, then I'd think he'd have to be pretty clean to hold that position."

"My thoughts exactly."

Detective Bowen lifted just one eyebrow this time. "Is there something going on between the two of you I should know about?"

"What? Me and Gordon? No. I barely know the man."

"What's Gordon's last name?"

"Ames. But that doesn't prove there's anything between us."

She chuckled. "Of course not. I just need his last name to run the background check."

Of course.

"Is there anything you can tell me about this letter?" She picked it up again. "Anything significant?"

"Not this time. I mean, it's about the meadow again." I strolled over to the front window. "The way it's described sounds like the same one where Billy died. But it's hard to say if it's the exact one."

"And that was in West Virginia, right?"

I nodded. "Other than that, she just describes it. Sounds beautiful. Peaceful."

"That's it?"

I looked out the window. The snow fell at a pretty good clip. "The writing seems more mature."

"Have you noticed? It seems like the person writing these is getting older with each one?"

I watched a singular snowflake float past the window. "Even though I was finding it hard to determine whether these were from a little boy or a little girl in the beginning, it is clear to me now that it was a little girl. This latest one was written by a woman. A young woman. You can still feel the hope in her voice. In her words. She still has a life ahead of her."

Unlike me.

Detective Bowen stopped asking questions and read the letter. "She supposedly played with a bear cub while the mother bear watched? Don't you find that a little hard to believe?"

Compared to all the letters? Are you kidding?

I turned around and stared straight at her. "No harder than writing to me about things from my past that can't be explained."

Detective Bowen folded the letter and placed it back in the box. "Since you put it like that, I suppose belief is a matter of perspective, isn't it?"

I turned back to the window. "I have no idea what to believe anymore."

She stood, grabbing the package, the letter and the money inside. "Is there anyone else you can think of who might be a person of interest? Someone who watches you every day, always seems to be around, always acts nice, always—"

The wife-beater.

I had wondered about him before but dismissed him as not the type for this sort of thing. But…

"There is this one guy. He lives in this building. He's Hispanic, I think. Maybe not. But definitely foreign. He's always wearing one of those wife-beater t-shirts, you know? The tank top kind? And he wears a coat with some basketball team on it. He hangs around with some other guys who all wear similar jackets."

"How old do you think he is?"

"Twenties. No older than thirty."

"And how many friends have you seen him with?"

"No more than three at any time. As a matter of fact, when I pulled up tonight, I was depressed. I just sat in my car and cried for like, fifteen minutes, at least. Then, all of a sudden, I heard a knock on my passenger window, and it was him. He asked if I was okay. Said he saw me pull up but stay in the car. When he walked up, he said he saw me crying when he looked in the window."

"Then what happened?"

"After I told him I was just having a bad day, he wished me a Merry Christmas and then met up with a couple of his friends down by the corner."

"So they were on foot."

"He's always on foot. I've never seen him or his friends use a vehicle. Not even a cab."

"Do you know his name?"

I frowned. "Afraid not. But he lives in 3-C. I did see him come out of that apartment the other day. And when I come home, he's often standing on the fire escape outside that apartment, watching me enter the building."

"Does he do that a lot?"

"What? Watch me? All the time."

"Sounds like I need to talk to him."

"Is it going to make living here more awkward than it already is?"

"Possibly."

"Then, I'd rather you not do that."

"I'll be discreet."

Monday

December 22, 2014

CHAPTER THIRTY-SIX

Sun Ridge National Bank
Manhattan, NY

I punched in my code and entered the bank through the employee entrance. The parking garage was under the bank, and it was nice to be able to go to your car in the evening and not have to scrape ice off the windshield.

Something to be thankful for, I guess.

I went through the motions for most of the morning. One customer after another. Each one blurring together with the one before and after. I was doing my job, handing out cash, taking deposits, doing much more of the former than the latter, yet my heart just wasn't in it. People would wish me a Merry Christmas, and all I wanted to say was, "Bah! Humbug!"

It was three days until Christmas. The only person I had bought a gift for was Joanie. Now, I didn't care whether she got it or not. I would probably return it now. Put that money toward the electric bill.

I had no idea what to get Momma. LIPC was so strict on what they could have in their rooms, it made gift giving difficult.

For the last three years, I had just decided to grace her with my presence and bring some cookies, but this year, with the way I felt, she was going to be lucky if I showed up at all.

The door to our teller section opened, and Gordon stepped inside and closed it behind him. "Hello, ladies. Everything going all right?"

"Wonderful, Mr. Ames," Natasha said. Natasha Bransen was twenty-something, model-thin, and bubbly. She wore dresses that usually rivaled the amount of cotton in an aspirin bottle, and always wore enough make-up for all of us. "It's been brisk, but that's to be expected, right? *It's the day before the night before Christmas, and we're busy-busy-busy being good,* right? Well, it's actually a couple of days before that, but you know what I mean."

Did she just sing that?

Oh, gag.

"That's true," Gordon said. A flustered flush of red swept across his face. "Busy time of the year, for sure."

Natasha handed the man at her window his deposit slip and wished him "Happy Holidays." Then, she turned toward Gordon. "Well, I just want to say, and I think I can speak for all of us, we love working here. You're the best, Mr. Ames. We hope you have a Merry Christmas."

No, honey.

This won't increase your bonus.

Gordon glanced at me and the other tellers. A small smirk appeared in the corner of his mouth. "Thank you, Natasha. You all are doing a wonderful job. I believe this may be the best group of tellers we've had in quite some time."

Natasha's eyes widened with delight. She giggled like a middle school girl standing in front of her movie star heartthrob for the very first time. She interlaced her fingers and pushed her palms toward the floor, apparently not knowing what to do with her hands. "Well, thank you, Mr. Ames. You just made our day."

No. That wasn't over the top at all.

Why don't you bow down, honey?

Kiss his feet.

Offer to bear him many children.

I could tell Gordon was uncomfortable, and I found it a little amusing. I watched him squirm for a couple more seconds before stepping in to help. "Uh, Mr. Ames, as you know, I'm the newest employee here. Just what? Five days? So, my feelings are a little different from Natasha's. Not bad, mind you, but having worked at another bank for four years, I do believe there are some things we do here at Sun Ridge that could be modified and improved. If you'd like, I'd love to discuss them with you. At your convenience, of course." I lifted my brow, hoping he understood.

He did.

"We're always looking for ways to improve, Miss Hamar." Gordon looked at the other ladies and the lines outside the window. "I think these ladies can handle the traffic for a few minutes. Miss Hamar, shut your window down, and let's discuss those ideas, shall we?" Gordon motioned toward the door.

"Uh, sure." I tried my best to act surprised. I looked around at the other women. A pained expression on my face. "Are you all sure it's okay? I don't want to leave you guys with it being busy."

"This won't take long, Miss Hamar," Gordon said.

I shrugged, offered a shame-faced grimace for dramatic effect, and set the Next Window Please sign in front of my spot.

We exited the teller area and strolled across the lobby toward the elevator.

"Go get your coat," Gordon said. "We're going to my other office. Meet you at the parking garage elevator in five minutes."

∼

THE ELEVATOR DOOR OPENED, and Gordon stood off to one side. "All aboard."

"Where's this other office of yours?" I entered the elevator.

"For me to know, and you to find out." He leaned forward and pressed the button for the basement.

"Okay, then." We both faced forward toward the door.

"Thank you for getting me out of the teller area," he said. "I try to stop by and encourage the employees, but Natasha can be over the top sometimes."

"My pleasure. I was about to throw up all over your shoes, so I had to do something."

Gordon blurted out a guffaw as the door shut. "Natasha's always been that way. You get used to it after a while. She means well."

"Are you that oblivious, Gordon?"

"Pardon me?"

"You didn't see it, did you?"

"See what?" The elevator started its descent.

"Natasha was coming on to you. Trying to butter you up. Get you to notice her."

"Natasha? Nah. She's been like that since we hired her."

I peered at Gordon. My "Hello?" face must have done the trick.

"No, seriously. She's…cute and all, but she's only three years older than my daughter. I could never be interested in someone that age. Not in that way. Too many obstacles."

"The gentleman doth protest too much, methinks." I nodded and looked straight ahead.

"I'm not protesting…"

I turned my head slightly, just enough to be able to see his face.

"Okay, maybe a little."

"Do you find her attractive?"

Gordon bit his lip. "A little."

"Just a little?"

"Okay, yes. She's very attractive. Is that what you wanted to hear? She's very pretty, in a Barbie doll kind of way. But, she's not my type."

The elevator door opened, and he motioned outside. "After you."

I walked through the door and waited for him to come alongside. "What is your type, Gordon? Because if she's not your type, then you apparently don't like hot, pretty, thin, athletically built blondes who could probably get any man they wanted."

"There's more to a person than the outside. All that fawning back there? Drives me crazy."

"Oh, Mr. Ames…You're so funny…You make me laugh. I love working for you. Thank you so much for hiring me. I'll never let you down. I'll be the best employee you've ever had because you're just so wonderful."

Gordon chuckled harder and harder as I added each sentence.

"Mr. Ames, there aren't enough words in the English language to describe how—and I think I can speak for all humanity everywhere when I say—how magnanimous and kind-hearted you are. I think they should put up a statue of your likeness in front of the bank. Then, all the employees could stop by it on our way to and from work and pay homage."

"Okay, you've made your point." He pointed toward the stairs. "This way."

"Where are you taking me, Mr. Ames?"

"It's on a need to know basis."

We plodded up a flight of stairs and out onto the street.

"This way." He pointed to our left.

"Why, Mr. Ames, this looks like the way to the coffee shop. You do know I'm on the clock, right?"

"Yes, and so am I. And you were going to share some ideas with me on how to improve our teller stations, if memory serves."

"Yes, but…"

"But what? Can't business happen anywhere? Why does it always have to occur in musty offices?"

"Your office is anything but musty."

"Musty is a state of mind, Miss Hamar." He drew in a deep breath. "I prefer the crisp air of a New York winter and the delicious smell of a fresh cup of coffee, don't you?"

I do.

"I've always preferred fall and winter to spring and summer. And who doesn't like the smell of fresh ground coffee?"

Gordon chuckled. "Natasha, for one. At last year's company Christmas party—you just missed this year's party, by the way, we hold it on the first Saturday of December—she went on for ten minutes about how the roasting process used to create coffee beans was one big cancer-causing agent. As it turns out, she's an organic chamomile tea drinker."

"With a spoonful of homegrown honey, no doubt,"

"How did you know?"

"She just looks the part."

Gordon squinted slightly. "She does, doesn't she?"

"Yep. Along with tai-chi, yoga, and tofu turkeys at Thanksgiving."

"Now that you mention it, she did say something about how eating turkey at Thanksgiving bordered on being an animal rights violation."

With a shake of my head, I laughed. "I have known a few turkeys in my day. All of them human, though. But now that you mention it, some acted like animals."

Gordon opened the door to The Columbian Coffee Shop. "Ladies first."

I walked inside, and smiling from ear to ear, standing behind the counter, was Heather. "Ohhh, look at the two of you," she said as Gordon stepped inside and allowed the door to ease shut.

"You two make a great couple." She pulled her shoulders in and turned her hands upward. "Just sayin'."

Gordon looked at me, and I shyly glanced at him. "Just the coffee, for now," I said. "Don't you think?"

"Uh, yes, of course."

Heather beamed and shook her head. "You guys are so cute. So, what will it be?"

Gordon waved me forward. "You first."

"I'm gonna try another one of those peppermint mocha frappes. Biggest one you have."

She grabbed a cup. "You liked the last one, I take it?"

"It was heavenly."

Heather smiled and scribbled my name on a cup. "And you, sir."

"I'll take my usual," Gordon said.

I unzipped my purse, and Gordon placed his hand on mine. "Don't you even think about it. My treat. Besides, this was my idea."

His hand remained just a split second longer than I thought was customary, but I didn't mind. "Thank you. Although I'm afraid you're gonna think I'm not only trying to get out of doing my job but also attempting to get a free drink out of the deal."

"Nonsense."

"Well, Mr. Ames, I just want to say how wonderful and generous you are. You're the best boss any girl could ever have in the entire city. What am I saying? The entire country. The world, even."

Heather turned slightly. An inquisitive expression etched in her brow.

Gordon must have seen it too. "Uh, she's just being…it's an inside joke."

"Oh, Mr. Ames," I said, feigning laughter, "you're so funny too. The whole package, you are."

"Would you stop it? People are gonna start talking."

I lowered my voice. "Uh, they already are, Gordon. You should hear what people say about Natasha and you."

His frustrated aspect morphed into one of concern. "What have you heard?"

"Not much. I've only worked there five days. But, what I have heard is—"

"Gossip?" Heather said, her back turned to us.

I looked Heather's way before turning to Gordon. "Precisely. The junk that starts office wars."

"That's not good." Gordon leaned against the counter. "Tell me. What have you heard?"

Heather stepped over to us and set our drinks down on the counter. "Yeah, what are people saying about my friend here?"

I stared at both of them. "Are you sure?"

"Yes," they both said in unison.

"You were seen walking her to her car one evening."

I could see the wheels turning in Gordon's head. "I walk out to my car with a lot of people. And yes, a couple of times she was one of them."

"But her car was supposedly on the other side of the parking garage."

"I don't remem—" Gordon stopped mid-sentence. The recollection became clear. "I do remember. She said she thought she had a flat tire and wondered if I would check it out for her."

"And did she?"

"No."

"Of course not," Heather said. "Oldest trick in the book."

"What else are people saying?"

"That she was seen in your office a couple of months ago. That she was in there for quite a while."

Gordon closed his eyes and huffed. "Her yearly evaluation was in October. Did anyone say that Mildred was also in there with us?"

"No."

"Of course not," Heather said again. "She probably talked about her evaluation and explained how you and she really hit it off."

I pointed at Heather. "Now that you mention it…"

"Please say she didn't?" Gordon said.

"She didn't," I said with a smile. "I was just messin' with ya."

Gordon lifted his finger, trying to connect the dots. "About what part?"

"I just made up the part about you two hitting it off. Everything else is true."

"Look, Gordon," Heather said, "you need to be careful. You're a good-looking man. A successful man. A man of integrity. All it takes is one little opportunist to ruin everything for you. Please promise me you'll be careful."

"It's apparent to me now that I need to be extremely careful." He looked at Heather, then at me. "Even this could be misconstrued as some romantic liaison. We did walk out of the lobby together, got on an elevator together. For all the tongue-waggers out there, we could be in my office, right now, doing who knows what."

"Well, Gordon," I said, holding my coffee up and gripping it firmly, "I know you don't know me very well, but if there's one thing I'm certain about, it's this: I made a pact a long time ago with myself. 'Never get your honey where you make your money.' So, as long as I'm employed at Sun Ridge, you have nothing to worry about. It's nothing personal. It's just that I've seen too many people ruin their lives and careers because they got mixed up with someone at work. Then, when the relationship fell apart, so did the job. And many times, their lives too."

"Well, there you go, Gordon," Heather said. She pointed back and forth between Gordon and me. "You have nothing to worry about unless you fire her, or she quits." She smiled.

Gordon missed her little joke. "I just hate it when people gossip and spread lies."

I placed my hand on Gordon's shoulder. "People are gonna talk. That's what busybodies do. So, let's get a table. We'll sit down and laugh and smile and talk and look like we are 'hitting it off.' And don't be surprised if we see one of your other employees out on the sidewalk spying in on us so she can report back to the gaggle of gossiping gals."

"That sounds like a plan to me," Heather said.

Gordon waved toward a back table with his head. "Maybe we'll be harder to see back there."

"Oh, Gordon, you sly fox."

The snow had stopped falling, and the sun was trying to peek through the clouds when we sat down. We sipped our coffees in silence.

Gordon checked his cell phone, texted someone, and placed it on the table. He grabbed his coffee, took another swig, and set it down but held onto it like a depressed sailor at a bar, clutching his scotch and soda. "You know, when my wife passed away, it was the darkest time of my life. I was suddenly a single dad with a son and a daughter. Getting along with my son was easy enough. However, I knew I would only be able to relate to my daughter half the time. There wouldn't be those conversations only a mother and daughter can have. No matter how hard I tried to understand her, I could only do so much.

"It made me appreciate all those single parents out there. Mothers feeling inadequate with the raising of their sons. Other fathers feeling like I did.

"So, I vowed to be a shining example to my daughter. I wanted her to be proud of me. I wanted her to feel comfortable enough to bring me anything. To not be afraid to talk to me about whatever she was dealing with."

"Did it work?"

"I don't know. I mean, she turned out great. But I'm not sure how much of that had to do with me. I've always thought the credit should go to her mother."

"I'm sure it had a lot to do with you too. Take it from someone who spent the majority of her life on the other end of those musings of yours. I longed for a father I could respect. One I could be proud of. As a little girl, I often thought that I wanted to marry someone just like my daddy. However, as I got older, and as he changed, I no longer wished that for myself.

"I often think that's why I never married. I didn't have any role model to judge other men by. I only knew what not to marry. And trust me, I've witnessed, been introduced to, and stumbled across a lot of what not to marry over the years. But I never got to see what was possible. I guess..." I took a sip of my coffee, trying to get a grip on my emotions. "In some small way, that's why I feel so inadequate and awkward when I am around men like you. Like Heather said. You're successful. You've obviously been an awesome dad to your daughter. You still love your wife even though she's been gone for some time now. You treat your employees with respect. You've made a good impression on Heather and her family. It seems that everywhere I turn, when someone is talking about you, it's always good."

Gordon's eyes moistened. "Thank you."

"And when I'm around men like you, I frankly don't know how to act. Don't know what to expect."

Gordon took another drink of his coffee. "I'm nothing special. Trust me on that one."

"Hey, I'm not so sure. Even Natasha thinks the world of you."

He frowned. "You just had to ruin a blessed moment, didn't you?"

"That's what I do." I grinned. "I don't get too many of those either. So, when a blessed moment comes, I don't know how to behave. So, I default to humor when I'm with people and self-loathing when I'm alone."

"That's a shame."

It is, isn't it?

"But hey, I did have a 'blessed moment' yesterday. Want to hear about it?"

"Sure." He took another drink of his coffee.

"I received a small box in the mail yesterday. Inside was what looked like a Christmas gift. Little box about this big." I demonstrated the size with my hands. "Inside, with a letter, like the ones I told you about a few days ago, was two thousand dollars in cash."

Gordon's eyes became saucers. "Wow."

"I know. My thoughts exactly. And I still can't imagine who would do such a thing."

"And it was addressed to you? Not someone else?"

"It was addressed to me. Just like all the letters. Same handwriting. Everything. Just in a gift box instead of an envelope."

Gordon wrinkled his brow and lifted his finger like he was trying to remember something. "Wasn't that about how much you needed for rent?"

"Yes." My eyes flared. "Isn't that wild?"

"That's a lot of money. Have the police gotten any closer to catching these people?"

"Afraid not." I grasped my cup of coffee. A sudden wrestling match in my gut ensued. "But there is one thing I should probably mention. I'd rather you hear it from me first."

Gordon didn't say anything. He just waited. Took another sip of his drink.

"Because I got a large sum of money, and because I work at the bank…"

"They think you stole it?"

"I'm sure that's crossed their mind. But because I self-reported it, and since the bank hasn't reported any stolen money—"

"They think there's someone on the inside?"

"No, silly. They're looking at anyone I know who might have the means to give me that much money."

Gordon's soft face hardened. "They're checking on me?"

I pinned my lips together in an embarrassed grin. "I told them to leave you alone. That you had nothing to do with this, but they said they had to at least do a background check on you."

He leaned back in his chair. "I'm not worried. Like I said before, I have nothing to hide."

"I'm so sorry. I tried to get them to drop the case, but they said it's proven to be too strange to just drop it now. Because of the letters and their content, they're afraid this whole thing may involve the welfare of a child."

"It's okay. I understand."

I studied Gordon's face, his movement. His words didn't seem to match. I could tell what little trust had been formed between us just eroded.

"You see?" I said. "I've hurt you. I can see it in your demeanor. And even though that's the last thing I would ever wish to do, it happened, nevertheless." I dropped my head. "Story of my so-called life."

"What are you talking about?"

"I'm a curse, Gordon. I'm a plague. This is why no one wants to be around me. That's why everyone in my life has abandoned me." I wiped my eyes. "Even when I think things are going to get better, when I see a sliver of hope, something happens that rips it out of my life."

"I'm still here."

"But I've hurt you."

"No. It's not that at all."

"But your face. You look sad. Like you've been offended."

"You said they were going to run a background check on me, right?"

"That's what they told me. Not sure when, though."

"Doesn't matter. Let them. They won't find anything except a couple of parking tickets from back when I was in college."

"That's it?"

Gordon smiled and leaned forward again. "I may be a good person, Rachel, but I'm not a saint."

I watched him as he spoke. The humble appraisal. The carefully chosen words. The slight squint of his left eye when he felt inadequate. It was amazing to me how much you get to know a person in just a few short days. That's why the actions of the police hurt me more, I think, than they did him.

I finally took a deep breath and did something I neither foresaw nor expected. I reached out and placed my hands around his, looking like I was helping him hold his coffee. "You're a saint to me. You give me hope, Gordon Ames. In mankind. In people. It's nice to find someone who, even though he doesn't know me well, still treats me with respect. Then, when that person learns more and more about my crazy past, my even crazier present, and has no idea what to expect from my future, he doesn't run away. He's still here. He still cares. He didn't get his coffee to go even though he could walk out with it at any time."

He smiled. "You're right. You do default to humor a lot."

I removed my hands slowly. "I've been told it's my coping mechanism. With my life, the way it's been, I've had to use it a great deal."

Gordon's eyes followed my hands. "Well, Miss Hamar, you don't have to worry about me leaving. I'm a good enough judge of character to know that you are definitely one, but in a good way."

Finally, a man with a sense of humor.

And he gets me.

I just may need to quit my job after all.

Or break my pact.

CHAPTER THIRTY-SEVEN

New York City Police Dept.
33rd Precinct

Detective Bowen sat at her desk, plinking away at her computer. The Technical Assistance Response Unit, better known as TARU, had gone over the video feeds from the Jericho post office. The video was authentic. No one had tampered with it.

Watching Mr. Singh disappear through the door after delivering one of Rachel Hamar's letters, she had decided to request the video feeds from every day a letter was mailed. Was Mr. Singh the only person mailing them? Were there others? If so, who? Did they disappear too? Or was that just a camera malfunction on the days in question? All these questions she hoped would be answered as she scrolled through one video after another, watching patron after patron walk in and out of the post office.

This was the tedious part of the job she despised.

She was also awaiting the arrival of a person of interest. He wasn't a suspect. Not yet. But his involvement warranted a conversation. Detective Witherspoon agreed. He was on his way too. Wanted to be there during the interrogation.

It had been about twenty minutes when two road patrol officers escorted a man inside.

"Take him to holding. I'm waiting on Detective Witherspoon to arrive."

"What's this about?" the man being escorted said. His New York Knicks jacket was unzipped, and a tank top t-shirt was the only thing on underneath.

"Sir, you're not under arrest," Detective Bowen said. "We just need to talk to you."

"You could've done that at my place."

"Sir, under the circumstances, we couldn't. When we talk, I'll explain everything. Then it will make more sense."

"You have no right."

"Sir, we have every right to question anyone we need to."

"But I don't have to comply. As a matter of fact, I can walk out of here right now, and there ain't a thing you can do about it."

"I hate to see this escalate into something that doesn't need to happen, but if you want to play hard ball, then I can too."

"You ain't got nothin' on me."

"Oh, you'd be surprised."

"Well? If you got somethin', then arrest me." The man jerked his hands out in front of him, pinning his wrists together.

"Do I need to arrest you, Mr. Rey?"

He dropped his hands. "And that's another thing. How do you know my name?" He pointed his finger at Detective Bowen. "You been illegally wire tappin' my place, man?"

"Nope. Didn't need to. Your name's on the contract of the apartment you lease. It's all public record, Mr. Jesus Salvador Rey."

"Do I need to call my lawyer?"

"Do you have something to hide, Mr. Rey?"

"No."

"Then, why don't you calm down, take a seat in our holding room, and—"

Just then, Detective Witherspoon walked up. "What's the problem?"

"Detective Witherspoon, meet Mr. Jesus Salvador Rey. We were just taking him to our holding room to have a little chat."

"Let me guess," Witherspoon said. "He wasn't cooperating?"

Detective Bowen looked at Mr. Rey with a fake smile on her face. "We've been doing this job a long time. He's been at it even longer than I have. There's not a whole lot we haven't seen, heard, or dealt with."

Witherspoon placed his hands into the pockets of his trench coat. "What she's tryin' to say, *hombre*, is the quicker you cooperate, the quicker this will be over, and you can go on your merry way and have a Merry Christmas. But if you cause problems, or impede this investigation, then you may need to write a letter to Santa and have your presents diverted to the county lockup. *Capisce?*"

Rey huffed and relaxed a little. "Let's get this over with."

The two road patrol officers led him to the holding room while Bowen and Witherspoon stayed back.

"We don't have anything on this guy," Bowen said, "so don't go in there full guns-a-blazin'. Capisce? If he clams up, then this was a big waste of time, and we're no closer to catching these guys."

"Roger that."

Bowen picked up a folder from her desk and opened it. "He lives two doors down from Rachel Hamar. According to her, he watches her all the time. He stands on the fire escape and watches her approach the building when she's coming home from work. He's bumped into her in the hallway. He's even confronted her out in front of the building. So, he's had some dealings with her. I want to know why he's so infatuated with her."

"Employment history?"

"Works a part-time job at a warehouse in the Bronx."

"That's it?"

"So far."

Witherspoon slipped off his coat and draped it over Bowen's chair. "Well, worst-case scenario…even if he's not part of this letter writing business, at least he'll be aware we know about him and his actions toward this Hamar woman."

"Exactly. If he's just creepin' her, then maybe it will make him stop."

"All right." Witherspoon motioned toward the holding room with a wave of his hand. "Let's get this show on the road."

"Remember: my precinct, my interrogation."

Witherspoon lifted his hands in surrender. "Yes, *kemo sabe.*"

"And would you knock off the foreign language lessons? They're annoying."

"Aye, Aye, *capitán.*"

Bowen groaned and headed for the holding room.

"I was just trying to have a little fun, Detective. It's only three days until Christmas. Where's your joy?"

"It arrives after I clock out."

"You know we never really clock out on this job."

She did. That's what kept her up at night. The Central Park Cameraman. Now, the letters to Rachel Hamar. It was the unsolved cases that caused the lack of sleep.

She didn't respond to Witherspoon's comments and opened the door to the holding room. The officer inside exited, and she told him and his partner standing outside they could go, thanking them for their help.

The two detectives entered and closed the door behind them. Bowen set a folder on the table and sat down opposite Mr. Rey. Witherspoon remained standing by the door.

"Mr. Rey," Bowen began, "I asked those two officers to bring you here for a couple of reasons. First, I figured questioning you in the neighborhood might give people the wrong impression, especially the boys you hang with."

"Ah, yeah, nothin' like being tossed into the back of a cop car to keep your street cred intact, huh?"

"Well, that was one reason why we did it this way."

"So, my crew might respect that, but what about all the other people on that block? Now they're gonna think I'm some drug dealer or gang banger." Rey snorted. "Nice job."

"That brings me to my second reason for bringing you here. Are you?"

"Am I what?"

"A drug dealer? Gang banger?"

"Man, I ain't got time for this." Rey stood.

Witherspoon took a step closer to him. "Sit down, and answer the question. You gotta know we wouldn't have you in here if you were just helpin' old ladies cross the street."

Rey's scowl remained as he sat back down. "I ain't none of those things."

"Mr. Rey," Bowen continued, "can you tell me what interest you have in a woman by the name of Rachel Hamar?"

"Who? I don't know no woman by that name."

"Rachel Hamar. She lives in your apartment building. Single, white female. Mid-thirties. Brown hair. About five feet six. Drives a Dodge Neon." Bowen waited for those details to sink in. "Ring any bells?"

"Okay, yeah. I think I know who you're talkin' about. But I don't know her."

"But you watch her."

"Watch her?"

"From the fire escape? From the street corner? In the hallway outside your apartment?"

Rey looked up at Witherspoon who had drifted back to his

original station. "Are you accusing me of stalkin' this lady?" He turned back to Bowen.

"You tell me. Why are you so infatuated with her?"

"I'm not infatuated with her. She lives with another woman. About the same age. Darker hair. They come and go a lot. Just like half of the other people in that building. I kind of keep an eye out for everybody in the place. You know how it can be in that neighborhood."

"We do."

"Then why don't more police cruise the streets?"

"We can't be everywhere, Mr. Rey," Bowen said. "Besides, you know as well as I do that if we did have units patrolling the streets, the real thugs would just wait until the coast was clear."

"Yeah, but you might roll up on somethin' goin' down."

"That's right. We might," Witherspoon said. "And watch as the perps scatter like roaches when the light comes on. And if we caught one of them, they'd tell us they didn't do anything. If we found a witness, they'd say they didn't see anything. Happens all the time."

Rey sucked his teeth, making a smacking sound. "That's because they live in fear for their lives."

Bowen played thoughtfully with the pencil in her hand. "Fear from whom, Mr. Rey?"

"Gangs. Police. Immigration. Lots of things."

"So, the very people who could help them, the police, are lumped together with the real enemies? Does that make any sense?"

Rey shrugged.

"And the people of the neighborhood realize those drug dealers and gang bangers are assisted with their terrorism of the neighborhoods by everyone keeping their lips sealed, right?"

"Hey, I'm just tellin' you straight up the way it is. And I get it. It's a messed-up world we livin' in. So, that's why I do what I do."

"What do you do, Mr. Rey?"

"You accused me of watching people. I don't watch them like you think I do. I ain't no creep or stalker or anything like that. I watch out for people. Like that woman you said I watch. From the fire escape, I can see the entire street. If someone came runnin' up to try and rob that woman, I'd see 'em comin'."

"And what would you do about it, tough guy?" Witherspoon said.

"Jump off the escape and help her."

"That fire escape is at least three floors up."

"But, if I slide down to the second-floor landing, then I can jump. I've done it before."

"And you'd chase after the bad guys?" Bowen said.

Rey nodded. "Done that before too."

"So," Witherspoon said, "we have a good Samaritan in our midst, Detective. Not a low life."

"I'm telling you the truth," Rey said. "Go ask anyone in my building. You can ask my friends too. They helped me out one time."

"Did they, now?" Witherspoon said.

"We were standin' on the corner one evenin', just chillin', when some young punks walked up the street, the whole time with their eye on that elderly lady who lived on the bottom floor. She was coming back home from Weston's Department Store. Had a couple of bags hanging from one arm. Her purse was over her other shoulder.

"Those punks followed her for three blocks, and then just as she rounded the corner of our building and stepped into that little courtyard, I guess they thought they was out of sight. Me and my boys ran into the courtyard just in time. They bashed that woman on the head and were stealing her bags and her purse."

"So," Bowen said, "what did you do?"

"We bashed in their heads. Ain't no one supposed to be doin' that stuff to widows and orphans."

"But what about the elderly lady?"

"Uh," Rey said, "she was okay. We tried to get her to go to the hospital. We even called for an ambulance, but she refused to go."

"No one called the police?"

Rey lowered his chin and peered at Bowen.

"Okay," Bowen said with a sigh, "so I get why you didn't call the police, based on our previous discussion. But don't you see, Mr. Rey? Now those punks are free to terrorize some other elderly lady instead of being locked up."

"I'm sorry, Detective, but please don't get angry with me if I choose to disagree."

"They would have been charged with assault and battery, robbery, probably with a deadly weapon because I'm sure one of them had a weapon, and stalking, just for starters. Link them to other unsolved crimes on the books, and the list gets longer."

Rey just peered back at her. Didn't nod. Didn't chuckle. Didn't smile. "And because they are juveniles, they'll get some slap-on-the-wrist juvy program and be back out on the street in six months, right? If not sooner."

"It all depends."

Rey looked away from her. "And that's why me and my boys do what we do. Your justice system…it lacks…how should we say it? Justice? Not for the innocent people who get attacked, eh? It only protects the criminals."

"This is where I disagree with you, Mr. Rey."

"Well, Detective, I know one of those thugs who attacked that old lady." Rey leaned forward and placed his elbows on the table. "Been in and out of juvy since he was ten. Got kicked out of his school too. Has to attend some special school for troubled teens. He never goes, though. Instead, he breaks into houses during the day when people aren't home and attacks weak people at night. Got himself a nice little crew too. And they know how to play the system." Rey smirked. "Ain't no justice in it. It's just a system, and those boys have figured out how to work it."

"So, you and your boys exact your own brand of vigilante justice in the 'hood then?" Witherspoon said.

"It's not much, but it keeps our building and our block safe. We ain't had any issues since those punks got beat down. That was over two years ago. If you don't believe me, check your own statistics. Word gets out on the street, you know?"

"And what did you do to those boys, if I may ask? Or do I even want to know?"

Rey smiled but in a painful sort of way. "You don't want to know. You probably wouldn't believe it, even if I told you."

DETECTIVES BOWEN and Witherspoon questioned Jesus Salvador Rey for another twenty minutes before releasing him. He declined a ride back to the apartment complex and chose to walk the three-to-four blocks instead.

"I had to let him go," Bowen said. "I had absolutely nothing on him."

"And you believe all that vigilante justice baloney he fed us back there?"

"He sounded pretty convincing to me."

"We need to find that elderly lady he talked about and interview her. See if his story checks out. We can talk to the landlord and get a name."

"I'll add that to my list of things to do."

"Oh, hey, speaking of lists of things to do." Witherspoon reached into his suit coat pocket and pulled out a small notebook. "I found one of the people who dropped off one of the letters at the On-Time Couriers' store in Queens. It was a lady. Her name is Beatrice Marino. She's an on-call LPN during the day. Floats from hospital to hospital, filling in when they're short-handed.

She then works for some kind of meal delivery outfit during the evening hours, delivering dinners to shut-ins."

"Record?"

"No. She's clean. Claims some man dressed in hospital scrubs was working at one of the hospitals she was filling in for. She said she overheard him say he had to mail this letter but didn't have time to before they closed, so she offered to mail it for him. Turns out, she was driving right by the Queens store on her way to deliver a meal that evening. She got to the Queens store at 6:50 p.m. They closed at seven."

"Good grief. There are too many rabbit trails. Whoever is doing all this is really good at planning things."

"Yeah. Tell me about it. Now I have to track down this male nurse who was working at that hospital at the time in question."

"Did you get a description?"

Witherspoon expelled an exhausted chuckle. "Male. Six foot. Dark hair. Cut short. Average build."

"Well, that should narrow it down."

"Needles and haystacks, Detective. Needles and haystacks."

CHAPTER THIRTY-EIGHT

West 173rd Street
Washington Heights, NY

Gordon and I spent the better part of an hour at the coffee shop. When we returned, the elevator dropped me off at the lobby, and he went upstairs to his office.

Sandy from Sun Ridge probably had the phone pinned to her ear as soon as he cleared her desk, spreading the news on her cheery, holiday gossip hotline.

All eyes were on me as soon as I entered the corridors leading out into the main lobby. I went back to my teller's station and opened my window.

I really felt like a fish in a bowl now.

All the hungry cats stared, smiled, and winked, waiting for me to spit out a tasty morsel.

Finally, one of them couldn't contain herself any longer. "So? How was it?"

I faced Barbara Howser and placed a hand on my hip. "How was what?"

"The coffee."

"So, we were right. You guys were spying on us."

"Oh, no. Nothing of the sort. Pamela Carson, the red head who works at the law firm next door, she's been a friend of mine for years. She ran down on her break to grab coffee for several of us. She happened to see you two in the corner. I believe she said she saw you holding his hand at one point, if memory serves?"

I dropped my chin to my chest. "It was nothing like what you're imagining."

"Oh, I don't know about that." A sly smile crept across her face. "I can imagine a lot of things."

I'm sure you can.

"It's not what it seems. Trust me."

"Did you tell him how we could make things more efficient around here?"

"I did. He said he would take those recommendations under advisement and bring them to their next leadership meeting."

Barbara studied me for a few seconds. "That's it?"

"That's it, Barbara."

"You're telling me that you went for coffee with the branch manager, and all you talked about was procedures for how we do things in this tank of ours?"

"Well, not entirely."

"See?" She looked around at our cohorts. "I told you."

I pursed my lips together and nodded with a painful smile. "We talked about you, Barbara. And you, Susanna. And you, Natasha. Even Reggie over there at the customer service counter. We talked about everybody. I mean, isn't that what we do here at Sun Ridge?" I then formed a delightful smile and turned to handle the customer at my window.

Barbara wanted to ask me a question so bad, I thought her head was going to explode.

To prolong her agony, I took my time with the customer until another stepped up to her window.

This little dance lasted the remainder of the day. By the end, I was exhausted. I was tired of the busyness of the job at this festive time of year.

And I was tired of the busybodies.

I drove home, hoping for a relaxing evening. I wanted simply to watch a Christmas movie, sip on some wine, and try to forget that Christmas was less than three days away.

When I got out of my car, the street was awash with the glow of the streetlights. Sporadic Christmas lights adorned certain store fronts and people's apartment windows. It was nothing like Rockefeller Square or Fifth Avenue, but it was something. An attempt to bring the peace of the season into a not-so-peaceful side of town.

I strolled into the mailroom. I felt lighter than usual. No hesitation. No apprehension. Just a desire to open the box and find letter number fifteen inside.

Sure enough, there it was, resting upright against the side like it had experienced a long day as well.

I opened it while I eased up the stairs, not giving thought to the effort but instead, wondering what words I'd find on the page today. Clearing the last step, I slowly made my way to the door of my apartment.

It's always wondrous to hear others singing. In perfect pitch. Perfect tone. Perfect harmony. The human voice just may be the best instrument ever created. As a matter of fact, now that I think about it, I've never seen any instruments around here. Yet music often fills the air.

The music here envelopes you. Resonates from the sky. Reverberates off the mountains. Echoes in the streams. Joins the wind. And as our household grows, the music gets louder, but not in an annoying way, like your eardrums are about to burst. Instead, the sound just grows bolder. Sharper. Like all the notes on the staff are being filled. Every possible harmony attained.

And the most amazing thing about it is, no matter whether I'm lying in the meadow or on my bed or anywhere in between, the music never goes away. You'd think that, in and of itself, would be irritating, but somehow, it's not.

Quite the opposite, actually.

I found myself several feet away from my door. Standing still. Trying to picture in my mind what in the world this person described.

I, too, loved to hear choirs sing. It was wondrous. To hear voices blend into perfect music. To make them blend and mix and meld into a sweet sound you could listen to over and over again. I knew exactly what she was talking about. "The Carol of the Bells" had always been my all-time favorite song this time of year. "O Holy Night" was another. With no instruments. Not even the chords to keep the singers on track. Just voices. Singing.

I entered my apartment and set the letter down on the coffee table with the other fourteen. I poured myself a glass of wine, and instead of watching a movie, I turned on the computer, got on the Internet, found my favorite Christmas song, and clicked Play.

Then I stretched out on the couch, closed my eyes, and listened. Like the girl in the letter.

To the picturesque arrangement of the words…

The rhythmic rhyme…

The heavenly harmony…

The perfect escape…

She was right.

It enveloped me too.

Tuesday

December 23, 2014

CHAPTER THIRTY-NINE

On-Time Courier Service
Main Hub
Brooklyn, NY

Detective Bowen spent the rest of Monday afternoon watching video tape from the post office in Jericho. She finally had to shut it off and go home. It wasn't because exhaustion overtook her. It wasn't because hunger ruled the day. Not because all the leads had dried up.

It was because of disbelief.

She had watched Kenneth Singh deliver all the letters in the beginning, right up until he was apprehended. Then, another On-Time courier took his place. This second courier continued the process until the day Detective Witherspoon determined which stores were used as the initial drop off points. When he made that connection, a different courier service was used to deliver the last few letters.

It was like someone was watching them. While she and Detective Witherspoon gained some ground, it seemed the perpetrator was one step ahead of them. Now, with a new courier service in play, Witherspoon would have to practically start all over.

Establish how this new company kept records.

Determine how these letters entered their courier system.

Visit those stores, request any security camera footage available, and ask around to see if anyone working at those stores remembered these specific letters being dropped off.

Then, after all that legwork, track down those anonymous faces in a crowd of eight million inhabitants of New York City.

"Needles and haystacks," she said, repeating Witherspoon's lament.

But that wasn't the most depressing part of it all.

In each instance, as the courier arrived at the post office in Jericho, he would mail it in the appropriate slot, and then head for the door. And in each instance, just like with Kenneth Singh, the courier would push on the door, exit the lobby, and disappear into thin air, only to reappear the next day.

Even the vehicle, used by the courier to arrive at the post office each time, vanished. Bowen had verified that with the other stores' parking lot camera feeds. At the exact same time stamp Mr. Singh disappeared through the lobby door of the post office, so did his motorcycle from the parking lot.

The same thing happened with the other courier and his minivan.

If it occurred one time, she could buy that. Video and security cameras fail in one way or another all the time. Often, at the most inopportune time. But multiple times? At the same exact moment? Every day? Two different cameras from two different businesses? Probably would have been one more time if they had not apprehended Mr. Singh that evening.

Unbelievable, she thought. And definitely too coincidental.

Someone had to be commandeering the feed. Regardless of what TARU said.

She and Detective Witherspoon were able to catch Kenneth

Singh. And he proved to be just a courier. Doing his job. Faithfully. Without fail. Sounded like a model employee, actually.

So, why would seeing him exit the post office be so bad? What could be so damaging and incriminating about vacating the premises to cause someone to go to all that trouble of changing the video feed? Was Singh receiving something from the person behind all this? Was that when Mr. Singh was getting paid a little extra? Picking up a little holiday cash from some designated location?

Or, was he meeting face-to-face with the person behind it all? Maybe that was it.

Maybe it wasn't the couriers in the video trying to be erased.

Maybe it was the mastermind behind the letters.

This person knew Kenneth Singh could be followed on traffic cameras when he left the post office.

At that moment, Detective Bowen decided she needed to see Mr. Singh one more time.

But tomorrow. Not at seven o'clock at night.

So, here she was, sitting in the On-Time Couriers manager's office at ten o'clock, Tuesday morning, two days before Christmas. Mr. Singh had been pulled off his route, and he was not one bit happy about it.

"I want to call my lawyer," he said. "This is turning into harassment. I told you people I had nothing to do with anything. I just deliver what I'm instructed to deliver. That's all. Tell them, Eugene."

"He has been a good worker for us," Eugene Hahn, the manager/owner, said. "No complaints, and that's important in this line of work, Detective. It's a very competitive business. Customer service is extremely vital."

"Look, Mr. Singh," Detective Bowen said, opening her

laptop, "I'm not here to accuse you of anything. I'm here because I have some questions that need answers, and you were the only person there who can answer them for me."

"Where?"

"At the post office in Jericho."

Kenneth rolled his eyes and held out his hands, pleading. "Not this again? I already told you everything I know. And I can't explain how I disappear."

"Please, I need you both to look at something for me. And yes. It's that video we talked about before. But just work with me here for a minute. Just watch this."

She clicked the mouse, and the video began running simultaneously. Two different camera angles sat side by side on the screen.

"Okay, so here you are, Kenneth, like we noted before." She pointed at the picture on the left. "You're walking up to the post office, and you enter through the main door. Now, here you are, entering the lobby. You stroll up to the mail slot, put the letter inside, and head for the lobby door. Do you both see that? And see how he pulls the door open and steps through?"

Both men nodded.

"Okay, now, watch this, and notice the time stamps. So far, they are completely in sync." She clicked and began the video. "See that?"

"I don't see anything," Eugene said.

"Exactly. We should see Kenneth walking out of the doors on the picture to the left. We saw him open the door from the inside to exit the lobby at time stamp 16:58:22. That's 4:58 p.m. Now, from this outside camera angle, at 16:58:22, the door opens, but nobody comes out."

Eugene and Kenneth looked at each other and shrugged.

"Kenneth, where did you go when you left the post office?" She motioned at the computer. "Point and show us where you went."

"I went that way." He jammed his finger into the computer screen in the upper right corner. "The same way I came. My motorcycle was parked way out towards the end of the grocery store parking lot. I'd driven by the post office, but all the parking spaces were full. So I drove around until I found an empty spot. I walked from there to the post office and back. That's it."

"You didn't deviate at all? Maybe go to the store next door or possibly change your mind and walk out the back of the post office?"

Kenneth's face scrunched into a screwball look. "Why would I do that?"

Bowen sighed. "I don't know. I'm just trying to figure out how you disappear."

"Maybe," Eugene said, "someone has tampered with the camera."

"I had our people go over it with a fine-toothed comb. They said it was authentic. As far as they could tell, no one had spliced anything together."

Eugene pointed at the computer. "How could a comb help you with this?"

Bowen closed her eyes for a moment. She counted to five inside her head. "It's a figure of speech. It means they checked it in every way possible." She sat down, exasperated. "Kenneth, you didn't happen to meet up with anybody, did you?"

He shook his head.

"Nobody stopped you on your way back to your motorcycle to speak to you? Maybe offer you something? Even stop you to ask for the time?"

He seemed to search his memory but could only shake his head again.

"And can you explain how your motorcycle disappears at the same time you exit the post office lobby?"

Kenneth twisted his face in a befuddled manner. "What are you talking about?"

"I have video evidence that shows it vanishing at the exact same time stamp as when you walk through this door." She tapped her computer. "It's there one second, leaning to the side, kickstand extended. The next second, the parking space is empty."

"Again, I do not know what to say." Kenneth pointed at the computer. "I rode my motorcycle to and from that location every time."

"Well then," she said, "it appears we have a real mystery on our hands." She folded up the computer and stood. "Thank you for your time, gentlemen. Sorry for any inconvenience this may have caused. However, if you remember anything, please call me." She handed both men a business card.

"We will, Detective," Eugene said. "Sorry we couldn't be of more help."

"Yeah. Me too."

CHAPTER FORTY

Hempstead Turnpike
Nassau County, NY

Detective Witherspoon sat at a stop light on the Hempstead Turnpike, wondering what his wife had fixed for supper. He was on his way home from the precinct when his cell phone rang.

It had been a long day. One of those one step forward, two steps back kind of days. He glanced at the screen and didn't recognize the number. "Detective Witherspoon."

"Detective, this is Stephanie Nunez, the postmaster here in Jericho. You came in a few days ago and spoke to me about some mysterious letters that've been mailed from here? Another detective asked for copies of our surveillance videos?"

"I remember, Mrs. Nunez. What can I do for you?" He made a lazy right turn.

"Well, you said that if I ever noticed anything suspicious, I should call you."

"Correct. So, I take it you have?"

"Well, I'm not sure what to make of it. But I just watched a man walk into our lobby. He had on one of those courier shirts, like the one you showed me before, but darker. Like a navy blue, but—"

"Yes, yes, Mrs. Nunez. That's the new courier service we are investigating. Their uniforms are darker. What about the man?"

"It's the most bizarre thing I've ever seen. He strolled inside right before closing, mailed something, a letter I'm guessing, although it could have been Christmas cards. He seemed to have several things in his hand, and I couldn't tell—"

Witherspoon waved his hand like that would speed her up. "Okay, so he had several things in his hand. Maybe letters. Maybe Christmas cards. Maybe a whole stack of flyers for the day after Christmas. What's so special about that?"

"Well, you don't have to be so rude, Detective."

He grunted a sigh. "I'm sorry, Mrs. Nunez. It's been a long day, but that's not your fault."

"You want long days? Come work for the postal service this time of year, buster. I'll show you long days."

"Point taken. So, about the man?"

"I was locking up the counter area and watched him through the door. I stuck my head out and asked if he needed to come inside and get anything, like stamps, perhaps. He turned around, looked me dead in the eye, gave me a huge smile, waved his hand, and vanished. I mean, *Poof!* Gone. He was there one second, gone the next."

"What did he look like? This man? White, Black, Hispanic?"

"Uh, he was a black man. About twenty-five years old. Maybe thirty. Clean-shaven. Short hair."

"Any noticeable tattoos or marks, like cuts, scars, glasses, anything?"

"It all happened so fast, but no, not that I can recall."

"Did you get a name?"

"He had a patch on his shirt. It started with a G, but it was written in a cursive script, and I couldn't make out the rest of the name."

Witherspoon spun his car around and headed in the opposite direction. "I'm going to need to see your security cameras."

"Right now?"

"Yes, ma'am. I'm on my way."

Witherspoon hung up and called Detective Bowen.

"Witherspoon, please tell me you have something."

"Hey, I need you to meet me at the post office in Jericho. The postmaster just called me. She claims another courier came into the lobby, mailed a bunch of something, and then vanished right before her eyes."

"You're not serious?"

"Don't shoot the messenger. I'd already left the precinct and was heading home when she called."

"So was I."

"Can you bring your laptop and any and all video footage we have acquired from the post office?"

"Yeah, sure, why not? I have no life."

"Do you want to catch these guys or not?"

Bowen fumed. "I'll be there as soon as I can."

CHAPTER FORTY-ONE

Santorino's Italian Grill
Manhattan, NY

Business was sluggish for a Tuesday night before Christmas. I thought things would have been hopping. People needing to eat while they did last minute shopping. Tourists celebrating with relatives. Others who lived here just wanting a break from the routine of cooking.

That's my motto during the holidays. "No cooking."

Well, that was my motto every day, actually. I hate to cook. But on my salary and with my bills, who could afford to eat out? Even with an employee's discount?

That was why I worked two jobs. Why I decided to work tonight. I was offered the night off, but since the restaurant was closed Christmas Day, I figured I'd switch.

I lost out on the deal. Twice. Lost out on the amount of tips I would have usually earned on a Thursday night as well as the night off.

Story of my life.

And now that Joanie was gone, I may have to give up my

Sunday and Monday nights and work at the restaurant. And if I couldn't find a cheaper place to live, then I'd have to pull a Joanie and get a third job.

And officially have no life left to live.

I walked around and asked the few patrons in my section if they wished to have their drinks refilled or look at the dessert menu. While I was pouring some man a cup of coffee, our hostess walked by me and let out a little squeal like she'd just won the lottery.

"What is it, Robin?" I looked behind her—

"Hello, Miss Hamar."

"Gordon. What are you doing here?"

He wrinkled his face. One eyebrow lowered. "This is a restaurant, correct?"

"Yes, but why here?"

He leaned in close, his face a few inches away but turned slightly so that his mouth was next to my ear. "I hear they have excellent eggplant parmesan here. I also heard their waitresses are the best looking in Manhattan." Straightening his stance, he gave me a quick wink and followed Robin to his table.

In my section.

My section.

He chose my section.

Or did Robin assign him to that table?

I watched Robin seat Gordon, hand him a menu, and tell him about the specials.

When she headed my direction, I spun around and walked beside her. "Did you seat him at that table, or did he request my section?"

Robin giggled. "Yes."

"Yes, what?"

"Yes! He requested your section, and I sat him at that table. When I saw how he looked around for you when he requested your section, I made sure I gave him the most private table you had."

"Thank you."

"Girl! That man is wearing a Hugo Boss. Don't let him get away."

"What's a Hugo Boss?"

"Don't you know anything about fashion? Hugo Boss is a very expensive brand of suits for men. Not the most expensive, but that suit probably set him back eight hundred bucks."

Eight hundred…

I looked down at my new shoes. From the sale rack at Weston's Department Store.

Robin started to laugh. "Hey, girl, you probably should close your mouth before you start drooling on the floor."

"I just bought these." I lifted my foot. "For eight hundred dollars, I could buy like…forty pairs of these. And still have leftover money."

"That's why I said don't let that one get away. If the outside speaks for anything on the inside, don't be a fool."

"But he's my boss. At the bank. Don't you think that'll make things a little awkward?"

"Honey, if that man can afford a Hugo Boss, he doesn't need you to work."

Don't get your honey where you make your money…

But you can send your honey off to work to make the money, right?

I took a deep breath and kept repeating that as I walked up to his table. "Good evening, sir. May I interest you in a beverage? A glass of wine, perhaps?"

Gordon looked up from his menu and gazed at me for an extended moment before returning to the menu. "I would love a glass of wine. What do you recommend?"

"Sir, I have to admit, I'm not much of a wine drinker, and most of the wines we serve here are out of my price range. I'm a grocery store, eight-dollar-a-bottle kind of girl. And I have to sip it slowly to make it last longer.

"However, I have had this one." I leaned over, scanning the menu. The scent of his cologne knocked me off my game for a second.

Focus.

I pointed at the one he bought me just a few days ago. "A very nice gentleman bought me a glass of this particular one to go with my eggplant parmesan. I have to admit, it not only was the best wine I've ever had, but it was an excellent choice as well. Complemented the meal perfectly."

"Well, that gentleman must have seen something in you he really liked to buy you a…" Gordon leaned forward and squinted at the menu. "A twenty-two-dollar glass of wine? He probably asked you for your phone number, too, didn't he?"

I formed a small smirk. "Actually, he did. Not in the traditional way, mind you."

Gordon's expression flipped from pleasant to perplexed. "He did?"

"Yes. On an application I filled out about two or three days later. He got everything, that sly dog. My phone number, address, all my previous employers' information. And now that I think about it, he even got my social security number."

"Hmmm. That's funny. I'll bet he never thought about your application." He peered at me with his adorable eyes and pointed his finger, like a thought just occurred to him. "I'll bet he's been thinking of how to ask you for your phone number and never once did opening your personnel file ever cross his mind."

"Well, if that's what happened, and it must be because he never called me, that actually sounds…refreshing."

"Refreshing? How so?"

"It means he's not a creep. He's not one to take advantage of a business situation for personal gain. Which tells me he's probably like that in his personal relationships as well."

Gordon cleared his throat and tried to keep a straight face. "You're probably right. Well, if he ever gets your phone number, I'll consider him the luckiest man in town."

"Aww, you're just saying that because I'm a lowly waitress working a second job, and you don't want to see me get hurt, especially during the holidays."

"That's true. I don't wish any harm on you whatsoever. Holidays or not. However, that's not why I said that."

We stared at each other for several seconds. I waited for him to say something, but he just kept looking into my eyes.

I finally looked away. "So, sir, was it wine you wanted?"

Gordon sighed but in a pleased manner. The smile said it all. "That wine the man sent you will be perfect."

"Coming right up."

I darted into the kitchen, and Robin was standing around the corner, waiting for me.

"I saw a bunch of smiillleess. He is totally into you, Rach."

"Yeah, I was kind of getting that impression."

"Penny told me he was in here a few days ago."

"Yes."

"Bought you an expensive glass of wine, and now he's your boss? Honeeey, does he have any jobs for me at that bank of his? I could use a man like him in my life."

"Isn't he a little old for you? What are you? Twenty-five?"

"Twenty-three, thank you very much."

"Yeah, well his daughter is your age."

"Age ain't ever been a problem for me. Older men usually have worked past that always lookin' in the mirror stage. They're usually more mature."

"And they usually have more money."

Robin's eyes flared. "Yes, baby."

I placed my hand on her shoulder. "I'll keep you posted on how things go, okay? You don't have to keep spying on us. It's a little disturbing."

"Girl, it's Tuesday. And we're not busy. We got time on our hands. Got to make this night interesting."

Just then, Penny joined us. "Hi, Rach. I see your secret admirer is back."

"Yeah, yeah. Will you guys just not ruin things for me tonight? Okay? Keep your distance, and let me play this out."

"Fine by me," Penny said. "You do know he talks about you all the time, right?"

"And how do you know that?"

"My brother told me. He said he's never seen Gordon like this since his wife passed away."

"He's a widower?" Robin said.

I nodded.

"Oh, honey, please, if you decide he's not your type, then will you put a good word in for me? Widowers are the best, I hear."

Momma's right. This world is going to hell in a hand basket. All the Robins of the world will be leading the march, digging up all the gold they can along the way. And the Natashas of the banking world will be right behind them, holding pom-poms, cheering them on. "I'll keep that in mind."

Robin placed her hands on my shoulders. "That's just in case, Rachel. I don't want things to get weird between us. He's all yours unless you decide otherwise. Okay?"

Please don't ask me to pinkie swear!

I just smiled and nodded.

Robin patted me on the shoulder and returned to her hostess station.

I grabbed Gordon's wine and delivered it to his table. "Here you are, sir. Are you ready to order?"

"Yes, but first, I have a question, and I'm thinking you may be able to help me."

"I might have an answer."

"Referring back to our conversation a few minutes ago...I

was just wondering…Since going through your personnel file would be a serious violation of several protocols and a couple of laws, how would you suggest he ask for your phone number? I mean, things change, right? Dating today is so different from back when I was a teenager and in college. And I know it was different for my parents back in the day, and different for their parents. What worked a few years ago is probably viewed as old school now, right?"

"That's for sure."

"So, how would he get your number without depicting himself as a stalker?"

"I'll be perfectly honest with you, I've only dated two guys in the last twenty years. Both of those relationships lasted about a month. Now, don't get me wrong. I've been hit on more times than I care to admit by guys at bars, guys in the grocery store, even one guy in my apartment building."

Gordon pointed at me. "And patrons at Santorino's, apparently, while you're on the job."

"True, but that guy seemed different from all the others. He bought me that glass of wine and never used it to make advances toward me. Like Penny, my friend, said, 'Good to see that chivalry isn't dead.'"

Gordon nodded slightly as I spoke before dropping his gaze to the table. "You know, the reason why he probably didn't use that wine as a conversation starter is because he's shy. Sounds like something I would've done.

"Buy a beautiful woman a glass of wine and then be scared out of my wits to follow up because she might not like me. And because she seems so out of my league, I'd ask myself, 'What in the world were you thinking?' So, in a nervous, knee-jerk reaction, I'd probably just walk away before she had a chance to get to know me and eventually reject me." He hesitated and looked up at me. "Wow. I sound like a real loser, huh?"

"No. Actually, that's about the sweetest thing anyone has ever said…"

And it was to me.

"So, how should that man go about getting your phone number?"

I bit my lip. I wanted to say something like, "Oh, I'm sure she won't mind if you happen to stumble across her number on your computer screen as you were, say, checking her personnel file to see if she qualified for a promotion and a hefty raise…" However, I said, "He should be patient. You know what they say. Good things come to those who wait."

He shook his head up and down in an animated fashion. A manifestation of nerves, I surmised. "If it's meant to be, right?"

"Exactly. It's Christmas time. Anything can happen at Christmas. Season of miracles and all that."

Wow! Listen to me pontificate, like I actually know what I'm talking about…

The sudden, eternal optimist.

"Okay then," Gordon said, repositioning himself in his chair, "while I enjoy the scenery on this fine holiday evening, I think I'm going to order the chicken scallopini."

"Excellent choice, sir. Anything else?"

"No, thank you."

"I'll get that order right in."

Forty-five minutes later, Gordon finished his meal, scraped the bottom of the bowl of his panna cotta with his spoon, getting the last vestiges of fudge sauce, and took the last sip of wine.

I watched him from the other side of the dining room when I wasn't serving other patrons. Noticing he was finished, I grabbed his bill and opened it. I snagged a napkin from the supply counter and sat down at an empty table. I pulled out my pen and began to write my original answer, albeit a bit modified:

In answer to your question about the phone number, under normal circumstances, it would be wrong. However, I think that guy who bought the wine could, just this once, look into her personnel file and retrieve her phone number. I think I know her well enough. She won't mind. Not this once.

I folded the napkin, placed it inside the bill holder, and delivered it to his table without mentioning it.

If it's meant to be…

CHAPTER FORTY-TWO

U.S. Post Office
Jericho, NY

*D*etective Witherspoon arrived at the Jericho post office at six o'clock. The miserable traffic slowed him down considerably, causing him not to be in the best of moods as he called, asking the postmaster to let him inside.

"Mrs. Nunez, Detective Witherspoon." He flashed his shield. "Thank you for sticking around. The traffic is horrible. And I had a little detour I had to make that took me ten minutes out of my way."

She led him to the back of the building. "Nothing like holiday traffic to cheer you up."

"Tell me about it." He scanned his surroundings as they crossed the small sorting area. "It's rush hour, there's always construction going on somewhere, and then you add all those last-minute shoppers clogging up the roads, it does set the mood."

"It really wasn't a problem, Detective. Gave me a chance to

catch up on some things. Besides, I had a truck that just got back about fifteen minutes ago. He was stuck in that traffic too."

"Well, I don't want to take up any more of your time than is needed. Do you have the video feed pulled up so we can look at it?"

"Right in here." She walked into a small office and sat down behind the desk. A computer, positioned off to one side, displayed pictures of mountains covered in snow. She tapped the keyboard, and mountains gave way to a security camera. "Here, let me turn this monitor so you can see it better."

"No, if you don't mind, I'll just come around behind you."

"Suit yourself." She waited for the detective to step around behind the desk before clicking a button. The frozen image snapped to life, and before them was the all-too-familiar lobby.

In walked a man wearing a dark uniform. He appeared to have several envelopes in his right hand.

"What would you say? Does that look like he's holding about ten, maybe fifteen, envelopes?" Witherspoon said.

She paused it. "Twelve. We found them in the bin after he disappeared. Luckily, one of my clerks had just emptied that bin right before this guy dropped them inside, so they were the only ones in there." She reached over and grabbed a stack of envelopes off her desk. "Got 'em right here."

Witherspoon slipped on a pair of gloves and took them from her.

Not your normal-sized envelopes.

More like Christmas cards.

Each one addressed to a different individual. No return address.

Similar to those letters that Hamar woman was getting, but not exactly the same.

"I need to see what's inside these envelopes."

"I can't authorize you to open them."

"Yes, you can." Witherspoon reached inside his overcoat and yanked out a folded sheet of paper. "I have a warrant." He handed it to her.

"That was fast."

"The purpose of my little detour I mentioned earlier."

"What do you think they have in them? Anthrax?"

"Probably not," he said, yanking out an oversized plastic bag from his coat pocket. "But do you want to take that chance?" He stuffed the envelopes into the bag and sealed it. "I'll have our lab take a look to make sure before I start opening all of 'em."

Her eyes narrowed. "How long will that take?"

"This time of year? Could be several days, but I'm gonna put a rush on it."

"What if they're just good, old-fashioned Christmas cards? By the time you examine them, reseal them, and send them out, they'll be really late."

"Better late than never, they always say." He peeled off his gloves and tossed them in the nearby trashcan. "Now, show me the rest of the video."

She grumbled something inaudible and clicked the mouse.

The man on the screen inserted the envelopes into the mail slot one at a time. Then just as he dropped the last one off, he spun around.

Mrs. Nunez stopped the feed and pointed at the monitor. "Okay, so here is where I was locking the service area door and saw him standing there. I thought I'd be nice and see if he needed anything from inside, like stamps or something, before I closed up for the night." She snatched a glance at Witherspoon. "Now, watch this." She clicked the mouse again.

The courier tilted his head slightly, formed a big smile, and waved with his right hand but never said anything. Then, in one brilliant flash, he was gone.

"Did you see that?" Witherspoon said. "That flash of light?"

"Yeah, just now, but I didn't see it when I was standing there. To me, he just vanished. Like, one minute he was there, and then he wasn't."

"How could you not see that light?"

"I'm telling you, he didn't flash like that when he disappeared. Trust me. I would have remembered something like that."

Witherspoon straightened his stance. "This is weird."

"I told you."

"Back that up. I need to see it again."

She did, and they watched it from the beginning.

"Stop it right there." He leaned in close.

"What?"

"Back it up slowly."

She clicked a different button.

"Keep backing up. Back, back, back, there. Stop. Can you enlarge it? Zoom in? I need to see the name on that patch."

She chose one button, and the video shifted to another camera. "Uh, that's not it." She changed it back. "Let me try this one." The video expanded to full screen, but didn't zoom in. "Does that help?"

"I still can't make out his name."

"Neither can I." She chose one more button, and a little regulator appeared on the screen off to the right. It read fifty percent. She grabbed the little lever with the mouse and slid it upward. The camera got closer to the courier. She manipulated the lever until she got it as good as it was going to get. "I can get closer, but it gets fuzzy."

"Does that look like a capital G?"

"Yes."

"And an A?"

"I think so."

Witherspoon leaned in closer. "G. A. B. E." He looked the postmaster in the eye. "Gabe."

Nunez picked up the pair of glasses resting on the desk and slipped them on. "G. A. B. E. Yeah. Gabe. That appears to be his name."

"And that says Next Day Couriers on his sleeve, right?"

"Yep."

Witherspoon snatched his cell phone from his coat pocket and dialed. "Hey, it's Witherspoon. I need a phone number for Next Day Couriers. I need it to be their main hub. Sure. I'll wait."

Nunez took off her glasses and bit the earpiece. "He waved at me like he knew me or something. But I've never seen him before in my life."

"We'll get to the bottom of this Mr. Gabe. I'm gonna—uh, yeah, hold on." Witherspoon made a writing motion. "I need to take this number down."

Nunez grabbed a pen from the coffee mug on her desk, which read, "Operator Not Responsible for Any Actions Taken Until the Medicine In This Dispenser Has Been Administered," and handed it to Witherspoon.

"Go ahead, Jim. 7-1-8, 5-5-5, 6-5-7-1...And this is the main hub in Staten Island. All right, Jim. Thanks...No, we're good... Okay, buddy, and tell your family I said for them to have a great Christmas. Disney should be fun, and warmer...you too. Later."

"I want to go," Nunez said.

"To Disney? You think there's a bunch of people here?" Witherspoon began punching the phone number into his phone. "They used to limit how many people could get in the parks back when Walt Disney was alive. My aunt used to tell me about how they would close the doors at eleven a.m. when the Magic Kingdom reached capacity. But not anymore. They keep the doors open all day. Cram 'em in like sardines." He hit Send.

"I still want to go. At least it would be warmer."

"That it would be—uh, yes, my name is Detective Witherspoon with the Nassau County Police Department. I'm investigating an incident which took place earlier today at the post office in Jericho, New York, involving one of your couriers, and I need to speak to a supervisor, or better yet, the owner, if either person is available." Witherspoon turned on the speaker so Nunez could hear.

"Our supervisor is the owner, but he is not here at the moment. He's out in the warehouse," a female voice said.

"I can wait if you could go get him for me?"

"Sure. Please hold."

Suddenly, the second stanza of "The Little Drummer Boy" blared from his phone.

"You have a family, Mrs. Nunez?"

"Yes. There's four of us."

"Tickets for Disney are over a hundred bucks a piece now. Per day. Unless you get some special deal. Then you have the airfare, hotel accommodations…"

"I said I wanted to go. I didn't say I could afford it."

"Sir, are you still there?" came the female voice over the phone.

"Yes."

"Please hold. I'm going to transfer you to the owner."

"Thank you."

Witherspoon heard a little click and then multiple voices and what sounded like a machine in the background. Maybe a delivery truck? "Hello?"

"Hello? This is Joe Cheema."

"Yes, Joe, my name is Detective Witherspoon. I'm with the Nassau County Police Department. I just have a few questions to ask, and I was wondering if you could help us."

"I guess."

"Well, I'm standing in the Jericho, New York, post office with the postmaster of this branch. We're in her office watching a security camera feed of the lobby. Are you familiar with this particular post office?"

"Uh, yes. We deliver there."

"Good. Do you have an employee by the name of Gabe? I'm sorry, but I don't have a last name."

"Gabe?"

"Yes. G-A-B-E. That's what it says on the name patch on his shirt."

"No, sir. We have no one by that name who works here."

"Are you sure? He's wearing a uniform with your courier service embroidered on the sleeve."

"Is it a navy-blue shirt with navy-blue pants?"

"It sure is."

"Is the stitching white?"

"Yes."

"Is the name patch on the chest on the right side? With a pocket for pens on the left side?"

"It's exactly as you describe it."

"Can you describe this man for me? What does he look like?"

"He's approximately how tall would you say, Mrs. Nunez?"

She stalled. "Uh, I'm five-four. He was probably two, maybe three inches taller than me."

"Sounds like he was about five-foot-seven. Clean-shaven. Short hair. It's hard to tell from the picture, but he looks like he may be African-American. But because the video is a little grainy when you zoom in, he could be from Ghana, Suriname, or a Caribbean island for all we know."

"I'm sorry, Detective, but I do not have anyone working for me who fits that description. All my employees are Middle Eastern, except for one white guy we just hired. And I am from Turkey."

"Do you have any other locations? Stores? Hubs?"

"No, this is it. We're small compared to some of our competitors. I only have eleven employees, including myself."

"So, no Gabe, Gabriel, Gabby, anyone who goes by any variation of that name working for you?"

"Sorry."

"You don't mind if I come down and look at your employees' personnel files, do you? Maybe this is a former employee who failed to turn in is uniform, perhaps?"

"Detective, you're more than welcome to come down and look at anything you wish. But I'm telling you, we do not have, nor have we ever had, an employee here by that name. Not even as a last name."

Witherspoon huffed in frustration. "Look, I'm sorry to bother you. I appreciate your time, Mr. Cheema. We'll be in touch."

"No problem. Goodbye, Detective."

Witherspoon pressed End and stared at his phone before lifting his eyes to the monitor again. "He says they've never had anyone working for them by that name."

Nunez scratched her cheek. "Maybe it was one of Santa's elves."

"Maybe I need a drink."

Witherspoon's phone rang. He checked the screen before answering. "Hey, you're not going to believe this."

"Well, can you let me in first? It's cold out here."

"Oh, sure." Witherspoon ended the call. "My partner on this case, Detective Bowen, is here. Can you let her in?"

Nunez rose. "Sure."

"We won't be much longer."

"After what we saw on that video, I'm not in any hurry to leave. No tellin' what's out there waiting for me." She left the office and returned a minute later with Bowen in tow.

"Detective Witherspoon, I brought my laptop like you requested."

"Great, but first, you've gotta see this." He pointed at the screen. "Mrs. Nunez, can you replay the whole thing, please?"

Nunez sat down again, slid the time bar back to 16:59 and change, and clicked Play.

The video showed the courier walk inside, mail the envelopes, turn around, wave, and vanish in a brilliant flash of light.

Witherspoon lowered his head as if he was peering over a pair of glasses and eyeballed his partner. "Have you ever seen anything like this before?"

Bowen leered at him. "Oh, yeah. Sure. Happens all the time."

"We called the courier service on his sleeve. They've never heard of this guy. The owner said they've never had anyone fitting his description working for them."

"Never?"

Witherspoon widened his eyes and shook his head. "This case is getting stranger by the minute."

Bowen didn't respond but instead opened her laptop and pulled up the video she'd shared with Kenneth Singh and his supervisor just a few hours ago. "Remember how this other courier guy just disappeared from the camera?" She spun her laptop around and then played the video for Witherspoon and Nunez. "He vanished too."

"But we found him," Witherspoon said. "And his boss knows him. We interviewed him. He's real."

"I know. I just spoke with him and his supervisor again today. I'm thinking this guy named Gabe is also real. We need to track him down."

"But, Bowen, we tracked down Kenneth Singh because he actually worked for On-Time Couriers. His supervisor knew who he was. This guy in the blue uniform doesn't work for this courier outfit. They have no idea who he is."

"But have you checked their personnel files yet? He may go by a different name, and the supervisor there is simply forgetting. He hasn't seen the video yet, right?"

"No."

"Maybe if he sees it, he'll recognize the guy."

Witherspoon stared at Bowen. "I was planning on going back to On-Time Couriers in the morning. We could stop by this Next Day Couriers afterwards. You want to go with me?"

"Sure. I really want to get these guys."

"You and me both."

CHAPTER FORTY-THREE

West 173rd Street
Washington Heights, NY

practically danced through the door of my apartment after work. Seeing Gordon, talking with him, and playing the little cat and mouse game turned out to be the most fun I'd had in years. I didn't want him to leave. I almost asked him to go sit at the bar and have a drink on me, just so I could stop by every now and then and talk. But I was afraid asking him to stay might appear too forward. Even desperate.

And that's the last thing I wanted to look like.

A thirty-five-year-old, single, white female, who drove a junker of a car and looked like she was pulling out all the stops to catch her Fifth Avenue sugar daddy.

Yeah. That'll win him over.

So, I stopped myself, and allowed my note to work its magic.

I just hope it does.

On the way up, I'd whisked into the mailroom, opened the mailbox, and pulled out what seemed like thirty pieces of mail.

Bills, flyers, letters, it all looked the same to me, and I didn't care about any of it as I waltzed up the stairs.

I'd tossed the stack onto the couch and spun my way into the bedroom, yanking off my Italian-smelling clothes in the process.

A shower sounds lovely.

I even sang in the shower.

I never sing in the shower.

That's what happy people do, I hear.

But not people like me.

Not people with pitiful lives. Painful lives. Lives filled with misery.

However, tonight? I wanted to sing.

And I did.

I was just glad no one was listening.

WITH MY FESTIVELY RED PJ's on and a warm, white robe wrapped around me, I poured myself a glass of eight-dollar-a-bottle wine and sat down on the couch. I flipped on the TV, and *It's a Wonderful Life* filled the screen. George Bailey was telling off Mr. Potter in front of all those men around the table. Saying how his father was twice the man Mr. Potter could ever hope to be.

You go, George.

I picked up the stack of mail and started sorting it. Junk mail went on the floor because the trashcan was too far away. The bills got the coffee table because I didn't want to open them this close to Christmas. Everything else was placed beside me to be opened.

First was a Christmas card from my doctor. Wishing me a Merry Christmas and secretly hoping I would pay my doctor bills on time next year.

Dear Santa, please give Miss Hamar some money so I can make the payments on my Mercedes-Benz.

I opened another Christmas card from my aunt and uncle in North Carolina. I'd received one from them every year since I moved to New York to be closer to Momma. I knew Momma gave them my address. And I knew the card was from my aunt, not Uncle Ronald.

Guilt offerings, Momma called them. Just like the letters Momma received from my aunt. Her way of dealing with the pain of not standing up to my uncle when I needed a home.

Another Christmas card from the lady in 4-D. She always gave everyone in the building a card. Every year. Without fail.

Lastly, another letter from the girl in the meadow. Same kind of envelope as the others. Same handwriting. Same everything. I opened it and began to read.

I love my daddy. He's always been there for me. He's taught me so much. He helped me become the person I am now. He sees the beauty in everything. He views life so differently than I do. I see, but not like he sees. I hear, but not the things he hears. I taste, smell, and feel, but he's so much better at it all. I love just walking around with him, listening, learning, bonding. It never gets old.

Just the other day, he walked me up to a tree. A maple tree. He pulled the branch out slightly, ever so gently, and bent it so the sun shone through the leaves. The intricate patterns the sun revealed in the leaves were amazing. I asked him what the spots were. It appeared to be made of little, lighter-colored dots with these veins running down the middle and branching out to the edges of the leaf. He told me those were the plant's cells. That every living thing was designed to be wondrous, and life was meant to keep us awestruck.

Today, I was awestruck. Not just by the leaf. But rather, by my daddy's love. Of life. By all the things around me. But most of all? By me. Who I had become. Thinking that if a simple leaf could be so astonishing in its simplicity, how much more so was I? Or the bear we met the other day? Or the birds in the air?

It's all pretty amazing, if you ask me.

I dropped the letter into my lap and wondered what that would be like. To have a father who spent time with you, taught you about life, helped you become "awestruck."

Awestruck.

What does that feel like? To be mesmerized by nature? To experience all the sights and sounds, smells and feelings this world has to offer? To—

The phone rang, and I jumped, knocking over my wine glass. "Ah, man."

That wasn't mesmerizing at all…

I set the glass upright and picked up my cell phone on the way to the kitchen to get some paper towels. I looked at the screen but didn't recognize the number.

"Hello?"

"Rachel? It's Gordon. I hope this isn't a bad time."

"Oh, no, no." I just spilled my wine all over the coffee table. That's all. I'm such a klutz. "Just sitting here reading the mail. Watchin' a movie on TV."

"Okay, good, because you sound winded, like you had to run to answer the phone."

"Oh, that. Noooo. I spilled my drink all over the coffee table. I was just cleaning it up. So, how are you? How was your dinner tonight?" I strolled into the living room and began wiping up my mess.

"It was great. The service was even better."

"Was it now?"

"I think I'm going to make a pact with myself, kind of like the one I have with the coffee shop. Only go there to eat if that waitress I had is working. If she's not, then go somewhere else."

I needed more paper towels. The wine was dripping off the edge of the coffee table.

Good thing it was white wine.

"As a matter of fact," I said, heading back into the kitchen, "I know her personally. She told me she works every evening, except Sundays and Mondays. However, she may have to work those too. Her roommate moved out. The rent is all hers now."

"Wow. That's a lot of hours if she has a day job, too, I mean."

I ripped off about ten towels. "She does. She works at a bank during the day. Leaves that job Tuesday through Friday and reports directly to the restaurant. On Saturdays, she works at the bank until noon, gets a short break, then heads over to the restaurant around four in the afternoon."

"She's quite the industrious one, isn't she?"

"Not by choice." I grunted as I knelt down on the living room floor. "Well, let me rephrase that. She chooses to live under a roof instead of on the street. So, yes, I guess you could say it is by choice."

"Good choice, I might add. Especially around the holidays."

I chuckled. "Yeah, well, the holidays don't always play nice with the budget, you know."

"How so?"

"Restaurant is closed Christmas Day, and that's one of her regular nights. And no paid holidays like there are at the bank. So, she was hoping to make up some money, thinking it was going to be busier than it was." I sniffed. "But hey, they had some waiters and waitresses who wanted the night off, and since she had nowhere else to be, she decided to help out." I sighed into the phone as I mopped up the last remaining puddles of wine. "At least she was able to help someone out in the happiness department at Christmas."

"I'm sorry she has to work all those hours."

"Yeah, it's a bummer, I'm sure. And now, with her roommate gone…" I paused before standing. "I worry about her. She rarely seems happy. I hear she's had a pretty rough life. Hasn't caught very many breaks."

"That's…sad."

"Yeah. It's two days before Christmas, and she has no one to spend it with, I hear. Except her mother. But she lives in a psych ward somewhere in the city."

I heard Gordon attempt to say something, but then he hesitated. "Could you do me a favor? Could you find out if she's available for dinner on Christmas Day? Say, around four o'clock? At my house? I'd like her to meet my daughter. Also, Heather and her family will be there. We'll be eating around five."

"You know, that's so funny." I trekked toward the kitchen. "She just told me a day or two ago that she was going to go spend the day with her mother at the, uh…center. She does it every year. There's a dinner around the same time as yours. She told me family members are invited to stay and eat with their relatives, and then they listen to some group of singers come in and sing songs…usually Christmas carols."

"Oh, of course. Family's important this time of year. I understand fully."

"However, since you said four o'clock in the afternoon, she may be able to juggle her plans."

"If she could, that would be wonderful, but tell her not to go out of her way. We're just having dinner and exchanging some gifts. Nothing extravagant. If it doesn't work out, we're also having a get together on New Year's Eve."

"New Year's might work better, but I'll pass this along to her. Why don't you text me the directions to your place, and I'll pass them along to her, just in case."

"I can do that."

"Okay, then."

"I'll, uh…I'll talk to you later then."

"I'll see you in the morning, Gordon."

"Oh, yeah, right. Good night, Rachel."

I stood in front of the garbage can holding the soiled paper towels.

If I left early enough, I could spend some time with Momma, go to her little cafeteria-style dinner, and cut out before the singers got going...

I opened the lid and jammed the paper towels into the overflowing garbage.

I could tell her I have a date. It wouldn't be a lie.

And she'd be happy for me. I know she would.

I grabbed a regular towel and was getting it wet under the faucet when the text came through.

"Valdemar Ave., Staten Island? He doesn't strike me as a Staten Island kind of guy."

I copied and pasted the address into a search engine. When the street view came up, it floored me.

Nice place.

I did a quick check on the appraised value.

Over one million? And it's a two-family home with a studio apartment…

Hmmm.

Then I remembered another pact we made, Joanie and me, several years ago. "Never move in where you get your lovin' unless there's a ring with the bling."

I wiped up the sticky places, but I did so robotically. My mind was elsewhere, thinking about Joanie. Wondering why she chose to break all the rules now. This late in the game.

Well, at least one of us is going to stick to the rules.

Christmas Eve
Wednesday
December 24, 2014

CHAPTER FORTY-FOUR

Sun Ridge National Bank
Manhattan, NY

The next morning, I stood at my teller window, bleary-eyed. The girl next to me had brought in a little plastic snowman and sat him on the ledge overlooking her window. It had a motion sensor, and every time a customer walked up to her window or strolled past it, it played a cheesy, poorly sung rendition of "Holly, Jolly Christmas." It might have been cute if I was well rested.

Really well rested.

But right now, I just wanted to kick the little snowman back to the North Pole so Burl Ives could teach him how to sing.

I tried to be nice to the customers, wishing them a Merry Christmas and Happy Holidays and whatever else people wish upon others at this celebratory time of the year, but I just couldn't wake up enough to sound pleasant. Although I'd gone to bed at a decent time the night before, I couldn't sleep. All I could think about was my conversation with Gordon at the restaurant. I kept replaying it in my mind again and again.

I had to be honest with myself.

I hadn't felt like this since I met Billy.

I'd forgotten what it was like to care for someone.

And I was also operating without my coffee. Heather was off today. So, I bypassed the coffee shop. Came straight to work.

Dumb move.

Bad coffee would have been better than no coffee.

"Hey, Natasha, do you mind if I run to the break room? I need some caffeine."

"No. Not at all."

"Thanks." I started to place my Next Window, Please sign in the opening when a man stepped in front of me.

I froze.

That looks like that Kenneth Singh guy…the man Detective Bowen had in the holding room the night I was in her precinct.

I stared at him for a couple of seconds with my sign in my hand.

"I'm sorry," he said. "Were you closing your window?"

"I was, but that's okay." I set the sign aside. "How may I help you?"

"I just have a deposit to make." The man handed me a deposit slip and a check, accompanied by two hundred dollars in cash.

I took the check and saw the name.

Kenneth Singh.

"Mr. Singh, I don't know if you remember me, but my name is Rachel Hamar. I believe the police questioned you the other day in conjunction with a case they're working on that involves some letters delivered to the post office in Jericho. Letters that were eventually delivered to my apartment."

"I'm sorry, your name is what again?"

I pointed to my nameplate off to the left. "Rachel Hamar."

Kenneth Singh's eyes widened. "Yes. Yes. They accused me of being some kind of stalker. I told them I was innocent. All I did was my job. I did exactly what I was instructed to do. Nothing more. Nothing less. I would never do anything to make my boss look bad."

I watched him as he changed from quiet and calm to agitated and bothered.

"I also noticed your check is for $48,000. You are aware that this check is for $48,000?"

He nodded. "Yes. What is that to you?"

"We'll have to put a hold on this check. The funds will not be available for use for up to ten business days."

"Not a problem."

"Very well, then." I went through the motions and processed his deposit, stealing a glance every chance I got. "Still working for On-Time Couriers, Mr. Singh?"

"Do you always make it a habit to interrogate your customers?"

"I wasn't interrogating you. Just making small talk." I finished the transaction and handed him his updated slip. "There you go, sir. Your check will take approximately ten business days to clear, but with the holidays, it could take longer."

"Thank you."

"Have a Merry Christmas, Mr. Singh."

"You as well."

I slid the sign into position, locked my cash drawer, and waited for him to clear the front doors. "I'll be right back, Natasha."

I exited the teller area and went straight to my locker. I grabbed my cell phone and called Detective Bowen.

"You're not going to believe who just came up to my teller window at the bank."

"Who?"

"Kenneth Singh."

"He came up to your window?"

"Yes."

"Are you sure it was him?"

"Yes. He just deposited a check with his name on it for $48,000 along with some cash."

"Really? So, where does a courier get that kind of money?"

"Exactly."

"Do you remember where the check came from?"

"It was from a bank in New Jersey, I think. It's in my money drawer."

"Listen, Miss Hamar, Detective Witherspoon and I are on our way to On-Time Couriers as we speak. We'll come to the bank just as soon as we're done there. Can you keep his paperwork somewhere where we can inspect it?"

"Sure. I'll just keep it in my drawer until you get here. But to be on the safe side, you better bring a warrant. I just got this job, and I ain't losing it over some legality issues from these letters. They've cost me enough, already."

"Not a problem. I believe we can get one without too much trouble."

"Oh, and remember, we close at noon today."

"We should be there long before then."

CHAPTER FORTY-FIVE

On-Time Couriers
Main Hub
Brooklyn, NY

Detective Bowen ended the call and held her cell phone in front of her, staring at it like she'd just been notified of a long-lost relative's unexpected passing. "That was Rachel Hamar. She said Kenneth Singh was just at her bank in Manhattan. He deposited a check from some bank in Jersey for forty-eight grand, and he had some cash to go along with it."

"What?" Detective Witherspoon said. "Forty-eight grand? Where does a courier get scratch like that?"

"I don't know what's going on, but there's something hinky about Kenneth Singh. I've thought that since the day we brought him into my precinct."

Witherspoon flipped on his left blinker and waited for the light to turn green. "If he's at her bank in Manhattan, then where is he going? To work? Has he already left to go on his route? Or is he off today?"

"It's almost ten o'clock. Eugene Hahn said they try to get

their couriers out on the street by eight. So, Mr. Singh should be gone for the day, making his deliveries by now."

"Or he could be off today. Although, I have a hard time believing a courier service would let an employee take off the day before Christmas."

"Yeah. Me too." Bowen rested her elbow against the window and placed her hand against her head in a thoughtful manner. "Maybe that deposit was part of his run? But, no, it couldn't be. Rachel said the check was made out to him."

"Maybe he sold something. A house, perhaps?"

"No. Remember? Singh rented an apartment."

"Maybe he sold somebody's Christmas gift. A forty-eight-thousand-dollar necklace or something."

"Could be, but we are really just speculating now. We're not going to know anything until we see that check."

Witherspoon whipped the car around the corner and parked in front of On-Time Couriers' main hub warehouse. "All I know is," he said, "if I get jerked around one more time by some disappearing magician, I'm gonna lose it."

"Then maybe you should let me go in and do the talking."

"You can do the talking, but I'm goin' in."

Both detectives got out and scanned their surroundings before entering the premises through a large, garage door-like opening.

Inside, a tall black man barked orders at some younger workers stacking boxes in one corner of the building. "Be careful with those! Those are all fragile! And expensive!"

"Excuse me." Detective Bowen held her shield in plain view. "I'm Detective Bowen. NYPD. This is Detective Witherspoon with the Nassau County PD. We're looking for Eugene Hahn and Kenneth Singh. Do you happen to know where we might find them?"

The black man held a clipboard and had a pencil tucked behind his right ear. "There's nobody here by those names."

"I'm sorry?" Bowen said. "I was just here yesterday. I spoke to both men over there in that office." She pointed to a small cubicle space in the opposite corner from the men stacking boxes.

"Detective, I don't know who you talked to, but I'm the manager here. I do all the hiring and all the firing. We don't have anyone by those names working here."

"And you are?"

"I'm Marvin. Marvin Belcher. I've been working here for ten years. Never had a Eugene or a Kenneth workin' here."

Witherspoon opened up his phone and pulled up Kenneth Singh's photograph. "Here. Can you take a look at this picture and tell me if you recognize this man at all?" He walked over to Marvin and handed him the phone.

Marvin pursed his lips and lifted an eyebrow. "Never seen the guy." He handed the phone back. "So, if I may ask, why were you here yesterday?"

Bowen explained the case without going into much detail. "I came back yesterday because I had some questions I needed answered, and Kenneth Singh and Eugene Hahn were the only two people who could help me."

As Bowen revealed another aspect of the case, Marvin's forehead wrinkled a little bit more.

"I stood right in that office yesterday." She pointed at it.

Marvin yanked the pencil out from behind his ear and used the clip to pin it to the board. "Well, I wasn't here yesterday, so I have no idea."

"That's right," Bowen said. "I didn't see you."

"You said you were the manager, right?" Witherspoon said.

"Yeah. What about it?"

"So, where were you yesterday?"

"I don't think that's any of your business."

"Marvin, we're just trying to solve a case. Detective Bowen was here yesterday. You weren't. She met with two men in your office while you were not here. Don't you want to know who was in your office? A man by the name of Eugene Hahn was acting as the manager-slash-owner of your business. Another man by the name of Kenneth Singh was acting like one of your couriers."

Marvin's eyes grew bigger and moved from Witherspoon to Bowen and then back to Witherspoon. "If you must know, I was in California attending my aunt's funeral. Okay?"

"That's all we needed to know," Witherspoon said. "That explains why you weren't here. And I'll bet, Detective Bowen, that Marvin here was gone for about a week. Isn't that right, Marvin?"

"Yeah. How did you know?"

"Because we picked up Kenneth Singh for questioning last Friday. I talked to his alleged supervisor, Eugene Hahn, the next day. They apparently have been here all week. Your employees over there had to have seen these two guys. As a matter of fact, when I came in here last Saturday, Eugene Hahn was holding a clipboard just like you're doing. He was standing right over there, talking to employees."

Marvin turned toward the men stacking boxes. "Hey! Dexter!" Marvin waved the man over.

Dexter, a twenty-something young black male with dreads and some assorted tattoos on his arms, jogged over to his supervisor. "Yeah, boss. Wuz up?"

"I got a question for you." Marvin pointed at Detective Bowen. "Has this lady ever been here before?"

Dexter took a quick glance at Bowen and nodded. "Yeah."

"She says she talked to the supervisor that day. As you know, Dexter, I was in California, so it couldn't have been me…"

"No, no, I remember. She was talking to Eugene."

"Who? We don't have no Eugene workin' here."

"Yeah, I know. But Mr. Hahn said he got sent to us from corporate."

Marvin's face twisted into a mass of frustration and confusion. "Corporate? We ain't got no corporate!"

"We don't?"

Marvin grunted in obvious anger. "Detective, can you show him that picture and see if he knows that guy?"

"Sure." Witherspoon opened his phone and held it out. "Recognize this man?"

Dexter started nodding. "Yeah. Sure do. That's Kenneth."

Marvin almost lost it. "Who the… Who is Kenneth?"

"According to Eugene, we were short-handed, so he had one of those temp services send us somebody. They sent him."

"I ain't believin' this." Marvin threw the clipboard at the wall behind him.

"Whoa, now." Witherspoon pocketed his phone and held his hands up. "Let's not lose our composure here. We're gonna get to the bottom of this."

Marvin stepped closer to Dexter. "You're tellin' me two men nobody knows walked in here and started runnin' the joint? And nobody questioned them?"

"They seemed legit, Marvin. There was a guy here from corporate who introduced Eugene and everything."

"What? There was a third guy?!" Marvin stormed away, shouting expletives

All the other workers stopped what they were doing and watched with eyes as wide as hubcaps.

"Dexter," Bowen said, "when did these men arrive? Obviously, Marvin left to go to California. So, when did the others show up?"

"The next day."

"And where was De'Ron?!" Marvin yelled from twenty feet away. "I left him in charge. Went over everything with him before I left."

Dexter wrinkled his brow. "You don't know?"

"Don't know what?"

"He got arrested. The night you left, he got into an argument with his old lady. She pulled a knife on him. He slapped her around. They both got arrested."

Marvin stumbled over to a chair and collapsed into it. "Are you kiddin' me?"

"No. I thought he'd call and tell ya."

"What's De'Ron's last name?" Bowen said. "We can check it out and see if that's correct."

"Chessom." Marvin sat there, shaking his head. "C-H-E-S-S-O-M." He turned, glared at Dexter, and then looked at Witherspoon. His voice waned. "De'Ron called me twice to tell me everything was okay." He paused. The expression on his face was like he was trying to understand the universe. "I called him on three different days. I texted him on the others. Spoke to him directly. He assured me everything was fine and not to worry about nothin'. How could that be, if he was in jail?"

"Somebody could have bailed him out," Witherspoon said.

Bowen felt sorry for the guy as she placed a call into her precinct. He'd come to work today, just trying to do his job and get packages out to people so they could have a merry Christmas only to find out his establishment had been run by unknown people for a week. "Hey, Marvin, when you got back," she said, waiting for an answer, "did you notice anything missing? Packages?..." She held up her hand for Marvin to hold that thought. "Yes, I need you to check a name for me."

"Marvin," Witherspoon said, taking over for Bowen while she talked to her precinct on the phone, "did you find anything missing?"

"No."

"Are you sure? Have you checked your logs? Your inventory? Your bank account? Kenneth Singh deposited a sizable check this morning that was made out to him."

When Witherspoon said "bank account," Marvin scowled.

He jumped up from his chair. "If they messed with my money, I'm gonna kill 'em!"

Witherspoon followed Marvin into the little office. Marvin sat down behind the computer and started pounding the keyboard like it was responsible. He finally retrieved his bank statement and began studying it. The more he stared at it, the more his face softened. "Huh? Ain't that somethin'?"

"What is it?"

"It doesn't appear any money is missing."

"That's good, right?"

"No, you don't understand. When I left, we had about five grand in there. I was gonna need to at least double that by the time I came back just to make payroll. I remember that distinctly."

"So, what's in there now?"

Marvin fell back into his chair. "There's over a hundred grand in there."

"Can I see?"

Marvin motioned for him to proceed.

Witherspoon stepped around the desk and leaned in for a look. "When were those deposits made?"

"All while I was gone. And it was only one. A big one. From some company in New Jersey I ain't never heard of for one hundred grand."

Witherspoon leaned in again with his notepad in his hand. "I wonder who Envoi Enterprises, Inc. is, and what they do specifically?" He jotted down the name of the company.

"How should I know?" Marvin said.

Witherspoon smirked. "No. What I meant was, the check Kenneth Singh deposited this morning was from a bank in Jersey. So, I 'm wondering if—"

"This Kenneth Singh dude uses the same bank as Envoi Enterprises?"

Witherspoon pointed at Marvin emphatically. "Bingo."

Bowen entered the office holding her cell phone. "Dexter was right. De'Ron Chessom was arrested last week for domestic battery. His wife was arrested for aggravated assault. According to the police report, he was drunk and sleeping on the couch around eleven p.m. His cell phone rang, and his wife answered it. Turned out to be another woman calling for De'Ron. His wife took offense and started hitting him, demanding answers. He woke up, retaliated, and told her it didn't concern her. She went to the kitchen, got a knife, and went after him. Looking at the photos, it appears she got a couple of good swipes in before he knocked her out."

Marvin grabbed his head in disbelief.

"Marvin," Witherspoon said, "what's the name of the bank in New Jersey who deposited that money into your account?"

Marvin leaned forward and squinted. He clicked the mouse a couple of times. "Banker's Trust."

"Thank you."

"So?" Marvin collapsed back into his chair. "What do we do now?"

"We need you to check your inventory," Bowen said. "Check your logs. Check anything and everything that will show us how that much money got into your account."

"What? You think these scabs are using our account to launder money or something?"

"That's why we need to verify the receipt of this money and where it came from. I hope for your sake it's legitimate. That would solve your payroll issues for a while, wouldn't it?"

"A hundred grand? Uh, yeah. But what if it's dirty?"

"Then you'll be talking to a whole different group of people very soon."

Marvin pinched his eyebrows together.

"The Feds, Marvin. They'll be crawling all over this place."

Marvin closed his eyes and turned away from the detectives. His shoulders slumped. "Great."

Bowen extended her hand. "Here's my card. We'll be back later to help you sort things out. For now, we need as much information as possible that can exonerate you."

"I'm on it. I ain't goin' to jail for nobody."

"Oh, Marvin," Witherspoon said. "One more question. You said you didn't have a corporate."

"That's right."

"And I know you guys have stores all over the city. Even one in Jersey, interestingly enough. But, who owns this business?"

Marvin tilted his head to the left and squinted again. "What are you talking about? This is the only place we own."

"No. I mean, I know this is your hub. Where all the packages come to be sorted and distributed. But you have drop off stores all over the city. There's a dozen of them. I've been to them. I've spoken to the employees there. They explained—"

Marvin held his hands up and stood. "Man, I don't know what in the world you're talkin' about." He tapped his chest. "I'm the owner. I own On-Time Couriers. And this is the only location I own. There ain't no drop off stores. We don't deal with the public directly. We're strictly commercial. This time of year, we handle a lot of the overload for some of the bigger companies out there. But mostly, we pick up and drop off business parcels, next day packages from law firms and stuff like that. Stuff that needs to be delivered within the city. Once in a while, we'll get some kind of bulk order to move outside the city, like those lightbulbs over there in those boxes. But most of our stuff can be handled on foot or by cyclists. I only own two box trucks. A couple of the drivers use their own cars. But that's it."

Witherspoon kept switching his gaze from Marvin to his partner and back. Now, he wasn't believing his ears.

"So, who did I talk to at those other locations?"

Marvin pointed at Witherspoon's phone. "Maybe you should talk to that guy and his alleged boss. Maybe they know."

"All right, Mr. Belcher. Thank you for your time." Bowen motioned at Detective Witherspoon. "We'll be in touch."

Marvin offered a half-hearted salute and sat back down.

Bowen and Witherspoon walked out of the building and got back into their car.

"We need to get to the bank and look over that check before we go to the other courier location," Bowen said.

"You know," Witherspoon said, starting the engine, "when we update our supervisors, they're gonna want to call in the Feds and turn this entire investigation over to them."

"Yeah, so they can wash their hands of this case before they feel the need to send us to Greystone Park. But before we report back to anybody, let's go to the bank first." Bowen grabbed her cell phone. "And while we're heading there, I'm gonna call a friend of mine to see if there's been any money laundering activity that matches this at all."

"No way. There can't be anything like this. It's too weird."

"I agree, but I'm gonna check anyway."

CHAPTER FORTY-SIX

Sun Ridge National Bank
Manhattan, NY

etectives Bowen and Witherspoon arrived at Sun Ridge National Bank around eleven o'clock. They filed into the lobby, spotted the teller windows, and made a beeline toward me.

"Rachel, we need to speak with you immediately," Bowen said.

"Is this about the check?"

Bowen nodded. "Do you have it?"

"Yes. Hang on." I grabbed the check and deposit slip from my drawer and then turned to Natasha. "Hey, I need to speak to these two people for a few minutes. I'll be right back." I slid the sign into my window.

Natasha looked at Detective Witherspoon as if his partner was invisible. She winked at me and shot me a coy smile. "Certainly. But, Rachel, aren't you going to introduce us first?"

"Uh, no." I spun around and exited the teller station. I heard

Natasha say something about being rude, but I didn't care. She could do her gold digging on her time, not mine.

I motioned for the detectives to follow me and led them down a hallway and into a small conference room. Witherspoon closed the door behind us and stood in front of it.

Bowen handed me the warrant. "It's all legal."

I read the warrant and handed it back to her. "All I have is the check and the deposit slip he filled out."

Bowen held out her hand, and I gave them to her. She inspected it and pivoted to see her partner. "Banker's Trust, Trenton, New Jersey."

"Looks like we have another connection between Kenneth Singh and On-Time Couriers' bank account," Witherspoon said.

"What?" I said.

Bowen explained what they had found out from their visit to On-Time Couriers that morning.

"You think this guy may be laundering money? That this check is dirty?"

"We're not sure yet," Bowen said. "All we know is a large deposit of $100,000 was made into the bank account of On-Time Couriers while the manager-slash-owner was out of state. He had no clue any of this had happened. I truly believe he was just as dumbfounded as we were."

"Yeah," Witherspoon said, "I'm pretty good at sniffing out drama queens and kings. This guy was for real. He's nervous too. He's afraid the Feds are gonna shut him down."

"Wouldn't you be?" Bowen said.

"Certainly."

Bowen faced me. "Can you check to see where these funds were deposited?"

"I already did. They went into an account that has Kenneth Singh's name on it."

"Are there any other names on the account?"

"No. Just his."

Bowen handed the check and deposit slip back to me. "So, what do we have thus far? A large sum of money gets deposited into the bank account of On-Time Couriers from this bank in New Jersey. A few days later, Kenneth Singh brings another large check from the same bank and deposits it into an account that only has his name on it. He's apparently the only person who can move money around in this account too."

"What we need to do now is go find out how that bank in Jersey is involved," Witherspoon said.

"And because this money came from New Jersey, it crossed state lines," I said.

"Making it all the more a federal case. But we can still question people there."

"But you know as well as I do," Bowen said, "that crossing state lines is gonna need some diplomacy first. If our supervisors find out we went into Jersey and started interrogating people maverick-style, we'll be on the night shift for a year, if we're lucky."

"And if we ask our supervisors for permission, they'll turn this over to the FBI in a heartbeat, and we'll be off the case."

"Before you guys do that," I said, "I need to apprise my supervisor of the situation. I would hate for him to be blind-sided by the Feds. Besides, he may be able to help us."

Bowen looked at her partner. They both shrugged.

"It can't hurt," Bowen said. "We're about to get kicked off this case anyway."

"If so," Witherspoon said, "let's wrap this up and hand it off to Uncle Sam before our shift ends. It can be our Christmas present to those glory hounds."

I plucked my cell phone from my pocket and dialed Gordon. "Hello?"

"Gordon, this is Rachel. Hey, I have a situation I think you need to be made aware of. Can we come up to your office?"

"We?"

"I'm here with two police detectives. It's concerning a check that was just deposited this morning."

"Yes. Most definitely."

"We're on our way."

I LED the detectives up the elevator, past Sandy from Sun Ridge's desk, and down the long hallway before knocking on Gordon's office door.

"Come in," Gordon said.

We entered as Gordon strode from behind his desk. A nonplussed look spread across his face.

"Mr. Ames, this is Detective Bowen from the NYPD. And this is Detective Witherspoon from the Nassau County PD."

Gordon extended his hand. "Detectives. I'm Gordon Ames, the branch manager. Please, have a seat." He offered the three chairs arranged in front of his desk. "How may I help you?"

"Mr. Ames," Bowen said, "we don't want to take up a great deal of your time, but Miss Hamar believed you may be of some help."

Gordon sat down behind his desk. "I hope I can be."

"Miss Hamar received a check earlier this morning for a deposit of forty-eight thousand dollars."

Gordon's eyebrows shot up. "She did?" He looked over at me.

"Yes, sir. It's a check from a bank in New Jersey called Banker's Trust."

Gordon nodded slightly. "We've done business with them before. Been around for about fifteen years, I think."

"So, they're reputable then?" Bowen said.

"As far as I know. I've not heard any industry news to the contrary."

"The check in question was brought here by a man named

Kenneth Singh. Would you happen to know anybody by that name?"

"As a matter of fact, yes. Miss Hamar has told me a little bit about the distressing ordeal she's been experiencing. I remember her mentioning a man by that name. Something about him being a suspect in the beginning? But I never heard how that turned out."

"Well, he was indeed a suspect early on in this case. However, until this morning, we had reason to believe he was just a man doing his job. Wrong place at the wrong time kind of thing."

Gordon narrowed his gaze. "But now, with this check, you're not so sure."

"That's right. And it's not just the check. We found out some additional information this morning that leads us to believe he is involved somehow, some way, with the letters you mentioned."

"So, Detective, how can I help you?"

"Well, we know this check was deposited into an account that only has Singh's name on it, so he's the only one that can make withdrawals."

Gordon drummed his fingers on the desk. "That raises some red flags for me."

"For all of us as well. We were wondering if there was anything you could tell us about the account. We have a warrant." Bowen held it up for him to see.

Gordon took it and examined it briefly. He thought for a moment and handed it back. "Miss Hamar, do you have the deposit slip handy?"

I gave it to him.

He awakened his computer, typed in the account number, and began scrolling through pages of information. Something I could have done, but I felt Gordon should do it. Besides, it got him involved in the investigation. Now, I just hoped it wouldn't ruin what began last night between us.

"There's really nothing terribly abnormal here that I can see," Gordon said. "Appears to be a normal account with some…sizeable deposits."

"Terribly abnormal?" Witherspoon said.

"Well, with most bank accounts these days, people have auto pay set up for their bills, etc. So, you'd see several withdrawal companies tied to this."

"Do you see any with this account?" Bowen said.

"Just one."

"Only one?" I said.

"That's it." Gordon said, tapping some keys on the board. "It's an internal account."

"Meaning?" Witherspoon said.

"If it was more of a normal situation, I'd see names here, like one for Con Edison to pay the electric bill or one for that person's cell phone provider. It would tell me when the payment is scheduled to come out and have some sort of authorization from the patron in the notes."

I shrugged. "Okay. So, maybe we hold Kenneth Singh's mortgage or something? And he wrote a check to pay off the balance."

"Let me check." Gordon jotted down the number for the internal account on a slip of paper and changed screens. He then held the sticky note up and punched in the number, clicked the mouse a couple of times, and suddenly dropped the hand holding the note on the desk with a *thunk!*

"What is it, Gor—, I mean, Mr. Ames?" I said.

"The account with Mr. Singh's name on it has a withdrawal authorization set up. The deposit today for $48,200 is scheduled to be transferred into another account…this internal one." He held up the sticky note. "Once the check clears, of course."

"Yeah," I said. "I did tell Mr. Singh that it would take ten business days to clear, and he didn't seem fazed by it at all."

"Where is the money scheduled to go?" Bowen said.

Gordon shifted in his chair to face us more directly. "Our bank's Christmas fund."

"And what is that, exactly?"

Gordon leaned forward on his desk. "For years, this bank has endeavored to give back to the community. One of the things we've done, for at least thirty years now, is set up a fund that goes one hundred percent towards buying a Christmas gift for each and every child who is hospitalized for an extended period of time in New York's area hospitals and will be in the hospital on Christmas Day. These children range from accident victims to children battling terminal illnesses and every child in between.

"At the beginning of the first week of December, hundreds of volunteers, many from our own bank on their own time, help the children create a list for Santa. Then, Sun Ridge purchases one of the gifts on the list, crosses it off, and then the lists are turned over to other benevolent organizations around the city who do the exact same thing. By handling it this way, these children get more than one gift, and hopefully, have their hope in mankind and the season strengthened a little."

"That's got to be at least...what? Fifty hospitals?" Bowen said.

"More like sixty-plus," Gordon said. "However, not all of them have wards which deal with long-term pediatric patients."

"The bank buys toys for all the kids who have been...what? Burned in a house fire? Suffered some broken bones in a car accident? Battling cancer? Those kinds of things?" Witherspoon said.

Gordon affixed the sticky note with the account number to his computer screen. "Yes. All those you mentioned, as well as children who are gunshot victims, domestic abuse victims, and every terminal illness you can name. The list is substantial in number, and it seems to grow each year too.

"So," Gordon said with a simultaneous sigh and a smile, "each Christmas season, we take donations toward the cause, as do other organizations and companies. Sun Ridge doesn't foot the entire bill. However, each year, the bank does pick up the tab on the leftover balance. Last year, we paid out almost forty thousand dollars to break even. With the economy the way it is, we're expecting that total to be higher this year."

"I didn't know we did that, Mr. Ames." I said.

Gordon offered a shy grin. "It's what we do."

"Your Christmas fund is scheduled to receive forty-eight thousand dollars from Kenneth Singh once the check clears?" Bowen said.

"Yes." Gordon tapped his keyboard. "It will be directly deposited into that fund and help pay for all the gifts for the kiddos. And help us get closer to the break-even margin. Every little bit helps."

"What if you go over your break-even amount?" Witherspoon said.

"Then, we'd just roll it over into next year's fund. But trust me, we've never been close in all the years of doing this."

Witherspoon nodded. "And we still have no idea where Mr. Singh got the money or why he's funneling it to your Christmas fund. That would concern me, if I was you, Mr. Ames."

"Oh, no, don't get me wrong. It concerns me too. I don't want any controversy to affect the bank's benevolent efforts. I've already flagged the check to have the money held in his account until I've given the word to release it into the fund's account. That money doesn't budge until I release it myself. Trust me. I've been doing this a long time. I've dealt with my fair share of federal investigations."

"We appreciate that." Bowen looked over at Witherspoon. "We also appreciate your generosity. I'm sure the kids and their families do too."

"Don't mention it. When you compare it to what those children are going through, it seems so small."

"Well, I for one am glad institutions like this exist." Bowen stood and pulled out a small wallet from her coat pocket. She reached inside and slid out a twenty-dollar bill. "Speaking of small, here. Please put this toward your fund. Maybe it'll buy one child some happiness this Christmas."

Gordon stood and took it. "Thank you. I will deposit this personally."

Bowen smiled and turned to her partner. "Is there anything else we need to know before we head out?"

Witherspoon stood and followed Bowen's lead, handing Gordon another twenty bucks. "Nope. Just this. Thank you."

Gordon accepted the money and shook his guests' hands. "Miss Hamar, would you get their contact information so that if we come across any additional information, we can let them know?"

"Oh, here, take my card," Bowen said. "Although, I have a profound suspicion the next people to contact you will be the FBI."

Gordon smiled. "We'll be ready."

CHAPTER FORTY-SEVEN

West 173rd Street
Washington Heights, NY

Santorino's closed at seven o'clock like they said they were going to do, although we were extremely busy with large parties. Very few couples. I chalked it up to guests coming into town for the holidays, and the hosts not wanting to cook for everybody. Instead, they were showing them the sights and grabbing a bite to eat along the way. I could tell. Almost every group had arguments over who was picking up the check.

> *"No, this was my idea, Harold. Let me pay for this."*
>
> *"I will do no such thing, Peter. We're imposing on your home. The least I can do is pay for an excellent meal. If you must, maybe you can treat us to dessert later."*

At least I knew they enjoyed the food.

And they had family, lots of family, to spend the holidays with.

I, on the other hand, had Momma.

That was it.

I drove past buildings with holiday lights aglow in the cold, crisp night air. Some white. Others multicolored. Some looking like dripping icicles. Others blinking and flashing in random order.

Tomorrow, on what was supposed to be one of the happiest days of the year, according to Tiny Tim Cratchit, I'd go to LIPC. Momma would open her gifts from me. She would apologize for not having anything for me since she never is allowed to leave. We'd eventually go to the dining room with many of the other patients and eat a cafeteria-style Christmas meal of turkey and stuffing, listen to some singers from a local theater group or church choir sing all the hits of the season. Then I'd escort Momma back to her room. I'd give her a kiss and a hug good-bye. And I'd leave. Christmas Day. Over by six o'clock.

Been that way for a long time. One psychiatric hospital after another. One sterile holiday to the next.

Antiseptically clean.

Emotionally draining.

Anticipatorily dull.

Again, I contemplated leaving a little early this year. Maybe before the dinner? Head for Gordon's place. He'd invited me over, so if I explained it to Momma, she would understand. She'd probably encourage it. Besides, if I went earlier in the day and spent more time with her before the dinner, she'd probably like that more anyway. And she'd doubtless be excited about me leaving to go on a date of sorts. Finally pleased I was being pursued by a man and actually pursuing the relationship in return.

Then, of course, Momma and I would more than likely spend a great deal of our time talking about Gordon. She'd want to know everything about him, sizing him up, making sure he was good enough for her little girl. I guess that's what mothers do.

What mothers do…

What do mothers do?

How did that feel?

To be a mother?

Tears bordered my eyes.

Stop!

Don't go there. Not tonight.

Not at Christmas.

But just imagine what Christmas Day would have been like all these years if—

Stop! Pleeease!

Having a little one ripping open presents on Christmas morning…

Please, stop…

Tears began to drip down my cheeks.

Watching their eyes sparkle when they see the gift they've always wanted…

I beg you, please.

To hear the laughter…the newfound joy…

I ran my hands over my eyes, attempting to dry them. The weeping blurred my vision, making it hard to drive.

The wrestling match between my mind and soul, the one that arose every Christmas, every Mother's Day, and on the anniversary of that regretful afternoon in Rosemont, Illinois, at the urging of Joanie, haunts me all the time. Lying on that cold table. Having the doctor assure me everything was going to be okay.

"It will all be over soon," he said, as the nurse gently rubbed my shoulder.

They lied to me, though.

It's never been over.

The sting, the torment, the inner hell…it springs forth from something as delicate as a smell, like that of a baby's blanket immersed in baby powder.

From something as wondrous as a sound, like that of a crying baby in a restaurant.

From something as ordinary and yet magnificent as watching another woman hold her child's hand as they cross the street. Or play in a park. Or pretend to play hopscotch on a sidewalk. Or walk up and down the aisles in a grocery store, filling their cart with goodies.

Just knowing, in each instance, like Christmas morning, when, of all things, the birth of a baby would be celebrated, that it should be a time for little ones to experience joy, happiness, and love.

But instead of those emotions, I experienced utter heartache.

On Mother's Day, particularly, I was—no, still am—hounded by what I allowed to be ripped away. A chance at joy, a chance at happiness, and chance at love, extinguished.

A part of myself…

It died that day.

What should have brought completeness and fulfillment now brings only regret, despair, and loneliness.

You have the power to make good choices, someone once told me, but you don't have the power to choose your consequences.

Nor the amount of guilt one must suffer.

"I am so sorry, my little one."

"Please, forgive me."

ARRIVING HOME AS AN EMOTIONAL MESS, I just wanted to go crawl into bed. Maybe pull a pillow over my head.

Or better yet, my face.

I plodded into the mailroom. With tomorrow a holiday, I expected to see two letters addressed to me, but when I opened the mail slot. I found only one, and nothing else.

Interesting.

I slogged upstairs, entered my apartment, and closed the door.

I realized, twisting the deadbolt, that I'd actually changed over time.

At the beginning, when the letters first arrived, I was puzzled. They made no sense. Scribbles on a page. Rudimentary pictures. Then, I felt apprehensive as they started to describe familiar, personal things.

Apprehension, however, gave way to dread as they continued delving deeper, almost like someone had been spying on me as a child and writing about it in an ambiguous, mysterious fashion.

But now, standing inside my door, I felt curious. To the point of being relieved I found one in my mailbox, if that makes any sense at all.

Maybe it was a release. An escape. A way to avoid my current situation with Joanie, Momma, and Billy. Or a way of simply sidestepping my sadness.

Lord knows I've had plenty of that.

I set my purse down on the coffee table and opened the letter like it was from a dear friend.

Today, I met a man. Daddy says he's my uncle. He's taller than me. The top of my head barely reaches his shoulders. He's definitely bigger too. Broad shoulders. Large hands. When I put the palm of my hand against his, the tips of my fingers only reach the first knuckle on his. Yet, despite his massive presence, he's such a nice man.

I slowly made my way onto the couch as I read.

My uncle told me that he's always lived here. Our home is the only one he's ever known. As I thought about it, the same was true for me. Actually, a lot of people here say that. Of course, I haven't spoken to everybody, but Daddy says I'll get to someday. He said, "It may take years, but who's counting, right?" Daddy's such a funny man. Kind and sweet too. The best Daddy a child could ever have.

I pulled my legs up beside me.

I have talked to other people here who have lived in different places before. No matter where they come from, it's always a joyous story. The memories are good ones. As a matter of fact, I can't recall meeting anyone who seemed anything but happy.

I've heard Daddy mention that some people come here from other places "depressed" or "down." He's even used words like "sad" or "confused."

Daddy says when that happens, all it takes is a gentle hug and a wipe of their cheek, and the things that make people sad and depressed disappear.

I have to admit, I'm not sure what words like "sad" and "depressed" mean exactly. I've heard of them, but I've never experienced them for myself. But how can you in a place like this?

As I write this letter, I'm lying under a sunny sky. Birds are tweeting overhead. The wind is whistling through the trees. There's a creek close by. Its gurgling sound is a lullaby. There are songs drifting over the mountains.

I think I'll take a nap and enjoy the peace.

Goosebumps scattered across my body.
What did she say about the creek?
"Its gurgling sound is a lullaby…"
Those were my words…
That's what I told Billy…
The night he…
I closed my eyes, fighting back the growing tidal wave of emotion rising in my chest.

Breathe.

In.

Out.

The creek. I remember the creek. It definitely was a lullaby. I just wanted to go to sleep in Billy's arms. Stay there forever. Listen to his heartbeat.

A tear dripped from my cheek and fell upon the page.

Breathe.

In.

Out.

Thoughts became difficult to sort out.

The meadow…Billy…Daddy being arrested…Momma in her room…The conversation in Gordon's office…A fund for ill children…How sweet…Making Christmas about someone other than yourself…People less fortunate…People in need…Making it about family.

About friends.

And loved ones.

Even if you only have one.

At least you have one, Rachel.

And at least you're not in a hospital bed. Wondering if you'll see another Christmas.

My cell phone rang, and I almost let it go to voice mail. I finally decided to answer it.

By the time I got up and grabbed my purse, the phone went silent. I unzipped the pouch and checked it anyway.

Gordon.

I started to call him back when the phone rang again.

"Hey, Gordon. Sorry, I missed your call. By the time I got to it, it went to voice mail."

"No problem. I was calling to see if you are able to make it tomorrow night for dinner. Again, no pressure. I know you're going to see your mom, and that's important."

"I was just sitting here on the couch when you called, trying to decide what to do, and you know what? It's becoming clear to me that I need to go spend this time with my mother."

"I understand completely."

"You know, uh…" I dried my cheek with the back of my hand. "It was the bank's Christmas fund that got me to realize what I needed to do. Well, actually, it was your little speech about the fund and how it works that got me to thinking. It's about others, Gordon. This holiday, right? Above all the other holidays, it's about those kids, others who are in need. Those who are hurting. Those who are lonely. Right?"

Gordon didn't respond immediately. I heard him clear his throat. "I couldn't agree more. That's why I've always wrestled with Christmas since my wife passed away. I get overwhelmed with loneliness this time of year because I miss her. Yet, when I start feeling sorry for myself, then I feel guilty."

"Well, I think everybody would understand your feelings of loneliness. It means you loved her very much."

"Still do."

I couldn't help it, but a tear escaped and raced down my cheek. Gordon was my friend, and he was hurting too. And his troubles had nothing to do with poor or selfish choices like mine did. "Well, I'll tell you what. How about I spend tomorrow with my mother, and New Year's Eve with you and your family…if the invitation is still open?"

"Of course, it is. That sounds like a plan. A good plan."

"Then, uh, it's a date?"

There was a slight pause on the other end. My heart almost stopped.

"I, uh, um…think that would be a very appropriate way of putting it," Gordon said.

Oh, Gordon. I know it's been a long time since you dated anybody, but you can't hesitate like that.

Sends a girl's heart into arrhythmia.

But it's okay. We'll work on it.

"I don't mean to pressure you or anything, Gordon. If calling this a date is—"

"No, it's not that at all. I think calling it a date is perfect. I just…uh, well, to be totally honest, I never thought anyone else would ever be interested in a guy like me."

"Are you kidding? You're a great guy. I'll bet there's a bunch of women who'd love to be hanging from your arm."

"Just my arm? And not my bank account?"

Okay, if you put it like that, the list probably does dwindle a bit.

"Well, let me make myself perfectly clear. I'm not interested in your money, Gordon. And I hope I've made that clear already, but it doesn't hurt to reiterate it."

"I believe you."

"Good. So, it's a date. New Year's Eve. Your place. And we'll discuss a time later?"

"Yes."

"All right, then. I should probably go. I just got home from the restaurant. I still need to take a shower."

"You have a blessed Christmas Day tomorrow with your mother. May it be a pleasant time for the both of you. And, I'll see you Friday."

"You enjoy your family tomorrow as well. Tell Heather I said, hi."

"I will. Merry Christmas, Rachel."

"Merry Christmas to you, Gordon."

He hung up, and I held the phone in my hand, looking at his name on the screen.

Christmas Day
December 25, 2014

CHAPTER FORTY-EIGHT

West 173rd Street
Washington Heights, NY

The alarm clock's red numbers said 8:42 a.m. when I rolled over.

Wow. I must have been really tired.

I rolled onto my back and stretched. The warmth of the covers beckoned, and I pulled them up over my shoulders and rolled the other direction.

Half of New York City has already opened all their Christmas gifts by now.

And I don't even have a tree.

Gave that up a few years ago. Joanie was never into Christmas, so I did all the decorating.

It started with a small, artificial tree sitting on an end table, which was pushed into the corner of the living room. A sparse set of twinkle lights wrapped around it. Half the lights would short out, so I'd have to jiggle them to come back on. A few ornaments hung from the branches. Most came from work.

Colleagues and bosses. One advertised my old bank. And, of course, an angel who sat atop the tree.

I also had little snowmen knick-knacks on the same table as the tree. Each one held a letter. One held a "J." One held an "O." The last one held a "Y." But that was years ago.

I huffed and pulled the covers tighter.

When Momma shifted to the ninth floor and life became progressively more difficult, the "J-O-Y," like Elvis, had left the building.

I rolled over onto my back.

I need to get up. I do not want to lie here and wallow. It's Christmas. I need coffee. I need to get dressed. I need to get ready and go see Momma.

She'll be shocked if I show up before noon.

"It's about others, Rachel Leah. Right?"

I whipped the covers off me and sat up.

Oh, my, it's cold in here.

I jumped up and shivered my way to the thermostat.

It's sixty-three degrees! No wonder I'm freezing.

I bumped the heat up a couple of degrees and went back into the bedroom. Grabbing my blanket, I wrapped it around me, and lumbered into the kitchen.

I dumped a few scoops of coffee into the basket and started the contraption, knowing the coffee maker was just a few more pots away from the trashcan. Joanie and I kept saying we needed a new one, but neither of us took the time or money to buy one.

Now, I guess it's my responsibility.

I walked over to the front window and parted the curtains. A fresh blanket of snow fell overnight, and just a few flurries fluttered about in the morning air. The plows hadn't been by, so the dirty slush of the salt and sand hadn't scarred the beauty yet. Only a couple sets of tire tracks left their mark, showing the whole world where they came from and where they went.

Why does snow always make Christmas brighter?

Is it the newness? Is it the magical feel it exudes?

I could have stood there forever, despite the fact my view was of West 173rd Street and not a mountain range. The couple walking across the street, hand in hand, didn't seem to mind either. The little boy on his new bicycle couldn't have been happier.

A poorer side of town.

And Christmas came here too.

Just then, I saw a man appear on the sidewalk. He looked like he came from our entryway. And he was wearing a mailman's uniform. A small pouch draped over his shoulder.

Wait a minute. I know they work on Sunday now, but not holidays. Right?

I watched him cross the street, follow the couple for about a block, then turn down an alley.

No. That wasn't a mailman. He would have a truck. No mailman is gonna be hoofin' it on Christmas Day.

As I scanned the street below, a mail truck emerged from an alley one block away, its right turn signal flashing. The truck waited for a cab to pass then pulled out onto the street and motored out of sight.

I stood there and wondered why a mailman would be working on Christmas Day.

Did he not get all his mail delivered yesterday? And who got mail today?

I closed the window and headed for the kitchen to get some coffee when I saw yesterday's letter lying on the couch.

No.

Surely not today.

I never got any on Sundays. So why on a holiday?

But you didn't get two yesterday…

I ran to the bedroom, threw on some clothes, and ran downstairs to the mailroom. I opened the mail slot, and there, leaning up against the inside of the box was another letter. I tore it open.

Since this will be my last entry, I've been wondering how to write what's on my heart. It seems each time I put words to the page, they can never quite explain how I feel. I could scribble on for paragraphs, use every descriptive word at my disposal, and ramble on like there's no tomorrow, yet somehow, the words would still fall short.

I began a slow walk up the stairs as I read.

I've tried as best I know how to give you a glimpse of life. As I see it. To be able to know that my life has meaning. My life is complete. I know why I'm here. How joyous and fulfilled my heart feels right this moment.

All I can say now is, you never gave up on me. You've always told me, "Love will always find you, if you look for it. It's all around you. Like the grass in the meadow on a beautiful summer's day. Like the trees in a serene forest. All you have to do is look." I believe you. You said it found me. The love here. The love I experience every day, and you're right. It did find me.

When I was in a dark place. When I experienced excruciating pain. It reached inside and found me. You wiped away my tears, and the pain went away. I now only know of dark places and terrible pain as words alone. They have no meaning here. Not where Love lives. I do not even truly recall what the dark place was or where it was. Or how the horrific pain affected me. But I do know this. It doesn't matter anymore. You have told me that death and pain and suffering have all died. They no longer exist here. And I believe it, because I experience it every waking moment.

I entered my apartment, locked the door behind me, and stood in the middle of the living room.

You said love is always available, always plentiful. I believe it because I've witnessed it. First hand. Daddy, you've always been there for me. From the day I arrived, I've known. You were the only one who loved me. The only one who cared. As I have learned, you are the only person I've ever needed. Sure, I have many friends. But you mean the most to me, Daddy. You're all I need. That's why I love you so much.

Thank you for bringing me home.

I went back to the window and opened the curtain, gazing upon the snow once more. Tiny snowflakes flittered past the glass and floated down upon the sidewalk, blending into a beautiful canvas of white.

Oh, how I long for that type of certainty.

That kind of peace.

That depth of feeling.

That kind of love.

CHAPTER FORTY-NINE

Long Island Psychiatric Center
Deer Park, NY

I arrived at the Long Island Psychiatric Center shortly after noon, dressed in my best effort to look the part of the happy, filled-with-the-joy-of-Christmas daughter, ready to see her mother in a place longing for hope.

Wearing a dark pair of slacks and a red blouse, I had also donned a sweater-vest that looked like wrapping paper, a gift from a co-worker at my old bank job. It had little penguins skiing to and fro, grasping ribbons and bows, racing around my torso, appearing to wrap me up like a present.

If Momma didn't like it, it was going in the trash.

I unzipped my coat and peeled off my gloves as I walked toward the receptionist's counter. A plastic grocery store bag hung from my left arm filled with all eighteen letters, organized chronologically, a rubber band around them to hold them together.

The usual suspects weren't working today. Instead, some

young girl I'd never seen before, no older than twenty, sat behind the desk, thumbing her cell phone.

Ah, the low person on the totem pole pulls the short straw of Christmas morning front desk duty.

How wonderful.

The girl glanced up at me as I crossed the lobby. She continued tapping away at the phone. Her thumbs of thunder pounded out something of note. The speed picking up, I noticed, trying to complete a semi-coherent thought before I said anything to interrupt.

Probably an emoji-filled, abbreviated to death, melodramatic exchange with a girlfriend about how lame her last boyfriend was.

Or possibly how unfair it is to be working today.

In 140 characters or less, of course.

For all the world to see.

Yet nobody will really care about it for more than two seconds. Because they are writing their own rants.

Same communiqués. Different words.

Our fifteen minutes of fame carved up into little groupings of characters on a screen. Slivers of seconds separated by profound lengths of soul-crushing anonymity.

Superficial. Paper-thin. Conversations.

Social media-style.

I stopped at the counter, and Britanie tapped the apparent last couple of letters.

I had a scone for breakfast last Tuesday, Britanie. Should I tweet that out?

She swung her head to the left, causing the long strands of blonde hair to reposition themselves over her shoulder, and set the phone down on the counter. Forming as big of a smile as she could muster for working on Christmas morning, she stood from her chair. "Good morning. How may I help you?"

I pulled out my driver's license and held it out. "I'm here to see Dorothy Hamar. I'm her daughter and on the contact list."

Britanie took my license and swiped it through the little card reader they'd used a hundred times before. After she saw I was indeed telling the truth, she clicked a couple of things while humming some tune I didn't recognize. "What's in the bag?"

"Oh, just letters I've received. I thought my mother would enjoy reading them."

"Wow. I didn't know people even wrote letters anymore."

I smiled, surprised but relieved she knew what a letter was.

Get your nose out of your phone, Britanie. It's a brave, new world out there, honey. One filled with advanced vocabulary, complete sentences, and punctuation.

A few seconds later, the machine spat out my printed pass. She grabbed it, pinched it together with my license, and handed me both at the same time. "Enjoy your stay." Again with the corporate smile.

"Thank you. Merry Christmas."

"Yeah. You too," she said, sitting back down, a hand already on her phone.

I made the trip up the elevator, hoping the nurses working today had a better temperament and sense of devotion toward their craft than Britanie.

When I reached the nurses' station on Momma's floor, it looked like Nurse Swanson sitting in front of a computer, facing away from me, entering some patient information. I cleared my throat. "Excuse me."

Nurse Swanson spun around in her chair. It took her a second to switch from data entry to facial recognition. "Oh, Miss Hamar, I didn't hear you walk up." She stood and came my direction. "Merry Christmas."

"Merry Christmas to you."

"How are you doing?" She worked her way around the tall counter.

"I'm doin' all right. How's my mother doing?"

She placed a hand on my shoulder. "She's as feisty as ever."

"That bad, huh?"

"No, no. Not bad." She twisted her face up and put her hands on her hips. "I'd call it more…"

"Mouthy? Cantankerous? Impossible?"

"No," she said with a slight chuckle. "I think opinionated would be the better word."

"Oh, well, she's always been that. Nothing new there."

"Honey, you don't have to convince me. I've seen it enough to know. But regardless, she's still a sweetie. She's one of my favorites. So, you ready to see her? I know she'll be so happy to see you today. You were all she talked about yesterday."

I motioned for her to lead the way. "What was she saying about me?"

We began a slow stroll toward Momma's room. "She had lots of stories about you when you were little."

"Oh, brother. That can't be good."

"It was cute." She nodded and then turned abruptly. "And speaking of that, I didn't know you had a brother."

"No, no, I don't. I was just saying, 'Oh, brother,' like 'Oh, boy,' 'Oh, bother.'"

She cocked her head slightly. "No, I mean, your mother said you had a brother. An older brother. Several years older than you."

"Lilly, I'm an only child. I've never had any siblings."

Her fallacious understanding morphed into a look of concern. "You're an only child?"

"Yes."

She pressed her lips together with obvious concern. "I'm so sorry. I thought…"

"Thought what?"

"I thought what she was telling me was true…" She gently grabbed my arm and stopped, shifting her stance toward me. The concern grew into more of a sorrowful demeanor. "One of the signs of the progression of the illness your mother is battling is a form of dementia. Patients who experience this begin to tell stories of people, places, and things they are convinced were part of their life but instead are probably recollections of stories they've heard others tell, either in person, on TV, or maybe have read about in the past. These stories come back to remembrance, and they get inserted into the mind as their own real-life experiences.

"So, if she's talking about an older brother, she's probably heard someone talk about one, and now, you have an older brother. For patients like your mother, these kinds of occurrences happen because the patient wishes something to be true or has regrets about something they wish had happened or didn't happen in the past."

I nodded, not really wanting to hear about how my momma was getting worse. Not on Christmas Day. "Like me being an only child, perhaps? I know Momma has mentioned that. Wished I had siblings to rely on at this time in my life."

"That's a possibility."

"She's mentioned more than once how scared she is about me being alone in the city."

"If she's voiced those concerns in the past, and wishes she'd had more children, then yes, a very typical response for patients like your mother would be to hear about someone else having an older brother and simply incorporate that into their life story. Now, as far as her mind is concerned, what brought sadness and regret now brings happiness and fulfillment. You now have a brother. One who can look after you."

Nurse Swanson's words cut to the heart. What she was telling me in psychological terms was, I was losing Momma too. First Billy. Then, Daddy. My baby. Joanie. Now, Momma. Different ways, but I had lost them or was losing them, nevertheless.

With each word about dementia and patients and older brothers, another tear formed in the corner of my eyes.

Finally, she stopped, realizing her explanation was getting to me. She placed her hand on my shoulder again. "Rachel, I'm so sorry. But don't lose hope. We're doing everything we can. And your mother still has her wits about her. She's still sharp as a tack in many areas. Still carries on conversations like she always has."

"But she's…slipping."

Nurse Swanson formed a frown at the corner of her mouth. "It appears to be slowly, but yes."

"It's probably from being locked up in here."

"She has plenty of interaction, if that's what you're afraid of. She sees a therapist once a day. She gets her two fresh air breaks every day. She goes to the dining room for all three meals twice a week now. She's even started being allowed to go to the rec room and watch TV or play board games with other patients."

"Does she? Play games with others?"

She shook her head. "Usually, she'll watch a little TV."

"But?"

Nurse Swanson grimaced. "But most of the time, she'll stand at the window and mutter to herself. When you ask her what she's talking about, she says, 'All sorts of things. That's what you do when you pray.'"

"At least that part hasn't changed."

"Oh, no. I've never seen a person, patient or otherwise, pray as much as your mother does."

"Can I see her now?"

She gave my shoulder a gentle squeeze. "Certainly."

We took the last steps leading to Momma's room, and Nurse Swanson peeked into the door's window. "Good. She's awake." She inserted her key into the lock. "She just got back from lunch."

She opened the door and led me inside. "Merry Christmas, Dorothy."

"Merry Christmas, Lilly." Momma was standing and pinned her eyes to me. "And to you, sweetheart. I'm so glad you came today." Her eyes shimmered, filling with tears.

I almost ran to her. We embraced, and I practically squeezed the life out of her. "Merry Christmas, Momma."

"Oh, baby girl."

"Well," Nurse Swanson said, "I'm gonna leave you two alone. If you need anything, just holler."

"Thank you, Lilly," I said, still hugging Momma.

I heard some footsteps and then the door closed.

Momma finally separated us just enough to look me in the eye. "I have been praying for you so much. I've been so concerned. I heard Joanie moved out, and I knew you'd be—"

"Wait a minute." I grabbed Momma by the shoulders and held her at arm's length. "How did you know about Joanie? I haven't talked to you since it happened."

Momma fashioned one of those little "I'm the Momma, I know everything" grins on her face and added a little roll of the eyes and head. "A little birdie told me."

"A little birdie, huh?"

"I guess you could say that."

"No, seriously. What do you have? A spy keeping tabs on me day and night?"

"I guess you could say that too."

"Momma..."

"Does it matter, sweetheart? Besides, if I told you, you wouldn't believe it anyway."

I released her and sat down on the bed.

If it has to do with God, then yeah, you're probably right.

"I told you," she said.

I jerked my gaze up to meet hers. "What did you say?"

"You're right. It does have to do with God."

"How did you—" I held my hands up in surrender. "Never mind."

I looked around the room. Everything was in its place. Nothing new in the way of furniture or decorations, except for some folded pieces of paper that looked like some kind of animal. "Momma, are you learning origami?"

"Yeah, whatever they call it. They say it's fun, but I know why they do it."

"Why?"

"To try and build up the dexterity in our fingers."

"Is that what they told you?"

"No. But why else would they teach me how to fold my napkin into a swan? It ain't like I'm gonna start working on some swanky cruise ship anytime soon."

I shook my head. Some things will never change. "Maybe they just want to teach you a skill, Momma. In this case, art."

Momma sat down beside me and patted me on the thigh. "There ain't nothin' they do here that doesn't have a purpose." She fixed her eyes on me again. "Even the prunes they feed us are on a mission."

"Ah, yeah, well,…let's change the subject before I lose my appetite."

She studied me for a moment. A motherly smile spread across her face before her eyes lowered to my arm. "What's in the bag?"

"Oh, that's right, I have something for you." I reached inside the bag and then stopped. "I know it's not much, but I wasn't sure what they would allow in here. Close your eyes, and hold out your hands."

She did. Her smile grew bigger.

I pulled out a box of chocolate-covered cherries, the kind she liked, wrapped up in red and green paper with a little silver bow affixed to the top. I set them in her waiting hands. "All right. Open your eyes."

Her eyes blossomed. She turned to me with a girlish giggle and proceeded to open the gift.

"I smuggled them in. The girl at the counter asked what was in the bag, but she didn't inspect it like they're supposed to. I figured, she didn't ask, so I'm not tellin'. If they get bent out of shape, I'll tell them they need to train their people better." I shook my head. "Makes me wonder what else gets in this place when no one's lookin'."

Momma, as she always did, finally unsecured the ends of the gift in such a way where someone could reuse the paper if they chose. She slid the box out without ripping the edges. "Ahhh. You remembered."

"Of course, I did, Momma. They're your favorite."

"They are. And I will eat every last one of them, unless your taste buds have changed, then I'll only share them with you."

I draped my arm around her. "Well, it appears I'm not the only one who remembered something. And no, my taste buds haven't changed. I still can't stand those things, so they're all yours."

She opened the box and gently plucked one from its little plastic bed. She popped it in her mouth and radiated a smile I found comforting. Her cheeks bulging as she chewed.

"Some things never change, do they, Momma?"

She shook her head but couldn't speak without drooling chocolate sauce all over her chin.

Then, she pointed at the bag and exaggerated her chewing, trying to finish her treat so she could speak. With a dramatic *gulp,* she said, "What else ya got?"

"Momma! Is that all you want from me today? Presents?"

She cleared out the remaining vestiges of the morsel with her tongue. "No. That's not what I meant. You know I don't care about presents. Never have. I mean, not that I don't like these," she said, hugging her box of candy, "but I always enjoyed watching you and your daddy open gifts. That's where I found my joy this time of year." She ran her fingers through my hair and tucked it behind my ear. "Always have."

"It was fun watching you open your gift just now."

Momma brushed my hair once more before allowing her hand to flop back into her lap. "I'm sorry I don't have anything for you. We don't get out much."

Momma's humor could be morbid sometimes. "You could make me an origami swan."

"Do you want an origami swan?"

"Not really, but from you, it would be nice."

"Then, that's what I'll do. I'll work on a special one and have it ready for your next visit."

"Deal."

Momma playfully pulled me close and gave me a quick peck on the cheek. "That's why I struggle so much around the holidays. Especially this one. Being in here. Not being able to go shopping." She paused. I could detect a catch in her throat. "Imagining you out there…My baby girl…Out there all alone in this big city. It troubles me."

"Momma, I'm fine." I gazed at the shiny tile floor. "I just have some issues to work through. That's all. And yes, Joanie moved out. She went to live with her boyfriend. So, now I have to figure out where I'm going to live. I can't stay in that apartment. It's too expensive."

She rubbed her index finger against the top of the candy box. "I wish I could help. That's why I pray. I'm stuck in here, but God isn't."

"Well, maybe the next time you talk to Him, maybe you could ask Him to help me find an apartment."

"I have been, and I will continue to do so. It may not wind up being an apartment, but you never know what God has planned sometimes until it happens. He may choose to help you in other ways."

"You know, now that you mention it, I did receive a large

sum of money the other day." I squinted at her. "Did you send me money, perhaps?"

"Me? Do I look like I have any money?"

"Don't you get social security?"

"I get Daddy's now. And what little pension he had built up. But, it all goes to this place. The bill for here is a lot more than what I get each month. Ain't nothin' left over for me."

I always wondered how that worked, but I never had worked up the nerve to ask. "I'm so sorry, Momma. I'll try to send you some money so you can—"

"So I can what? There ain't nothing here to buy."

"Do you get to go online and shop?"

"There is a computer in the rec room, but I don't know how to work the thing."

"I could teach you."

Momma wrinkled her nose and shook her head. "I probably wouldn't be allowed to buy anything. They're very strict about what we can have in our rooms. Just the other day, a man on the floor below us ripped his extra pair of pajamas into tiny strips, tied them together, and made himself a long rope."

"Oh, my."

"It's sad in here. Lots of battles going on. We lost that one."

I didn't know how to respond, so I simply opened the bag and retrieved the letters. "Speaking of unexpected happenings, I've been receiving these." I pulled the letters from the bag and flattened it beside me so it wouldn't fall to the floor. I unwound the rubber band from the bundled letters. "Started getting these about two weeks ago. They're all addressed to me. None of them have return addresses." I sorted through them so Momma could see. "As you can see, almost all of them, except for this one in the red box, came in this kind of envelope.

"However, each letter is different." I opened the first one. "They started out like this." I gently removed the paper and unfolded it. I handed it to Momma. "We thought it was some little child. Got ahold of a pencil and started scribbling."

She turned it over and examined both sides. Her expression wasn't what I expected but instead was hard to read. She didn't say anything. She simply folded the letter and held it. "What about the others?"

I opened the second one and handed it to her. "More scribbles. And what looks like a little child trying to write his or her alphabet."

Momma set the first letter beside her and took the second. When she saw the picture, her eyes welled up.

"What is it, Momma?"

There was a long pause. I could tell she was trying to get her thoughts together without becoming a blathering idiot, as she always liked to say.

"These remind me of when you were little. Always such the little artist. You would hold your tongue just so," she said, mimicking what she remembered, with her tongue sticking out just a little. Her lips pressed against it like she was thinking really hard. Her hand held out like she was writing something. "I used to sit at the dining room table and watch you go to town on one drawing after another. You'd scribble something, fling it in my direction, tell me it was this and that, then be right back at it on a new sheet of paper." She began to laugh. "Oh, those were good days. I remember telling your daddy that we needed a bigger refrigerator to hold 'em all."

"I remember some of that. Especially the phase where I had that paint by numbers set. You remember that?"

"I sure do. You thought you were Rembrandt's daughter. It was so cute. And you'd get so mad if you accidentally painted outside the lines and got one color lopped over onto another." She guffawed. "You'd ask me to paint it white and redraw the lines so you could start over. You were such a little perfectionist back then."

"I was, wasn't I?"

"Yes, you were."

"So, what happened to that? I don't see myself as a perfectionist now."

"Oh, you'd be surprised how much of it has stuck with you."

"What's that supposed to mean?"

Momma held up the letter in her hand. "Take these, for example. You say you got eighteen of these?"

"Yes. Well, they're not all like that one, but yes. Eighteen in all."

"And you have no idea where they came from?"

"Nope."

"But they're all addressed to you?"

"Yep."

"At your apartment? Not your work?"

"Yes."

She looked me in the eye like only a mother can do. "And you just read them? Then put them in this bag? And brought them here?"

"Not exactly."

Momma's head began to bob in affirmation. "Of course, Miss I-have-to-know-everything-about-these-letters-or-I'm-gonna-die."

"I'm not like that."

"Didn't you call the police?"

My shoulders slumped. "Yes."

Momma's frame bounced as she laughed to herself. "You've always been that way. No stone unturned, and no one could convince you of nothin' unless you figured it out for yourself. I always thought you would've made a great detective. Like that Sherwood Holmes character."

"Sherlock, Momma. Sherlock Holmes."

She waved me off. "Sherwood, Sherlock, Sherbet. Whatever his name is, that's not the point. When Detective Bowen came here to see me, I thought to myself, 'That could've been my Rachel Leah.'"

"I don't think I could do her job. I'd probably faint at the first sign of blood."

"Maybe. It takes a tough cookie to deal with the scum of the earth day in and day out. It's gotta affect you. But, I know you well enough to know you got the police involved in this matter." She held up the letter again. "Probably thought some stalker was after you, didn't you?"

"Now, how do you know that?"

"I'm just guessing." Her chin lifted a little higher, but her eyes remained fixed on mine.

"Uh-huh." I wasn't convinced. "Did Detective Bowen tell you all that?"

"She did not."

"So how did you know about these letters?"

"Detective Bowen told me about them…briefly…when she paid me a visit."

"What did she tell you about them?"

"Not much. Only that you were receiving some mysterious letters in the mail." Momma opened the letter in her hand again and stared at it. Her change in tone made me shudder. "She wanted to know if I knew anything about them at all."

"Momma? What did you tell her?"

"Nothing."

I studied her facial expression. I watched her eyes scan the letter. "What did you tell Detective Bowen? About the letters?"

"Nothing. We really didn't get a chance to talk about them. Dr. Hausberger was in one of his moods. Tried to take over the entire conversation with his psychobabble."

"So, what did Detective Bowen talk to you about? What did you say? What did you do?"

Momma's finger retraced the letters on the page. "Only what I was asked to do."

"You're talking in circles." I held up the stack of remaining letters. "Momma, I can see it in your eyes. You're not being truthful."

"I'd never lie about such things, Rachel Leah."

"Then, tell me the truth. What did Detective Bowen—"

Momma lifted her hand. "I sent them."

What?

I glanced around the room, looking for signs of her ability to do such a thing. Paper. A pencil. A box of crayons. Anything that would've been used to write the letters. I only saw origami swans. I furrowed my brow. "You sent them?"

Momma nodded.

I shook my head. "Nope. I'm not believin' it."

She stalled, waiting several seconds before answering. "I was asked to."

"By who? No, wait." I held my hand up and pinched my eyes shut. "Please don't tell me it was God, or I'm walking out of here right now."

Holding the letter still, she rubbed her thumbs gently against the page. "It wasn't God, honey."

"That's a relief."

"Mary asked me to do it. She told me what to write, and I wrote it down for her."

"Mary? The Mary you talk to all the time? The one who came after Jesus and Joseph?"

Momma nodded again.

Well, maybe it's not such a relief after all.

"So, Jesus' mother told you to write this stuff down?"

"No, silly." Momma broke out into laughter. The kind of laughter people exhibit when they need to release some tension. "Not that Mary."

"I thought they were one and the same."

Suddenly, her soft expression exploded into wild laughter.

"So, that's what everybody's been thinking all these years? That I was talking to Jesus and his parents?"

I blinked. "Yes."

She continued to laugh. "Now that is hilarious. No wonder they have me locked up in here."

"So, who's Mary then?"

Still holding it, Momma held up the second letter I received and retraced the four letters scribbled on it. "Do you know what these are, Rachel?"

"Yeah. They're letters. So what?"

"But what letters?"

"Two A's and Two B's. So?"

Momma held it up so both of us could see it. "Yes. The first two letters of the alphabet. Written twice. But do you know their significance?"

I shrugged in frustration.

With her finger, she pointed at the letters like a teacher in a class. "A-B-B-A. It's the Hebrew word for 'Daddy.' *Abba.* Rachel, this child was writing to her Daddy. She was writing to God."

"Who? What child?"

"Mary."

"But Mary isn't a child."

"We're not talking about the Mary of the Bible, sweetheart." Momma dropped the letter into her lap. "I'm talking about my granddaughter."

An eeriness swept into the room. Goosebumps shot in every direction. It was like all time stopped on a dime. "But you don't have any grandch…"

Momma began to nod. My facial expression must have confirmed her suspicions. "Thaat's right, sweetheart…You're starting to understand now." She held my hand. "Here," she said, pointing toward the corner of the room. "I want you to meet someone."

I slowly faced the corner. Fear swelled in my gut.

A sudden sparkle emerged from nothing, just mere feet in front of me. The twinkling of what looked like stars blended into a swirling, roiling, cloud-like mass. From the churning smoke, a child's face came into view. A girl. Dark hair. A small child. Maybe one-year-old. No older than two. Yet, not like a child at all but instead, a teenage girl. Full of life and years. Her face like a tender flower, without blemish. Yet not like a young woman, but like a bustling child no older than ten. Her face and arms flailing in happiness, like someone was tickling her incessantly. The extremities appeared to be long, like those of an adult. Now, a child's. Flailing again, but like that of a baby fresh from the womb. The cackles of laughter transforming into the cries of a newborn.

I leaned back, away from the apparition, but Momma wrapped her arm around me and pulled me tight. "It's okay, Rachel. I want you to meet Mary. My granddaughter." Then, Momma looked at me. "Your daughter."

I couldn't speak. I don't know why, but my lips wouldn't budge. All I could do was pull back, like I was trying to clear the image. The way a child shakes an Etch-a-Sketch.

The vision slowly came into focus, and, standing before us, was a little girl. Four years old. Maybe five. Wearing a cute little spring-like dress. Barefoot. With a flower tucked into her long, flowing, dark hair.

A buttercup.

As I stared at her, she smiled, and for a quick instant, I saw Billy's face. That person I so loved. Loved still. It was in the way she curled her lip. The way her right eye squinted slightly. She had his smile.

"Rachel, are you okay?" Momma said.

I pointed at the girl with a trembling hand.

She slowly changed into a baby just old enough to crawl. On all fours. Rocking backward and forward. A look of determination on her face. A white robe-looking garment draped around her.

"Can…can she…speak?"

"She can." Momma gazed upon the vision before us. "Mary, as I had hoped, and as your Daddy had promised, if we could get her this far, you would be allowed to talk to your mother."

Then, before us, morphing from a newborn, stood a young woman. Seventeen. Maybe eighteen. Dressed in a long, flowing gown, she became as clear and distinct as Momma.

"Hello," Mary said.

I simply sat still. I didn't know what to say.

Momma nudged me. "Well? Aren't you going to say something?"

I looked at her and back at the girl. "Hi."

The young girl nodded slightly. "Did you get my letters?"

"Your letters?"

"Yes. I spoke to Daddy when I arrived here, and He saw how sad I was. He wiped the tears from my eyes and assured me everything would be all right. I told Him that I felt bad because you blamed yourself for sending me here, and I wanted to tell you not to fret or be discouraged. I was, as you often say in your world, 'in a better place,' and I wanted to convey that to you.

"Daddy said, 'Would you like to write her? I'm very good at sending people messages.' He told me He had been doing that for a long time."

I turned to Momma. My befuddled expression must have been amusing, because she let out a small chuckle. "She's talking about the Bible, sweetheart. She's never seen it, you know."

"How could she have never seen the Bible…" Then, it occurred to me.

She never had a chance.

I closed my eyes for a brief moment. "Mary, I am so sorry for what I did." Sorrow overwhelmed me, and I began to cry. "There's not a day that passes where I don't think about you, wishing you were here with me…wondering what you looked like…imagining how you would have grown up…wondering what kind of woman you would have become…" I wiped my eyes but to no avail. "Look at you. You're an angel."

The girl shifted again, growing shorter. Now, under four feet tall and appearing as an eight-year-old. "No, I'm not an angel. There are angels here, but I'm not one of them. They look a lot different than I do. I'm Daddy's child. That's what He calls me."

I grabbed the letters, slid off the bed, and knelt down before the girl. "You wrote these? For me?"

"I did."

"Because you wanted to let me know you were okay?"

The little girl nodded. "Daddy told me that it was not a common request. And He does not do this every time. But in this case, He said, it was for the best."

I sniffed and tried to gain a little composure. "So, when you wrote about the buttercups and the bear named Buttons, you were recalling times from my life, right? Your Daddy must have told you about me when I was growing up, perhaps?"

The little girl's face scrunched up for a moment before smiling. "No. I was telling you about my life. I picked that buttercup and asked Daddy to make sure He put it in the letter for me. That is my favorite buttercup of all time."

My heart melted at the thought of my daughter giving me her favorite anything. Tears streamed down my face and neck.

"And I have a bear named Buttons. See?"

Just then, the little girl changed into a five-year-old holding a stuffed animal before transforming into a young teenager. "Daddy said I was just like you when you were little."

"I guess you are."

The girl nodded and held out her arms.

I looked at Momma. The question on my face apparent.

"Go ahead, sweetheart. With God, all things are possible."

I rose up to meet her and extended my arms, and before I

could get fully off my knees, the teenager switched back to the five-year-old and clutched my neck.

A warmth I'd never felt, not before and not since, wrapped around me like a heavy, welcomed blanket. I couldn't contain myself. My grief. My regret. My sorrow. It all came bursting forth. Tears gave way to sobs. A massive groundswell of mourning, rooted deep within my soul, broke loose.

Mary patted me on the back just like a little girl her age would do. "It's okay, Mommy. I forgive you."

That did it.

The sobs gave way to wailing.

"I'm okay, Mommy. I know you didn't mean to hurt me. I know."

I couldn't hold myself up anymore. I began to fall, faint with overwhelming anguish, when stronger arms gripped me and pulled me up.

Now I was standing, holding my eighteen-year-old daughter.

"I've always loved you, Mom."

I seized her tighter. "And I have missed you so much. All the years I've wasted. All the times I've regretted not having you in my life." I pulled away slightly and looked her in the eye. The pool-blue circles…carbon copies of Billy's.

He would have been so proud.

"Look at you. You've turned out to be such a wonderful, beautiful young lady." I began to stroke her hair. "I am so, so sorry."

Mary reached out and wiped away some tears spilling down my cheek. "There's no need for these here," she said. "Not where I live. And I would love for you to come live with me some day. I could show you the meadow."

"You mean the one in the letters?"

Mary nodded with delight. "We could spend the rest of… forever there, if we wanted to. It is an amazing place."

"It sounds like it."

"It is. I go there all the time. It's so peaceful. I love to look up at the sky and listen to the creek. It is like a—"

"Lullaby."

Mary's eyes effervesced. "Yes. And the music. The voices never stop singing. It is—"

"Wondrous?"

Mary tilted her head. "Yes."

"I would love to see it with you. And listen to the music. I love choirs. Angelic ones must be the best, huh?"

"They are."

"You must take me there someday and show me."

Mary nodded and gripped me tight. "Then, you know what you must do."

"I do?"

"Yes."

I turned to Momma. She was sitting on the bed, crying. But in a happy way.

"I don't understand."

"You will," Mary said. "And when you do, promise me you will say yes."

The look in Mary's crystal-clear blue eyes was one I would never forget. So innocent. So full of life. So pure. Something was different about her eyes. They were unlike any others I'd gazed into before. "I promise."

She hugged me tighter than before. "I can't wait!"

"I love you, sweetheart."

Mary tittered. "Look, Grandma, did you hear what she called me? She called me sweetheart, just like you do."

Momma nodded.

Mary looked me squarely in the eye. "I love you, too, Mom."

I hugged her and began to sob again.

"Rachel," Momma said, "there's someone else I want you to meet."

I held Mary close, not wanting her to ever leave my side again. "Who?"

In the other corner of the room, a similar cloud-like formation appeared, and at once, a man stood facing us. He towered over Mary and me. At least a foot taller, maybe more. Broad chest. Big hands. Short-cropped hair. He wore a robe similar to the one Mary wore, but a much larger one and a little darker.

"Rachel," Momma said, "I want you to meet Joseph."

I glanced back and forth between Mary, Joseph, and Momma. "So, they're the Joseph and Mary you were talking to all these years?"

"Uh-huh."

Mary allowed me to turn and face Joseph. He looked familiar yet not so much. It was the face. The square jaw. The serious forehead. The way he looked at me. "Do I know you?"

"No," Joseph said.

"But I know that voice."

Momma stood and walked over beside me. "Joseph is your brother, Rachel."

"My brother? But I don't have a brother."

"Actually, you do. When I was a teenager, your daddy and I..." Momma tried to continue but became overwhelmed.

Joseph stepped over to Momma and put his arms around her.

I attempted to process it all, but my head was swimming. I was in another world. Another life. Another existence. What I saw, heard, smelled, and felt seemed so real, but yet, it seemed like a dream too. Like I was living a dream. The most real dream imaginable.

"Momma? Are you saying...," I pointed back and forth between her and Joseph, "you had an abortion too?"

All she could do was nod as the tears fell.

"Was that the secret, Momma? The one you asked a person named Sarah to keep? Something about a barn...and don't tell anybody."

Momma used her sleeve to dry her eyes. "Where did you hear all that?"

"When you were in the hospital the day Billy died. You were drugged pretty good that night. And I came in and cuddled up next to you. While I was there, you started mumbling about someone named Sarah. You asked her, 'Please don't tell anybody. We have to keep this a secret.'"

Momma's shoulders slouched. Her tears dried up. "That was the secret, sweetheart. Sarah was my best friend. We were a lot like you and Joanie. She was the only other person to know about Joseph besides your daddy."

I looked up at the man who would have been my big brother, both literally and figuratively. "Joseph?" I said. I gave Mary a big squeeze. "Are you...I mean,...Do you and Mary...live together?"

"We do," Mary said.

Joseph smiled at Mary. "We all live with Daddy. All of us. Every one of us."

We all...?

Ohhh.

"All of us" ...

"Every one of us" ...

People like them.

Oh, my.

My heart sank at the thought.

Just then, I felt a hand on my shoulder. I spun around, and standing beside me, with the most innocent look I'd ever seen, stood the man in the wife-beater t-shirt. "Don't be afraid, Rachel."

I jumped back a couple of steps and pointed at him. "You. You? What are you doing here?" I flipped my gaze back and forth between Mary and Joseph.

"Haven't you ever heard of a guardian angel before?" the man in the wife-beater t-shirt said.

"But you…you were just a…a…man who lived in the building. Right?"

"The Father sent me to look after you. So, that is what I did."

"But what about the other guys you were hangin' around with?"

The angel smiled.

"Them too?"

"Yes, Rachel. And we're not the only ones."

My knees began to falter more, and Mary pulled me closer. She led me over to the bed and helped me sit down. Then, before I could get fully situated, my teenage-looking daughter was a seven-year-old girl, leaning against me with her arms holding me tight. I pulled her up on the bed with me and held her in my lap.

"You have a gorgeous daughter, Rachel," came a voice from the other side of the room.

I peered around Momma, and standing beside the bed, near the window, stood Heather. Her blonde hair shimmering like gold.

Heather stepped out into the middle of the room. "She looks just like you."

"Are you telling me you're an angel too?"

"Isn't it obvious?"

I shook my head. "I'm not sure what's real anymore."

"It all is, Rachel. What you experience with your senses… and this," Heather said, arms outstretched. "There are two worlds. One of stones and dust and flesh and death. Another of the Spirit and life. They coexist. They intertwine. The former cannot exist without the latter, yet mankind has been working hard at trying to separate them from the beginning. Sinful man is quite happy with acknowledging our world, the one you see this very moment," she said, lifting her arms and motioning at Mary, Joseph, and the man in the t-shirt. "When it is convenient.

"However, these two worlds cannot be divided. They cannot be severed from one another. They are inextricably linked together, for that is how The Father intended it to be from the beginning. And one day very soon, it will be as it was intended to be, forevermore."

I looked at Momma for clarification.

Momma shrugged. "You know how I've always told you to read your Bible?"

I nodded.

"Well, for times like these, that's when it's most helpful."

"I'm not following."

"Isaiah, sweetheart. The prophet Isaiah spoke about this centuries ago." Momma stopped and began to pray. "Oh, Lord, like in the days of Elisha, open the eyes of Your servant, that she may see You in all Your Glory."

I watched her close her eyes. I listened to her pray. As she did, everything fell silent, just as I have imagined the vacuum of space would be. No sound whatsoever competed against her request.

The room instantly filled with the brightest light I'd ever seen. A blinding light. I couldn't even see anymore. Yet before me, instead of five people around me, I witnessed six.

Then, it was like the roof of the building had been lifted off by a pair of hands. The brilliance flooded the room. From the heavens, a voice thundered from the light:

"BEHOLD, I will create new heavens and a new earth. The former things will not be remembered, nor will they come to mind. But be glad and rejoice forever in what I will create, for I will create Jerusalem to be a delight and its people a joy.

"I will rejoice over Jerusalem and take delight in my people; the sound of weeping and of crying will be heard in it no more. Never again will there be in it an infant who lives but a few days, or an old man who does not live out his years; he who dies at a hundred will be thought a mere child; he who fails to reach a hundred will be considered accursed.

"They will build houses and dwell in them; they will plant vineyards and eat their fruit. No longer will they build houses and others live in them, or plant and others eat. For as the days of a tree, so will be the days of my people; my chosen ones will long enjoy the work of their hands. They will not toil in vain, or bear children doomed to misfortune; for they will be a people blessed by the LORD, they and their descendants with them.

"Before they call I will answer; while they are still speaking I will hear. The wolf and the lamb will feed together, and the lion will eat straw like the ox, but dust will be the serpent's food. They will neither harm nor destroy on all my holy mountain, says the LORD."

I SHOOK IN FRIGHT. My eyes were closed. I was hugging Mary tight. Overwhelmed by it all.

Completely astounded.

Mary became a teenager again, slid down off my lap, and sat beside me instead. Her strong arms encircled me. "It's okay, Mom. Don't be afraid."

"How can I not be afraid?"

She took my face in her hands. "You know what you must do."

I peered at my daughter. "That's the second time you've said that."

Mary gave a little nod. "And I will continue to say it until you keep your promise."

I swiveled my gaze toward the ones standing before me. The light had subsided, and the ceiling appeared to be untouched. "So, all of you have been sent here? To Earth? For my benefit?"

They all nodded.

Mary gripped me tighter. "That's how much Daddy loves you, Mom."

"Yet He loves others too," Heather said. "The Father didn't just send me to look after you alone. I've also been sent to look after someone else. A person you know, by the way. A mutual friend."

My face lit up, and my mouth parted in surprise. Heather giggled when she saw it. "Is it Gordon?"

"It is."

"Who's Gordon?" Momma said.

"A friend of mine."

Heather pointed at me. "Are you sure that's all he is, Rachel?"

"Excuse me, but we are just good friends."

"Rachel Leah." Momma turned toward me. "Don't sit here and lie in front of, well, God and everybody."

Mary searched me with her blue eyes. "Is he a nice man?"

I beamed at her. "He is. I think you'd really like him."

"Gordon is a good man. A righteous man," Heather said, brushing Mary's hair with her fingers. "He's been through a great deal of turmoil himself, as have all who have walked the Earth since the Beginning. He once was a strong believer, but his faith has been shaken. That is why I was sent."

I considered Heather's words. Although we'd been together a couple of times, Gordon had never mentioned anything about church...or God...or anything like that.

He was a strong believer, she said, but his faith was shaken...

"Rachel, do you know why?" Momma said.

"Do I know why...what?"

"Why his faith was shaken?"

I searched my memory. "I would imagine it has to do with the passing of his wife."

Momma gave an affirming nod. "He, too, lost someone who was dear to him."

Mary transformed again into a small child of no older than six. "You two have a lot in common."

I took Mary by the hands. "It would appear so, sweetheart."

"Now, Rachel," Momma said, holding out her arms, "do you see? I've prayed for you every day. Prayed that one day you would have your eyes opened just like Elisha's servant did."

Heather, Joseph, and the man in the t-shirt all stood before me now, shoulder to shoulder, smiling. Mary hopped up on the bed and sat beside me. "Well, I see Heather, and Joseph, and…" I pointed at the man in the wife-beater, "Do you have a name?"

"My name is Malachi."

"And Malachi." I said, still pointing. "And of course, my dear Mary." I brushed her cheek with the back of my fingers before turning triumphantly toward Momma.

"You misunderstood me, Rachel. I wasn't asking you who you saw. I was asking if you see now."

Mary crawled into my lap again, reached up with her hands, and gently cupped my face. "Mommy, do you believe what Grandma has been talking about all these years?"

"How could I not?"

Malachi stepped forward. "The enemy is strong. Do not underestimate him. He has used others around you in an attempt to shield you from the truth."

"Just as he has done with Gordon," Heather said. "When you are sad and depressed, or tempted, or full of pride, that is when the enemy is at his strongest. You cannot withstand him on your own. You need the power of God to overcome the evil one."

"Rachel," Momma said, "listen to them. They are here for your reclamation."

Reclamation?

I pondered their words as Mary slid down off my lap and joined them.

"Wait, Mary, don't leave me," I said.

"Mommy, you know what you need to do. If you keep your

promise, then I will see you again. Very soon. And I will never have to leave your side again."

I jumped to my feet. But before I could reach her, the swirling, churning cloud from before appeared again. Her form, her silhouette, all of it was visible until the cloud dissipated like the morning fog. And in an instant, my little girl was gone again.

I collapsed to my knees in a sobbing heap.

Heather knelt down beside me and grabbed my shoulder firmly. "Do not despair, Rachel. What you have been given is a wonderful gift. You have been allowed to see a glimpse of Heaven. Not everyone is so fortunate."

"But the pain…My heart aches for her."

"That is how sin operates. And until you leave this realm and see fully what God has in store for you, like Mary and Joseph, the effects of sin will remain." She pulled on my arm. "Now, stand."

I did so, and standing at the far side of the room was Kenneth Singh.

"What are you—" My shoulders slumped. "You too?!"

Kenneth beamed a healthy smile, waved his fingers, and then vanished into thin air.

I faced Heather. "What just happened?"

"You got to meet the courier too," Heather said.

"He's also an angel?"

"And not the only one."

"How many are there?"

"More than you can count."

"Rachel," Momma said. "The orderly who received each and every letter from me was an angel too. He would take it to the courier service where Kenneth Singh was—"

"Yeah, yeah. And he would take them to the post office and mail them. Yeah, that's how the police caught up to Kenneth."

"But did you catch the little tidbit God threw in, just for fun? That's why I love Him so. He's so creative."

"What are you talking about, Momma?"

"Kenneth was instructed, as were all the other couriers, to make sure those letters got postmarked in Jericho, New York."

"Right. I knew that. But why is that so important?"

"Sweetheart, it was in Jericho where the walls fell down. God's people marched around the city seven times, blew their horns, 'and the walls came tumblin' down,' as the song says." Momma walked up to me and peered into my eyes. "That's what God is trying to do to you. To get those thick walls of your stubborn heart to come tumblin' down so He can come marching in, trumpets sounding, all of Heaven rejoicing, and have you live in His presence."

With those words, Heather, Malachi, and Joseph swirled out of our sight until it was just Momma and me standing in the middle of the room.

However, as they did, I heard a small child's voice call out. "You know what you have to do, Mommy!"

CHAPTER FIFTY

West 173ʳᵈ Street
Washington Heights, NY

spent the rest of the afternoon and evening with Momma. We talked. We laughed. We enjoyed each other's company so much. Of course, I had a bevy of questions after meeting Mary. Even more after seeing Heather and Malachi.

Joseph was a harder subject to breach, and Momma spoke very little about him, and I understood why. Talking about Mary with anyone, even Momma before today, would have been problematic at best. The pain was real. The regret was beyond harsh. Forgiveness for taking a life was difficult to accept at any level. When it was your own flesh and blood, though, it became unbearable.

So, you played the blame game to help cope with the empty feelings. Blame was easier to dish out, especially when there are others who encouraged you, helped you, told you it was the better choice.

But as the person who must live with the decision, you always ended up with the biggest piece of that pie.

That's what sin does.

It beats you down. Stomps on your throat, and vows never to allow you the opportunity to get back up.

And that's how I felt when I entered LIPC earlier today.

I had given in. Decided to remain on the ground. Allow sin to apply pressure until life was no more.

Thank God for Momma. She never gave up.

WE FINALLY HAD to say our goodbyes. Visiting hours were over, and the staff kept knocking on the door, hurrying my departure along.

I waved goodbye to Momma and left her in her room for the night. The orderly closed the door and secured it with a key. I wondered if he was the letter deliveryman about whom Momma spoke, but I didn't have the nerve to ask, so I simply thanked him for his help and headed for the elevator.

It was empty when I stepped inside, so I walked to the back and snuggled into the corner, hugging myself. My plastic grocery bag full of letters draped over my forearm.

As I dropped nine floors, each one dinging its proximity, I closed my eyes and relived the events of earlier that afternoon.

Mary's face. At one moment, a baby. The next, a small child. The next, a young woman. All of them, full of life.

And my brother. Joseph. Such a strong, handsome man. Looks so much like our daddy.

Then, Heather, the little barista with the golden hair and all the smiles.

And Malachi. Oh, how I misjudged him. Forgive me. Please.

And God…Your magnificence, the light, the thundering words. I really don't deserve any of this.

"You have been given such a magnanimous gift," I heard someone say.

I opened my eyes, but the elevator was empty.

"You got to see a glimpse of Heaven, Rachel."

God, is that You?

"You know what you have to do."

Mary?

The elevator chimed, and the door opened. I strode out into the lobby feeling new. Even exuberant. I had envisioned leaving LIPC as depressed as I was when I arrived. Instead, I didn't want to go home. I didn't want to entomb myself and waste my life away any longer. I wanted to live.

I wanted to live.

Forever.

I burst out onto the sidewalk. The brisk air scratched against my face, but I didn't mind. I cinched up my coat, slipped on my gloves, and began singing on the way to my car.

I jumped inside, cranked up my rundown car, and pulled out into traffic. Riding down the street, everything looked so different. I don't know how to explain it, but somehow, the Christmas lights looked brighter. The decorations appeared more festive. The snow more charming.

I took a serious detour and stopped by Rockefeller Center. I got out of my car and stood amongst a large crowd overlooking the area. The ice skaters circled and zigzagged on the ice while the enormous Christmas tree and lights illuminated the scene in a marvelous, jovial array. I inhaled deeply. Even the crisp air smelled cleaner somehow.

A choir stood down in the corner, singing songs of the season. The music of "The Twelve Days of Christmas" faded as I sauntered up to the crowd, and the beginnings of a rendition of "O Holy Night" surrounded us with several members of the choir producing the sound of a cold night wind into their microphones.

My skin erupted with goosebumps as the remaining voices unified into the first lines of the song.

Standing there, amongst people I didn't know, with my eyes closed and my face facing the night sky, I swore I'd never hear that song the same way again.

The words meant so much more now.

I remembered what Malachi said about how the world fights against God.

I began to recall all the times I had fought…

> *Long lay the world in sin and error pining*
> *Till He appear'd and the soul felt its worth.*

That was what I'd been doing. Lying, no, wallowing in sin and error. Pining away in depression. Misery. Lamenting, all the time, about my woes. Hating life itself.

Then, with thunderous light, He appeared.

In Momma's little room.

Now, my soul feels its worth.

My soul feels.

For the first time.

The choir got to the chorus, and all the voices joined in…as did my heart…with tears streaking down my face.

> *Fall on your knees*
> *O hear the angel voices*
> *O night divine*
> *O night when Christ was born*
> *O night divine*
> *O night*
> *O night divine*

I relived Mary's hug. The warmth I felt…penetrating to my bones…through my bones.

How I long for that again…

Mary's little voice. Trying to soothe my heartache.

"I forgive you, Mommy," she said.

I forgive you…

Her tiny hands clasping mine.

My little, little daughter…sitting on my lap.

As a child.

I looked out upon the skaters on the square. The tree in all its splendor. The backdrop was amazing. Yet, in all its wonder, it paled in comparison to Momma's room.

When God was present.

Maybe that's why Momma changed the subject when I suggested she come live with me. Maybe she was not ready to leave that room yet. Maybe God and Momma had some unfinished business to conduct before she was released.

"He allowed me to be here for a reason, sweetheart," she said a while back. "And when He's ready, He'll tell me it's time to go."

I got into my car and drove straight home. Walking up to the building, I stopped and looked up at the fire escape, but Malachi wasn't there.

I shrugged and lilted through the front door. I almost raced past the mailroom, but a thought caught me in mid-stride. I stopped and went directly to my mailbox. I opened it, and for the first time, it was empty.

No letters.

No packages.

I reached inside, just to make sure, and toward the back, in the shadows, I felt something. I grabbed it and pulled it out.

It was a button.

A beige button.

Just like the one on my stuffed bear when I was five.

Just like the one Mary held today.

I gripped it in my right hand and pulled it close to my chest. Although the tears flowed heavily, they were jubilant.

Of remembrance.

Of life.

Of *a* life.

One I thought I would never see.

Now, one I hoped to see soon.

Very soon.

For all eternity.

"Everything okay, miss?"

Startled, I spun around to see Malachi. "It's you!" I ran and hugged him. "I was afraid I wouldn't see you again."

He whispered in my ear. "My mission is not complete yet."

I pulled away and looked him in the eye. "It is with me, I think. I don't know how I can ever be the same."

"That is wonderful news, Rachel. When the time fully comes, my brethren in Heaven will be rejoicing, I am sure of this. In the meantime, you know what you must do."

"Hey, that's what Mary said to me."

He placed his hands on my shoulders. "She is a delightful child of God. You should listen to her."

"I will."

Malachi smiled and nodded. "I must go."

"Merry Christmas, Malachi."

"Merry Christmas to you too." He stepped back. "Oh, and by the way, my name around here is Jesus Salvador Rey. But people know me as Rey."

I winked. "Got it."

"You have a wonderful evening, Rachel."

"Thank you."

He gave me a little wave and walked outside.

I bounded up the stairs, bolted the door behind me, and ran into the bedroom. I fell on the bed and began opening the letters one at a time.

Reliving their life.

Their vibrancy

Their words.

From the first to the last, setting each one around me, forming a semi-circle as I did, I read each one again. New meaning leapt from the pages. What was written made so much more sense now.

I slowly, methodically, read each line. Each word. Until I made it to the last line of the last letter. I pressed it to my chest and closed my eyes.

I felt the warmth of Mary's embrace.

I heard her words.

"You know what you have to do."

I looked heavenward, then dropped my head and hugged the letter even tighter.

God, please forgive me…

Friday

December 26, 2014

CHAPTER FIFTY-ONE

The Columbian Coffee Shop
Manhattan, NY

Having parked my car at the bank, I made the usual trek down to The Columbian Coffee Shop. I laughed to myself about all the times I'd been in there recently, wondering if Heather was working. Wistful when she wasn't.

Well, of course, she's gonna make the best coffee ever. How can you out perform an angel?

I opened the front door, and standing at the counter with his back to me, was Gordon. He was chitchatting with none other than Heather.

Heather listened intently while she glanced up to see who had just walked inside. When she saw me, she beamed a gorgeous smile and gave me a quick wink, but continued to carry on the conversation with Gordon as if nothing else happened.

I strolled up with my finger over my lips, motioning to Heather not to give me away.

I gently placed my hand on Gordon's shoulder and stepped around him so he could see my face.

"Rachel, hey. How are you?"

"Gordon," I said, "I can honestly say, 'I'm in heaven.' I had such a wonderful day yesterday. I'm…I'm still floating."

Heather continued making his coffee, but I could see her grasp every word with her smile.

"You know, we had a great day too. Didn't we, Heather?"

"We sure did."

"It takes days like that to help you refocus, you know?"

"Refocus?" Heather said, handing him his drink.

Gordon reached out and took it. "Yeah. It's so easy to let the busyness of the season get in the way of why we celebrate in the first place. Does that make sense?"

"Perfect sense," I said. "And it isn't just the hustle and bustle. Past regrets can also take their toll." I looked at Heather again, trying not to cry.

Heather began to make my drink without even asking. "Here! Here! So, you two had a good day off. I'm glad."

"I sure did," Gordon said.

I winked at her. "I did too. I'm hoping for a repeat next year."

Heather handed me my coffee and spoke in a hushed voice. "I'll have to see what I can do."

Gordon's happy expression turned to puzzlement. "So, Heather? Did you two spend time together yesterday before you came over to the house?"

"Yes," she said, looking at me as she spoke. "We had a great time, didn't we?"

"The best."

"Huh. I didn't know you two knew each other that well."

I began to chuckle. "Neither did I," fixing my eyes on Heather, "but…we seem to have more in common than meets the eye."

Heather laughed. "I couldn't have said it any better myself."

Gordon held his cup high. "Well, thanks, Heather, for

another great cup of coffee." Then, he leaned in close. "I know I've said it before, but you're gonna need to train these other people how to do it. They just can't seem to get it right like you do."

"I'll look into that too," she said.

I sipped my drink. "I agree. It's heavenly."

Heather didn't respond. She simply smiled and waved us goodbye before I blew her cover.

Gordon and I exited the store.

"So," Gordon said, "remember that guy who came in and made the big deposit toward the Children's Christmas fund?"

"Yes…" I wasn't sure how to reply after the revelations of yesterday. "Did the police ever figure out how he got so much money? I mean, the guy was a courier, not a millionaire."

"I haven't heard yet about that, but the day before Christmas, in the afternoon, after we close for the day, we usually check the fund to see how short we're going to be. So, we did, and it appears we're going to break even this year. That money your courier guy deposited turned out to be the exact amount we needed to break even. Of course, that's if his check clears and the police allow us to keep it."

"Somehow, I think everything's gonna be all right."

"I hope you're right."

"I'm pretty confident. It's amazing, isn't it? The exact amount?"

"Yeah. It's like he knew…somehow."

"Maybe he did."

Gordon turned to get a better look at me while we walked. "And how would he know that information?"

I grinned. I couldn't contain myself. "Maybe a little birdie told him."

"Yeah, that makes a lot of sense."

It does when you know the birdie.

"Well, anyway, it's good news for the bank. And our employees. Because we're going to break even, we'll be able to give our employees a bigger bonus this year."

"That's great news."

"It is. I know it's not before Christmas when everybody could have used it, but better late than never, right?"

Man, you're tellin' me.

"Everybody loves more money."

"They do. Hey, speaking of more money, because of the success of the Children's Christmas Fund this year, I wanted to celebrate. I know you usually work Friday nights, so I'll understand if you can't, but I was wondering if you wanted to go out for dinner tonight? Help me celebrate?"

"I'd love to. And it won't be a problem finding someone to swap with me or take my shift. Not on a Friday night. I'll call my supervisor as soon as we get to the bank and let him know."

"So…" Gordon stopped and turned toward me, "it's a date?"

Good for you, Gordon. You didn't get all tongue-tied.

"It's a date."

He began walking slowly again. "I know of this great Italian place, if you're interested. They have the best service ever."

"And if you knew me better, you'd know I'm not that into Italian food. However, I'm willing to allow you to get to know what I do like, if you're interested."

He took a swig of his coffee. "I would love for you to grant me that opportunity."

I glanced up at the sky and smiled before giving way to a joyful laugh.

I was so happy.

And I knew Mary would be happy for me too.

This is what the LORD says, "A voice is heard in Ramah, mourning and great weeping. Rachel weeping for her children and refusing to be comforted because her children are no more."

— JEREMIAH 31:15 NIV (CF. MATTHEW 2:17-18)

"Sing to God, sing praise of his name,
extol him who rides on the clouds—
his name is the LORD—and rejoice before him.
A father to the fatherless, a defender of widows,
is God in his holy dwelling."

— PSALM 68:4-5 NIV

ABOUT THE AUTHOR

 Kevin is a husband, a father, a grandfather, and a kid at heart. Often referred to as "crazy" by his grandchildren, it's only because he is. He's a writer. Need he say more? He is an award-winning author, having his debut novel, THE SERPENT'S GRASP, win the prestigious Selah Award in 2013. His second novel, 30 DAYS HATH REVENGE, earned a Silver Medal in the Reader's Favorite Awards in 2013, too. Reviewers have referred to him as a "mastermind" when developing a plot. Readers have claimed, "they are glad he is on their side" after reading the "very realistic" plot for his Blake Meyer Series.

Kevin is a huge fan of the TV series 24, The Blacklist, Blue Bloods, NCIS, and Criminal Minds. He's also a fan of the British shows Broadchurch, Shetland, Hinterland, and Wallander. He loves anything to do with Star Trek and is a Sherlock Holmes fanatic, too. With him, the game is always afoot, but you'll never catch him in a deerstalker. Ever.

ALSO FROM EXPANSE BOOKS

The Seer

Book One of The Kalila Chronicles

Viktor has one order to follow:

Kill the girl before her eyes are opened.

For thousands of years, his job has been to torment and kill seers: humans that have the gift of seeing the spiritual realm. So it was no surprise when his brother Matthias was once again sent to stop him and protect the girl.

Now the last of the seers' bloodline hangs in the balance, as the estranged demon and angel brothers are forced to work together to save a girl's life and escape to the sanctuary city of Bethesda.

∾

The Gathering Dark

Quest of Fire Series – Book One

After a thousand years of light, a teen's world teeters on the edge of utter darkness.

Jason is an expert at running from his past. But when it catches up, he finds himself hiding in a peculiar inn listening to a tale from centuries past.

The story is Anargen's, a teen who is pulled from all he loves to follow his oaths of loyalty to the fabled King of the Realms. Together with his mentor, Cinaed, he rides north on a special quest to mediate peace talks between ancient foes—the men of Ecthelowall and the dwarfs of Ordumair. Nothing goes as planned. Many on both sides of the dispute despise Anargen's Order. Worse, an arcane evil has returned to the North. This "Grey Scourge" seeks to ruin the peace talks and ensure a lost treasure held by the dwarfs is never found by those for whom it is meant.

As Anargen's story unfolds, Jason begins to wonder whether it is truly just a fable. He soon finds himself drawn into the conflict Anargen faced. A battle that has shaped and can destroy his world.

The Gathering Dark is a finalist in the 2020 Selah Awards for

Speculative Fiction.

∾

Kokopelli's Song

Book One of the Four Corners Fantasy Series

Three teens race against a waxing moon to prevent an ancient evil from tipping the universe into chaos.

New Mexico

When seventeen-year-old Amy Adams finds her father's family and a lost twin brother on the Hopi reservation in Arizona, she stumbles into a struggle between shamans and witches that spans a thousand years. After Mahu is attacked and a Conquistador's journal stolen, Amy and her new friend Diego set out on a dangerous quest to find and perform the ceremony that can stop ancient evil from entering our world.

But Amy and Diego are not alone as they race against time measured by a waxing moon. Kokopelli's song, the haunting notes of a red cedar flute, guides them along the migration route sacred to pueblo peoples: West to Old Oraibi, South to El Morro, East to Cochiti Pueblo, North to Chimney Rock, and finally to the Center—and the final confrontation —in Chaco Canyon. (Releases August 2020.)

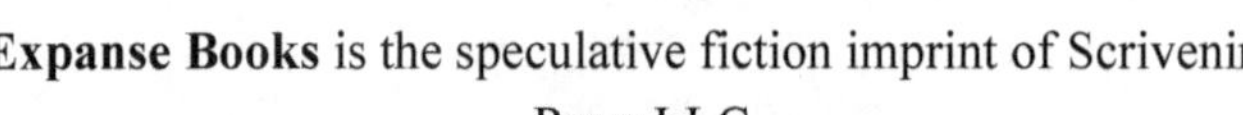

Expanse Books is the speculative fiction imprint of Scrivenings
Press LLC.

Stay up-to-date on your favorite books and authors with our free e-newsletters.

ScriveningsPress.com

www.ingramcontent.com/pod-product-compliance
Lightning Source LLC
Chambersburg PA
CBHW060609100726
47907CB00006B/1554